THE ANGEL OF DEATH

BOOK

ELICIA HYDER

Inkwell & Quill, LLC

GET A FREE BOOK

Robbery · Arson · Murder
And the one-night stand that just won't end.

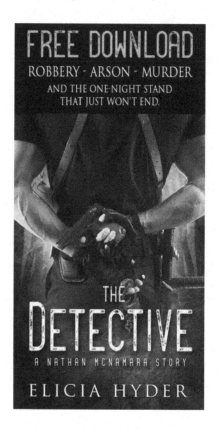

The Soul Summoner Series Order

Book 1 - **The Soul Summoner**
Book 2 - **The Siren**
Book 3 - **The Angel of Death**
Book 4 - **The Taken**
Book 5 - **The Sacrifice**
Book 6 - **The Regular Guy**
Book 7 - **The Soul Destroyer**
Book 8 - **The Guardian**
Book 9 - **The Daughter of Zion**

Standalones:
The Detective
The Mercenary
The Archangel

For Rena.
Thanks for saving my life.
Literally.

ACKNOWLEDGMENTS

Special Thanks to everyone who made this book possible:

To my badass husband…the inspiration behind all my heroes.

To my kids who have sacrificed many home-cooked meals during the writing of this book.

To my Mom who has been my #1 fan and wing-woman in all my travels this year.

To my dad for being my most anxious beta reader.

To Chris Osteen, Aleesha Baker, Jennifer Kelly, Trish Longnecker-Potter, Delefay McCoy, and Kris Arnett for contributing names for this story!

To Tango. Dude. Your support and encouragement is priceless.

To Karen for all the comedic relief during the final proof of this book. Appalachia here we come!

And finally, thanks to all the fans who patiently—or not so patiently—waited for the release of this book. We aren't done yet.

TO MY AWESOME LAUNCH TEAM
THE BOOK SUMMONERS
I would be nowhere without you!

(Alphabetically):

Kris Arnett, Elsbeth Balas, Karla Barker, Tracie Bechard, Lorelei Buzzetta, Connor J. Bedell, Lynn Biggs, Lilia Bingham, Betty Bowers, Cindy Brown, Ellen Burghardt, Gabriela Cabezut, Tiffany Cagle, Marsha Carmichael, Shweta Chopra, Mary Cooper, Céleste Couture, Lisa Cowens, Andrea Delaney, Estee Del Padre, May Freighter, Donna Geoffroy, Sarah Gillaspie, Venice Gilmore, Rick Gottinger, Melody Hall, Lina Hanson, Judith Hartsock, Bridget Hickey, Kira Hodge, Melissa Hongisto, Wendy Howell, Kathryn Hughett, Paula Hurdle, Misi Hurst, Martina Hutchinson, Susan Huttinger, Ashley Huttinger, Kristin Jacques, Ara James, Deborah Jay, Sandy Johnson, Tango Jordan, John K. Park, Ramona Kekstadt, Katorah Kenway, Russelin Kisiel, Erani Kole, Debra L. Rutschman, Erica, Linda Levine, Sue Lopp, Micaela Lowe, Juliet Lyons, Lori Mahan, Samantha Malizia, Chuck Mason, Sal Mason, Kellie Milon, Michel Moore, Debi Murray, Rebecca Nickleson, Marie Nicoll, Susan Oates, Tammy Oja, Teresa Partridge, Danielle Plain, Rena Pratts, Wendy Pyatt, Jenny Quinn, Lucy Rhodes, Kim Roberts, Megan Robinson, Tamara Ruth, Sandy Ryan-Earl, Marsha Sanderlin, Sonya Sargent, Bill Sbrocco, Lisa Shaw, Vandi Shelton, Ana Simons, Sherry Skiles, Stephanie Smith, Tanya Spencer, Rata Stevens-Robinette, Heather Grace Stewart, Ann Stewart-Akers, Debbie Stout, Leigh W. Stuart, Christine Sturgill, Tina Torrest, Dee Tracey, Sharon Tweede, Laura Theraalt, Angela

Tinkham, Nina van Vlierden, Ana Victoria Lopez, Ronnie Waldrop, Susie Waldrop, Lennie Warren, Shanna Whitten, Russ Williams, Stephanie Williams, K. Williams, Bridgett Wilson, Natalie Wolicki, Terrilynne Work, Ann Writes

CHAPTER ONE

"You're going to put that thing *where?*"

My eyes were double their normal size as I peered at Dr. Grayson Watts over the bridge the paper sheet formed between my knees. The long device in her hand looked more like a lightsaber than a medical instrument. My mouth was gaping so wide that I should have been at the dentist's office rather than the OB/GYN.

Dr. Watts cocked her head to the side and raised an eyebrow. "It's a transvaginal ultrasound, Sloan. It will be a little uncomfortable, but this is the only way we can get a clear picture of your uterus at this stage and determine how far along you are."

I winced. "It looks like you're going to battle the Empire."

She wasn't amused.

I sighed and flopped back on the exam table. "Go ahead."

"Relax your knees," she said.

I focused on the speckled ceiling tiles and gulped. "Oh, boy."

I sucked in a deep breath and whimpered as she impaled me like a jousting knight.

"Relax," she said again.

I considered kicking her in the face.

A moment later, she turned the screen on her computer toward me, and I rose up on my elbows again. "Here is your uterus." She was pointing to a cloud of white fuzz on the screen. "And this black blob is the gestational sac." She shifted her magic wand around some more. "And this little spot right here, that's your baby."

I squinted my eyes. A small, gray misshapen bean was inside the black blob.

My chest tightened, and I fell back onto my pillow again and took a few deep breaths.

"It looks like you're about eight weeks along," she said.

"Eight weeks?" I shook my head. "No. That can't be right. I know exactly when I got pregnant. October 19th."

I counted backward in my mind. So much had happened in the past few months it was hard to place the events and catastrophes in the order in which they occurred. It had been three weeks since my boyfriend, Warren Parish, was reactivated with the Marine Corps. The week before that, my biological mother—a demon, literally—tried to kill me. Two weeks before that, my adoptive mother died from brain cancer on October 19th. The tiny speck on the screen was the product of emotional, grief-stricken sex, when my boyfriend hadn't bothered to remove his boots or use any protection. I couldn't be eight weeks along.

"It's only been about six weeks," I told her.

She closed my legs when she removed the wand. "The weeks are calculated starting with the first day of your last period, so mid-October is right for the conception date."

"I knew it," I said. "Warren should be very glad the military has him because if he were still here, I might kill him."

Dr. Watts was trying hard to suppress a giggle. Her latex gloves snapped as she removed them. She pulled a sliding, paper wheel from her pocket and adjusted it with her thumbs. "This puts your due date as July 11th."

As she scribbled in her notes, I stared out the window. On one hand, July 11th felt like an eternity away. On the other, if I had learned anything in the previous four months, it was how much could radically change in such a short time period. Warren was lost to me in November, and there was no guarantee he would find me by July.

"Are you all right?"

I groaned and covered my face with my arms.

She rolled on her chair till she was by my head. "Sloan?"

I let out a deep sigh. "I'm all right. This wasn't exactly planned."

"I can tell." She helped me sit up. "Can I ask about the father?"

There was so much to say about my baby's father that I didn't even know where to begin. He was the son of an Angel of Death. He was a Recon Marine Sniper and then a mercenary. He had a body that could only be ranked on a scale of one to oh-my-god, and he made love like he should require a height restriction. Of course, none of this was the kind of information Dr. Watts was interested in.

"He's not here because he's off in Iraq or Israel or somewhere," I said.

"Military?" she asked.

I smoothed the paper sheet over my bare legs. "He's in the Marines, but I don't know where he is. He can't tell me anything."

She frowned. "I'm sorry to hear that. Does he know you're pregnant?"

"No one outside this room knows." That was true, unless you counted the supernatural world. "You won't tell my dad, will you?" My father and Dr. Watts worked in the same building.

She dumped her gloves in the trashcan. "I wouldn't dream of it. And legally, whatever you say in this room is protected under doctor-patient confidentiality."

"Really?"

"Absolutely."

I was skeptical. "What if I sound crazy? Could you tell someone then?"

"Not unless I thought you might harm someone else or your-self," she answered. "Do you need to talk about something?"

There were only a handful of people on the planet who knew I was part-angel, and none of them knew I was pregnant. So no one had heard the fears all my over-thinking had produced since those two pink lines popped up on the home pregnancy test. *Is it fair to bring a baby into the mess that has become my life? Will the baby be normal with parents like me and Warren? Can I even live through child-birth if the kid inherits Warren's big head and broad shoulders?*

I hesitated. "Did you notice anything abnormal about the baby?"

Her eyes widened with surprise, and she shook her head. "No. Nothing at all. Are you worried about something specific?"

I was worried about many specific things, none of which I could discuss with Dr. Watts. "My body has been through a lot lately, before I knew I was pregnant."

"Trauma?" she asked, pulling out my medical chart and a pen.

My fight with Kasyade was certainly traumatic. I had suffered a broken hip, a broken nose, several broken ribs, and was slammed into the concrete more times than I could count. Again, I couldn't tell the doctor about that either, since then I would have to explain how my body had healed itself on the way to the hospital.

"I've been through severe emotional trauma," I said, which wasn't at all a lie.

Her face twisted into a frown full of pity. "I heard about your mother passing recently. That must have been painful for you."

My mother had complained of a headache on Monday and was dead by Saturday. To describe the incident as 'painful' was almost insulting. I had successfully managed to not cry over it yet that day, and I wasn't about to start while I was naked from the waist down with my dad's colleague. So I bypassed the conversation altogether.

"I also have a panic disorder, and I take Xanax."

She grimaced. "You should avoid taking it, unless it's absolutely essential, especially for the first twelve weeks or so. It does carry a risk for your baby."

I cringed. "I've taken it a few times recently. Since my mom died, I've had nightmares that sometimes trigger panic attacks in the middle of the night."

She made some notes. "Pregnancy will probably increase your dreams."

I groaned. "That's just great." I thought for a second. "Also, I won't be able to do parts of my job without it."

She pulled her head back in surprise. "Your job induces anxiety? Aren't you the publicist for the county?"

"I am," I said. "I have to work at the sheriff's office some, and it's inside the jail. I always have attacks there."

"Fear of enclosed spaces?" she asked.

I laughed. "Sure. That's it." It wasn't, but it was a better reason than the truth.

"Maybe you should think about seeing a psychiatrist."

I laughed again but didn't comment. Any truthful explanation would only validate her suggestion. "What do I need to do as far as being pregnant? I'm a first-timer."

She scribbled something on a pad of paper. "Here is a prescription for generic prenatal vitamins, and I want to see you again in a month."

I nodded. "I'll make the appointment before I leave."

"Do you smoke?" she asked.

"Nope."

"Do you drink alcohol?"

"All the time."

She looked up with alarm. "How much do you drink?"

"I usually have a few beers a week," I said.

She tapped her pen on my chart. "Like, more than four in one sitting?"

"Never. I'd pass out around four."

She pointed the pen at me. "No alcohol."

"I figured."

"What about other meds?" she asked.

I shook my head. I had a prescription for migraines, but I wouldn't need it.

She looked over her notes. "So, no Xanax, and don't take any over the counter pain meds except Tylenol and only if it's absolutely necessary. Go easy on caffeine and stay away from raw and undercooked meat and seafood. Other than that, drink plenty of water and no heavy lifting. Have you had a flu shot this year?"

I shook my head.

"Get a flu shot," she said.

"OK."

She stood and pulled open the cabinet over the sink. She retrieved a thick paperback and handed it to me. "This book answers most questions I'm regularly asked, so I bought them for my patients. If you can't find an answer in there, call me."

I gripped the book, *What to Expect When You're Expecting*, with both hands. A lumpy looking woman with a suburban haircut, 1980's red trousers, and an orange smock was seated in a rocking chair on the cover. My face soured. "Do I have to dress this way?"

She laughed and patted my shoulder. "We're all done here. You can get dressed." She walked across the room but paused before she reached the door. "Sloan, please tell someone you trust that you're pregnant. You'll need support through this."

I took a deep breath. "I will."

"Oh, and happy Thanksgiving," she said.

A wave of nausea hit my stomach. "Happy Thanksgiving."

Before I left her office, I made an appointment for the next month. On my way outside, I shoved the baby book in my purse and checked the screen of my brand new cell phone. It had been on silent since the nurse took me back to see the doctor. There were two missed calls and a text message from Warren.

Call me ASAP. Getting ready to board the C-130 and have to turn off my phone.

I hit the call button, and he picked up on the first ring. "Thank God, I was afraid you wouldn't call me back in time." He was out of breath. "Where have you been? I've been trying to reach you for about thirty minutes."

"I was in with my doctor," I told him as I sank back against the wall. A lump rose in my throat.

"The doctor? Is everything all right?" he asked.

"Yeah, everything is fine. I had a checkup." At least it wasn't a complete lie. "So, this is it?"

"This is it," he said. "We are flying out today. I may not be able to have contact for a while after this. I had to hear your voice one more time."

"Still no idea when you will be back?" I asked.

"Nope," he said. "Although, I think it will be shorter than we expected. Maybe three to six months."

I picked at my cuticle. "And you still can't tell me where you're going or what you're doing?"

"You know I can't, babe." There was a loud rumble in the background. "I've got to go. I'll be in touch as soon as I can," he said over the commotion.

God, I wanted to tell him about the baby. "Warren!"

"Yeah?"

I bit my lower lip and hesitated. "Uh…" *Say it.* "Be careful."

"I will if you will," he said, laughing. "I love you, Sloan."

"I love you too."

"I'll be back before you know it." He disconnected the call without saying goodbye.

My back was glued to the wall in the hallway. I couldn't move. I just stood and stared at the phone in my hand, thinking about what Dr. Watts had said before I left. *Tell someone you trust.* I stepped onto the elevator and pressed the button for floor three. If I trusted anyone in the world the most, it would be my dad.

Dad's office was almost empty when I opened the door to the waiting room. There was only one elderly patient waiting to see him. Thankfully, Dad had been keeping his workload light since Mom wasn't there to help him. She had been his primary nurse since he opened the practice. When Mom was alive, I rarely visited during work hours, but since her funeral, I made it a point to drop in a few times a week to check on him.

The receptionist greeted me, far too bubbly before lunch. "Hey there, Sloan."

"Hey, Patty," I said. "Is my dad busy?"

She looked down at a piece of paper on her desk. "He's in an exam room with a patient, but you can wait in his office if you'd like."

I glanced around the small lobby. "I'll wait out here. Can you let him know?"

She stood from her desk. "Of course."

I took a seat next to an old man with sporadic white hairs encircling his mostly bald head. His skin sagged around his dark eyes and his jaw line. He turned a wide, toothy grin toward me. "Hello, Sloan," he said, his voice deep and raspy.

My eyes widened with surprise. "Hello."

He nodded. "You don't know me, but I've seen your picture on the desk in your dad's office. He's awful proud of you."

I felt my face flush. "Yeah, he is."

He offered me his hand. "My name's Otis Cash."

"Nice to meet you, Mr. Cash." Something about the old man caught my attention. I had gotten the same feeling from my mother before she died. Mr. Cash had cancer. "Do you come see my dad often?"

His head bobbed up and down. "Ever since they found the tumor in my lungs a couple of months ago," he said. "Your dad's been checking up on me every few weeks since I refused to see that cancer doctor they wanted me to go to." He laughed, wheezing heavily. "I told 'em, I don't need a cancer doctor. I'm eighty-nine years old. I've lived through World War II and Vietnam. My wife's been gone for twenty years, and my youngest granddaughter just had her first baby last year. I've lived too good of a life to go out sick with chemotherapy."

His chuckling turned into a fit of coughing. Sympathetically, I put my hand on his back. "Sounds like you've lived a pretty full life." I closed my eyes and focused on Mr. Cash's cancer.

"I have," he said. "It'd be swell to see it through Christmas one last time with my kids, but I'm ready to go on home when the good Lord wants me."

With my other hand, I patted his arm. "World War II and Vietnam, huh? That's pretty impressive."

"Yep." He paused to cough and catch his breath. "I was in one of the first groups that arrived at Hiroshima after they dropped the bomb on 'em. There was nothin'. I mean, no people, no military, no stray dogs even. It was all ash and black." He shook his head as my hand warmed on his back. "Then I was in Saigon for a year during Vietnam."

"That's incredible, Mr. Cash," I said.

He took a deep and easy breath and looked over at me. "You feelin' all right, young lady? You seem awfully warm to me."

I leaned into him. "I'm fine. Want to hear a secret?"

"Sure."

I lowered my voice and looked carefully around the room. "I'm pregnant."

He laughed. "No kidding? I'll bet your daddy's a happy man."

"He doesn't know yet," I said. "I think I might tell him today."

He pulled back and eyed me curiously. "I didn't know you were married."

I shook my head. "Oh, I'm not. So you'd better say a prayer for me before I go back there and break the news."

He pointed down at the carpet. "You're going to tell him right now?"

I sighed. "That's the plan."

He chuckled. "Well, that man is over the moon about you. I'm sure you'll be fine. Where's the baby's father?"

My hand cooled as the last ounces of my power left my fingers. I slowly removed it so Mr. Cash wouldn't notice.

I shrugged my shoulders. "He's a military man too. He's deployed right now."

"Really?" he asked. "What branch?"

"The Marines."

He laughed, this time with no rasp in his voice at all. "I was an Army man myself," he said. "But I won't hold it against 'ya that your man is a *jarhead*."

I clasped my hands together over my knee. "I try not to hold it against him myself."

The door into the waiting room swung open, and my dad stepped out with an elderly woman clutching his arm. "Now, don't you forget," she was saying, "to bake the casserole at 350 degrees for an hour."

"I won't forget," he replied.

Dad turned, his face brightening when he saw me. He looked down at the old woman. "Mrs. Hannigan, you be safe on your drive home now."

She patted his hand. "I will, Robert. I will."

The woman left the office, and Dad walked over to me and Mr. Cash. "Otis, I hope my daughter isn't causing you too much trouble out here," he said, reaching out to shake his hand.

I rolled my eyes.

Mr. Cash smiled. "She's just as wonderful as you say she is."

Blushing, I nudged him with my elbow. "You old charmer."

He laughed.

We both stood. Dad looked at me. "Mr. Cash is my last appointment before lunch. Do you have time to wait?"

I opened my mouth to answer, but Mr. Cash cut me off. "You know, Dr. Jordan, I'm havin' a pretty good day today. I think I'll reschedule my appointment and let you chat with this lovely girl." The old man winked at me.

Dad's mouth fell open a little. "Are you sure, Otis?"

"Yeah, I don't mind waiting," I told him.

Otis shook his head. "I'm sure. Maybe I'll go see my own daughter."

I smiled as he turned to leave. "Mr. Cash?"

He looked at me in question.

I hugged him. "Happy Thanksgiving, and if I don't bump into you again beforehand, have a Merry Christmas too. I hope you enjoy it with your family."

He cocked his chin to the side and beamed at me. "The good Lord willin'." Without another word, he turned and left the room.

Dad looked down at me and raised an eyebrow. "You healed him, didn't you?"

I pressed my lips together. "Maybe."

He sighed and shook his head. "People will start thinking I'm a miracle worker if all my patients keep ending up suddenly cured around here." He put his arm around my shoulders and steered me through the door toward his office.

"Is that such a bad thing?" I asked, looking up at him.

"Well, no, but it will raise questions. Mr. Otis has stage four terminal cancer," he said.

I grinned. "Not anymore."

He rifled through some files on his desk while I sat in the leather wingback chairs meant for patients and pharmaceutical reps. "How come you're not at work today?" he asked. "Are you already off for the holiday?"

I crossed my legs. "I had an appointment with Dr. Watt's downstairs."

He carried a folder to the filing cabinet in the corner. "A checkup?"

I scrunched up my nose. "Sort of. Dad, you need to sit down."

He turned and looked at me. "Is everything OK, sweetheart?"

A deep breath puffed out my cheeks. I slowly expelled it. "Well…"

His eyes widened, and he moved over in front of me, sitting down carefully on the edge of his desk. "What is it?"

"Warren just called," I said. "He left the States."

Relief washed over Dad's face, like he was sure I was about to tell him I was dying. "I hate that. He still doesn't know when he will be back?"

I shook my head. "Nope."

"Well, that's not exactly a surprise—"

I cut him off. "There's more, Dad."

His face fell again. "Oh no. I hate it when you say that."

I rubbed my fingers against my eyes. "Do you promise you won't freak out?"

He laughed. "Sloan, last month you told me your migraines were supernatural. Then you told me you were half-angel. After that, you informed me your birth mother was a demon, and she tried to kill you. Do you really think you could say anything to me at this point that would shock me?"

"I'm pregnant."

Dad slipped off the corner of his desk. He caught himself before hitting the floor. His mouth was gaping as he straightened. "What?"

I pulled the ultrasound picture from my purse and handed it to him. "I'm due July 11th."

His mouth was still hanging open as he looked at it.

"Dad?"

He glanced up. "Can I assume Warren is the father?"

I folded my arms across my chest and scowled. "Seriously?"

He held up his hands in defense. "It's a legitimate question that I'm sure Warren will probably ask as well."

This time, *my* mouth fell open. "He'd better not!"

"He's aware things aren't strictly business with you and Detective McNamara."

"That may be true, but Warren knows I'm not sleeping with Nathan. I'm surprised, and pretty disappointed, it even crossed your mind."

He sighed. "I'm sorry. I didn't mean it the way it sounded. Have you told him?"

I smirked. "Warren or Nathan McNamara?"

He frowned. "Sloan."

"I haven't told anybody, Dad. Not even Adrianne," I said, and it surprised even me. I'd been telling my best friend, Adrianne Marx, everything since I was thirteen.

"Why didn't you tell Warren?"

"Because I found out after he left. I figured it out when we dropped him off at the Marine station in Charlotte last month and I didn't get a migraine. It made everything make sense. My demon-mom trying to murder me, my sudden ability to heal, oh —and I saw Warren's soul for the first time ever."

"That's right. You could never see his soul," he said.

"But I can now. I can sense him like I can sense everyone else," I said.

He rubbed his palms over his face.

I leaned forward and rested my elbow on his desk. "Am I wrong for not telling Warren? It didn't seem right because he's already so worried about me, and I'm sure he's worried about the crap with me and Nathan..." I cast my gaze at the carpet. "He needs to focus on whatever dangerous stuff they have him doing. He doesn't need anything else to freak out about."

Dad sighed. "I don't know, Sloan. If it were me, I would want to know. Imagine what it will do to him when he shows up and you've got a belly out to here." He was holding his hand about a foot out from his stomach. "Or worse. What if you've got a baby in your arms when he comes home?"

I groaned. "You're probably right. Maybe I'll tell him if I get to talk to him again on the phone. I'm not writing it in a letter though."

He shook his head. "No, don't do that." He handed me the ultrasound picture. "Does this mean you'll marry him?"

"We talked about it before he left, but he said I needed to take the time while he's gone to figure out what I want for the rest of my life," I said.

"Him or the detective?" Dad asked.

I nodded.

"Well?" he asked.

I turned my palms up. "Aside from the obvious fact that I'm in love with Warren, doesn't it kind of make up my mind if we're having a baby together?"

Dad was thoughtful for a moment. "Sloan, you can't put that kind of pressure on your child. You can't just marry him because of the baby. You still have to choose for yourself." He laughed a little. "I will say you won't come across another man like Warren. I wouldn't be so understanding if I were in his shoes."

Tears pooled in my eyes. "I can't help it. If I could turn off my feelings for Nathan, I would. I swear I would."

Dad got up and knelt down beside me. "Come here." He pulled me into his arms and let me cry on his shoulder.

"I don't know what to do. Why can't I just love them both?"

He pulled back to look at me. His eyes were serious. "You *can* love them both. But sometimes, the most loving thing we can do for someone is let them go."

I sniffed and wiped my nose on my sleeve. "I don't know how."

He tucked a loose strand of hair behind my ear. "You have to figure out how, sweetheart, because three-way relationships don't work. Pretty soon you won't have a choice, and you might lose them both." He handed me a tissue from the box on his desk. "May I ask you a question?"

I braced myself.

He studied my face. "What is it about Nathan?" He held up his hands. "Don't get me wrong, he's a good man. It's just you and

Warren seem so perfect for each other. It surprises me you're still struggling with a decision."

I had asked myself the same question over and over since the fall. "You know, for years I pretended to be normal because I feared if people found out what I was really like, they'd be afraid or they'd hate me. For years no one knew except Adrianne, not even you and mom."

Dad squeezed my hand.

"Then Nathan showed up," I said, smiling. "The first day we met, he had me so flustered that I basically blurted it out." I took a deep breath. "And he did the opposite of reject me. He found out everything I wanted to keep hidden, and I think he liked me even more."

"And then Warren showed up," Dad said with a sad, soft expression.

"Yeah, and like you said, Warren's perfect. It's like he was made for me," I said. "Sometimes it feels like the universe shut everything down with me and Nathan and neither of us had a choice in it."

Dad grinned. "I wouldn't say it shut *everything* down. Otherwise you wouldn't still have to choose."

"Yeah."

He squeezed my shoulder. "Well, if your old man's opinion matters, I really like them both. I don't think you could find two better men to pick from."

I whined. "That is so not helpful."

"I know."

"You really won't tell me who you think I should be with?" I asked.

He shook his head. "Maybe someday but not today." He winked at me. "I don't want to give up any leverage I may have in case they start bribing me with gifts or money."

I wadded up the tissue and threw it at him.

CHAPTER TWO

My ability to summon people had drastically improved since I found out I was pregnant. So when my phone rang as I left Dad's office, it wasn't a surprise that Detective Nathan McNamara's face popped up on the screen.

I tapped the answer button and pressed the phone to my ear. "I was just talking about you," I said in lieu of a greeting.

He chuckled. "You know, it's not always you putting your voodoo on me. Sometimes I call or come by all on my own."

I squinted against the sunshine as I unlocked my car and got inside. "Whatever you say, Nathan. What's up?"

"Where are you?" he asked.

"I stopped in to visit my dad, but I'm heading back to work now." I started my engine and backed out of the parking space.

"Good. Come by my office on your way in."

I slammed on my brakes, bringing the car to a lurching halt. Nathan's office was located inside the jail, and I could no longer take my Xanax. "No."

"No?" he asked. "Trust me. You want to see this."

I groaned and put the car in drive.

"I'll see you in ten minutes," he said and disconnected the call.

Nathan knew how much being at the jail affected me, and he wouldn't ask me to come if it wasn't important. So, on the drive there, I practiced deep breathing exercises and tried to think about anything but the panic attack I knew was on its way.

A few minutes later, I pulled into the jail parking lot and parked in the space beside Nathan's county-issued SUV. I took the steps to the front door two at a time and sucked in a deep breath before pulling the door open.

I breathed a small sigh of relief when I saw Virginia Claybrooks stuffed into the office chair behind the front desk. Her uniform was screaming at the seams, and her shoulder-length black wig was sitting a little too far back on her forehead. She was on the phone, and her bright red lips bent into a fake smile when she saw me.

She held up a long manicured fingernail, signaling for me to wait before continuing her animated verbal assault on whoever was on the other end of the line. "Honey, if you wanted to have Thanksgiving dinner with your baby boy, you shoulda raised him better so his ass didn't wind up in jail! I don't give a turkey's butt about whatchoo think is fair and not fair. Not fair is me having to sit my ass on this phone, listening to the whinin' and complainin' of you people when I oughtta be...Hello? Hello?"

She stared at the phone for a moment in disbelief. "That bitch done hung up on me!"

I tried to suppress my laughter, but I wasn't successful.

She rounded on me. "You think sumthins' funny?"

I covered my mouth with my hand and shook my head. "No, Ms. Claybrooks. I'm sorry."

"How 'you know my name?" she barked at me.

"Ms. Claybrooks, I've worked with the sheriff for years." I tapped my chest. "I'm Sloan Jordan."

She tossed her head from side to side. "I don't know no Sloan Jordan."

I sighed. "Can you please tell Detective McNamara I'm here?" I asked. "He's expecting me."

She looked me up and down so skeptically that I half-expected her to throw me out the front door. "Mmm-hmm," she said, pressing her lips together. She picked up the phone and pushed a few buttons. "McNamara!" She waited. "De-Tec-Tiv Mc-Na-Mara!" Her voice bounced off the concrete walls around us.

She slammed the phone down and looked at me. "He ain't answerin'."

Her phone rang, and she picked it up. "Hello?" She rolled her eyes toward the ceiling and huffed. "They's six thousand offices up in this buildin'. How do you people expect me to remember 'em all. I got close enough for you to hear me so stop your bitchin'." She looked over at me. "You got a girl up here askin' for ya…Uh-huh, OK." She hung up the phone and forced a smile in my direction. "He'll be right with you."

Rather than sit, I paced the lobby. Evil reverberated off the walls like a heartbeat. The whole place pulsed with dark energy, and it tightened around my throat. I took a deep breath in and blew it out slowly. The mechanical doors slid open, and Nathan stuck his head out. "Sloan!"

I jumped, then scurried over.

Even my rising anxiety wasn't enough to completely suppress the butterflies that were disturbed every time I laid eyes on Nathan McNamara. He was in his standard outfit of khaki tactical cargos and an olive drab green fleece pullover. He wore his badge around his neck and a ball cap with an American flag patch on the front pulled low over his face.

Nathan was the guy mothers wanted their daughters to marry, and the one fathers warned them about, all wrapped up in one. He was the blond-haired boy next door with a baby-face smile and the ability to put a bullet between someone's eyes. He was also the kryptonite to my better judgement, and he had been nothing but trouble for me since the day we met.

"Hey stranger," he said. "Long time, no see."

That was a joke. Nathan had come by every night for the past three weeks. Warren had asked him to keep tabs on me since we found out I had a cosmic bounty on my head.

His eyes widened when I stepped through the door. "You OK?"

I pumped the collar of my blouse forcing cool air down the front. "You know I'm not. I hate this place."

He nudged me forward. "Come on. We won't be here long."

We walked past his office, and I jerked my thumb toward his door. "Where are we going?"

"Women's solitary," he answered.

I shuddered. "Isn't that where they keep the really bad people?"

"Sometimes."

"Nathan," I whined, dragging my feet.

He urged me on. "We'll be on the medical hall. I promise it'll be worth it."

My rising blood pressure stirred my doubt in him.

Once we were deep inside the jail, we went through one more heavy metal door that opened to a long hallway. Nathan escorted me by four locked rooms that reeked of evil before stopping in front of an empty cell. "What is this?" I asked.

He nodded toward the door. "Look through the window."

Curious, I peeked inside.

The stale white room was flooded with blinding light from the overhead halogens. There was a steel frame bed shoved against the wall, a metal toilet, and a matching small sink. "I don't get it," I said, looking back at him.

He looked in, then took a step back. "Under the bed."

I leaned toward the glass again. This time I saw long strands of red hair laying across the concrete floor, and the edge of a corpse peeked out from the shadows. I gasped. "Why is there a body in there?"

"Keep watching." He knocked his knuckles against the metal.

A hand shot out from under the bed in our direction. I jumped back. "What the hell?"

He put his hand on my shoulder and ushered me forward again. Covering my mouth with my hands, I watched an emaciated woman, paler than anyone I'd ever seen, drag herself out from under the bed. I scrambled to get away, but Nathan held me still.

He put his lips to my ear. "She can't get to you."

"She's not a *she*, Nathan." I gripped his sleeve as I looked at him. "She's not human."

He looked only mildly surprised. "They found her wandering around the Vance Memorial completely naked. She doesn't speak English, but she kept saying one thing very clearly."

"What was that?"

"Sloan Jordan."

My mouth fell open. "What?"

Then her soulless eyes settled on me. They were the color of flawless sapphires. "*Id vos, Sloan!*" The woman banged her fists against the glass, her nails caked with dirt, or blood, I wasn't sure which. I'd put my money on blood given the heavy white bandages on her forearms. "*Id vos! Id vos! Utavi! Ename utavi.*"

Had I not already been mid-panic attack, she would have triggered one. I stumbled back into Nathan.

"*Nankaj morteirakka!*" she screamed.

My heart was pounding. The air was as thick as soup. "Nathan, I can't stay in here."

He put his hand on the back of my neck. "Did you take your Xanax?"

I shook my head. "No. I forgot it," I lied.

The woman threw her body against the door. "*Ketka, Sloan! Ename utavi!*"

Nathan took hold of my arm, just as my legs wobbled. "Come on. Let's get you out of here." He hooked an arm around my waist.

She was still wailing in her cell. "Sloan! *Sloan!*"

My heart was pounding so loud I could swear it was echoing off of the walls. I feared my head might pop right off my shoulders. Nathan was carrying me more than I was actually walking. "Hold on," he said, pushing a door open.

When we got to the front of the building, we reached a door that could only be opened by Master Control. Nathan pressed the button and held it down. When no one answered, he groaned and pushed it again. Finally, Ms. Claybrooks came over the speaker. "Seriously!" she shouted. "They's only one of me up here, ya know!"

I bent at the waist and rested my hands on my knees for support as the floor spun in and out of focus.

"Ms. Claybrooks, it's Detective McNamara. I need you to open the door immediately." He was trying to sound calm but not doing a convincing job of it.

"Hold your horses! I'm just one woman," she said.

Finally, the door slid open, and I sprinted through it. I was panting when Nathan caught up with me at the front door. "Happy Thanksgivin', y'all," Ms. Claybrooks called as I bolted outside into the crisp, cold mountain air.

I sucked in an icy breath and blew it out toward the sky. "Oh my god."

He gripped the sides of my waist, and angled his head to look me in the eye. "Geez, Sloan. You about gave me a heart attack. Breathe."

I took a few deep breaths. "Please get me out of here."

He clicked the unlock button on his SUV. "Come on. I'll buy you lunch."

I didn't have time for lunch, but nothing in me wanted to argue. He opened the passenger side door, and I climbed in and rested my forehead against the dashboard. He got in and cranked the engine, peeling his tires as he exited the parking lot. When we were a safe distance away, my heart rate slowed to normal. I sat back in my seat and opened my eyes.

"I'm sorry. I had to leave," I said.

He shook his head. "It's not your fault. I didn't think it through before calling you."

I turned toward him. "What was that thing?"

He shrugged. "I was hoping you could tell me. Deputies brought her in this morning. They called me when she kept rattling on about you. No name, no ID. Nobody even knows what language she's speaking."

My stomach felt sick. "You've heard it before. I'm pretty sure that's my demon mom's language."

"You think so?"

I was still panting. "Yeah. And I don't understand much Latin, but I think whatever she was saying had something to do with someone dying." I tapped my chest. "Probably me."

He scowled. "Don't talk like that." He jerked his thumb back toward the building. "Do you think she's like you and Warren?"

I looked over at him. "Maybe. Or she could be like Abigail."

He drummed his fingers on the steering wheel. "Do you think there's a chance she could *be* Abigail?"

I cringed at the thought. I'd watched the body the world knew as Abigail Smith turn to dust, but the angel Samael had told us she would procure another body. I chewed on my fingernail. "Abigail doesn't strike me as the type to allow herself to be locked up."

He nodded. "I thought the same thing. That's the only reason I even considered letting you near her." He leaned toward his door and wedged his hand into his pocket. He produced his cell phone and handed it to me. "Look in my photo gallery."

After a moment of searching, I navigated my way to the pictures on his phone. I saw my own face before I saw anything else. There was a succession of photos of me making funny faces that I'd taken one night when Nathan left his phone lying on my sofa. It had been weeks before, and he hadn't deleted them.

"Check the folder called 'work' in the gallery list," he said, snapping me back to reality.

I tapped the work folder open, and immediately cringed at the sight of blood. "Eww."

"Look at the first few," he insisted. "That's what's under those bandages on that girl."

It took me a second to figure out I was looking at pictures of the red-head's forearms. Two different words were written on... no *carved into* her arms. The first one was a little hard to read. "Kot...*kotailis?*" I asked, looking over at him. "Is that what it says?"

He shrugged. "I'm not sure, but that's what it looks like."

"What does it mean?"

He shook his head. "I don't know that either. Could be something from a video game. Could be an online company in the UK. Could be crazy-person-speak for 'let's give McNamara a headache.' Beats me."

My bottom lip poked out as I looked at the second word. "Nathan, why does she have my name carved into her arm?"

He cringed and turned his palm up. "Sorry. I'm striking out with answers today." He held out his hand for his phone, and I gave it to him. "Is there any way I can get the info on her to Warren? I'd like him to see it."

I sighed and shook my head. "Nope. He called this morning. He's officially on his way to wherever they're sending him."

His face twisted into a frown. "That sucks. How are you doing with it?"

I shrugged my shoulders. "I hate it, but we knew it was coming sooner or later."

He pointed his finger down the road ahead. "Want to blow off work and go to the bar?"

"As tempting as that sounds, I can't" ...*because I'm pregnant,* I silently added. I rested my head back against the seat, and the cloth ceiling of Nathan's SUV caught my attention. It was covered with patches for his hat. "This is new," I said, giggling as I read some of them.

Finish your beer. There are sober kids in Africa.

My idea of 'help from above' is a sniper on the roof.

I'm here to kick ass and chew bubblegum and I'm all out of bubblegum.

He grinned. "It's become somewhat of an obsession. People at work are giving them to me now."

"It's definitely a conversation starter." After a moment, I rolled my head toward him. "What will the jail do with her?"

He turned his palm up on the steering wheel. "Probably release her to the mental hospital. She's not stable enough to be released into public, and they can't keep her locked up."

"What if she comes after me?" I asked.

He looked over his shoulder at me. "You know I won't let that happen. Besides, you won't be home this weekend to worry about her."

I straightened in my seat. "Oh, yeah! We're going to Raleigh. I've had so much on my mind, I almost forgot. When are we leaving?"

Nathan's family had been waiting for months to finally be able to lay his baby sister, Ashley, to rest. I'd promised to be moral support for the burial service.

He pulled into the parking lot of my favorite restaurant, Tupelo Honey. "Well, my mom invited you to come to our house for Thanksgiving tomorrow, but I told her you would probably want to spend the day with your dad. So we can leave on Friday if you want."

"Sure," I said. "What are you doing tomorrow?"

He shrugged. "Getting take out and watching football, I guess."

I rolled my eyes. "No, you're not. You'll come eat with us. Dad and I are cooking, so the food might suck, but it would be nice to have another body at the table."

He smiled as he put the car in park. "I'd love to. What can I bring?"

I laughed as we got out. "A backup plan."

My nerves were frayed for the rest of the day. Every time I blinked, I saw the red-haired woman's crazy blue eyes frantic with terror. Her screams were on replay in my brain like the theme song to my own personal horror movie.

When I pulled into my driveway and parked next to Warren's black Dodge Challenger, it was dark in Asheville. Mile markers could have ticked off the distance between my car and my front door and it wouldn't have seemed any further away. I was frozen in the driver's seat, unable to even will myself to turn off the engine. Gripping the steering wheel with both hands, I swallowed hard.

Nathan had offered to escort me home from work, but like the idiot I was, I insisted I was fine.

I wasn't fine.

I was very, very far from it.

Laying my face against the back of my hands on the steering wheel, I focused on breathing.

A car horn blasted behind me.

My foot slipped off the brake and onto the gas pedal, sending the car barreling forward into the large rhododendron that crowned my driveway. I cursed.

Adrianne's red sports car pulled up behind me as I backed out of the bush. When I was completely on the gravel again, I put the car in park.

My best friend was laughing as I got out. "Are you drunk?"

I slammed my car door. "You scared the crap out of me!" I walked to the front of my car and shined the light from my cell phone onto the hood. "What are you doing here?" I began plucking leaves from the grill.

"Your dad dropped by my shop today and said I should check in on you. He was really worried, so I figured we'd need this." She held up a bottle of tequila. "Are you OK?"

I swiped my hand across the hood. Thankfully, I didn't feel any major scratches. "It's been a rough day."

She looped her arm through mine as we walked up the sidewalk. "I heard Warren left."

I frowned up at her. "That's only the beginning of it."

A faint ripple against the night sky caught my attention. It was an angel, or *angels*, I wasn't sure. I'd been seeing them regularly since we returned from Texas. Adrianne didn't notice.

"What else happened?" she asked, leading me up the front steps.

I unlocked the door and unwound my scarf as we walked inside. "Well, a crazy woman—who may or may not be a demon—was arrested downtown today. She was walking around naked with my name carved into the skin on her arm."

Her eyes widened as she shrugged out of her coat. "I heard about a naked woman downtown. I didn't hear anything about you though."

I followed her into the kitchen where she went straight to the cupboard containing my shot glasses.

"Nathan called me down to the jail to see her for myself. She started screaming in some crazy language, then I almost passed out from a panic attack." I plopped down in a chair at the table. "It was fun."

She filled two shot glasses full of golden liquor and pushed one in my direction. In one swift motion, she drained hers. "Who was the woman?" she asked.

I shrugged. "Nobody knows."

"What does she want with you?" she asked, refilling her glass.

"Don't know that either." I slouched in my seat. "Nathan almost had to carry me out of there, so I didn't have a chance to talk to her."

When she picked up her second shot, she noticed my first one was still sitting in front of me. She glanced up expectantly.

I looked at it, then back at her. "I can't drink it."

"Why not?" Before I had a chance to answer, her mouth fell open. She pointed at me. "Oh my god. You're pregnant!"

I slumped over the table. "And you accuse *me* of being psychic."

She gently shoved my shoulder. "Are you serious? When did you find out?"

"I figured it out when we dropped Warren off in Charlotte and I didn't get a migraine. Four positive pregnancy tests and then an ultrasound today confirmed it," I said.

She tossed her hands up. "You've known for a month and didn't tell me!"

I grimaced. "I didn't tell anyone till today."

"Have you told Warren?"

I shook my head.

"Nathan?"

"No. Just my dad. Nobody else knows," I said.

She rubbed her hands over her face. "Warren will be fine, but Nathan will freak out. You know that right?"

I felt a familiar hitch in my throat that always preceded tears. "Please don't make me cry again. I've cried all day." I blinked a few times to keep my tear ducts in line.

She pointed a perfectly manicured fingernail at me. "This is what you get for not figuring out your feelings before you hooked up with Warren."

I shook my head. "That's not helpful."

She drank her second shot. "Didn't mean for it to be." She screwed the cap back on the tequila. "Just stating the facts."

"Adrianne, how am I supposed to tell him?"

She sighed. "I don't know, but you need to tell him soon. The longer you wait, the worse it will be. And you've got to have some boundaries with him. You guys can't be together all the time like you are."

"I know." I slouched in my seat. "I'll tell him this weekend. We're visiting his parents' house in Raleigh for his sister's memorial service."

"Well, wait till after the funeral and then break it to him. Cut the poor guy some slack."

I nodded, still pouting. "You're right."

She drummed her nails on the table. "So, what does you and Warren having a baby together mean?"

"Samael, the angel that was with us in Texas, told me demons would try to kill me."

She rolled her eyes. "Not what I meant. I was wondering if you've decided to marry Warren, but I can see how that would take a back seat to being murdered."

I chuckled. Only Adrianne could make that statement funny.

"Why do they want to kill you?" she asked.

I shrugged my shoulders. "I'm not really sure, but I do know I've got a bunch of angel guardians floating around me all the time."

Her eyes searched the ceiling.

"You can't see them," I told her. "They don't come inside, anyway."

"That's creepy."

"Tell me about it." I put my hand on her arm. "Thanks for coming by tonight. I really didn't have it in me to be alone, and I know I can't keep relying on Nathan."

She patted my hand with her own. "Call me anytime, Sloan. I may be as much of a wimp as you, but at least we can puss out together." Getting up from the table, she offered me her hand. "Enough supernatural B.S. for tonight. We've got important things to discuss."

"Like what?" I asked as she pulled me to my feet.

She spun around and put her hands on her hips. "Like redecorating. Where the hell will you put a baby in this tiny dollhouse?"

Where the hell, indeed.

CHAPTER THREE

The redecoration plans began and ended with: Sloan needs to buy a bigger house. After that, I heard all about the new stylist her salon had hired and the rising rent crisis in downtown Asheville. Adrianne left when I could no longer hold my eyes open, despite my pleas for a slumber party. Once she was gone, I packed for my trip with Nathan, then stared at the ceiling fan for most of the night and seriously contemplated taking my Xanax against my doctor's advice. I should have had her define "absolutely essential" before I left her office. My fingernails were bloody by midnight.

After fading out of consciousness sometime around four in the morning, I awoke to the shrill ring of my cell phone. I picked it up and saw Nathan's picture on the screen. It was eight forty-five. I groaned and tapped the answer button. "What did I ever do to you?" I asked. "It's my day off."

"Good morning to you too, sunshine," he said.

"Screw you, Nathan."

He laughed. "I'm outside and it's snowing. Come let me in."

With a huff, I disconnected and dropped the phone on the mattress. I sat up, draped my blanket over my head, and wrapped it around my body instead of getting dressed. Barefoot, I trudged down the cold hardwood steps, through the living room, and to the door. I yanked it open.

His head snapped back with surprise. "Whoa. You look terrifying."

I rubbed my eyes. "I didn't get much sleep. Why are you here?"

Dusting the snow off his shoulders, he stepped inside and wiped his boots on the welcome mat. "It's Thanksgiving. You invited me."

I scowled as I closed the door behind him. "I invited you to eat with us later at my dad's. It's the butt crack of dawn."

He slipped off his camel colored jacket. "Thanksgiving is an all-day gig, Sloan. The parade starts at nine."

I tightened the blanket around me and cocked my head to the side. "The parade?"

"The Thanksgiving Day Parade."

I smiled. "I know what it is. You get up early to watch it?"

He held up his hands in confusion. "Doesn't everyone?"

I laughed and shook my head. "Not everyone over the age of seven."

"Shut up, Sloan."

The patch on the front of his hat said, *I'd be thankful if you'd shut the hell up.* Chuckling to myself, I rolled my eyes and turned toward the stairs. "I'm going to get dressed. You woke me up, so I expect coffee when I come back downstairs."

"What do I get in return?" he called after me.

I started up the steps. "You get to not die today."

Fifteen minutes and a hot shower later, I was much more alert when I went back down to the living room to find Nathan lounging on my white sofa. His socked feet rested on the coffee table, and his thighs cradled a bowl of dry cereal. The Thanksgiving Day Parade was live on my flat screen. It was kind of adorable.

He looked up at me. "You look less lethal now."

I was pulling my hair up into a ponytail. "I still might kill you."

"The coffee's fresh."

"Bless you," I whispered as I walked past him toward the kitchen.

On the third shelf of the cupboard above the coffee pot was one of Warren's man-sized travel mugs. I stretched on my tiptoes to retrieve it. One cup of coffee simply wouldn't be enough. As I filled the mug, Dr. Watts' voice came to mind. "Go easy on the caffeine," she'd said.

My shoulders slumped and I whimpered.

"Everything OK in there?" Nathan called.

"Yeah."

Damn it.

I put Warren's cup back and got my regular mug. I fought back bitterness as I poured it half-empty. I shut off the coffee maker and went back to the living room. "You ready to go?" I asked, taking a tiny sip of my drink.

Nathan looked over his shoulder. "Can we wait till a commercial?"

I giggled. "Sure." Stepping over his legs, I plopped down beside him. I eyed the bowl he was holding. "Where did you find Lucky Charms cereal?"

He offered me a rainbow marshmallow. "Brought it from home. I thought you'd have milk. I'm not sure why."

"Sorry," I said, taking the rainbow from his fingers.

He pointed at the screen. "You just missed the new Snoopy and Woodstock balloon."

I turned toward him. "It's like I've never met you before."

Laughing again, he funneled a handful of cereal into his mouth.

When the program went to a commercial break, Nathan picked up the remote and shut the television off. "Come on. Let's hurry and get to your dad's. I don't want to miss Joan Jett."

Before we left the house, I picked up the suitcase I'd packed and left in the foyer the night before.

He cocked an eyebrow as he eyed it in my hand and opened the front door. "You running away?" he asked, taking it from my hands.

We walked outside together, and I turned to lock the front door. "I'm crashing at Dad's tonight. You can pick me up there in the morning."

"Really? How come?" he asked.

I grimaced. "I'm kinda becoming a wuss at being alone. Nightmares and such."

A snowflake landed on my cheek. He brushed it away. "You don't have to be alone."

The nerve endings on my cheek tingled from his fingertip. "I know. Thanks."

He gestured toward the truck. "Ready?"

"Yeah." I paused before walking down the front steps and saluted the ripples in the sky. "Hold down the fort while I'm gone, boys."

Nathan looked around. "What the hell?"

I looked to the sky. "I'm talking to my guardian angels."

He laughed. "Are you cracking up on me?"

I pointed. "There's an angel right there, or maybe more than one. I'm not sure. They've been following me around since we got back from Texas."

He looked in the direction of my finger. "I don't see anything."

Rolling my eyes, I shook my head. "Mortal."

He sighed and offered me his arm as we headed out into the flurries. "You weird me out sometimes."

I gripped his sleeve as we carefully went down the stairs. "I know. I don't want things to get too boring."

My foot slipped on a patch of slush.

Nathan's bicep crushed my arm against his chest, while his other arm shot behind my back as my feet flew forward. Wide-eyed and panting, we both stared at each other a moment as I regained my footing.

He burst out laughing. "Boring? No one can ever accuse you of being boring!"

We took Nathan's pickup to my dad's house on the outskirts of downtown Asheville. The roads were wet and empty as we wound up the mountainside. It was that time of year when Mother Nature was stuck in limbo between the decay of fall and a glistening winter. The oaks and maples were bare, jutting out from the mountains like a dark skeleton of the forest. The thick branches of the hemlocks sagged with the weight of the almost-snow dropping from the gray sky in clumps. Soon, North Carolina would be a winter wonderland, but that day it was just soggy and cold.

Dad's stone chimney was pumping out smoke when we pulled in the driveway.

Nathan grabbed my arm when I reached for my door handle. "Get out over here on my side so we can avoid any holiday catastrophes, please."

I laughed and scooted across the bench seat toward him. He held me steady with both hands as I slid down from the cab.

When we walked in the front door of the house, a crash of metal clanged against the tile floor in the kitchen. "Dad?" I called out as I took off my winter coat.

"I'm all right!" he answered.

Nathan followed me to the kitchen where we found my father with a pile of pots and pans scattered around his feet. He shrugged his shoulders as he looked around at them. "I pulled out the bottom one, and they all fell," he explained.

We helped pick them up.

Once all the cookware was tucked back in the cabinet, Dad's eyes settled on Nathan. "Detective McNamara, I wasn't expecting to see you this morning."

Nathan stuffed his hands into his pockets. "Sloan invited me. I hope that's OK."

My father squeezed Nathan's arm. "Of course it is. You're always welcome here. I just assumed you would be with your family today."

Nathan shook his head. "Sloan and I are heading to Raleigh tomorrow to see them."

Dad's eyes widened, and he cast his gaze down at me. "Oh, really?"

"His sister's burial service is this weekend, so I'm going with him," I said.

"Oh." Dad's shoulders sagged. "Please send my condolences."

Nathan nodded. "I will, sir. Thank you."

Dad stepped over to the coffee pot. "Would you like some coffee, Detective?"

"Please, Dr. Jordan. Call me, Nathan," he said.

My dad smiled. "As long as you promise to call me Robert."

Nathan grinned as Dad handed him a cup. "Deal." Nathan motioned toward the den behind us. "Do you mind if I turn on the television?"

I giggled. "Nathan wants to watch the parade."

Dad held out his hands. "Be my guest."

I pulled out a barstool at the counter. "I want some coffee, Dad."

He shook his head. "Not in your condition, Sloan. It isn't healthy."

Nathan glanced back at me as he turned on the parade. "You can't have coffee now?"

Dad poured his own mug full and shook his head. "No. Caffeine isn't good for the ba—"

"My panic disorder!" I shouted to interrupt him with a loaded glare. "I'm not supposed to have caffeine due to my anxiety. Right, Dad?"

Dad looked at me, then at Nathan and back at me before a

mental light bulb flickered on. "Oh, yes. Caffeine is no good for your anxiety, Sloan."

Nathan settled onto the barstool next to mine. "Oh man. That's bad news for everyone if Sloan can't have coffee in the morning. That was the only thing standing between all of us and a beheading before ten A.M."

I elbowed him in the ribs. "Shut up."

He grinned over the rim of his cup.

"So, Dad, what's on the menu for today?" I asked, leaning on my elbows.

He stepped across the kitchen. "Well, I went to the grocery store this morning and bought a turkey." He pulled the refrigerator door open and lifted out the plastic covered bird. He set it down with a heavy thud on the marble counter top.

My eyes doubled in size. "How big is that thing?"

He looked at the tag. "Twenty-two pounds. Do you think it's big enough?" He wasn't joking.

"It's only you, me, and Nathan eating, right?" I asked.

He nodded.

I exchanged a smile with Nathan and chuckled. "Surely, it's plenty." I got up and walked over to the turkey. "Now, does anyone know how to cook one of these things?"

No one answered.

I looked around at them. "Fantastic. Nathan, can you Google directions on your phone for how to cook a turkey?"

He whipped out his cell phone, and I carried the bird to the sink. "This thing is frozen solid," I said. "Can we cook frozen meat?"

My dad shrugged. "I don't see why not. It will thaw as it cooks, right?"

I shrugged. "I guess so."

"All these directions say to thaw the turkey first," Nathan said, glancing up from his phone. "Then you cook it on 325 degrees for 4 to 4 ½ hours."

Dad cocked his head to the side. "Well, if we start with it frozen, why don't we kick up the temperature a little to help it thaw and cook faster."

I studied the knobs on the oven. "That's a good plan. What should I set the oven on?"

"How about an even 400 degrees?" he suggested.

"Sounds good to me," I said, dialing it up to 400.

"I also got potatoes, green beans, and rolls from the bakery," Dad said.

I looked up at him. "What about dessert?"

He grimaced. "Oh, I forgot dessert."

Nathan jerked his thumb toward the front door. "I can run to the grocery store and pick up something. We passed an open grocery store on the drive here."

"OK, great." I looked around. "I need a knife."

Nathan stood. "Here you go." He produced a tactical knife from his pocket, opened it, and passed it to me.

I sliced open the plastic wrapping around the bird, and Dad handed me the biggest pan they owned. The bird clanged against the metal when I dropped it in the center.

"Let me lift that," Dad said, stepping in between me and the pan when I went to put it in the oven.

I opened the oven door, then set the timer for 4 ½ hours as Dad put the turkey inside. I washed off my hands and wiped them on my jeans. "All right, when should we cook everything else?"

Dad shrugged his shoulders. "I don't think the potatoes will take long, and the green beans are in a can."

I shook my head and laughed. "Somewhere, Mom is rolling her eyes and laughing at us right now."

Dad chuckled and put his arm around my shoulders. "I'm sure she is."

Nathan jingled his keys. "Sloan, do you want to go with me to the store?"

"If you don't mind, I'll hang out with Dad. I think you can

manage dessert by yourself." I was still hugging my father around his middle.

He held up his cell phone. "Call me if I need to get anything else."

When he was gone, my Dad looked down at me and raised an eyebrow. "So you haven't told him about the baby?"

I walked to the den and plopped down on the sofa. "No."

He sighed and sat in his recliner. "You understand you won't be able to keep a secret like this for long, right?"

I kicked off my boots and curled my feet underneath me. "I know. I guess I was hoping I'd be able to tell Warren first."

"Do you think he'll call today since it's a holiday?" he asked.

"I doubt it."

"How would he feel about you spending the weekend with Nathan?"

I looked over my shoulder at him. "He wouldn't be surprised. Warren's aware I was planning to attend the service. It's really not a big deal."

Genuine concern had contorted his face. "Can I be honest with you, Sloan?"

I hugged a couch pillow to my chest. "Of course you can."

His crumpled brow suggested he was struggling to choose his words. "You aren't doing anyone any favors by spending so much time with Nathan, especially time alone with him. Both of you may have the best of intentions at keeping the relationship appropriate, but I feel like you're playing with fire. I don't want to see you do anything you might regret once Warren gets home."

Dad was right and I knew it. "I appreciate the word of caution. I'll tell him about the baby after the funeral and work on figuring out how to put some space between us."

He cut his eyes over at me. "Please be very careful."

I nodded. "I will."

The familiar guitar riff of *I Love Rock and Roll* came over the television speakers. Joan Jett was performing Nathan's song, and he was going to miss it.

Almost two hours later, I was sound asleep on the couch when the doorbell rang. Dad slept in his recliner, snoring with his mouth hanging open.

I shuffled across the house in my socks and opened the door to find Nathan shivering in the cold, holding two grocery bags. His eyes were wide, his face pale, and he shook his head as he stepped inside. "You do not want to go to the grocery store on Thanksgiving."

I laughed and took the bags from him so he could take off his coat. I glanced at the clock on the wall. "You've been gone for hours. You were at the grocery store the whole time?"

"The whole time," he said. "That place is like the third ring of hell. People are freaking crazy. I considered getting my taser from the truck."

I peered into a bag. "Did you get dessert?"

He grimaced. "Sort of."

We walked to the kitchen, and I opened the bags. He'd bought a half-gallon of mint chocolate chip ice cream, Swiss Cake Rolls, and an economy-size bag of Skittles. I put my hand on my hip and glared at him. He held his hands up in defense. "There were no pies left! I even checked for frozen pies! Zero. So I improvised."

I rolled my eyes and put the ice cream in the freezer.

"Uh, Sloan," Nathan said behind me.

I turned to see smoke pouring from the oven. "Oh my god!" I screamed.

Dad sat up so fast that the foot rest slammed closed, jerking the seat back upright so violently he catapulted to his feet. He ran to the kitchen as I yanked the oven door open. Billows of black smoke rolled out into the room. Coughing, I waved my hand furiously in front of my face.

"Move!" Dad shouted.

The fire alarm wailed through the house.

Dad grabbed two pot holders and pulled the pan from the oven. The turkey was black, and one of its wings was on fire. Dad was chanting, "Oh no, oh no, oh no..."

Nathan doubled over laughing.

I smacked him on the back of the head. "Open the windows and shut off the alarm!"

Dad was horrified as I threw a wet dishcloth over the turkey to extinguish the flames. I wondered if he might burst into tears.

Instead he burst into hysterical laughter. "We are not responsible enough to do this!"

"I'm not going back to the grocery store!" Nathan shouted from where he fanned the smoke alarm with a newspaper.

I leaned against the counter and laughed. I pulled out my phone, took a picture of the charred bird, and sent it to Adrianne with the caption, *Happy Thanksgiving!*

Dad picked at the blackened skin. "Do you think we can save any of it?"

I grimaced. "I'm not eating that mess."

The bird was still smoking, so Dad carried the whole thing out to the back porch. Once the fire alarm stopped screaming through the house, Nathan came over and draped his arm around my shoulders. "Best Thanksgiving ever," he said, chuckling.

I elbowed him again.

Dad came back inside and closed the door. He turned and looked at us. "Well, what do we do now?"

Nathan shook his head. "Seriously. I'm not going back to the store."

I folded my arms across my chest. "Then we're having mashed potatoes, green beans, rolls, ice cream, and Skittles for Thanksgiving."

Nathan beamed down at me. "And Swiss Cake Rolls."

Dad laughed. "Do you think anyone is delivering pizza today?"

I rolled my eyes and went back to the den. On the end table next to the sofa was a picture of Mom and Dad, smiling arm in arm. I picked it up and sighed as I ran my thumb over my mother's face. A haze of smoke still clouded the entire downstairs of the house. "I miss you, Mom."

An hour later, Dad was nervously watching the rolls brown through the window in the oven, Nathan was opening the can of green beans, and I was attempting to mash the potatoes with a fork when the doorbell rang.

I walked to the foyer and pulled the front door open. Adrianne and her parents were holding covered pans and casserole dishes.

"Happy Thanksgiving!" the trio sang in unison.

I laughed and stepped out of their way. "What are you doing here?"

Dad and Nathan joined us in the foyer.

Adrianne thrust a large pan covered in tin foil into my arms. "We brought Thanksgiving to you," she said as she unwound a fluffy white scarf from around her neck.

I felt tears prickle the corner of my eyes.

Gloria Marx, Adrianne's mom, gave me a giant bear hug and kissed my temple. "We can't let our favorite family eat burnt turkey on Thanksgiving," she said.

Adrianne wrapped her arms around me and looked down from where she towered over me at six feet some odd inches in her high heels. "I think we have a whole lot to be thankful for this year, don't you?"

I smiled. "Yes, I do."

CHAPTER FOUR

The next morning, Nathan sent a text message warning me at six a.m. that he was on his way to pick me up. I'd already been awake for an hour battling the first pangs of what I assumed was morning sickness. I was bloated, nauseated, and craving coffee, but I was dressed and ready to go when he rang Dad's doorbell fifteen minutes later.

Dad opened the door as I was coming down the stairs. "Good morning, Detective."

"Good morning, sir." The corners of Nathan's mouth twitched when he saw me. "Nice hair."

"Shut up," I said as I finished tying my unruly locks in a knot on the top of my head.

Dad closed the door. "Nathan, I must run. I have a patient I need to see at the hospital, but I'll be thinking of you and your family this weekend."

Nathan shook his hand. "Thank you, sir."

Dad pointed at both of us, but gave me a warning glance. "You two be careful."

I gave him a side hug. "We will, Dad."

He kissed the side of my head, then released me and headed toward the garage. "I'll see you at dinner on Monday, Sloan?"

"Yes. Love you, Dad."

He smiled back over his shoulder. "Love you too, sweetheart."

I did a double-take when I turned back to Nathan. He looked completely different. It was the first time I had ever seen him dressed like a normal guy. He was in blue jeans and a dark green plaid shirt over a white thermal. I blinked. "What are you wearing?"

He looked down at his outfit. "You don't like it?"

"It's weird. Aside from Mom's funeral, I've never seen you in anything but your GI Joe getup." I was still eyeing him suspiciously. "This is weird."

"You'll get used to it." He looked down at his watch. "How long till you're ready?"

My head flopped to one side. "I am ready."

His eyes went from my pink hoodie, down to my blue sweatpants, and then to my fuzzy brown boots. He sighed and shook his head. "It's a good thing you're hot."

I held my arms out. "What's wrong with my clothes? I thought I looked cute."

He chuckled. "Yeah, if we were popping popcorn to watch a movie in bed, but we're going to see my family."

I pulled down on the corner of my eye to show off my mascara. "I put on makeup."

"Those ugly boots cancel out the makeup."

"Hey!"

Laughing, he rolled his eyes and picked up the suitcase I'd put by the door. "Come on. I told my mom we'd be there by lunch."

It was a four hour drive to his parents' house outside of Raleigh in Durham, North Carolina. Half-way there it started snowing again, and by the time we pulled up in front of the blue, two-story farmhouse, there was over an inch on the ground. It was a grand, older home with white shutters, a wraparound porch, and a small barn in the back. Christmas garland twisted around the porch spindles, and two large wreaths with giant red bows hung over the front double doors.

I marveled at the house. "This is like something from a fifties Christmas movie. You grew up here?"

"Yep." He pointed up to the second floor. "I broke my arm in the second grade trying to jump off the porch roof and fly like Superman."

I motioned to a line of cars around the side of the house. "Who all is here?"

He turned off the engine. "Oh, my whole family is here, I'm sure."

I blinked with surprise. "Your *whole* family?" I asked. "How many are there?"

"Well, my parents are here. My sister, Karen—"

I cut him off. "You have another sister?"

He nodded. "I have two other sisters and a brother."

I cringed. "Are you joking?"

A thin smile spread across his face as he shook his head. "Is that a problem, Madam Sweatpants?"

"No," I lied, tugging on the strings of my hoodie. "You just never told me you have such a big family."

"I also have a bunch of nieces and nephews."

"And they'll all be here?" I asked.

"I'm pretty sure they all got here yesterday."

I looked back at the house. "None of them are serious criminals or anything, are they?"

He laughed. "What?"

I shrugged my shoulders. "Well, I have panic attacks around scary people, and I can't take my medicine."

"You can't take your medicine?" he asked surprised. "I thought you said you forgot to take it."

Dang it.

I scrambled for a recovery. "Well, the doctor took me off of it because of some of the side effects. You didn't answer my question."

He shook his head. "No criminals around here. I promise." He stretched his arm across the back of my seat. "Relax. You'll love them."

I took a deep breath. "All right. Let's do this."

When we got out of the truck, the front door swung open and a short, plump woman with straight white hair that curled under around her shoulders ran out onto the porch. She was wearing a white sweater with a red collar and a big sequined poinsettia on the front. She was clapping her hands and had a smile so wide I thought her face might crack in the cold. "Noot-Noot! You're here!" she cheered.

I spun around toward where he was pulling our bags from the back seat. "Noot-Noot?"

He pointed a warning finger at me. "Don't even start."

I laughed and followed him as he jogged up ahead of me to meet his mother halfway up the steps. She squealed softly as he put the suitcases down and hugged her tight. He turned toward me when I stepped up onto the bottom step. "Mom, this is—"

She came down the stairs to meet me. "This is Sloan. I know exactly who she is." She stretched out her arms and hugged me. "I'm Nathan's mom. You can call me Kathy."

I shivered. "It's nice to meet you, Kathy."

She curled her arm protectively around my shoulders. "Come on, honey. Let's get you in the house where it's warm."

The smell of cinnamon and apple pie made me close my eyes and inhale when we stepped through the front door. "Oh my goodness. This must be what Heaven smells like," I said, looking over at her.

She was smiling from ear to ear as she took our bags from Nathan. "Thank you. I hope you're hungry, Sloan. You got here just in time to eat!"

"I'm famished," I said as I unbuttoned my coat.

Tiny squeals and the sound of little rushing feet filled the hall-way. "Unca Nate!" a munchkin voice squeaked.

Two children, a boy with long blond hair and a girl with brown curls, latched onto Nathan's legs. He laughed and picked up the little girl. "How are you, princess?" he asked.

She tossed her hair over her shoulder. "Gramma says I can't have cookies till after we eat."

He growled. "She's so mean."

His mom smacked him on the back of the head and he laughed.

The little girl rubbed her nose and pointed at me. "Who is this lady?"

He touched my shoulder. "This is my friend, Sloan. Sloan, this is Gretchen."

I shook her tiny hand. "Hi, Gretchen."

The boy tugged on my pant leg. "And I'm Carter!"

I laughed. "Nice to meet you, Carter."

Nathan put Gretchen down, and they took off running down the hallway again. Kathy headed up the stairs behind us. "I'll put these in your room, Nathan. You can go on into the kitchen."

"Thanks, Mom," he said.

I grabbed Nathan's arm as we walked down the hall. "Your room? Are we supposed to share a bedroom?"

"Calm down. I'll sleep on the couch, so you don't have to worry about me spoiling your virtue."

I rolled my eyes. "Does your mom think we're a couple?"

"Beats me," he said. "I haven't told her we are."

I cocked an eyebrow. "Have you told her we're *not*?"

He just winked at me.

We passed a formal dining room and a living room with a massive Christmas tree in it. There were no ornaments on the tree, but the smell of fresh pine was intoxicating. At the end of the hall, loud chatter was coming from behind a swinging, white door. He pushed it open, and stepped aside so I could enter. It was a large kitchen, but it was crowded with the McNamara clan all dressed in holiday sweaters.

And there I was, *Madam Sweatpants.*

No one seemed to notice, however. They all cheered when we walked inside and, instinctively, I clapped my hands over my ears. Nathan ceremoniously introduced me to everyone.

Nathan's sister Lara looked like she could be his twin. She and her husband, Joe, were Carter's parents. They lived about twenty minutes down the road.

His other sister, Karen, was married to Nick, and they lived in Columbia, South Carolina. Karen and Nick had four kids. The oldest two were out Black Friday shopping, but the younger two were ignoring us all in the adjoining den off the kitchen.

Nathan's brother, Chuck, was the oldest sibling and was the exact opposite of Nathan. He looked like a lumberjack with a thick brown beard, dressed in camouflage from head to toe. He was recently divorced and living in Tennessee. He was Gretchen's dad.

In five minutes, I was completely overwhelmed.

"Sloan," Nathan said, turning me around again. "This is my dad, James McNamara."

My head snapped back with surprise. James McNamara was a silver-haired, gray-eyed Paul Newman in a sweater vest. He was Nathan in thirty more years.

He shook my hand. "It's nice to finally meet you, Sloan. We hear about you quite a bit."

I blushed. "Really?"

"Absolutely. We owe you so much for helping us find Ashley after all these years of searching and wondering. You'll never know how grateful we are."

"I'm glad I could help, and I'm so sorry for your loss," I said.

He squeezed my hand again. "Well, we're happy you're here. I hope you'll make yourself at home."

"Thank you, Mr. McNamara," I said.

He shook his head. "Call me James."

"Ok."

Someone shoved a plate into my hands, and Nathan led me toward the counter piled with leftover Thanksgiving food. He leaned close to my ear. "See? You're the big hero here. They love you."

"They all seem really nice." There was a half-carved turkey at the end of the counter. Its skin was golden brown, not black. I pointed to it. "Maybe I can get your mom to teach me how to cook a turkey while I'm here."

He chuckled. "Still, best Thanksgiving *ever*."

Nathan's mom had reserved us seats at what everyone referred to as the 'adult table' in the formal dining room. Everyone else scattered throughout the house. I sat between Nathan and his mother. She patted my hand. "Sloan, we are so excited you could join us," she said.

"And we are so glad you're not Shannon Green," Lara added with wide eyes and a chuckle.

I covered my mouth so I didn't laugh and spit food all over the table.

Nathan's cheeks turned bright red, and he dropped his eyes to his plate. "Don't start, Lara."

Lara looked at me. "Sloan, have you met Shannon?"

I laughed. "Oh yes. I grew up with her."

Lara rolled her eyes and groaned. "I am so sorry."

Nathan draped his arm across the back of my chair. "Don't feel too sorry. Sloan convinced their whole high school that Shannon had syphilis."

The table erupted in laughter.

Nathan's mom was hiding her red face behind her napkin. "Is that true?"

I held up my hands and gave a noncommittal smile. Nathan's ex-girlfriend, Shannon Green, had been my nemesis since we were teenagers. He had broken up with her about a month before, apparently pleasing more people than only me.

"That's terrible," Kathy said through her giggles.

Lara pointed her fork at both of us. "So what is this? Are you two finally a *thing?*"

"Lara!" Kathy snapped. "That's none of your business." Despite her words, her questioning eyes turned slowly toward us.

I glanced at Nathan for help.

"It's not like that," he said. "We're close friends. That's all."

I swallowed the bite of cornbread stuffing in my mouth. "I have a boyfriend. He's deployed with the Marines."

There was a collective, sorrowful moan around the table accompanied by condolences.

"How long will he be away?" Kathy asked.

I shrugged my shoulders. "He left a few days ago, and I have no idea when he'll be back."

"I was a Marine right out of college," James said. "I never saw any combat though."

"Dad's an engineer now," Nathan added.

"What kind of engineer?" I asked.

"Civil," James answered.

Kathy smiled. "James is working on the gridlock problem in Raleigh."

I nodded and looked at Nathan. "I remember you telling me you wanted to be an engineer before you went into law enforcement."

He tilted his glass of sweet tea toward his father. "Yeah. I think Dad's still a little bitter about it."

James shook his head. "No, son. We're all very proud of you."

"I know, Dad."

Lara mocked a cough behind her hand and said, "Golden boy."

Chuck did the same, but coughed out "mama's boy" instead.

Nathan wadded up a napkin and threw it at his brother. We all laughed. Kathy stood, waving her hands. "None of that! There will be no food fights in this house this year!"

That evening with the McNamaras was my first real experience with a big family. It was delightful. There was so much laughter and chatter, and it was nice to be a part of it. After dinner, we all gathered in the living room and helped his mom decorate the Christmas tree. The after-Thanksgiving tradition had been put on hold till Nathan and I arrived.

When all the ornaments were in place, James motioned to me from his spot by the tree. He held up the end of the Christmas lights' string. "Sloan, would you come and do the honors?"

Smiling, I pushed myself off the couch. "I'd love to!"

He handed me the plug, then rejoined his wife by the fireplace. I plugged in the tree and it lit up in a colorful glow. A melody of "ooo's" and "ahh's" echoed around the room. Nathan beamed at me as I settled back down next to him on the sofa.

Watching them all laugh and carry on as Kathy passed out hot cocoa to the kids, I felt a strong wave of guilt wash over me. Somewhere, Warren was off doing god-only-knows-what, and I was with another man, like part of his family. And I was enjoying it. A lot. My hands went to my stomach.

"You all right?" Nathan's voice was concerned.

I forced a nod. "Yeah. This is amazing."

He squeezed my hand, smiling as he looked down to where his fingers wrapped around mine. He took a deep breath and released it.

When it was time for bed, everyone became a little somber. The next day wouldn't have the same laughter and joy the evening had. It was hard for me to even imagine how devastated this sweet family must have been when their baby girl went missing ten years before.

Nathan followed me upstairs. "Did you enjoy yourself?" he asked.

I smiled back at him. "Yeah, I did. Your family is great."

"You were the star of the night." He put his hand on the small of my back to steer me down the hall when we reached the top. "Second door on the right."

It was obvious Nathan's bedroom hadn't changed much over the years. Sports trophies lined the walls, along with plaques and ribbons from different events. He had a queen sized bed with a navy blue comforter and a stuffed brown bear perched against the pillows. I pointed at it, looked back at him, and giggled. "Is that Noot-Noot's teddy bear?"

He grabbed my finger. "You leave my bear outta this."

Laughing, I pulled my hand away.

He picked up his suitcase and dropped it on the bed. He fished out a t-shirt and a pair of flannel pants. "That door is for the bathroom," he said, gesturing to the right side of the room. "It adjoins to Lara's room, so I suggest locking it from this side if you don't want Carter wandering in and out of here."

"Thanks for the tip."

He draped his clothes over his shoulder and walked toward the bathroom. "Are you sleeping in the same pajamas you've worn all day?"

I picked up his bear and threw it at him.

When he returned dressed and ready for bed, I was putting my black dress for the next day on a hanger.

"That's pretty," he said.

I smoothed out the front and hung it from the top lip of the closet door. "Thank you. I'm determined to make a better second impression on your family than I did the first."

"I'm only giving you a hard time," he said as he folded his clothes and zipped up his suitcase. "I couldn't care less what you wear, as long as you're here."

I smiled and pulled the comforter down on the bed. "Nevertheless, I plan on looking spectacular by breakfast."

He put his suitcase in the corner of the room, then walked past me to grab a pillow. He nodded toward the bed with a devious grin. "What Warren doesn't know won't hurt him."

I crossed my arms over my chest. "You want to take that chance with a guy who hunts people down for a living?"

He laughed and walked to the door. "I'll be on the couch downstairs if you need anything."

"Thanks, Nathan."

He paused in the doorway. "Goodnight, Sloan."

"Goodnight."

CHAPTER FIVE

"Miiiswoooan…"

"Miiiiiiiissssswoooooan…" The voice came again, the second time a little more sing-song.

I rolled over in the dimly lit room and hugged my pillow. I had to be dreaming. Something was touching my face. My right eyelid was slowly pried open. Big blue eyes were inches from my nose.

I screamed.

Carter screamed.

I bolted upright in the bed.

With his tiny fists clenched at his sides, he screeched as loud as he could.

I stretched my arms toward him. "Carter! Carter! I'm sorry, bud! I'm sorry!"

He threw the door to my room open and screamed all the way down the hallway, then all the way down the stairs. I flopped back onto the bed and groaned. *I'm going to be a great parent.*

As if on cue, my stomach churned with nausea.

When I finally felt like I could stand without hurling all over the shag carpet, I walked to the window and peeked out through the blinds. A fresh blanket of snow covered the ground making the McNamara's front yard look like a scene from a Thomas Kinkade painting. I looked at the driveway and hoped I'd be able to walk in my heels.

My heels. Oh crap!

I ran across the bedroom and dropped to my knees beside my suitcase. Frantically, I tossed out every shred of fabric onto the floor. I'd forgotten to pack my shoes. I looked at my dress on the hanger, then down at my brown, sheepskin, fuzzy boots. Sitting back on my heels, I let out a frustrated huff toward the ceiling.

The morning got worse from there.

Half-way through my shower, just when I'd finished lathering up my hair, the water ran cold. Ice cold. Then my hair dryer shorted out with half my hair still soaking wet, and it took out all the lights in the bathroom. My teeth were still chattering by the time I trudged downstairs *not* polished and ready for the day like I'd wanted.

Kathy and Lara were in the kitchen when I walked in. "Good morning," Kathy said, her welcoming smile fading to wide-eyed concern when she looked me over. "Are you OK, dear?"

I slumped down onto a barstool next to Lara at the kitchen island. "I'm a train wreck. Please don't hate me."

She laughed and covered my hands with her own. "Nonsense. You look like you could use some coffee. May I pour you a cup?"

I sighed. "No, thank you. I'm trying to cut back on caffeine."

She looked around the kitchen. "How about orange juice or milk?"

The thought of milk made my stomach queasy again. "Juice would be great."

She stepped back toward the counter against the wall and pulled a glass from the cabinet overhead. "Lara, would you like some juice?"

Beside me, Lara slurped her coffee. "Mother, I haven't had juice not laced with some form of alcohol since elementary school."

I laughed, but Kathy sighed and shook her head.

When she handed me the orange juice, I smiled up at her. "Thank you."

Lara handed me a large wire basket lined with a red checkered cloth. "Mom made muffins," she said. "There are blueberry ones, and there may be chocolate chip ones if Carter and Gretchen didn't eat them all."

I plucked a blueberry muffin from the basket and put it down on a napkin Kathy handed me. "These smell amazing. You made these?"

"From scratch," Kathy replied.

The sugary topping crumbled between my fingers as I broke off a bite and popped it into my mouth. It melted on my tongue. "Mmm," I moaned. "This is delicious."

She was beaming. "Thank you."

I turned toward Lara. "I have to apologize. I may have scarred Carter for life this morning."

Her eyes widened. "All that yelling earlier. Was that to do with you?"

I grimaced. "We scared each other half to death."

Lara groaned. "He came into your room?"

I nodded. "And pried my eyeball open while I was sleeping."

She hid her flushing cheeks behind her hands. "Oh god, Sloan. I'm so sorry. That boy is impossible."

I laughed and squeezed her arm. "Don't worry about it. I doubt he'll do it again after the way I screamed out in terror."

"Other than the rude awakening, did you sleep well?" Kathy asked.

I sipped my juice. It was delicious. I needed to start buying it to keep at home. "I did, but my morning was a nightmare."

"Oh?" she asked.

"I forgot my shoes at home that go with my dress, and I may have blown a fuse in the bathroom upstairs when my hair dryer died."

"It happens all the time in this old house. James will set it right." Kathy's gaze rose to my crazy hair. "I have a hair dryer you can borrow."

Lara nodded. "And what size shoes do you wear?"

"Seven," I answered.

She sucked in a sharp breath through her teeth. "Well, none of us will be any help with that. We all have giant clown feet."

"Thanks anyway," I said. "You'll just understand now when I look like an Eskimo from the shins down later."

They both laughed.

"Have you seen Nathan this morning?" I asked.

Kathy pointed toward the back door. "He went out with his dad and brother early this morning to scout the woods for deer tracks."

Lara smiled over her mug. "That's what they call it, but they're really out there drinking Daddy's stash of whiskey and bitching about Chuck's ex-wife."

Kathy pulled out the stool on the other side of Lara and sat down with her coffee. "Mind your mouth, Lara Jane."

Lara chuckled.

I looked over at Kathy. "I'm sorry Nathan missed Thanksgiving with you all."

She waved her hand in my direction. "Don't apologize. I assumed he would be wherever you are."

That made me feel bad for a few different reasons. I scrunched up my nose. "I appreciated your invitation here, but I didn't want my dad to be alone."

Kathy put her cup down on the tiled countertop. "Nathan told us your mother passed away. I was sorry to hear it. She must have been young."

"She was fifty-one," I said. "It was a very aggressive brain tumor."

Kathy shook her head sadly. "I'm so sorry." She patted my hand. "I wish I could tell you that you'll get over it in time, but it never goes away. You learn to deal with it differently, and the day-to-day gets easier."

The way her eyes were fixed on the wood grain of the table, I knew her mind was on Ashley.

Thankfully, before we both burst into tears, Carter exploded into the room. He froze when he saw me, then quickly ducked between his mother and grandmother. He slowly peeked his head up, and I gave him a little wave, but he ducked down again.

Lara twisted around in her seat. "Carter, what have we told you about going into people's rooms when they are sleeping?"

I heard a faint "not to" come from the other side of her.

"You owe Ms. Sloan an apology," Lara said.

His eyes lifted just above Lara's knees. "Sowwy."

"It's all right," I told him. "I'm sorry if I scared you."

Without another word, he ran from the room again.

Lara sighed. "Kids."

"I've never really been around kids." I ran my finger along the rim of my glass. "I come from a really small family."

"Only child?" Kathy asked.

"Yes. I was adopted, and my parents never had any children of their own."

Lara laughed. "This circus must scare the bejeezus out of you."

I shook my head. "Not at all. It's been really nice. It's sort of like being in a Hallmark movie."

Lara put her hand on my forearm. "Don't be fooled. It's sometimes more like the Bundys than the Bradys around here."

The back door of the kitchen swung open and Nathan, his dad and brother, stepped inside. Kathy jumped up from the bar. "Take those nasty boots off on the porch! You're not tracking mud and snow in here!"

They all grumbled and walked backward outside again. A moment later, Nathan came in and pulled off the toboggan that covered his head. He smiled at me, then his eyes widened when they fell on my hair. "Morning."

I shook my head. "It's not my fault this time. I tried."

He pointed at my glass. "What is this?"

"Orange juice. It's amazing."

Nathan grinned. "Is vodka in it?"

Beside me, Lara laughed.

I stuck my tongue out at him. "How was the *hunt*?" I asked using air quotes around the word.

He winked. "It was cold." He pointed to the ceiling. "I'm going to hop into the shower. Do you need anything in the bathroom?"

"No, but I'm not sure the shower is a great idea." I cringed. "Something may be wrong with the water heater."

He looked confused for a second, then he laughed. "Oh! You got in late."

Lara patted my back. "The curse of big families."

"Did we run out of hot water on you?" his dad asked as he came in from the porch.

I was shocked. "I guess so."

Chuck was still dusting snow off his hat as he walked in. "Gotta get up early if you want a hot shower around here."

Kathy glanced at the clock. "It's probably had time to warm up now. Karen and Nick took the kids to see his parents earlier, so no one has been in the bathrooms."

Nathan squeezed my shoulder. "You OK?'

I smiled. "Yes."

"I'll be upstairs," he said and left the kitchen.

"Nathan!" his mother called out.

He stuck his blond head back through the door.

"You'll have to reset the breaker for the bathroom." She looked at her husband. "It blew again this morning while Sloan was getting ready."

"That explains a lot," Nathan teased.

She pointed at him. "You leave her alone."

He nodded. "Yes, ma'am." Then he was gone.

James poured a cup of coffee. "I'll fix it tomorrow."

Kathy rolled her eyes. "Tomorrow," she mimicked. "It's always tomorrow."

James kissed her on the cheek as he walked by to the den behind us. He turned on the television to the morning news. I hated the news. With all the evil in the world, it was like watching the inside of the jail through a thin piece of glass. I shuddered and turned away.

In my back pocket, my cell phone vibrated. I pulled it out and saw my dad's picture on the screen. "Hey, Dad," I answered.

"Hey, sweetheart. Are you with Nathan?" he asked.

"Sort of. He's upstairs. What's up?" I asked.

"The FBI was just here at my house. They were looking for you," he said.

My spine went rigid. "Are you kidding? Did they say why?"

"No, but it didn't seem like a social call," he said. "She left a card. Agent Sharvell Silvers."

My chest tightened. I swallowed the growing lump in my throat. "OK. Thanks for telling me, Dad."

"How are things there? Do you like Nathan's family?"

"Yeah. They're great. You'd like them too."

"I have no doubt," he said. "I'll let you go. Just thought you should be aware."

"Thanks. I love you."

"I love you. Bye."

Kathy put her hand on my arm. She must've noticed when my face fell. "Is everything all right?"

I forced a nod. "Yeah. Everything's fine." Slowly, I pushed my chair back and stood. "Excuse me," I said to the group before walking out the door. I took the steps two at a time till I reached Nathan's bedroom. The door was open, and I could hear the shower running in the bathroom.

I knocked on the bathroom door. "Nathan, get out of the shower!"

"What?" he shouted.

"Come out here! I need to talk to you!"

The water shut off, and I sat on the edge of the bed with my knees bouncing like they'd been electrified. The door opened and Nathan stepped out of the bathroom in a cloud of steam. He wore a pair of black dress pants and a belt. That was it.

"Sloan?"

I jerked my eyes up to meet his and immediately felt my cheeks heat up.

He was drying his head with a towel. "Are you blushing, Ms. Jordan?"

"No."

"Liar."

I held up my phone. "Put on a shirt. We need to talk."

A lone water droplet slid from his chest down the center line of his stomach. I thought about catching it with my finger, or my tongue.

Sweet Jesus.

"Sloan?" he asked again. This time he was laughing.

I shook my head in an attempt to clear it. "My dad called."

His brow scrunched together as he walked to his suitcase. "Congratulations. You got me out of the shower to tell me that?"

"The FBI showed up at my dad's house looking for me," I said, my voice elevating with every syllable. I watched him pluck a white t-shirt from his bag. "It was that agent from Texas."

He stopped with one arm in and one arm out of the shirt. "Silvers?"

I nodded. "Why would she come all the way to North Carolina looking for me?"

He didn't speak. Which was *never* a good sign with him.

"Nathan, I don't want to go to jail!"

His eyes snapped to mine. "You're not going to jail. They're probably following up with you because they're still looking for Abigail."

"That's not the reason. She wouldn't get on a plane for that." I pointed at him. "I'll bet anything she knows we were lying."

The corners of his mouth tipped up in a smile. "You're willing to bet *anything*?"

"Nathan! This is serious!"

He sat next to me. "Maybe, but don't jump to conclusions. It's a holiday. For all we know, she might have family in Asheville and she wanted to bring you a fruitcake."

"You're a terrible liar." I dropped my face into my hands. "Nathan, what will we do?"

He was quiet for a moment, and he put his hand on mine. "I'll find out what's going on as soon as we get home." He squeezed my fingers and let out a deep sigh. "But honestly, I don't have the headspace to worry about it today."

My shoulders slumped. I'd completely forgotten what the day would hold for him. My bottom lip poked out. "You're right. I'm sorry for being insensitive."

He released my hand, then stood. "Don't apologize."

"Are you wearing a suit today?" I asked.

"No. I've got a button up and a black sweater," he said.

I scrunched up my nose.

"What is it?" he asked.

"I forgot my shoes, so I'm wearing my pretty black dress with my ugly brown boots."

His shoulders shook with laughter. "Of course you are."

"What time are we leaving here?"

He looked at his watch. "Probably in about an hour. The service is at one."

The graveside service for Ashley was held at a small cemetery outside town. Nathan and I rode with his parents in the back of their SUV. In the snow, James had to use the four-wheel drive to make it up some steep hills. No one spoke in the car, allowing me plenty of time to consider the implications of the FBI's visit to find me.

When we arrived at the cemetery, about fifty people had gathered under a green tent surrounded by sprays of flowers. A shiny mahogany casket rested over a giant hole in the ground.

It reminded me of my mother.

The moment I stepped out onto the cemetery path, a strange sensation came over me. *Death.* Warren had once tried to verbalize his ability to detect the presence of the dead. He said it felt like a vacuum. It was an accurate description. Death pulled at my attention in every single direction.

I felt it because the baby felt it.

Nathan's hand on my back snapped me out of a daze. "I'm going to go talk to some people," he said.

My smile was gentle. "Do what you have to do. Don't worry about me."

He straightened the angel pin on the lapel of my coat. "Are you warm enough?"

I lowered my voice. "My boots may be hideous, but they're nice and toasty."

He laughed softly, but his eyes were sad.

I wandered the grounds as Nathan and his family mingled with people I didn't know and would probably never see again. It was eerie to be able to distinguish the empty grave plots from the occupied ones as I left my tracks in the untouched layer of snow. Unlike Warren, the awareness creeped me out, and I suddenly realized how far I'd strayed from the group. Turning on my heel, I double-timed my pace back to the tent.

Rows of chairs faced the casket, and I sat in the back and watched mourners come by and pay their respects. But something beyond the ornate box caught my attention.

Transparent against the scenery, three rippled figures hovered near the casket. Everyone but me was ignorant of their presence.

Family members passed by and through them undeterred. It was chilling. Even more disturbing was, despite their lack of faces, I knew they were watching me.

They didn't strike me as sinister, but I got up and backed out of the tent nonetheless. Their gazes followed me, but they didn't leave their post. It was like they were guarding her, but I didn't know why.

As I watched them, my mind went to dark places. Had the angels been there in the woods where she was discarded and hidden for ten long years? Were they standing watch during her rape and torture? Did they really do nothing to intervene?

With everything I had experienced in the past few months, I could no longer believe the supernatural existed only in fairytales and Bible stories. God was real, and I knew it. But the more I found out, the more pissed off I became.

A tall, stout man who looked more like a politician than a minister, walked up in front of the chairs, clutching a brown Bible in his hands. "Everyone, I'd like to ask that the family please be seated. Friends and loved ones, please gather close for a word of prayer and a message of thankfulness for the life of sweet Ashley McNamara."

The crowd filed in, and I kept my distance near one of the back poles. Then Nathan waved to me from the front and motioned me forward. When I approached, I saw he'd saved a seat for me between him and his brother. I squeezed my way across the cramped second row and into the seat beside him.

The pastor opened with a prayer, then read a few letters written by various friends shortly after Ashley disappeared. Nathan's body tensed next to me, and when I looked at him, his face was frozen, staring ahead. I rested my head against his shoulder, and he wrapped his hand around mine.

I squeezed.

He squeezed back.

The pastor hugged his Bible to his chest. "Can I be honest?"

Everyone looked up at him.

He let out a heavy sigh and slowly shook his head. "For the life of me, I can't understand this tragedy." He took a step closer to Nathan's parents. "James, Kathy, I've looked at my little girls this week and wondered how a God who claims to love us like a father loves his children could let something so horrific happen. I'm sure you've wondered the same."

Kathy wiped tears away with a cloth handkerchief as they both nodded.

The pastor looked out over the crowd. "We've all asked this question, haven't we?"

A few people answered out loud in agreement while others bobbed their heads.

He shrugged his shoulders. "I honestly don't know why. No other memorial I have ever preached has stirred my doubt as this one has."

I withered with disappointment in my chair.

He held up his Bible. "But I know a few other things." He pointed to the casket. "I know Ashley's not here."

"That's true," I whispered to no one in particular.

The pastor tapped his chest. "This body—this temporal, decaying, grayer-every-day body—is just a container." He lifted the Bible again. "And if I believe what this book tells me, then I know to be absent from this body is to be present with the Lord! This life is only the beginning. Jesus told his disciples, '*Do not let your hearts be troubled. You believe in God. Believe also in me. My Father's house has many rooms. I am going to prepare a place for you. And if I go and prepare a place for you, I will come back and take you to be with me.*'" He looked around the group. "Ashley hasn't been missing all these years." He pointed up. "She's been at the Father's house."

Kathy dabbed at her eyes again, and her husband rubbed her back. Chuck reached up and squeezed her shoulder.

The preacher approached the family. "While I can't give you a reason why this happened, I can assure you this wasn't God's will.

However, if we allow Him to be in this grief with us, He will use even this to do His good work. He promises us that. We won't see it for a while because right now our vision is obscured through the darkened glass of this world. But someday, when we stand face-to-face with Him in eternity, we will see clearly. We will see how even this evil, which was meant to destroy us, He used for good." He held his hands out. "Let us pray."

When he finished, a man with a guitar sang *Amazing Grace*, and Ashley's childhood friend read a poem. After a final prayer, each family member placed a single red rose on the lid of the casket. I held Nathan's hand during his turn.

When we were close to Ashley—close to the angels—I realized why they were there. Peace stirred in my soul, and they were the source. The angels weren't there for Ashley's bones. They stood guard for us.

We waited till the casket sank into the ground, then Kathy was ready to leave. The drive back to the house was even quieter than the drive to the cemetery had been. I stared out the window, watching small snowflakes drift to the ground, and thought about what the preacher had said again.

Typically, Bible verses frustrated me the same way poetry always had. All the words seemed to be a step beyond my comprehension level. Like there was a great message in there, but I was too dumb to get it.

The pastor that day, however, actually made sense. Maybe a positive ripple effect from all the crap we endure in this life *will* be unveiled in the next. It was a nice thought, whether or not it was true.

Nathan's hand touched my arm, drawing me back into the solemnity of the car. He didn't speak or look at me, but I understood his need for reassurance that the world was still real. I had felt the same when my mother died. Like a world without my mother in it, simply couldn't exist.

I wished my power to heal included the ability to mend broken hearts. Unfortunately, the divine didn't seem to work that way. The body I could touch; the soul I could only see.

The snow had stopped by the time we reached the McNamaras' home. Kathy's eyes were red and swollen, and she walked into the house and to her room without a word. James stopped with us at the stairwell and hugged his son. The other cars pulled into the driveway as I followed Nathan up the stairs.

When we reached his room, he walked over and picked up a framed picture. It was the first photo I had ever seen of Ashley. She wore a cheerleader's uniform next to Nathan in his football gear. His football number sparkled with glitter on her cheek. She had disappeared a week later.

For the first time all day, Nathan broke. He pinched the bridge of his nose while his shoulders shook with silent sobs. I put my arms around him from behind, and he laid the picture down and gripped the ledge of the dresser so tight his knuckles turned white.

When his breathing returned to normal, he turned around and pulled me into his arms. The subtle essence of fading cologne and testosterone made me light-headed.

He rested the side of his face against my hair. "Thank you so much for being here."

The soft fuzz of his sweater tickled my nose. "I wouldn't dream of being anywhere else. Can I do anything for you?"

He shook his head. "You're doing it."

We stood melted together for a long time, his fingers trailing up and down my spine, and his heartbeat quickening in my ear with each passing moment. Finally, he brought his hand under my chin and tilted my face up to look at him. He studied my mouth for a moment, then leaned in and kissed me.

The kiss was gentle at first, his mouth tenderly lingering on mine. Then his hand slid back into my hair, and he parted my lips with his tongue. Sidestepping toward the door, his free arm pushed it closed before he pinned my body against the wall. As the kiss deepened, his hands slid down my sides, and his fingers dug into my hips. The whole room seemed to spin.

I could empathize. A similar scene when my mother died spawned the predicament I was in. Frantically, I scrambled to muster the ability to stop him before things escalated any further.

I put my hands on his chest and pushed.

He stopped moving and pulled his lips away. He rested his forehead against mine, his eyes pressed close. "Please, Sloan," he whispered. "Please."

I gripped the collar of his shirt. "Nathan, I'm pregnant."

CHAPTER SIX

Nathan stumbled back like I had told him I was infected with the plague. I stayed glued to the wall. His face twisted with shock and confusion...and anger. "Pregnant?"

I nodded.

He raked his fingers through his hair and walked across the room. "You're pregnant?" he asked again.

I flinched at the tone of his voice. "About eight weeks."

He turned to look at me. His face was as pale as I had ever seen it—even when he was dead for a brief time. "Does Warren know?" he asked.

I shook my head.

He ran his hands over his face as he continued to pace. He was making me nervous, like he might spontaneously combust at any moment.

"Nathan, please say something."

"How long have you known?" he asked.

I took a small step away from the wall. "I realized it on our drive back from Charlotte when we dropped off Warren. It made sense when I didn't get a migraine that day. I found out from the doctor for sure a few days ago."

He stopped walking and tossed his hands in the air. "When were you planning to tell me?"

"I...I was trying to figure out how," I stammered.

He waved his hand toward me. "Well, I'm glad you figured it out before I tossed your dress onto my bedroom floor!"

I walked toward him. "Nathan, please—"

He held up his hand to stop me and shook his head. "No." He turned toward the door. "I can't do this anymore." He walked out of the bedroom and slammed the door behind him.

I started after him, but as soon as the door was open, I heard the front door downstairs slam. I sank back into the bedroom. Uncontrollable tears streamed down my cheeks, and I curled into a ball on the bed and cried.

At some point, I cried myself to sleep, and I awoke to the creak of the bedroom door. I opened my eyes and saw Nathan crossing through the room in the fading light of sunset. He stopped at the edge of the bed and looked down at me. I half-expected him to yell again.

Instead, he whispered, "Scoot over."

I slid over in the bed, and he stretched out next to me. He reached for my arm and pulled me close. I rested my head on his chest. "I'm sorry," he said, stroking my hair.

"I'm sorry too."

He tugged the blanket up around my shoulders. "This has to be over with me and you." His tone was low, serious, and unsteady. "I love you. I've loved you since that first day I walked into your office and you smacked your head on your desk." He sucked in a deep breath. "But this has to be over now."

I didn't speak.

"As much as I hate him sometimes, Warren's a good guy, and he really loves you. You're supposed to be with him," he said.

"Nathan, I—"

He cut me off. "Please, don't. Please, don't say it." His hand was still tangled in my hair. "I can handle being shot at and having my body broken in half by a demon, but I can't stand hearing you tell me you love me."

I closed my mouth.

He pressed a kiss to the top of my head, and silent tears dripped onto his sweater. My father's words floated to my mind. If I really loved him, I had to let him go.

I just wish I knew how.

After lunch the next day, we said our goodbyes to his family, promised his mother we would get our flu shots, and headed back to Asheville. We rode for a while in silence. Me staring out my window, and Nathan staring at the road ahead.

He finally looked over at me. "What are you going to do?"

"About the baby?"

The word made him flinch, but he nodded. "With you and Warren being whatever it is you are—"

"Seramorta."

"Right. Angel hybrids. What does that mean your kid will be?"

I sighed. "I don't know, but I'd guess it's why the supernatural world is so interested in me now. It's a big deal for an Angel of Life and an Angel of Death to even be together. I can only imagine the repercussions of us having a baby."

"Is that what you are? An Angel of Life?"

I shrugged my shoulders. "I guess so. That's what Kasyade told me before she went full demon on everyone."

He shook his head. "Life with you is starting to feel like a Hitchcock movie."

I leaned my head against the cold glass. "I can't argue."

"And you believe her?" he asked.

"Samael, the angel that helped us the day we fought her—"

"The day I died?" he asked.

My heart deflated. "Yes. The day you died. Samael said basically the same thing, and he's a good angel."

"Is it because you're pregnant that you could bring me back from the dead, and now can fully heal people?" he asked.

"Yeah. All the powers I had before are magnified like crazy. My summoning power works like a GPS now," I said. "I also seem to have developed Warren's ability to sense dead bodies. It was overwhelming at the cemetery yesterday."

"That must be weird," he said.

I nodded. "It was." Another thought occurred to me. "I wonder if I can kill people too."

Nathan looked at me with raised eyebrows. "So Warren can kill people?"

I grimaced. "I wasn't supposed to tell you that."

He sighed. "I already knew, but it's still alarming to hear it said out loud." He looked back out the windshield. "Is that what really happened to Billy Stewart and Larry Mendez?"

I didn't answer because I didn't have to.

After a minute, Nathan groaned.

"What?" I asked.

He rubbed his forehead. "I'm considering what Warren could do to me if he finds out what happened with us last night."

I laughed. "What did you think 'Angel of Death' meant?"

He shrugged and draped an arm over the steering wheel. "Honestly, I still have a little trouble believing all that."

Some days I still had trouble believing it myself.

When we reached my house, the sun was sinking behind the mountains. I was half-asleep with my head against the window listening to the moody drone of nineties grunge rock.

"This isn't good." Nathan switched off the radio.

Rubbing my eyes, I straightened in my seat. "Huh?"

"You've got company," he said.

A dark blue sedan was at the curb in front of my house.

"Oh god," I said. "It's the feds. I'm going to prison."

Nathan rolled his eyes and pulled to a stop behind the car. "Calm down and let me do the talking."

A man got out of the driver's seat, then the passenger side door popped open. FBI Agent Sharvell Silvers angled out of the car and tightened the belt on her wool coat as she marched to the curb.

I was sweating.

"Get out of the truck, Sloan," Nathan said.

I looked over and he was leaning against his door. I hadn't heard him move. Exhaling slowly, I opened my door and slid off my seat.

Even in the four inch black pumps she was wearing, Agent Silvers didn't quite reach my eye-level, but she made me feel about two inches tall. Technically, she was one of the good guys, but she could be one hell of a villain if she so desired. And I wasn't sure which side of the law she thought I was on in that moment.

Swallowing my fear with a heavy gulp, I extended a hand toward her. "Agent Silvers, it's nice to see you again."

"Good afternoon, Sloan." She looked at Nathan. "Hello, Detective."

Nathan stepped forward and shook her hand.

She looked toward the man with her. "This is Agent Clark"

Nathan shook his hand, then turned his attention back to her. "What brings you to Asheville?"

She looked me up and down. "I'd like to have a private word with Ms. Jordan, if you don't mind."

Nathan crossed his arms. "Absolutely not without a lawyer."

She shot him a daring look. "I could detain her and put her in jail on a temporary hold."

He smirked. "You have to have probable cause for that."

She held up a padded legal folder. "How about suspicion of conspiracy to commit sex trafficking, conspiracy to harbor aliens, and conspiracy to commit money laundering. I have a whole file full of probable cause." Sharvell looked at me. "Would you prefer a holding cell, Ms. Jordan, or shall we step inside?"

The spike in my blood pressure was enough to make my knees wobble. I shook my head furiously. "Of course we can go inside, Agent Silvers."

Without waiting for me to lead the way, the two agents turned toward the steps to my house. Nathan grabbed the tail of my shirt. "What are you doing?" he whispered.

"I can't go to jail, Nathan!"

He pointed at me. "You watch what you say in there, Sloan. They can hold anything against you."

We followed them, and I passed the agents on the porch. My hand was shaking so much I fumbled the keys, twice. Sharvell noticed. Once we were inside, I motioned toward the living room. "Please make yourselves comfortable. Can we get you some water? Or I can make coffee," I offered.

Agent Silvers shook her head and walked around my living room like a cat on the prowl. She stopped at the mantle and picked up a photo of my family. "Is this your mother?"

I looked at Nathan. He nodded.

"Yes, ma'am," I said.

She traced her finger over the edge of the frame. "I hear she passed away."

"In October," I answered, a familiar pain creeping through me.

Gently, she placed the frame back on the ledge. "How did she die?"

"Cut the interrogation tactics. Using her mom to rattle her is a low blow," Nathan interrupted.

Her gaze cut to him. "I simply wanted to offer my condolences."

"Bullshit," Nathan said.

Without further argument, she stalked to the sofa and sat down. The rest of us took that as our cue to find a seat. Nathan sat so protectively close to me, his hip touched mine.

Sharvell opened the business folder and balanced it on her

thighs. "Sloan, I would like you to tell me again about your involvement with Abigail Smith."

I shook my head. "I'm not involved with Abigail and haven't seen her since Texas."

"What was your involvement with her prior to Texas?" she asked.

I turned my palms up in question. "We weren't involved. I only met her a couple of times."

She pointed at me. "You're lying."

My mouth fell open. "No, I'm not."

She pulled papers from the portfolio and handed them over the coffee table. "These were found inside her residence in San Antonio. Can you explain them?"

They were photographs. Of me.

One was a picture of me locking the front door of the apartment I lived in during my senior year of college. The second was me on the playground at school when we still lived in Florida. And the third was of me and Warren carrying boxes of his stuff into my house. A chill made me shudder. I felt naked. Exposed.

"I don't know what these are," I said.

Nathan was looking over my shoulder. "These are obviously surveillance photos taken without her knowledge."

I flipped back to the picture of me as a child. It was the same playground where I'd received the scar over my eye as a kid. Kasyade had been watching me the whole time. I thought of the teacher who had terrified me that same year and realized she'd been planted there on purpose. My chin quivered.

"Why would Abigail be watching you?" she asked.

I held up the photos. "I would love to know the same thing."

"Sloan, we recovered boxes and boxes of photographs like these, along with notes, newspaper clippings, medical records, school transcripts..." She tapped her finger on the folder. "For someone who claims to have only just met this woman, I find it odd she has a lifetime of information on you."

Nathan shook his head. "All this proves is Sloan has a stalker."

"And what does this prove?" She leaned forward, passing Nathan a manila folder from her portfolio.

Nathan opened it, and I leaned over his shoulder.

Uh oh.

"I believe that's an information packet about a woman you were investigating here in North Carolina, is it not?" she asked, her voice dripping with haughty derision. "You lied to me, Detective. You both lied."

The folder contained the original information he had gathered on Abigail when we still assumed her name was Rachel Smith and that she'd been murdered by our serial killer.

"My question is *why* would you lie?" she asked.

Nathan closed the folder. "I was out of my jurisdiction while investigating—"

"Now who's spouting off bullshit, Detective?" she snapped. She wagged her finger between the two of us. "I also know the two of you aren't a couple. Never have been."

I scowled at Nathan.

He ignored me and stood. "Well, unfortunately for you, Agent Silvers, our relationship status isn't governed by federal law. So unless you're going to charge us with a crime of which you have zero proof, our conversation here is over."

I was surprised Nathan didn't fall over dead under the heat of her glare.

Sharvell stood, as did the man with her. They walked toward the front door and we followed. She turned on her heel in the foyer and looked up at me. "I promise you, Ms. Jordan." Her eyes shrank into angry slits as she snatched the photos I was still holding. "I will find out what you're hiding from me. Make no mistake of it."

My skin prickled at her tone, and I shuddered as they walked out the door.

Nathan leaned toward my ear. "Stay inside. I'll get your bag from the car."

I couldn't have moved if I'd wanted to. And I didn't want to.

Nathan stood on the curb with his arms folded across his chest till the agents drove away and disappeared around the curve. Then he went to his truck and retrieved my bag. I was still frozen in front of the door when he came back in and closed it.

He waved a hand in front of my staring eyes. "Earth to Sloan. Are you OK?"

Snapping out of my daze, I nodded. "Yeah. At least she didn't arrest me." I turned toward him as he put my bag down by the stairs inside. "What did she mean by she could detain me on conspiracy of all that stuff? Is that true?"

He came back over and stood in front of me. "Technically, they can hold you without charging you, but they won't do that. Not if that's all the probable cause they have." His face wasn't convincing.

"That woman is going to bury me under the jail!"

He shook his head. "They have no evidence you're involved in this because no evidence exists." He bent to look me in the eye. "I won't let them bury you anywhere."

I wished his words were comforting.

"Just to be safe, we should look for a federal defense attorney," he suggested.

I smirked. "And tell them what?"

"It's still a good idea." He glanced at his watch, then around the room. "Are you staying in for tonight?"

"Yeah. I need to try to get some rest. *Try* being the keyword in that sentence."

He hesitated as he turned toward the front door. "I can sleep in the guest room if it will help you relax."

I squeezed his hand. "This has to end, remember?" I asked. "You moving in with me—no matter how noble the reason—isn't good for anyone. I can always go stay with Dad if I need to."

He looked down at the floor and sighed. "You're right."

"I'll call you if anything happens," I said.

He put his arms around me. "I hate this."

"I know."

From the door, I watched until he got into his truck and drove away, then I sucked in a deep breath and looked out over the horizon. The faint ripples were thicker and covered more of the sky. I wondered how many angels were out there, and if it was a good sign or a bad one that their numbers were multiplying. Slowly, I closed the door and walked back into my quiet house.

As I lay in bed, waiting for sleep to come, my brain replayed the events of the weekend. The FBI and the funeral were both overshadowed by the memory of Nathan's arms pinning me against his bedroom wall as we kissed. I still felt his fingertips on my hips and the weight of his body pressing against me. My stomach fluttered with the taste of desperation on his lips and the plea for escape dripping from his eyes. *Please*, he had whispered.

With so many emotions between us, that neither of us could reconcile, how would it ever be possible for me and Nathan to just be friends? Someone in our triangular affair was destined for heartbreak. I suspected it might be all three of us.

I didn't deserve the unnatural patience and understanding that Warren Parish afforded me. If he struggled between love for me and love for another woman, I would be devastated and possibly homicidal. I pictured his face and washed myself in the memory of the intoxicating buzz of energy I felt whenever we touched.

Into the darkness, I reached out with my gift to find his soul. He was there, but he was so far away. Lost in the delusions of a faceless embrace, I drifted off to sleep as tears dripped to my pillow and thunder rumbled in the distance.

The sound of my alarm clock came too early the next morning.

Nothing in me wanted to get up and go into work. I briefly considered grabbing my phone and typing out a resignation email with my thumbs. *If I quit my job, I can go right back to sleep.*

I didn't. I got up instead and blindly crossed my bedroom to the master bath. When I flipped on the light, two bulbs blew out. There was barely enough light for me to see to brush my teeth, much less fix my hair and do my makeup. Just my luck.

I picked up my hairbrush and pulled it through the tangles in my long brown hair. My eyes were tired, and I blinked a few times to get them to focus. I put my brush down to wash my face, but my reflection in the mirror didn't change. I was still brushing my hair.

I wiped the sleep from my eyes and looked again. I stared back at me. "Sloan." The sound of my own voice, though it didn't come from my lips, was jolting as it echoed around the bathroom.

My reflection moved closer to the glass. "Sloan."

To my horror, blood spread over the midsection of Warren's gray t-shirt I wore. I looked down to see nothing amiss with the real me standing at the sink, and when I looked back again at the mirror, the eyes staring back at me were solid white and empty. I held up my shirt, showing a long bloody gash across my stomach. The inside was hollow. My baby was gone.

My scream echoed throughout the house.

I sat up in bed, sweat pouring down my face, when I looked at the clock on my nightstand. It was 2:13 in the morning. Instinctively, I grasped at my stomach. There was nothing wrong with me.

In the corner of my room, I saw something move.

A shadow, with the shape of a small person and bright, amber eyes, moved toward me. With my heart pounding so loud it reverberated around the room, I scrambled back as far in the bed as I could before the figure overtook me and slammed my body against the mattress.

I tried to scream, but no sound would come. I tried to fight, but the shadow had nothing to grab onto. Two chilly hands pushed through my chest and gripped my heart, squeezing and twisting. I fought to breathe, but the crushing weight on my chest wouldn't allow for any air. The veins in my eyes exploded as the life slipped from my body.

There was a flash of bright light, and then I was sitting up again. I looked at the clock. 2:13.

This time, I lunged for the lamp on my nightstand and jumped out of bed. There was nothing in my room. I was wearing Warren's shirt, and it wasn't covered in blood. I walked to the bathroom and turned on the lights. All the bulbs flickered on.

As I splashed cold water on my face, I avoided looking at my reflection—just in case.

"It's only a dream," I said, still panting. "It's only a dream."

There was no use in trying to go back to sleep because it wouldn't happen. I got up and walked downstairs to the dark living room. I grabbed the pregnancy book from the doctor and sat on the couch. An entire section dedicated to dreams and fantasies confirmed increased nightmares were normal during pregnancy. It made me feel slightly better. I pulled the fleece blanket off the back of the couch and curled up underneath it. The clock on the wall said 2:26.

The unmistakable sound of footsteps came from my front porch.

Slowly, I got up and moved against the wall. Whoever it was had seen my light come on. They knew I was home, and if they'd been watching my house for any period of time, they also knew I was alone. I should have let Nathan stay. My phone was upstairs.

My heart was racing so fast I was dizzy. Closing my eyes, I sent out my *evil radar*, as Nathan called it. There didn't seem to be anything sinister waiting for me, so I crept into the foyer and looked out the peep hole. On the other side of the door, the silhouette of a man flashed against the distant glow of the dim city lights.

I blinked and he was gone.

Gripping the sides of my head, I wondered if I was losing my mind. For a moment, I considered driving to Nathan's apartment, but I decided the idea was worse than staying home alone. I could have gone to my dad's, but if I woke him up that early, he'd never go back to sleep.

Wind howled in my chimney.

A branch cracked outside the window.

Screw this.

I ran upstairs, threw some clothes into a bag, then drove to the only place that made sense.

Adrianne's.

Adrianne was rubbing her eyes with her knuckles when she opened the front door. She leaned against the doorframe and surveyed my wild hair, disheveled pajamas, and the overnight bag in my hand. "This can't be good," she said through a yawn.

My teeth were chattering. "Can I come in?"

She stepped out of the way, and I rushed into her two-story loft apartment. She locked the deadbolt behind me. "What's up?"

I pulled the scarf from my neck. "There might be a demon at my house. Can I sleep here?"

"Did you bring the demon with you?" she asked.

I shrugged my shoulders. "I don't think so, but I can't be sure."

She shuffled toward her kitchen and flipped the light on. She pointed at the table. "Sit." Obediently, I sat down as she poured two glasses of water. She handed me one and sat across from me. "OK, what happened?"

Without pausing to breathe, I told her everything.

She was cradling her skull in her hands by the time I finished. "Are you sure you were still dreaming when that thing attacked you in your room?"

"I have no idea. I'm not completely convinced I'm fully awake right now."

She reached across the table and pinched my arm. Hard.

I yelped with pain. "Ow!"

She shook her head. "You're awake."

I scowled and rubbed the stinging spot on my arm.

"Did you call Nathan?"

I groaned. "No. He would have insisted on coming over to my house."

"Is that such a bad thing?" she asked.

I covered my face with my hands. "*Things* happened with us this weekend."

She rolled her eyes and sipped her water. "Oh, geez. What now?"

I blew out a long puff of air. "I told him about the baby, and it didn't go well."

"I thought you were going to wait to tell him," she said.

"Well, I was, but after the funeral, things got a little heated in his bedroom, and I sort of blurted it out."

Her jaw dropped. "You told him you were pregnant during sex?"

"No. Geez, get your mind out of the gutter, Adrianne."

She tossed her hands up. "How else am I supposed to take 'heated in his bedroom,' Sloan?"

I groaned. "I told him before things went that far. He freaked out."

"I told you he would."

I raked my fingers through my hair. "We're all right now, but he stormed out of the house. I was afraid he'd never speak to me again."

"*Pshhh*," she said. "He's too in love with you for that."

I ran both hands down my face, pulling my lips down into a frown. "I know, which is why I came here instead of going to him."

She pointed at me. "Smart girl. You need to tell him about this though. This is major."

"He'll be even more protective of me, and that's the opposite of what either of us need," I said.

"You need to work on having some boundaries with him, I agree. However, if you don't tell him, I will. I'm a hair expert, not a bodyguard," she said.

I nodded but said nothing.

A smile crept over her face. "So what happened in his bedroom?"

My mouth fell open. "We're not talking about that."

"Tongue or no tongue?" she pressed.

I got up and walked toward the bathroom.

She followed me. "Was there nakedness?"

"Adrianne!"

I tried to shut the bathroom door in her face, but she blocked it with her long arm. "Serious question though."

I put my hand on my hip.

"If you weren't pregnant, what would've happened?"

My shoulders dropped.

She pointed at me. "Bingo."

CHAPTER SEVEN

Adrianne made up the couch for me to sleep on, but sleep never came. My brain replayed the nightmares over and over again. Every time I closed my eyes, I saw the figure in the corner of my room. At six, I gave up and got ready for work.

Sleep wasn't so elusive once I got to my office. I woke up drooling on my desk, not once but three times during the day. By five o'clock, I was running on autopilot, but I'd promised my dad we'd have our regularly scheduled Monday night dinner, and I was desperate to talk to him more about the FBI.

When I walked out of the building, Nathan was walking up the steps. I narrowed my eyes. "Did Adrianne call you?"

He met me half-way. "She sent me a text message to come by today. I thought it was strange. What did you do?"

My brow wrinkled. "Why would you assume I did something?"

He crossed his arms over his chest and glared.

I rolled my eyes and walked down the stairs. Nathan fell in step beside me.

"Adrianne's worried because I had a pretty bad nightmare last night. I showed up at her house at three this morning." From the corner of my eye, I saw he was suppressing a smile. I pointed at him. "Don't you dare laugh at me. You don't know how bad it was."

"Tell me about it," he said.

"I dreamed someone cut the baby out of my stomach, then when I woke up screaming, something—or someone—was in my room, and it tried to crush me in my bed," I said as we crossed the lot.

He stopped walking. "Were you really awake?"

I shrugged my shoulders. "I don't know. After that, I got up and went downstairs, but I heard something or someone outside. I looked through the peep hole and maybe saw a man, but when I looked again, he was gone."

"Why didn't you call me?"

I kicked my toe against the gravel on the asphalt. "Because things are weird with us right now."

He rested his hands below the sides of his tactical belt.

"That's when I drove to Adrianne's. She thought I should tell you."

For a few moments, he stared down at the ground. Then he cut his eyes up at me. "I'm coming to your house tonight."

"I'll sleep on Adrianne's couch—"

He pointed at me. "No, you're not. What if that was a person standing on your porch or in your room? I'll sleep in the guest bed till we figure something else out."

"Nathan, I—"

He cut me off again. "Stop arguing. We've already seen what Kasyade is capable of, so we're not playing around with this shit anymore." He sighed. "I promised Warren, Sloan."

I put my hands on my hips. "He might feel differently given what's already happened."

He crossed his arms over his chest. "Do you not think he weighed that out before he asked me? He was worried enough to still take that chance, obviously with good reason."

I scowled but had no argument.

"When and where are you having dinner with your dad?"

"Red Stag in half an hour."

"Then I'll be at your place around eight." He turned on his heel and headed toward his tan SUV.

"Nathan, this is a bad idea," I called after him.

He stopped and looked back at me, laughing sarcastically. "When have we ever done anything that's been a good idea? I'll see you in a couple of hours."

Before I could protest further, he got into his car and slammed the door.

Thanks to Nathan's untimely visit, if I didn't hurry, I would be late for dinner with my dad.

There was a little-known shortcut through town involving a questionable road by the park and passing through two parking lots marked with No Entry signs. When I exited the first parking lot, I noticed a set of headlights in my rearview mirror.

When I entered the second parking lot, the lights were still behind me. I reached out with my gift, but my sixth sense was choppy and vague because I was distracted by driving.

I hoped Nathan was being overprotective and had decided to follow me. I dialed his number.

"McNamara," he answered.

"Hey, it's me." I turned left onto the main highway toward the Biltmore Estate. "Where are you?"

It was loud wherever he was. "Just walked into the jail to wrap things up."

"Someone might be following me," I said.

"Where are you?" he asked.

I checked my surroundings. "On highway twenty-five, near Biltmore. I'm almost at the Red Stag."

He was quiet for a second. "As soon as you get there, park in a well-lit area and get inside as fast as you can. I can't leave right now, but stay at the restaurant till I get there. I'll follow you home."

"OK."

"Sloan!"

"What?"

"Don't do anything stupid," he said.

I rolled my eyes and pulled into the parking lot of the Bohemian Hotel. "I won't."

"Stay on the phone with me till you get inside," he said.

When I put the car in park, I looked back over my shoulder. A car stopped on the curb of the street a block down from the hotel. "I can't be sure because it's dark and there are so many cars, but they might have parked near McDonald's."

"Can you tell what kind of car?" he asked.

"Of course not." I grabbed my purse and bolted from my car toward the entrance. When I slid to a stop in the lobby, I was breathless. "I'm inside."

"Stay there," he said. "I'll be there by the time you're done." He disconnected the line.

I loved the Red Stag Grill for its ambiance and perfect mix of gnarly mountain cuisine and trendy pretension. Only around Biltmore could venison and rainbow trout feel snobbish. The room flaunted rich shades of brown and red with a warm glow from honey-colored lamps illuminating its many guests. In the corner, an enormous Christmas tree, trimmed with holly berries and flameless lanterns, stood beneath the mounted head of a twelve-point buck. My father waved from a table between the bar and the silent baby grand piano.

A hardwood path wove in and out of crimson, candlelit tables across the room. When I reached my dad, he offered his cheek for a kiss. I obliged before pulling off my pea coat and sliding into my seat. "I'm sorry I'm late," I said, draping the cloth napkin over my lap. "It was a weird drive here."

"Weird drive?" he asked.

"Yeah. I think I was followed."

"Followed?" The alarm in his voice drove his pitch up an octave.

I nodded. "I called Nathan. He's meeting me here before we leave to make sure I get home OK."

Dad's shoulders relaxed. "That's good. I expected him to be with you."

"Not for dinner, but I'm sure you'll get to see him before the night's over." I opened the menu and looked over the choices. "I wonder what wild boar tastes like. What are you ordering, Dad?"

He pointed to his menu. "I believe I'll have the halibut."

I scanned the entry and frowned. "What on earth are duck fat baby potatoes?"

He chuckled and took a sip of his water. "They're tiny little potatoes. Very tasty. How's Nathan?"

"He's good." I looked over the top of my menu at Dad. "Do you think they yank the trout out of the river out back?"

Dad smiled. "I doubt that." He leaned toward me. "Why do I feel like you're avoiding Nathan as a topic of dinner conversation?"

I forced my lips into a smile. "I'm not," I lied. The truth was I knew I couldn't talk about my weekend with Nathan without blushing, and the last thing I wanted was for Dad to know Nathan was going home with me after dinner.

By the grace of God and all the good karma in the universe, our waiter appeared at the table with a basket of sliced multigrain baguettes. "Ma'am, would you be interested in a glass of wine?"

I blew out a sigh that puffed out my cheeks. "Oh, I'm interested, but no. Water will be fine."

"May I take your dinner order, then?" he asked.

I pointed across the table. "Start with him."

Dad ordered his fish, then both men stared expectantly at me.

I looked up at my dad, tapping my fingers against the sides of the menu. "Can I just have the chocolate lava cake?"

"No."

I frowned. "Then I guess I'll order the meatloaf." I closed my menu and handed it to the waiter.

Dad buttered a slice of bread. "How was the funeral?"

Heat rose in my cheeks. "It was very emotional." I picked up my water goblet and drained half of it.

Dad chuckled. "Are you OK?"

"Yup."

His brow rose in question. "Sloan?"

"Yeah?"

"You're as red as a beet," he said. "What happened?"

"Nothing."

He pointed his butter knife at me. "You're lying."

I scrunched up my nose. "That's twice in two days I've been called a liar."

He put the knife on the plate and lifted the bread. "Well, at least half the time it's been true. Who else called you a liar?"

"The FBI."

His hand froze midway to his mouth. "They found you, then?"

"Yeah. They were waiting at my house yesterday when we got back, and my guess would be they're following me now," I said.

He looked around the room. "What do they want with you?"

I turned my palms up. "I'm not really sure, except they believe I was lying in Texas about my relationship with Abigail."

"You *were* lying to them in Texas," he said, taking a bite of his bread.

"Was I supposed to tell them the truth?" I scoffed at the thought. "Do you want them to lock me up in the loony bin?"

Dad pressed his lips together in a tight grimace. "It'd be better than prison."

I groaned. "What did they say to you?"

The waiter returned with our salads. I smiled and thanked him.

Dad poured dressing over his wedge of iceberg lettuce. "Not much. They asked where they could find you. I said you were attending a funeral out of town with a friend. They inquired about Nathan. Apparently, they were under the impression the two of you were a couple. I set them straight."

"Ahh...that makes sense," I said.

"What makes sense?" he asked.

I skewered a grape tomato. "Nathan told them we were together. I was wondering how they found out we weren't."

Dad's eyebrow peaked. "Why would he do that?"

I rolled my eyes. "Because he's an idiot."

He folded his arms on the tabletop. "While we're on the subject…"

My fork clinked against the china when I dropped it onto the salad plate.

"Are you taking my advice and minding your boundaries with him?"

He wasn't going to let it go. I sat back hard in my seat and stared at him. "Dad, I've had two attempts made on my life in the past two months and have been promised that more will come. I've done my best to keep a safe distance from Nathan, but he's staying close to protect me like he promised Warren he would. Please stop insinuating I'm becoming the Harlot of West Asheville."

Dad couldn't suppress his laughter. "Are you a little defensive, my dear?"

"Yes."

"Pregnancy hormones will do that to you," he said.

I picked up my fork again and stabbed an innocent crouton. "So will meddlesome fathers."

He chuckled behind his napkin. "All right. No more questions about Nathan, I promise."

"Thank you."

His head fell to the side. "Is he following you home so he can stay with you?"

"Dad!"

Nathan arrived at dinner in time for dessert, and he pulled up a chair to our table set for two. He shook my father's hand. "Sorry to crash your date, Dr. Jordan."

Dad waved his napkin. "Nonsense. I'm glad you're here."

I handed Nathan the dessert menu. "Did you see anything strange outside?"

He shook his head. "No, but I'll keep an eye out on our drive to your house." He pointed to my plate. "What is that?"

"Chocolate lava cake. Do you want some?" I asked, offering him the bite on my fork.

He leaned over and opened his mouth. As the tines scraped across his teeth, I caught my dad rolling his eyes in my peripheral. I credited myself with paying attention to my father and not to Nathan's lips as he licked a drizzle of chocolate off them. Damn hormones.

The waiter stopped by and Nathan ordered a cup of coffee.

"No cake?" I asked, surprised.

He patted his flat stomach. "Trying to watch my figure."

I laughed. "Whatever, Captain Skittles."

He smiled at me, then rested his elbows on the table and lowered his voice. "What makes you think someone followed you here?"

I wiped crumbs off my mouth. "I took a few obscure back roads and headlights were behind me the whole way."

"Was the driver human?" he asked barely above a whisper.

"I'm not sure. They were far away and I was driving so I couldn't concentrate."

The waiter returned with Nathan's coffee, and he wrapped his hands around the steaming mug. "I'm sure it's the FBI. You've probably got eyes on you in this very room."

I carefully scanned the other tables. "Right now?"

He nodded and scooped a finger full of chocolate icing off my plate. "You need to be careful. They could tap your phone and bug your house too."

I pushed what was left on the plate toward him, and he grinned and picked up my fork.

"Can they do that?" Dad asked.

"They can if they get a warrant for it." He grimaced. "And I hate to say it, but if I were a judge, I'd issue one in this case."

I dropped my face into my hands.

Nathan squeezed my shoulder. "They still can't prove you're involved because you're not. I'll make some calls tomorrow and see what I can find out. Don't worry till there's a reason to."

I looked up at him. "Easy for you to say."

"If they're investigating you, they're investigating me too."

I scrunched up my nose. "I guess that seals the deal on no FBI job for you."

He finished what was left of my cake. "I'm sure it does."

I was yawning by the time we said our goodbyes to my dad in the hotel lobby. Dad hugged me and kissed the side of my head. "Are you all right to drive yourself home? It looks like it's flurrying outside."

I nodded against his shoulder. "Yeah. I'll be fine."

He shook hands with Nathan. "Thanks for looking out for her, son."

"It's my pleasure, sir."

Dad pointed a finger at me. "You be careful." His warning tone was loaded with double meaning.

Nathan walked with me to my car. "I'll be behind you the whole way," he said.

"Thank you."

Knowing the headlights behind me belonged to Nathan, I relaxed on the drive home. I called Adrianne and yelled at her, but I also thanked her for looking out for me by calling him. We chatted until I pulled into the driveway.

"Gotta go. We're home now," I said to her.

"OK," she said. "No staying up past eleven with him and always sleep in Warren's shirts."

I laughed. "Is that your recipe for chastity?"

"Yes. And don't let him wear cologne in the house. You're a sucker for that shit," she said.

She was right.

"Goodnight, Adrianne."

"Call me if you get weak."

Nathan was waiting by his car door behind me when I got out. "Sorry," I said, holding up my phone. "That was Adrianne."

"What did she have to say?" he asked.

I chuckled. "You don't want to know."

"Probably not." He froze when he noticed the crushed rhododendron in front of my driveway. "What happened to the bush?"

I squished my mouth to one side.

"Sloan?"

"I drove over it."

He cocked his head to the side. "Why?"

I looked down at my feet. "Adrianne scared me."

He pointed at me. "You scare me." We turned toward the sidewalk leading to the house. "Well, you don't have to worry about anything sinister that can be stopped by bullets. That's the upside of having the FBI on your tail."

"They're following me?"

He grimaced. "That would be my guess. Someone certainly is."

I dropped my arms and looked up at the sky. "Why?" I asked the angels, or God, or the universe. I scanned the dark street. "Where are they now?"

He jerked his head to the side. "They're in a truck a street over."

"Fantastic," I muttered as we walked up the steps to the porch.

As I unlocked the front door, he nudged my side. "Maybe you should give me Warren's key while he's gone."

Smirking, I pushed the door open. "Sometimes I worry you have a death wish."

"Been there, done that, Sloan."

I laughed as we walked inside.

CHAPTER EIGHT

The rest of the week was remarkably uneventful considering an army of angels and the federal government followed me wherever I went, the world's hottest cop was sleeping in my guest room, and a person the size of a duck fat baby potato was growing inside me. On Friday afternoon, I was packing up my files and laptop when my boss walked into my office.

"Hey, Mary," I said.

Mary Travers was so small she could easily be mistaken for a child from behind if it weren't for her fondness of tweed and polyester skirt suits. She'd recently gotten a new hairstyle, an asymmetrical long pixie cut—a daring leap from her boring straight brown bob—and contact lenses to replace her thick black frames. In our office, it was the most peculiar metamorphosis since Kafka.

"I'm glad I caught you." She handed me a white envelope.

I blinked with surprise. "What's this?"

"Your valet vouchers for tomorrow night," she answered.

My brain raced. "Umm…"

"The office Christmas party at the Grove Park," she said, wide-eyed.

I laughed. "Oh my. With everything going on, I completely forgot about it."

"I hope everything's OK," she said.

I sank down into my office chair and motioned to the chairs across from my desk. "We need to talk."

Mary sat, worry lines creasing her brow.

I shifted uncomfortably on my chair. "I recently found out I'm pregnant."

She covered her mouth with her hand. "Really?"

"Really. I'm due in July."

She looked a little uneasy. "I hope congratulations are in order."

I smiled. "Yes. I'm happy about it." And it was true, despite my raging nerves and confused hormones.

Mary reached across the table and squeezed my hand. "Congratulations, Sloan."

"Thank you."

She tapped her fingertips together. "Have you considered how your job will fit into your new life as a mother?"

I shook my head. "I haven't even thought about it, but I'll let you know if I forsee any major changes."

"We'll do whatever we can to make your life easier so we can keep you here."

"I appreciate that," I said.

She glanced at the envelope. "Will you make it to the party tomorrow night?"

I stood and straightened my shirt. "If I can stay awake, I'll be there."

Laughing, she got up. "Wonderful. I'll see you then."

"Goodbye, Mary."

When she left, I crammed my laptop and files into my bag and locked up my office. It was freezing outside, and I saw my breath against the last rays of pink and orange sunshine. There were ripples watching me in the sky and a black truck watching me from the corner of the parking lot. I waved to both of them.

The truck followed me home.

Nathan, who had been camped out in my guest room all week, was idling at the curb when I pulled into my driveway. When I came around front, he was waiting by his SUV. He was carrying a pizza box from Asheville Pizza and Brewery.

I smiled. "I could get used to living with you."

He laughed. "Don't."

The patch on the front of his ball cap said, *The ATF should be a convenience store, not a government agency.*

I pointed at it. "You didn't work today?"

He took my bag from me as we walked up the stairs. "I went in for a few hours this morning, but I wasn't on the schedule. How was your day?"

"Exhausting." I looked over at him. "Do you have plans tomorrow night?"

"I'll have to check my social calendar." He shook his head as we went up the steps. "I've got this chick in my life who wears me the hell out—"

I playfully backhanded his arm. "Shut up."

"Why do you ask?"

"My office Christmas party is tomorrow night at The Grove Park Inn," I said. "I forgot about it."

He groaned.

"Have you ever been to the Grove Park Inn?" I asked as I put my key in the deadbolt.

He laughed. "I dated Shannon. What do you think?"

Rolling my eyes, I pushed my door open. "Have you ever been at Christmas time?"

"No."

"It will be nice," I said as we walked inside.

He locked the door behind us. "Does that mean I have to dress up?"

"Yes."

He groaned again. "How dressy are we talking about?"

I thought for a moment. "I'll probably wear a black dress and—"

He spun toward me. "The black dress you wore at the bar?"

I froze as I unbuttoned my coat. "What?"

"Short black dress, kinda shiny with a belt. You wore it to the bar the first night I met Adrianne," he said.

I closed my eyes and thought back to the first night I'd ever seen Nathan outside work. We were at a nightclub downtown. He'd shown up with Shannon. Ugh. I shook my head. "No. I hate that dress."

He pulled off his hat and hung it on a hook by the door. "I liked it, but it probably wouldn't fit you anymore."

I gasped. "Excuse me?"

He nudged my arm. "It's not bad. It's normal to have a baby bump."

"I don't have a baby bump."

He carried the pizza to the kitchen. "I've been looking at your body for six months. You have a bump."

I shrugged out of my coat. "I'm not sure what offends me more, your admission of checking me out all the time or you pointing out I'm gaining weight."

"If that offends you, then you'll really be pissed to know I've noticed your boobs getting bigger also," he said over his shoulder.

"Nathan!"

He was snickering as he pulled two plates out of the cupboard. "I thought you wanted bigger boobs."

Stalking into the kitchen, I punched him in the shoulder. "We're not talking about my boobs!"

"I meant it as a compliment." He laughed. "If you're putting on a few pounds, at least you're doing it in the right places."

"Please stop talking." I yanked open the refrigerator to retrieve two bottles of water.

Thirty minutes later, most of the pizza was gone. I ate half. I put my plate down on the coffee table and pointed a warning finger at Nathan. "Don't you dare say a word about how much I ate."

He laughed and swallowed his last bite. "I wouldn't dare."

I pulled the blanket off the back of the sofa before positioning the throw pillow against the arm of the sofa. I stretched out, tucking my cold feet behind Nathan's back.

He tapped my shin. "Hey, isn't that the guy you think they sent Warren after?"

On the television was a photograph of an Arabic man who Warren had shown me before he left. The terrorist, whose name I couldn't pronounce, had no soul which meant he was dead or he wasn't human. Since videos and stories kept flooding the news about him, I suspected it was the latter.

"And there's more breaking news out of Lebanon. Abdelkarim Abdulla Khalil Shallah, has released a new video on a known terrorist website claiming responsibility for the beheading of US Marine, Alexander Diaz..."

They showed a paused video image of another man in a black robe and face mask, standing next to a person who was on his knees in the dirt wearing multi-cam fatigues. A black pillowcase was over his head, and his hands were behind his back. I covered my mouth and gasped. "That's horrible."

The video played, and the pillowcase was ripped off the man's head. A tangle of long black hair fell around his shoulders, which the terrorist grabbed to pull him upright. Warren's eyes locked on mine, pleading in horror through the camera. Then a machete swung and blood splattered across the television screen.

I screamed.

"Sloan, wake up!" Nathan was shaking my arm.

When I opened my eyes, we were still on the couch, the news was still on, and a gray-haired man was showing a cold front moving into Western North Carolina. I rubbed my eyes and tried to catch my breath. "What happened?"

He helped me sit up. "You dozed off and then started screaming."

"There was a Marine on television," I said, pointing at the screen.

He nodded. "Yeah. Alexander Diaz died in Israel, but we saw that fifteen minutes ago."

I gripped my head. "Geez, I'm losing it."

"No, you're not. You're just exhausted. Go to bed," he said, pointing up the stairs.

Just then, a blast of thunder rattled the house. We both jumped.

Nathan got up and went to the back door. He pulled it open and a rush of wind blew inside, carrying a flurry of dead leaves into the room. My heart constricted—like it had the night the figure attacked me in my bed. I hugged my knees to my chest. "Nathan, close the door."

He looked over his shoulder at me. "What?"

Before I could answer, he was knocked backward off his feet. I leapt off the couch, stepping over him to shut the back door. I tumbled the deadbolt, then sank to the floor against it.

Nathan's eyes were double their normal size. "What the hell was that?"

I shook my head and crawled over beside him. "I don't know, but I've only ever felt like that in Texas and in my nightmares. Pinch me."

"Huh?"

I pinched his arm.

He yelped. "What was that for?"

"I guess I'm not asleep," I said.

He got up, jerking his sidearm from its holster. "How does you pinching me prove you're not asleep?" He walked over to the door and pulled back the curtains over the window. "There's movement out there. Lock the door behind me."

I scrambled to my feet and grabbed his arm. "Don't. Please don't leave me."

His mouth opened like he was about to argue, but he didn't. "I won't." He walked to the table and picked up his radio. "Dispatch this is 2201, off duty."

The radio beeped and a woman's voice came over the line. "Officer 2201, this is dispatch. Go ahead."

"Dispatch this is 2201. Current location is 7506 Bradley Avenue. Requests you dispatch the zone two unit to this area for patrol. Be on the lookout for suspicious activity or persons at current location. Unable to investigate at this time."

"Officer 2201, this is dispatch. 10-4. I'll have the zone two officer en route to your position."

He hooked the radio on his belt, then walked to the kitchen. I followed close on his heels as he peeked out the blinds behind the dinette. "No unusual cars on the street."

I was right over his shoulder. "Nathan, forget the cars. There's no wind, or storm!"

He didn't respond.

Pressing my eyes closed, I sent my evil radar out into the night, sincerely hoping to detect an armed robber or an axe murderer. They would be easier to deal with than what I feared was out there. There was no one. No humans, anyway.

Through clenched teeth, I let out a squeal. "Nathan, it's her. It's Kasyade. She's going to kill me."

He turned around and leveled his gaze at me. "You don't know that."

"Yes I do."

He shook his head. "It could have been a transformer blowing or kids setting off fireworks."

I pointed at his face. "Nathan, you know better."

He pushed my hand down. "Maybe it was Thor, God of Thunder."

I bit down on the insides of my lips to keep from laughing. Nothing about the situation warranted jokes, no matter how funny they were.

He winked at me. "Go to bed. I'll stand guard."

I smirked. "Right. Let me get right to that." I paced around the kitchen.

"Sloan, you'll trigger a panic attack if you don't calm down," he warned.

I was wringing my hands. "I'm trying."

He tucked his gun back into its holster and grabbed my hand. "Sit," he instructed, pulling a chair out at the dinette table for me. "Talk about something else."

"Like what?" I sat on my hands to keep from fidgeting.

"What will you name the baby?" he asked, opening a cabinet and retrieving a water glass.

I blinked with surprise. "I haven't really thought about it."

He filled the glass at the sink. "Don't all girls keep lists of what they want to name their babies? Or was that just Shannon?"

That time, I laughed. "It's not just Shannon, but it's never been me."

He handed me the glass and sat next to me. "Never?"

I shook my head. "No. I guess I always assumed kids wouldn't be in the cards."

His head snapped back with surprise. "That's crazy. Why would you think that?"

I shrugged and pulled the water close. "I've never been in a relationship long enough to imagine it going anywhere. I've always kind of been alone."

"Bullshit," he said, sitting back in his chair.

I sipped the water. "True story. The longest relationship I've ever been in was a few months, and it was long distance so it doesn't count."

"But everybody loves you, so why?" he asked.

A dog barked outside, and my eyes flashed back to the window.

Nathan snapped his fingers in front of my nose. "Focus on me. Why are you romantically defective?"

I took a deep, calming breath and thought for a second. "Adrianne once accused me of taking things too fast, not slowing down enough to get to know someone before deciding it won't work." I leaned on my elbow. "But it's the exact opposite. Immediately, I know people too well."

His brow lifted. "So that's why you jumped in so fast with Warren. He was mysterious."

I smiled. "The tall, dark, and smoking hot thing didn't hurt either."

He rolled his eyes. "Yeah, that too."

I drummed my nails on the sides of the glass. "It's different with him. I never worry that he's attracted to me because of my magnetic qualities." I added some finger flair to the last part of that statement for dramatic effect. "What most people feel for me isn't real."

He leaned toward me, cutting his eyes. "You still believe after everything we've been through that I care about you because of"— he waved his hand toward me—"whatever it is you are?"

"Nathan, Kasyade told me—"

"I don't care what she told you!" His voice was a little louder than he obviously intended. He dialed his decibels back down. "I'm not here because I'm some weak-willed mortal who can't resist the charms of the county publicist."

Whoa.

"Nathan, I didn't mean it like—"

He cut me off again, this time standing up so fast his chair legs squeaked across the tile floor. "How else could you mean that?" It was his turn to pace the kitchen. "Is that really the whole reason you and I aren't—"

The doorbell rang.

He muttered a few profanities before stomping across the room to the foyer.

How the hell we'd gone from a demon trying to blow my house down to the subatomic foundation of our relationship was beyond me. At least he kept my panic at bay. I was still scratching my head when a uniformed sheriff's deputy walked into my living room.

"Russ, this is Sloan. Sloan, Russ Hughes," Nathan said, not looking directly at me.

I waved to the deputy.

"Nate, I didn't see anything out of the ordinary, and we circled the area a few times," he said.

Nathan folded his arms over his chest. "Did anyone else report hearing some kind of explosion? Or have you gotten any calls about power outages from a transformer in the area?"

Russ shook his head. "Not that I'm aware of."

"How about a surveillance car? Usually a truck parked over on Hyde Lane. Did you see it?"

"I didn't see one," Russ answered. "Do you have a tail?"

"Maybe." Nathan offered him his hand, and Russ shook it. "Listen, thanks for coming out and checking."

"Not a problem. I'll be around tonight. I'll swing back by a few times and keep my eyes open."

"Thank you," Nathan said.

"Hey, did you hear the news about Gollum?" Russ asked.

Nathan looked at me, then back at Russ. "No. What news?"

"She busted out of the psych ward. They just called it in that she's gone missing," he said.

Nathan groaned. "I'd better keep my scanner on. Call me if you hear anything."

"10-4." Russ gave a slight nod in my direction. "Good evening, ma'am."

"Thanks, Russ," I said.

When he left, I looked at Nathan. "Who's Gollum?"

He swirled his finger around his ear. "Red-headed crazy chick."

I perked with alarm. "The demon lady who's looking for me?"

"That's the one."

I pointed to the door. "Perhaps that's what all the noise and wind was about."

Nathan shrugged but didn't look convinced. "Whatever it was, it's over now." He paused, but his mouth was still open and ready to speak. After a moment, he looked in my direction but not exactly at me. "I'm sorry for raising my voice."

"It's OK."

He finally made eye-contact. "No, it's not. Please forgive me."

"Forgiven."

He glanced toward the stairs. "You're exhausted. You may not sleep, but you still need to rest."

I walked toward the stairs but stopped in front of him. "I'm sorry too."

He cast his gaze at the ground, bobbing his head in acknowledgement. "It's over. Let's not bring it back up."

I nodded, but we both knew whatever *it* was, it certainly wasn't over.

It was far, far from it.

CHAPTER NINE

The last time I'd had a social night out was the night before Warren's reactivation with the Marine Corps. He had almost proposed to me then, but he didn't because of Nathan McNamara.

Oh the irony, I thought as I stood in front of a full-length mirror in the ladies' room of The Grove Park Inn. I was polished and primped for a date at the most romantic hotel in all of Asheville…with the wrong man in my life.

"This is not a date," I corrected myself out loud. "This is *definitely* not a date."

A woman stepped out of a stall I didn't realize was occupied behind me. She had a teasing smile.

I shook my head. "It's really not."

The lady chuckled.

After tucking a loose curl back into the bird's nest Adrianne had sculpted on my head, I walked out of the bathroom, but Nathan wasn't where I'd left him by the piano. I walked around the Great Hall fireplace and all around the crowded bar, but I couldn't find him anywhere. I thought about calling him on the phone, but I remembered my cell was still plugged up at home on my nightstand.

I heard a familiar whistle somewhere in the distance behind me and turned to see him on the far side of the room, sitting in the back of a big red Santa sleigh.

I held out my arms as I walked over. "What are you doing?"

He stood, holding two full wine glasses. "All the other seats were taken," he said, stepping out of the sleigh. "What were you doing in there? You were gone for half an hour."

I rolled my eyes. "I was not."

He handed me a glass.

I frowned. "Umm?"

He smiled. "It's grape juice. It's *sparkling*," he added with a lisp.

I laughed and accepted it. "Thank you."

Halfway through the lobby, I heard my name over the commotion. It was a woman's voice. I turned and looked, as did Nathan. Finally, I spotted a waving arm in the crowd. "Sloan!" she called again.

My brain scrambled to place the older woman's familiar face.

A half a second later, three and a half feet of bounding energy burst through the crowd of legs in the room. Blond haired, blue and green eyed, Kayleigh Neeland sprinted toward me, her red patent Mary Janes click-clacking against the marble as she ran.

I knelt down in time to catch her in my arms. "Kayleigh!"

"Miss Sloan!" she cheered, throwing her tiny arms around my neck.

"How are you, sweet girl?" I asked.

She pulled back, pushing her curls out of her face. "We came to see the gingerbread houses. The one with the Barbie in the castle is my favorite."

"Really?" I asked, tugging on the hem of her sparkly red and green Christmas dress. "You're so pretty. Is this new?"

"Uh huh," she said, nodding.

Over our heads, Nathan greeted Kayleigh's grandparents.

Kayleigh pointed back behind her. "Did you see Santa?"

I shook my head. "No. I didn't know Santa was here. Did you sit on his lap and tell him what you want for Christmas?"

"Uh huh. I want the new Mary Ashley doll. The one that talks and goes to school. Not the Mary Ashley doll that cries and wears diapers," she said.

I laughed and bobbed my head like I knew what she was talking about. "How's kindergarten?"

She shrugged. "It's OK." Her head tilted to the side. "Miss Sloan, when's your baby coming?"

I blinked. "H...how did you know about that?"

She pushed her hair back again. "I saw your baby tummy."

Nathan nudged my leg with the toe of his dress shoe. "Told you."

I swatted his leg away, then turned back to her. "Well, my baby is coming this summer. Isn't that exciting?"

She bit her lower lip, swaying from side to side. "She's going to be pretty, just like you."

"Thank you," I said. "Oh, look what I still have." I held out the collar of my coat so she could see the angel pin she'd given me.

She touched it with her tiny finger.

"I wear it every day," I said.

"Nana says if I'm good we can have hot chocolate before we leave," she said.

I pinched her nose. "I'm sure it will be delicious."

She looked up at Nathan. "You're the police man."

He dropped to a knee beside me. "You remember me?"

"Uh huh." She rocked back and forth on her heels. "You found me that one bad day."

He sucked in a deep breath and smiled. "Yes, I did." He playfully touched the tip of her nose. "It was a bad day, but it was also one of the very best days."

She laughed. "Yeah."

I looked up at her grandmother. "It's so good to see you. How long are you in town?"

"Just tonight," she said. "We had a custody hearing yesterday, so we decided to make a weekend out of it. Few places are more beautiful than Asheville at Christmas."

"That's the truth," I agreed. "How did the hearing go?"

Kayleigh's grandfather nodded. "It went well. The judge granted us full custody."

"It was a bittersweet victory," Nana said. "But you can only imagine how happy we are."

I tucked a strand of Kayleigh's hair behind her ear. "Yes, I can." I opened my arms. "Can I have another hug?"

She lunged into me, squeezing my neck again.

"I hope you have a very Merry Christmas, Kayleigh," I said, kissing her on the side of the head.

"Merry Christmas, Miss Sloan."

Nathan gave Kayleigh a high-five, then helped me to my feet. I pulled one of my business cards out of my purse and handed it to her grandmother. "The next time you're in town, let me know so we can plan to meet. This has made my night."

The woman nodded. "I will."

"Merry Christmas," I said to them.

"Merry Christmas," they echoed back.

Nathan's hand at the small of my back turned me toward the hallway. I closed my eyes and let out a melodic sigh. "I love that kid so much."

He smiled when I looked at him. "I know you do. She's cute." He pointed toward the banquet room. "You ready to go in?"

I took a deep breath. "Yeah. Let's do this."

The annual Christmas party was the only social event my office ever had, and the county went all out for it. The room glistened with Christmas trees and twinkle lights, but the centerpiece of the decor was the view. Beyond the panoramic glass walls, the sun dipped behind mountains speckled with snow-covered pines, splashing the dark blue sky with violet and fuchsia swirls. I'm pretty sure if Heaven exists, then Asheville at Christmastime was modeled after it. It was so stunning that I almost didn't notice how every eye turned toward me and Nathan as we crossed the room.

"Why are people staring at us?" Nathan whispered behind me.

I shrugged.

Sheriff Davis, Nathan's boss, sauntered over in a black suit with a bright red Santa Claus tie. "McNamara!" He extended his hand as he approached. "Glad to see I'm not the only one representing our office tonight. You clean up pretty well."

He was right. Nathan's black pants and charcoal button up couldn't have fit any better if they were melted onto his body. He had a fresh shave and a haircut. And he smelled even better than he looked.

Nathan caught my eye and winked. "Thank you, sir, but no one is looking at me tonight."

This is not a date. This is not a date. This is not a date.

The sheriff turned toward me. "Sloan Jordan, you look like a million bucks." He gave me a side hug, jostling my shoulders with his large hand. "How 'ya feelin' these days, young lady?"

I nodded. "Pretty well, thank you. How's Mrs. Davis?"

He looked around the room. "She's good. Around here somewhere."

"If I don't have the chance, please wish her a Merry Christmas for me."

"Will do." He looked at Nathan. "You heard any more from the feds?"

Nathan crossed his arms over his chest. "No, sir. Though I believe they're still following Sloan."

I held my hands up. "Gentlemen, this is a party. Can we please not talk about things that might make me cry?"

Sheriff Davis laughed with a hearty chuckle. "I remember those tearful days when Rosie found out she was carrying our first. One time I told her we were out of egg salad; you'd think I told her our dog was dead."

I laughed, but I turned my wide eyes toward Nathan.

He shrugged.

The sheriff grabbed Nathan's shoulder and shook it. "On that note, I need to find my wife. You two have a fun night. You've earned it." He paused as he turned away. "Oh! And congratulations," he said with a wink.

As he walked away, I put my hands on my hips. "He knows I'm pregnant. Who did you tell?"

Nathan held up his hands. "I didn't say a word. Who did *you* tell?"

"Just my boss but only yesterday."

He helped me out of my coat. "Well, this is a pretty small town. News travels fast." He motioned toward an empty table near the exit. "Want to sit where we can make a quick getaway?"

Smiling, I nodded my head. "Please."

The room filled up over the next few minutes. I often forgot how many people worked for the county. Half of them I didn't recognize because they either worked in a completely different division or they were so dressed up I couldn't place them. Mary was one of those. I had to do a double-take when she appeared at our table dressed in a red gown that sparkled like a disco ball. She was even wearing makeup. "Hello, Mary. Don't you look beautiful!" I said, standing up to hug her.

"Thank you, dear. So do you!" When she stepped away from our embrace, she noticed Nathan. "Detective McNamara, I wasn't expecting you here tonight!"

He squeezed her hand. "I'm here against my will, I assure you."

I laughed. "Don't let him fool you. He's here for the open bar."

He grinned at her. "That too."

Mary blushed. He had that effect on people. "You two kids have a lovely evening. I'm going to go join my date."

I blinked with surprise. "Your date?"

She looked like she might squeal with excitement. "You're not the only one around here with a juicy love life these days."

My eyes widened. "Well, don't hold out on me! Who is it?"

"Calvin Jarvis."

The name sounded familiar. My brow crumpled.

Nathan laughed. "We were sworn in together."

I grabbed her hands. "Oh, I'm so happy for you!" Mary had called him a fox the first time we'd seen him—the day I met Nathan.

She was so excited, I was worried she might pass out. Glancing from me to Nathan and back again, she squeezed my fingers. "I guess both our wishes came true."

It wasn't till she was gone that I realized what she meant. I plopped down in my chair. "Everyone's staring at us because they all think we're having this baby together."

He popped the collar on his shirt. "What can I say? I'm a stud."

I laughed and swatted him with my cloth napkin.

After a delicious meal, dessert, and coffee—decaf, Nathan leaned into me. "You've yawned nine times in the past four minutes. You ready to head home?"

Home.

"Yes."

My eyes were watery with exhaustion while we waited for the valet to bring around his SUV. It was freezing outside and flurrying again, and all I wanted was to curl up in my warm bed. I was dozing in and out by the time we reached the bottom of the mountain. Soft Christmas music floated through the speakers.

Thoughts of what the next Christmas would be like danced around in my mind. I'd be a mother by then, and Warren would be home, hopefully. We'd have a tree; I'd never bothered to put one up before. And my dad would buy lots of expensive toys that were completely unsuitable for a baby. I smiled and leaned my head against the cold glass window as the car gently shifted around a curve.

"Whoa!" Nathan yelled.

I looked up in time to spot a skeleton shaped figure with stringy red hair standing in the dead center of the road. She was barefoot in a hospital gown. An IV dangled from her withered and scarred arm.

Nathan swerved to miss her, sending the SUV careening off the side of the road. We missed a telephone pole by inches and tore through a cluster of mountain laurel before going off an embankment.

The last thing I saw was the French Broad River in front of us before my face smacked the dashboard.

CHAPTER TEN

Nathan was screaming somewhere off in the distance. I was bobbing up and down, floating on a faint stream of consciousness. Something was gurgling. My feet were cold. *I should have worn thicker stockings,* I thought.

When my eyes swirled into focus, Nathan was frantically jerking on my seatbelt. I blinked.

"Sloan!"

I blinked again. "Nathan?"

"Sloan, we've got to get out of here!"

I shook my head from side to side. It hurt like hell. I touched my fingers to a throbbing spot on my forehead, and when I pulled them back, blood dripped down my palm.

Water was everywhere.

Outside my window, water and ice sloshed up and down against the glass. I pressed my hand to it, trying to make sense of what was happening. Nathan's SUV was bobbing in the river. My feet were wet. One of his hat patches pinned to the ceiling above my head said, *All Work. No Pay.*

I chuckled. *It's sad all of Nathan's patches are going to drown in the river...*

"Sloan!"

I'm going to drown in the river.

Realization hit me like a freight train. Confusion gave way to panic. My fingers fought with Nathan's over the seat belt. He grabbed my hands. "Sloan," he said, trying to keep his voice calm. I focused on his gray eyes. "I need you to stay calm so we can get out of this. Unbuckle your seatbelt. I'll break the windshield."

I nodded my understanding.

Cold was spreading from my wet feet, up my legs, and deep into my bones. I shuddered as I fought with the seatbelt latch. It must have been damaged in the crash, but after a moment, I worked it free. Nathan turned around on his seat and yanked the headrest out of the seat. The water was sneaking up the glass on both sides of us, and we were moving downstream in the current.

I tried the button to roll down my window, but the electric opener was no longer functional. Perfect snowflakes were freezing on the windshield.

"Can you swim?"

My teeth chattered. "Yes."

"Take off your coat and your shoes. We'll have to get to the bank as quickly as possible before we freeze to death," he said.

The water was over two inches up my window. My hands were shaking but only partly from the cold. "We can't die in here!"

"Nobody is dying today," he said. "Take off your shoes."

I slipped off my heels and struggled out of my thick wool coat. I detached the silver angel pin and shoved it down into my bra.

Nathan slammed the posts of the headrest against the windshield. The glass cracked, but it didn't shatter. "It would be easier to bust out the side, but I'm afraid the car will sink before we can both get out. Problem is, the windshield's bulletproof," he said. "This could take a minute."

The water was at least four inches over the window, and it was up to my calves in the floorboard. Looking down at the water swirling around my feet, I noticed my hands—seemingly of their own accord—shielding my stomach. *My baby.* That was all the motivation I needed. I got up on my knees and pounded the windshield with the balls of my fist.

"Sloan, stop! You'll wear yourself out!"

"I'm not going to drown in your stupid car!" I screamed.

With all my desperation focused on getting out of the windshield, I slammed my fist into the glass again. This time, it splintered beneath my hands, and ice cold water gushed in. I sucked half of it down my lungs before realizing the barrier between me and the oxygen above was gone. My feet pushed against the sinking passenger's seat and kicked till my face pierced the surface.

I thrashed around in the freezing current until I saw Nathan pop up a few feet away. He gasped and began thrashing toward the river bank. The ice felt like needles in my skin as I forced my legs to kick for the shore after him. A small crowd of people had gathered on the snowy bank. Everyone was screaming. Flashlights were blinding me as they flailed in the dark sky.

I kicked and kicked, but I couldn't feel anything below the water anymore. As my arms reached for the riverbank, the burning sensation slowly faded. *A few more feet...*

The pain in my chest exploded as I went under the surface again. The beams of light from the shore grew more and more distant. I thought I was swimming, but there was enough light to see my arms floating motionless up toward the surface of the water. I could no longer close my eyelids.

Then a hand wrapped around my wrist, and a warm, familiar buzz of energy flowed into me. Only one other person had that touch. His energy ignited the life inside me. Warren's face was inches from mine under the water. *I'm dreaming again...*

We broke through into the icy night air.

For a split second, I saw his face.

Then the world went black.

"Get blankets!"

"Bring her here!"

"Get those wet clothes off!"

The world faded in and out for a few moments. Someone ripped off my dress, and another pair of hands wrapped a fleece blanket around my shoulders. I opened my eyes to look for Warren, but I couldn't find him. I was inside a minivan. Nathan was there, and I could hear his teeth chattering beside me.

I couldn't hold my head up on my own. I thought of my baby and slipped into oblivion once more.

Halogen lights blinded my eyes when I opened them again. The wheels of the bed underneath me squeaked as I rolled down the familiar hallway. Between Adrianne's accident, my near-death trauma with Billy Stewart, and Mom's death, the Mission Hospital emergency room was becoming like a second home.

A nurse with long dark hair bent over me when we stopped moving. Her name tag said, *Rena*. My jaw wouldn't stop trembling. "Wh...wh...where's N...N...Nath...than?"

Rena put her hand on my shoulder. "He came in right before you did. He's fine. Can you tell me your name and what happened?"

"M...my n...ame is S...S...Sloan J...Jor...Jordan. I w...was in a ca...car cr...rash. A w...woman w...was s...standing in th...the r... road," I replied.

She nodded. "Ms. Jordan, we've notified your father. He should be here soon. We need to check out your head, but your body temperature is coming back up."

"I'm pr...pr...egnant," I said.

Her eyes widened. "I'll let your doctor know."

"Is m...my b...boyfriend, here? W...W...Warren P...Parish?" I asked.

She looked around the room. "Just you and Detective McNamara were brought in."

When they wheeled me behind a curtain across from the nurses' station, they covered me from head to toe with warm blankets. I wiggled my legs and realized I wasn't wearing any pants. At least I'd worn pretty panties with my dress.

"Sloan, is th...th...at you?" I heard Nathan ask on the other side of the curtain divider. His voice was as shaky as my own.

"Y...yeah. Are y...you ok...k?" I asked.

"C...cold," he answered. "You?"

"A...l...live," I chattered.

Rena came back into my cubicle. She pulled the curtain back between me and Nathan enough so we could see each other. She winked at me. When I looked over, Nathan's face was blotchy and red. He was in a similar blanket cocoon.

Two deputies from the Sheriff's office walked in and went to talk to Nathan. My nurse returned and hooked me up to a warm IV bag. She paused after sticking the needle in my arm and cocked her head to the side.

My eyes widened at the look on her face. "Wh...what is it?"

Her brow scrunched together. "The gash on your forehead... It's closed now."

Because I was so cold, I hadn't felt it. "I'm a f...fast healer."

"That's impossible," she said.

I gave a sheepish shrug.

A doctor, a man I hadn't seen on any of my previous visits, walked in behind her. She motioned for him to come over. "Dr. Lambert, five minutes ago this mark on her forehead was a gaping wound. I've never seen anything like this before."

He pulled at the skin on my forehead with his thumbs. "Are you sure?" he asked.

"Positive," she replied.

He rubbed his chin. "That's strange." He looked at me expecting an answer.

"M...maybe I d...didn't hit my h...head as hard as w...we thought."

He scribbled something on my chart. "I'm still ordering a CT scan to make sure the bump on your head is OK. I've also paged the obstetrician on call to check on the baby."

Just then, I saw my dad walk up to the nurses' station behind them. "D...dad!"

He turned, and panic flashed across his face when he saw me. "Sloan, thank God you're OK." He walked over and kissed my forehead. "You're freezing."

"Your daughter is lucky," the doctor said. "The water temperature could have killed her."

"I know." Dad leaned down toward me. "How are you feeling?"

"C...cold," I answered.

He blew out a long sigh. "Are you hurt?"

I shook my head. "I d...don't think so. I'm gon...na need some dry c...clothes."

He squeezed my shoulder. "I'll take care of it once they confirm you're stable."

I nodded. "H...have you s...seen W...warren?"

His head snapped back with surprise. "Warren?"

"He p...pulled m...me out of the w...water," I stammered.

Dad looked around the room confused. "Honey, Warren isn't here."

I'm officially crazy.

Just as I suspected, the CT scan came back clear. If I had sustained any injuries to my skull, they would have healed before I reached the hospital. My teeth had stopped chattering, and I could once again feel my arms and legs.

Nathan was sitting in a chair, dressed in a dry outfit, and he stood when I was wheeled back into my curtained cubical. When they parked my bed, without a word he closed the space between us and bent over me. I wrapped my arms around him and squeezed the back of his neck. I cried into his shoulder.

"Shh..." he said. "It's over. You're safe." He eased down onto the bed beside me, and he brushed the tears off my cheeks with his thumb. His eyes were glassy. "I looked back and saw you go under." With each word, he struggled to not fall apart.

He pressed a long kiss to my forehead.

My father walked in behind him, followed by another doctor in a white coat. Dad motioned toward me. "Dr. Rhodes, this is my daughter, Sloan."

Nathan stepped back, drying his eyes on the back of his sleeve as he turned away.

The woman held up a fetal doppler. "Sloan, are you ready to check the baby's heart rate?"

I sniffed and sat up in the bed. "Absolutely."

Dad laid a black backpack on the chair beside the bed. "I got your clothes, sweetheart."

Nathan took a step back next to my dad.

A few moments later, a muffled *bump, bump, bump, bump, bump* echoed around the room. I covered my mouth with my hands. "I've never heard it before."

She smiled.

Dad walked over and put his hand on my shoulder.

Nathan was beaming in our direction.

"The heart rate's a little slow, but that's normal due to the drop in your body temperature," she explained. "I'll come back and check on you in a little bit."

"Thank you, Doctor."

When she was gone, I looked at Nathan. "Did they find the lunatic who was standing in the middle of the road?"

He shook his head. "No. The Sheriff's office is looking for her, but so far they haven't found anything."

"The FBI guys following us didn't see anything?" I asked.

He lowered his voice. "As far as I know, no one from the FBI was there."

Interesting.

In the cubical to my left, someone erupted into a violent coughing fit. Then a woman cried out in pain.

I pointed toward the bag on the chair Dad had brought from my house. "Hand me my clothes, please."

"You haven't been cleared for release yet," Dad said.

I shook my head. "I don't care. I can help her."

He hesitated. "This isn't a good idea."

"Dad, nothing I ever do is a good idea."

He tried not to, but he cracked a smile.

I held my hands up. "What will they do? Kick me out of the hospital? Hand me my clothes!"

Dad dropped the bag onto my bed and put his hands on his hips.

I unzipped it and pulled out a sweatshirt. It was a black hoodie with S.W.A.T. written across the back in bold white letters. I laughed. "Nathan, look," I said, holding it up for him to see.

He glanced over and chuckled. "That's hilarious."

"What's so funny?" Dad asked.

"It's Nathan's shirt," I said. "It's a long story."

Nathan had given me the shirt to wear the night we saved Kayleigh Neeland, and Warren hated I still had it. Thinking of Kayleigh reminded me that the angel pin she had given me must still be in my bra, wherever it ended up…or maybe it was at the bottom of the river.

I couldn't put the shirt on with the IV still in my arm. "Dad, can you take this thing out?"

He looked around for the nurse. "Sloan, I really don't feel right about this."

I cocked my head to the side. "Are you going to let me jerk this needle out of my arm and bleed all over the emergency room?"

He groaned and stepped over beside my bed. "You're so stubborn."

I winked at him. "I get it from you."

He rolled his eyes and removed the IV.

I slipped the sweatshirt over my head and caught Nathan grinning over at me. "It still looks good on you," he said.

I laughed. "Glad you think so."

Carefully, I wiggled into a pair of black yoga pants underneath my blankets. Almost all the feeling had returned to my extremities, so I was even able to tie on my sneakers without any help. I swung my legs off the bed and looked up at my dad. "Do you see anyone coming?"

He looked around the hall behind him. "Your nurse is two stalls down."

"Can you distract her?"

He frowned but nodded his head.

My legs wobbled a bit when I stood, so I gripped the bed for support.

"Where are you going?" Nathan whispered.

I didn't answer him. Instead, I quietly tiptoed over to the curtain, pulling it back slowly as to not make a sound.

In the cubicle next to me was Virginia Claybrooks, the guard from the jail. I gasped. "Oh, Ms. Claybrooks."

Perspiration was beaded on her forehead, and her cheeks were streaked with tears. A young man was holding her hand. She looked at me, full of fear. "How 'you know my name?"

I touched my fingers to my chest. "I'm Sloan Jordan from the county office. Don't you remember me?"

Her eyes narrowed. "You're the cute blond boy's girlfriend, aren't you?"

I laughed. "Detective McNamara and I are friends. Are you ill?"

She began coughing again. With each convulsion, she winced

and more tears spilled out. "They say I got fluid in my lungs. Feels like I'm drowning from the inside out. I'm gonna die here."

I stepped to her bedside and took her hand. "You're not going to die, Ms. Claybrooks."

She moaned, triggering another coughing fit.

Gently, I sat on the edge of her bed and put my hand on her clammy forehead.

"Your hands are ice cold," she said, shivering.

"Well, speaking of drowning, I almost drowned in the river tonight," I said.

Her eyes widened. "What the heck were you doing in the river, child? Don't you know it's winter time?"

I laughed. "If I didn't know it before, I know it now." I put both my hands on either side of her face.

"What are you doin' to me?" she asked.

"Maybe my cold hands will help with that fever," I said, smiling gently. "Hey, that cute blond boy is here. Do you want to see him?"

She shook her head. "Don't nobody need to see me. They say this thing could be contagious. My son, David"—she gestured to the man beside her bed—"he's as stubborn as a bull, and he won't leave."

I laughed. "My dad just said the same thing about me." I glanced at her son. "Hi, David."

He waved. "Hi."

Ms. Claybrooks shuddered again and winced with pain. When she coughed again, it already sounded less congested. My hands warmed against her face as my whole body buzzed with energy.

"I feel all twisted up inside," she cried.

"Shh," I said. "It will be over soon."

"Cuz I'm gonna die," she whimpered.

"Virginia, look at me." Her swollen eyes focused on mine. I shook my head. "You're not going to die. Not today. And certainly not from a cough."

Her face relaxed, and she looked at me with fierce curiosity. "What are you?" she whispered.

I winked at her. "I'm a publicist."

Before the doctors caught on to the rounds I was making through the emergency room, I was able to heal Ms. Claybrooks from pneumonia, a single mom of three kids from a severe case of strep throat, and two old ladies who were dreadfully sick with the flu.

When the nurse brought my discharge papers, she was frowning. "Make sure you stop by and say hello when you're back in here with a productive cough and a fever in a couple of days."

I smiled and tucked the papers into my bag. "I'm sure I'll be OK. Thanks for taking such good care of us, Rena."

She pointed at me. "I don't want to see you again, Ms. Jordan." She turned toward Nathan who was standing next to my bed. "Or you, Detective."

"Yes, ma'am," Nathan said.

My dad looked down at me. "Are you ready to go?"

I nodded and he helped me to my feet. "Yeah. Can you drop us off at my house since neither of us have a car?"

"Of course. You about gave me a heart attack. I may never let you out of my sight again." He kept his hand on my back. "I'm so thankful you're both alive."

Nathan took my backpack and slung it over his shoulder. "We've all got Sloan to thank for that. She saved us by shattering the windshield." He looked over at me as we walked out to the lobby. "How did you do it?"

I thought about the way Kasyade had once thrown a car down a San Antonio street and how Samael was able to lock and unlock doors without touching them. "I think it must have been part of my power, but I have no idea how I did it."

"That's near death experience number three in the time I've

known you, Sloan," Nathan said as he held the door open to the parking lot. It was still snowing, but it was wet and clumpy.

"I think I came a lot closer to death than you did this time," I said.

Dad looked at both of us. "It's not a competition, kids!"

I put my hood up over my head. "I never would have made it to the shore if..." I stopped before sounding completely nuts again.

"If what?" Nathan asked.

"I could have sworn Warren pulled me out of the water," I said, bringing our little group to a halt.

Nathan's brow crumpled. "Impossible. You had to be hallucinating."

"Nathan, I saw him. I felt him when he grabbed me. I didn't hallucinate that feeling."

"It's impossible," he said and started walking again.

I did a double-step to catch up with him. "Did you see who pulled me out?"

Nathan was quiet till we got to the car and Dad unlocked the doors. "I was in and out of it, and I remember seeing a man carrying you up the riverbank, but it wasn't Warren. It couldn't have been."

We all got into the car, and Dad started the engine. "It isn't uncommon to imagine things when you come so close to death, Sloan. I agree with Nathan."

I leaned my head back against the seat. "I know you're right, but I also know what I saw."

Dad sighed. "Well, I'm grateful to whoever pulled you out of the river."

"Me too," Nathan agreed.

We had an uneventful drive home, but when we turned on to my street, a black truck was parked in front of my house. Nathan pointed over my seat. "That's the truck that's been following you."

I strained my eyes in the dark. "That doesn't look like the FBI."

"No, it doesn't," Nathan agreed.

My father pulled to a stop behind the truck.

"Stay in the car," Nathan said as he wrenched his door open.

I smirked and pulled on my door handle. "You can't tell me to stay in the car at my own house."

Dad tossed his hands up. "What good is it to have the boy to protect you if you never listen to him?"

The street was dark, but in the moonlight, I saw a man standing on the front steps of my house. I couldn't sense his soul. I grabbed onto Nathan's hand and ducked behind him. "Not human," I whispered.

When we got closer, the man turned toward us, and light from the moon flashed across his face.

It was him.

CHAPTER ELEVEN

"Warren?" Nathan asked, cautiously moving forward.

I hesitantly side-stepped around him, but Nathan blocked me with his arm.

The man didn't move, making us come all the way to him at the foot of the stairs where he towered over us. I doubted it would be much different if we were on equal footing. Beneath him, I felt very small and was keenly aware Nathan had lost his sidearm in the river. We were completely unprotected.

The man was dressed in dark clothes and had short black hair. It wasn't Warren, but it could have been his clone. I gasped and covered my mouth with my hand. "Oh my god."

"Who are you?" Nathan demanded.

"My name is—"

"Azrael," I said, pushing Nathan's arm away from me and taking a step forward. "Your name is Azrael."

The man's black eyes widened with surprise. "Yes. My name is Azrael. How did you know?"

"Lucky guess," I said.

Nathan looked at me. "Who?"

"He's Warren's father." I studied Azrael. "It was you who saved me tonight. You were following me."

He nodded slowly.

"You've been following her?" Nathan asked, anger rising in his voice.

Azrael stepped down one step. "And where would she be if I hadn't been?" His voice was dark and dangerous, just like his son's.

"Are you here to kill me?" I asked, summoning courage I didn't know I had.

"If I were here to kill you, I would have let you drown," he answered. "You're in danger and, as I am Warren's father, I came to protect you...and your unborn daughter."

"How do you know about the baby? And what makes you so sure it's a girl?" Nathan asked.

He smiled, but it was more creepy than comforting. "Your child is well known in my world, Sloan."

My neighbor's porch light flickered on. My eyes darted down the street. "Can we go inside before someone calls the police?" I asked.

"I am the police," Nathan reminded me. "And no, we can't go inside." He stepped protectively in front of me again and looked up at the angel on my porch steps. "If you're here to protect her, then why all the secrecy? Who the hell do you think you are?"

Azrael took a step toward Nathan. "My name is Azrael, the Archangel of Death."

I swallowed and cowered behind Nathan's back.

Nathan smirked. "Sure you are."

I pressed my lips together and shrank back even more. I tugged on his arm and lowered my voice. "I don't think it's a good idea to get mouthy with him, Nate."

Azrael's face was inscrutable. "You don't have to believe me. It doesn't make it any less true. I am also her child's grandfather."

Nathan cast me a skeptical glare.

"Who, may I ask, are you?" Azrael said.

Nathan folded his arms over his chest. "I'm Detective Nathan McNamara. Sloan and I are close friends, and I promised the baby's father I would look out for her while he's gone."

"You know my son?" Azrael asked.

"How do we even know he's really your son?"

"Look at him," I said. "They couldn't look any more alike if you put Warren through a Xerox."

Nathan turned toward me and put his hands on his hips. "People think my dad looks like Paul Newman, but it doesn't mean they're related!"

"Your dad *does* look like Paul Newman!"

Nathan's head dropped to the side. "Focus please."

"Sorry."

"Even if he is Warren's dad, who's to say he's not a psychopath like your sadistic mother?" he asked.

I put my hands on his forearms and cut my eyes up at him. "Nathan, this is one of those leap of faith moments you'll have to take with me. I believe him, and I really want to hear what he has to say."

He ran a hand down his face in frustration. "You're impossible."

"I know."

I turned back in the direction of the car and waved for my dad to come, then Azrael stepped aside as I walked up the steps past him. When I reached the front door, I realized my keys were sitting at the bottom of the French Broad River. I patted my empty pockets. Azrael must have understood because he lifted his hand toward the door, and I heard the deadbolt slide open. My mouth fell open a little as I stared up at him.

He looked like he wanted to smile, but he didn't.

It was unnerving how much he looked like Warren. The jawline, the cheekbones, the tanned skin stretched smooth and taut over his face…it was all the same. What wasn't the same was the cavernous scar running from the inside of his eyebrow, across the bridge of his nose, and down the opposite cheek. I wondered what the other guy must have looked like.

Azrael followed me into the house with Nathan and my father quick on his heels. I flipped the light switch.

My father shrugged out of his wool coat. "Can someone please explain to me what is going on?"

I touched his elbow. "Dad, this is Azrael. He's Warren's father."

Dad blinked with bewilderment. "His father?"

"Angels don't age," I explained. "Azrael, this is my dad, Dr. Robert Jordan."

Dad extended his hand, but Azrael just looked down at it until my father awkwardly pulled it away. "Well, it's nice to meet you, I think, Azrael," Dad said, stumbling over each word.

"Come in and have a seat," I said, motioning toward the living room. "Make yourself comfortable."

Nathan and my father cornered me in the foyer.

"I don't like this, Sloan," Nathan said.

I rolled my eyes. "Surprise, surprise."

Dad pointed at him. "I agree with Nathan."

I looked at both of them and motioned toward the door. "Then you can both go home. You don't live here."

In unison they scowled at me.

I pushed through the middle of them, but Nathan's hand to my chest stopped me. He lowered his face to my ear. "You don't need to talk in here. I told you, the FBI's probably listening."

"It's OK," Azrael called out from across the room. "I swept the house for bugs before you got home."

We all turned toward him.

"How did he hear that?" Nathan asked quietly.

"I hear lots of things," Azrael replied without looking over.

He was settled in the corner of the loveseat, his black boot resting over his knee and his arm stretched across the seat back. He even occupied the sofa like Warren.

Cautiously, I walked over and sat in the middle of the couch across from him.

His dark eyes were taking a close inventory of me. "How did you know who I was?"

"Well, for starters, you look exactly like Warren," I said. "I thought you were him earlier tonight."

"How did you know my name?" he asked.

My knees were bouncing nervously. "Warren told me a story of when he was in Iraq a few years ago, and an old man freaked out when he saw him. He called Warren by your name, and it left such an impression on him that Warren had the name tattooed on his side. I'm assuming now, by looking at you, the old man had once seen you in person."

He nodded. "It's possible. I've spent time in Iraq. I think I was memorable for the few people I met there."

I didn't doubt him.

"You're in the military?" Nathan asked as he came across the room. He sat on my left side, and my father sat to my right.

Azrael shook his head. "Not exactly, but I have been present for most of the major world wars."

My father looked as though his brain was cramping. "I don't understand. How old are you?"

"Older than the ground you walk on."

That was sobering.

"How did you find me?" I asked.

"I've stayed close to Warren since he was born. Your union with him is quite notorious," he said.

I scrunched up my nose. "So I've been told."

Nathan straightened in his seat like he'd been electrocuted. "It was you!"

We all turned to stare at him.

He pointed at Azrael. "You were in Chicago when Warren was a kid!"

Azrael nodded.

My head swirled around with bewilderment. "How the heck did you put that together?"

"Remember when we found out your demon mom was in Chicago?" he asked.

I covered my gaping mouth with my fingers. "We wondered why Warren never got a migraine when she left." I looked at Azrael. "It's because you were there the whole time."

He nodded again.

I thought of Warren and his childhood foster-sister, Alice, being placed in a home with a child molester and stiffened. My hands clenched into tight fists. "You were there the whole time," I said again, my voice deepening with anger.

"Had I not been there," his tone was a warning, "Warren would not have been able to access his power and use it that first time."

My breath caught in my chest. "You're the reason he's so much better than me."

Azrael didn't respond.

Dad leaned toward me. "What are you two talking about?"

"Kasyade told me my exposure to Warren increased my ability to use my power. Warren's been around Azrael his whole life without knowing it. That's why he's so much better at using his gift than I am," I said.

"I don't think it hurts that Warren's more disciplined and focused than you are," Nathan added.

I pinched his side.

Azrael's foot dropped to the ground with a heavy thud. "You've met your mother, then?"

I smirked. "Oh yeah. We've met. She tried to kill me a few weeks ago."

Azrael's brow scrunched together. "I doubt that."

Nathan and I exchanged a puzzled glance. "Azrael, she tried to kill me." I pointed at Nathan. "And she succeeded at killing him."

"Him, I can believe she would kill. Not you. That would be counterproductive," he said.

"She beat Sloan within an inch of her life," Nathan argued.

Azrael leaned forward, resting his elbows on his knees. "Perhaps, but she would not kill Sloan." He tapped his fingertips together. "Not until my granddaughter is born, anyway."

No one spoke.

"She wants the baby?" my father asked. "Why?"

"Because Sloan is carrying the most powerful angel in all of history."

I couldn't help it. I burst out laughing. Beside me, Nathan was laughing too. Dad joined in as well, but his was more of a wide-eyed, nervous chuckle.

Azrael didn't move.

Or speak.

Or laugh.

Our cackles quickly faded with all the decrescendo of a cartoon balloon losing its helium.

I looked at Azrael. "You're serious?"

He turned his palms up. "Do I look like I make jokes?"

After a second, Nathan stood and wiped his hands on his pants. "That's my cue to get a beer. Dr. Jordan?"

"No, thank you," Dad said.

"Azrael?" Nathan offered.

Azrael shook his head. The way he was staring at me made me contemplate crawling behind the sofa. He pointed at my stomach. "I'm fairly certain this was planned before you were ever born."

Nathan returned from the kitchen, twisted the top off his beer bottle, then tossed it across the room into the fireplace. "I'm going to need some more information." He sat next to me again. "Why don't you start at the beginning?"

"Of time?" Azrael asked.

I snickered.

Nathan glared at him, but Azrael didn't seem to care...or notice.

He looked at me. "What do you know about my world?"

"Nothing good," Nathan muttered.

"Ignore him," I said. "We know Warren and I are Seramorta, part angel and part human."

Azrael nodded. "That's correct. But to understand what that means and why your child is so important, you must first understand what I am."

This was about to get interesting.

He held up seven fingers. "There are seven choirs of angels in Heaven. Messengers and the Ministry choir are the lowest ranked. Then there are Angels of Prophecy, Knowledge, and Protection. The Angels of Life—your mother—make up the second choir. First, are the Angels of Death." He tapped his chest. "That's what I am."

I wondered if I should get a pen and piece of paper. "Samael is an Angel of Death."

Azrael's brow rose. "That is correct. Samael is a guard of the spirit line. He decides who is permitted to cross, who must suffer the second death, and who must be turned over to The Destroyer."

I liked the sound of *none* of that. I gulped and kept my mouth shut, but Nathan didn't.

"The Destroyer?" he asked.

"The truly wicked souls are turned over to The Destroyer at their death." Azrael spread his hands out. "He is aptly named."

I closed my eyes. "My head hurts."

"Shall I continue?" Azrael asked.

I nodded.

"Each choir has an archangel like myself, and above the archangels was The Morning Star," he said.

I raised my hand. "Satan?"

He shrugged. "For simplicity's sake, sure."

"What makes him so special?" Nathan asked, sounding more annoyed than interested.

"The Morning Star was given both the gift of life and the gift of knowledge, making him more powerful than the rest of us."

Nathan seemed satisfied with the answer.

Azrael stretched his arm along the back of the sofa again. "Long after the angels were created, God created humans. Comparatively, humans were weak and inferior, but He favored them above all His other creations, even us. They were given a gift none of the rest of us had."

"What was that?" Dad asked.

"Free will," Azrael answered. "The angels were solely created to carry out the will of the Father. We have no right to choose which orders we will obey and which orders we will not. We rarely questioned it because we knew no different. Then humanity was born, and they were given the option to serve only themselves. And if that wasn't insulting enough, then God placed the angels in service to his new creation."

Nathan drummed his fingers on the arm of the couch. "You sound bitter about it."

Azrael gave a noncommittal shrug. "None of us were happy, but I'm certainly not bitter. The Morning Star, however, was furious. He argued that because the angels had been with God since the beginning, we should have dominion over humans. Not the other way around. When God refused the Morning Star rebelled and incited a war to take the throne. Of course, he and his followers were defeated and cast out of Heaven, exiled here."

I raised my hand again.

Nathan pushed it back down. "Knock it off. We're not in school. Just ask."

Azrael almost looked amused.

"Why would they be cast down here to Earth? Why not send them to Saturn or Pluto where they can't bother anybody?" I asked.

"Heaven is not up or down. Heaven is here"—he motioned

around the room—"and Heaven is all throughout the universe, but it's across the spirit line."

I stopped myself before I raised my hand again. "Like a different dimension?"

"Sort of."

Nathan began humming the theme song to *The Twilight Zone*.

I rolled my eyes. "Azrael, please continue."

"The Morning Star vowed to torment man." He pointed at us. "Including all of you."

I held up my hands. "Why man? What did we do?"

"I can answer that one," my father said.

Nathan and I turned our curious eyes toward him.

"Because there's no greater pain than when your children are in danger," he said, looking right at me. "The worst punishment he can inflict on God is to attack his children."

Azrael nodded. "Exactly."

Nathan took a long drink of his beer. "But what does all that have to do with Sloan and this kid?"

"I'm getting there." Azrael leaned forward on his elbows and looked at me. "The Seramorta, like you and Warren, are children born to angels," he said. "There are few Seramorta in the world, and only twice before in the entire history of mankind, have two Seramorta borne children together. The child is born with both gifts and no human spirit at all."

My father's medical brain was trying to process the information, but it was clear from his face that it wasn't doing a good job of it. "So...like biology," he began, "the angel gene is the dominant gene, so that's what Warren and Sloan passed on to their child."

Azrael pointed at him. "Correct. That's a good analogy. It's like a loophole in the laws of the universe. Angels can't copulate with other angels to prevent this very thing from happening, but because Sloan and Warren are also human, they can have a child together."

Nathan looked over at me and pointed between us. "So let's say you and I had a baby. Would it get the angel gene?"

Azrael shook his head. "No. The angelic line would end, and the child would be a normal human. That's typically what happens. The odds of two Seramorta finding each other are minimal."

"You said this has happened twice before. What happened to those children?" Dad asked.

"Their bodies matured as a normal human would, but they never died. They were escorted across the spirit line by the Father himself, and their human bodies were frozen as they were."

My hands instinctively went to my stomach. "They never died?"

Azrael shook his head. "Metatron possesses both the gifts of life and ministry, and Sandolfin possesses the gifts of prophecy and knowledge."

Nathan rubbed his forehead. "So what's so special about Sloan and Warren?"

Azrael rose from his seat and slowly walked back and forth in front of the coffee table. He was wringing his hands as he paced. "Do you remember what I told you about the hierarchy? The Angels of Life and the Angels of Death are the most powerful choirs in Heaven."

I looked at Nathan. "I feel like I'm missing something."

He nodded in agreement.

Azrael stopped walking and knelt down in front of me. He gripped my hands. "Sloan, the birth of the child you carry will be the greatest event in angelic history. She will be known as the Vitamorte, born with the gift of free will as well as the power to control life and death. Your daughter will someday take the empty seat of The Morning Star." He leaned toward me. "The Vitamorte will be more powerful than Satan himself."

CHAPTER TWELVE

My mouth was gaping as his words sank in. Then I burst out laughing again, this time in his face. I doubled over, resting my forehead against Azrael's hands that still covered my own. "What the hell?" My voice was an octave higher than normal. I straightened and looked at him. "Do you hear yourself? Oh, geez. Maybe we're both delusional." I quickly sobered as a rational thought occurred to me. I grasped his massive forearms. "Maybe this is another one of my crazy dreams!"

Azrael sank back onto the floor and stared at me with a clear mix of confusion and frustration. "You're not dreaming."

I pushed myself up out of my seat and stepped over him. "Oh, Azrael. I'd better be dreaming, or this world is in trouble."

He got up and followed me to the kitchen. Since I couldn't drink alcohol, I reached into the freezer for a carton of ice cream. As I retrieved a spoon from the drawer, Azrael grabbed me by the arm and spun me around. His eyes were pleading. "Sloan, I know this is a lot to process, but you have to understand the seriousness of what I'm saying."

Dad and Nathan walked in behind him. My father looked like he had been punched in the stomach.

Nathan put his hand on my shoulder. "I don't think he's lying to you."

"Oh, don't tell me you're buying into this now too," I whined.

Nathan stepped closer in front of me as I shoveled a spoonful of mint chocolate chip into my mouth. "Think about all you can do now, Sloan."

Azrael nodded his head. "You possess and can use the power of the Vitamorte."

Everyone was quiet for a moment.

Dad pointed at me. "Then doesn't that make Sloan the most powerful angel in history?"

I sucked a chocolate chip down my windpipe and erupted into a fit of coughing. Nathan took the ice cream carton from me as Azrael thumped his large hand on my back. I leaned against the counter and gasped for air. Dad was ready to perform the Heimlich...or CPR.

When the coughing subsided, reality settled on me like the fallout from a nuclear warhead. My demon mother's final words echoed in my mind. *"This is what you were born for."*

Huge tears spilled out onto my cheeks. My hands were trembling so much I dropped my spoon, and it clanged against the kitchen floor. I felt my knees give way underneath me, and I would have fallen if Azrael hadn't caught me.

The buzz of his energy was consuming, and immediately, my nerves settled. "Now you know why I've come," he said quietly in my ear. "And I will not leave you."

My father wedged himself between me and the angel who held me. Protectively, he curled his arm around my shoulders and guided me back to the sofa. Tears were still streaming down my face. As we sat down, I was shaking my head and quietly chanting, "I can't do this."

Nathan and Azrael followed us, and Nathan sat on the coffee table in front of me. He looked up at Azrael. "Why can't you find Kasyade and kill her?"

"Even I do not have the power to destroy another angel." Azrael reclaimed his spot on the loveseat. "And Kasyade is but a cog in a larger wheel. For thousands of years, Kasyade has kept close counsel with two other Angels of Life, Ysha and Phenex. I'm sure they're as much involved with this as she is."

"Involved how?" Dad asked.

Azrael laced his fingers together. "Have you seen the red-haired woman?"

"Yes!" Nathan answered.

Dad was shaking his head, but I straightened in my seat, anxious to hear Azrael's commentary.

Nathan was sitting on the edge of his seat. "Who is she? And what does she have to do with all this?"

Azrael pointed at me. "She's Sloan, or a different version of her, rather."

"Excuse me?" Nathan asked.

"As I said earlier," Azrael began, "I believe this child was planned before Sloan was ever born."

I didn't like where the conversation was headed.

"My son is unique," he said. "Never before has a Seramorta born of an Angel of Death ever existed."

"Warren's the only one?" I asked.

Azrael nodded. "The only one in history."

"So?" Nathan asked.

"When Warren was born, I believe Kasyade, Ysha, and Phenex saw it as their opportunity to create a weapon. The red-haired woman confirms to me they each created a daughter." He was watching me, like he was waiting for a light-bulb in my mind to flicker on. When it did, I suddenly felt nauseated.

"Kasyade said she created me for a purpose. She gave birth to me so I would someday breed this super angel." My voice sounded small and pathetic even to me.

"I believe so," Azrael said. "They planned for one of the daughters they created to have a child with my son."

Nathan scratched his head. "Why? So they can start another war?"

Azrael shook his head. "No. Their war with God is finished, but they're still subject to the law of Heaven. Think of this place as their prison. It's their goal to cut off the warden. The Vitamorte will have the power to destroy the spirit line, forever separating this world from my world, and they'll be free of the restrictions set forth to protect humanity."

"They'll rule the Earth," I added.

Azrael bowed his head slightly in confirmation. "And eventually wipe out the human race altogether."

Nathan bent forward, resting his elbows on his knees and pressing his palms against his eye sockets. He groaned. "I keep waiting for a movie director to walk in and yell 'Cut!' at any moment."

My stomach was churning. "I'm going to be sick." Covering my mouth with my hand, I ran up the stairs to the guest bathroom and barely made it to the toilet before losing the last remnants of my prime rib dinner.

Somehow I managed to flush before melting into a puddle of tears on the cold floor.

My father came in to find me sobbing in the fetal position. He sank down next to me and gathered me into his arms.

Nathan appeared in the doorway. "What can I do for you?" he asked.

I wiped my eyes. "I don't want any of this."

Dad squeezed the back of my neck gently.

Nathan knelt down beside my knees, a teasing smile on his lips. "Sloan, we all know, if I had any control over this situation whatsoever, *this*"—he gestured to my stomach—"would have never happened to begin with."

Through my tears, I chuckled.

"On a more practical level, what else do you need?" he asked.

"A toothbrush," I whimpered.

"That, we can manage." He glanced at his watch. "It's really late. Maybe you should brush your teeth and go on to bed. I think you've had enough excitement for tonight."

"Or a lifetime," Dad added.

"That's the truth," Nathan agreed.

The two of them hoisted me to my feet. Dad's arm around my waist steadied me as they escorted me to my bedroom. Nathan stopped at the door, and Dad helped me across the room. "What about Azrael?" I asked, sitting down on the edge of my bed.

Nathan waved his hand. "I'll grab blankets and a pillow for him or something, or who knows? Maybe he sleeps in a coffin in your backyard. Whatever. Don't worry about him."

Dad bent to look me in the eye. "Angel and demon nonsense aside, are you feeling all right? Your body went through quite an ordeal today."

"Yeah, I'm all right," I lied.

"I'm going to make a bed on the floor by the fire—"

I waved my hand to cut him off. "No, you're not. Go home and sleep in your bed. I'll be fine, Dad. Really. I won't sleep at all knowing you're on the floor."

It was clear from my father's pained expression he was torn. "Well, I'll call and check on you first thing tomorrow." He pressed a long, lingering kiss to my forehead. "I love you, Sloan."

I gripped his arm. "I love you too, Dad."

Dabbing his eyes with the cuff of his sleeve, he straightened and walked toward Nathan. They shook hands. "You'll stay with her?" Dad asked.

"I wouldn't dream of leaving," Nathan replied.

My father looked pleased. "Call me at any time if something happens."

"I will, sir."

When my dad was gone, Nathan pointed to the bathroom. "Do you need help getting ready for bed?"

I shook my head.

"OK. I'll deal with Azrael, then I'll come back and make sure you're squared away," he said.

"Thank you."

A little while later, when I finally climbed under my covers, it was Azrael who knocked on my door instead of Nathan. "May I come in?"

I didn't sit up, but I nodded.

Slowly, he crossed the room to my bedside and sat next to me. "I am truly sorry to be the bearer of such news, Sloan."

I didn't respond.

"But I am here, and I will not let anything harm you or the child," he said.

"The nightmares," I whispered. "They were real, weren't they?"

"In a sense," he said. "The veil between what is seen and what is unseen becomes thin when your mind isn't alert. The dreams were designed to torment you, to break you. If they can break you, they can control you."

"So last night, the thunder...that was you?"

He nodded.

"And the figure I saw in my room?"

"It was very real." He put his hand on my shoulder.

I blinked up at him. "And you got rid of it?"

"While I stand guard, no evil shall befall you. Now rest."

Azrael laid his massive hand on the top of my head, and the room swirled out of view.

In the morning, the aroma of sausage and fresh coffee roused me from the deepest slumber I had enjoyed since Warren left town, or maybe ever. Hysteria has some positive side effects, I guess, and having a father-in-law who can induce comas doesn't hurt either.

Part of me wanted to curl into my pillow and doze off again, but the other part—the rumbling in my stomach—urged me out from under the heavy warmth of my down comforter.

On the nightstand, the little light on my cell phone was blinking red. I picked up the phone and saw I had a voicemail from my boss, a missed call from Sheriff Davis, and a string of text messages and two missed calls from Adrianne.

Did you make it home OK?

You and Nathan are on the front page of the Citizen Times.

You really need to answer me.

Are you dead??

I dialed her number, and she answered on the first ring. "I was about to drive over to your house and kick your ass! Why haven't you answered the phone?" She was yelling into the receiver.

"I'm sorry," I said. "It was a really, really messed up night."

"I would say so! You almost drowned in the river, and I had to read about it in the newspaper!"

"I'm sorry," I said again. "I was going to call you, but things got weird."

"Weird?"

"Warren's dad was at my house when we got home last night," I said.

She was silent for a second. "Are you kidding me?"

"Nope." I rubbed my hand over my face. "He's been following me around in an attempt to protect me."

"Where is he now?"

"I'm guessing he's cooking breakfast downstairs."

"What the hell?"

"I told you things got weird."

"Does Nathan know?" she asked.

"Oh yes. And my dad," I said. "We all stayed up half the night talking about angels and demons and a cosmic war between Heaven and Earth. It was thrilling."

"Sounds like it," she said.

My stomach growled so loud I could hear it. "I need to go eat. Can I call you later?"

"You'd better," she said.

"I will."

I disconnected the call and trudged across the cool hardwood floor to my bathroom. I brushed my teeth and pulled my unruly hair into a knot on the top of my head before following my nose downstairs.

Azrael, who was dressed for the day in black cargo pants and a fitted white thermal shirt, was hunched over a frying pan which belonged to his son. "Good morning, Sloan," he said, recognizing my presence in the room though his back was turned.

Weird.

I pulled open a cupboard door and retrieved a glass. "Good morning. Did you go to the grocery store?"

"The contents of your refrigerator was quite abysmal." He flipped an egg over onto its yolk and turned to look at me as I ran tap water into my glass. "There's orange juice in the refrigerator."

My heart fluttered. "You bought juice?"

He pointed at the pink sticky note I'd put on the refrigerator door when Nathan and I returned from Raleigh. "The note said 'buy orange juice', so I did."

I dumped the water in the sink, then clapped my hands together with glee as I walked to the fridge. "Yay! Thank you."

"Did you rest well?"

"I slept like the dead." I poured my glass full and raised an eyebrow in his direction. "Which is ironic."

Either he didn't get the joke, or he didn't think I was funny. Instead, as if anticipating my next move, he handed me my bottle of prenatal vitamins. "Are you hungry?"

"Starving. Has Nathan come down?" I asked as I dropped a pill into my mouth.

"Yes," Nathan answered behind me.

When I turned around, he was rubbing sleep from his eyes. He was dressed in similar attire as me, sweatpants and a tank top.

"Good morning," I said.

He yawned. "No, it's not."

I poured him a cup of coffee, snuck a sip of it, then handed it to him. "You look like you need this."

He accepted the cup and carried it over to the table. "How are you feeling this morning?" he asked.

I pulled out a chair next to him and sat down. "I slept better than I have in weeks, so that definitely helps."

"You're not sore from the accident?" he asked.

I shook my head. "You?"

"Not even a little bit."

Azrael put plates piled with sausage, eggs, and biscuits from a can in front of both of us. Nathan looked up in amazement. "Breakfast prepared by the Angel of Death. Do you think his cooking will kill us?"

"I hope not." Smiling, I scooped up a forkful of eggs. "I'm kinda surprised these aren't deviled."

Nathan and I snickered quietly at the table. It felt good to laugh after the severity of the night before. Azrael carried a plate to the seat opposite mine and sat down. He wasn't amused.

Nathan sandwiched a piece of sausage between two halves of his biscuit. "What's on the agenda for today?"

I sighed. "I've got to figure out our living situation. I'm running out of space in this house."

Azrael nodded. "I need to gather my things from the hotel, and at some point, I'd like to find the woman who was in the road last night."

"I'd like that too," I said.

"Something tells me, she'll be back all on her own," Nathan said.

I looked at Azrael. "You said all three of them gave birth to daughters. Who is the third?"

He put his fork down. "When Warren was very young, Phenex arrived in Chicago. She was pregnant with a daughter. It was then I first suspected their plan because angels don't often decide to procreate."

"Why?" Nathan asked.

"Our gift is passed on to the child, creating a bond between us and our offspring that cannot be willingly severed," he explained. "As long as the child lives, the angel is confined to this earth. That's not an easy sacrifice to make for any angel, good or evil."

I was confused. "But I thought you said none of the angels who were cast out can cross the spirit line, regardless?"

He shook his head. "They can't cross back into Heaven; that is true. But they can move through time and space here unhindered as long as they aren't tied here. The bond with the child is a lot like gravity in a sense."

"What happened to Phenex?" I asked.

"I dispatched her from her human form," he said.

My eyes doubled in size. "You killed a pregnant woman?"

"No. I told you, I don't have the ability to destroy an angel." Azrael looked frustrated by that fact.

Truthfully, I was frustrated by it as well. If he couldn't destroy my demon mom, no one could. "That's why Samael couldn't kill Kasyade in Texas," I said. "He said she'll come back."

"That's correct," Azrael said. "It will take a full moon cycle, then Kasyade will be able to take human form again."

"How is that done?" Nathan asked.

Azrael held up two fingers. "Two different ways. We can either be born into a body or a body can be taken. I suspect it will be the latter because it doesn't take as long."

I shuddered. "So that exorcist stuff is real?"

"Quite real, but she won't be able to do it alone. She'll need an angel to help her. Therefore it is imperative we find Ysha and Phenex."

"How?" I asked.

Azrael smiled. "I have my resources."

"We are getting way off topic here. What about Phenex's baby? Did it die?" Nathan asked.

Azrael shook his head. "The child was full term, and she was born perfectly healthy and completely human."

I thought for a moment. "She wasn't part angel?"

"Only human," he said. "If the angelic spirit is severed while the child is in utero, no part of the spirit is passed on at birth."

Suddenly, I was no longer hungry. "What if something happens to me while I'm pregnant?"

Azrael hesitated.

"I want to know," I said despite every one of my feelings to the contrary.

He folded his arms on top of the table. "If something happens to you before the child can survive outside your womb, then you'll both pass into the spirit world."

He was quiet again.

Nathan and I exchanged a worried glance. "And if something happens once the child *can* survive?" Nathan asked.

Azrael took a deep breath. "If Sloan dies, then Kasyade will no longer be tied to this world. She'll be able to move across time and space freely, and she will get to the child before any of us can stop her."

Nathan said a bad word.

"Even you can't stop her?" I asked.

He shook his head. "Not if she's in spirit form and I am not. This is why Phenex is particularly dangerous. She has no bond here. She can come and go at will."

Resting my elbows on the table by my plate, I cradled my face in my hands and stared down at my eggs.

A surge of energy flowed into me when Azrael's hand

stretched across the table to grasp my forearm. "Look at me," he said.

Numb and completely overwhelmed, I looked up at him.

"I won't let anything happen to you or the child. I am a formidable adversary, even as I am." He smiled and pointed at me. "And you are not easy to kill."

I wasn't so sure I believed the last part.

He nudged my plate toward me. "Eat. You need your strength."

Frowning, I dropped my head. "What strength?"

"Eat," he insisted.

Nathan offered me his coffee cup. "Here, have another sip. I know juice is your thing now, but this will make you feel better."

"Thank you."

As I drank it, he winked at me.

Azrael must have noticed the exchange. He split a glance between the two of us. "What is your relationship? I've been watching the two of you for weeks, and I rarely find one of you without the other."

Nathan blew out a sigh. "It's complicated."

Azrael sat back in his chair. "I was able to work that much out for myself."

"We're friends," Nathan said. "Warren asked me to take care of Sloan while he's gone."

"And does he know you're in love with her?" Azrael asked.

His blatant candor startled both of us.

Nathan tapped his fingers on the table. "I told him."

My head snapped up with surprise. "You did?"

"Yeah, I did."

"When?" I asked.

"When he moved in with you before we all went to Texas," he answered.

"Before Texas?" My voice rose. "That was months ago!"

Nathan shrugged. "He asked. I answered. It's not like it's some big secret. Everybody knows."

Azrael shook his head. "My son did not get his patience from me. I would have killed you."

I cringed. *Yikes.*

Nathan's head tilted. "I'm sure he's thought about it."

"Speaking of relationship drama," I said, looking at Azrael. "Who is Warren's mother?"

Azrael stared at me for a moment, then looked at his plate without answering. He devoured a piece of sausage like I hadn't even spoken.

"Kasyade all but admitted she raped the man who fathered me," I said, conjuring up a surprising amount of bravery. "Is that what happened with Warren?"

Anger flashed through Azrael's dark eyes, and I shrank back in my seat. Even from across the table, I could hear his teeth grinding. Warren did that too in the rare moments he was mad.

After a moment of steely silence, he spoke. His voice was tight and even. "I knew Warren's mother. I loved her very much."

My mouth fell open. Azrael didn't strike me as having the ability to love anyone. "You loved her?"

He slowly nodded his head. "She's the reason I tied myself here."

It was obvious Azrael didn't want to elaborate, but I didn't care. If he could inquire about my love life, then I entitled myself to knowing about his. "How did you meet her? What was she like?"

There was more teeth-grinding.

Nathan nudged my leg with his socked foot under the table. He was warning me with his eyes.

I didn't care. "Where is she?"

Azrael picked up his half-eaten breakfast and carried it to the sink.

"Where is she?" I asked again.

His head whipped toward me, his eyes fiery and his jaw set like stone.

We stared at each other. I could feel my blood pressure rising as we engaged in a silent battle of wills.

Finally, his shoulders dropped. "She's dead."

His words echoed around the room, and his anger melted into raw pain.

I'd won, but I was infinitely sorry I'd asked.

CHAPTER THIRTEEN

Azrael walked out of the house and didn't return for an hour. When he came back, he carried in a large black duffle bag, a rolling suitcase, and a backpack. He deposited them in the foyer. I didn't remember an official agreement of him moving in, but I'd been so tired the night before, anything was possible. No matter, we all knew he wasn't going anywhere and as much as he made me nervous, I was glad.

None of us brought up Warren's mother again.

Despite the falling snow outside, Nathan had to go into work that afternoon. The city had extracted his SUV from the river early that morning, and he was called in to prepare a written report of the accident and list the contents of the vehicle that would have to be replaced. He also needed to go pick up a new cell phone since his sank to the bottom of the river with everything else. It was obvious when he left the house he was hesitant to leave me alone with Azrael, but I assured him I would be safe until he got back.

After we said our goodbyes at the door, I surveyed the stuff Azrael had brought in. With my hands on my hips, I sighed. "I need a bigger house." He walked up beside me, and I looked up at him. "I have no idea where you're going to sleep."

He shook his head. "I don't usually sleep."

I frowned. "That's creepy."

"My body doesn't require sleep in the same way yours does. I can sleep, but usually I prefer not to. The couch is fine," he said.

I groaned. "But what will we do with all your stuff?" I pointed toward the ceiling. "I'm going to see how much space is left in the guest room-slash-Nathan's room-slash-the armory upstairs."

When I got to the room, the sight was a little overwhelming. There was a dresser already filled with most of Warren's clothes sandwiched between the wall and two oversized, fireproof gun cases. Blocking the only window in the room, was a cabinet filled with ammunition. Nathan had two stacks of clothes on the floor beside the bed, along with two pairs of tactical boots and a spare belt. Surprisingly, the bed was made, but his toiletries bag and a laundry bag were deposited on top of the comforter. In the small closet were more of Warren's clothes and most of my summer wardrobe.

There was no place for Azrael's belongings, and even worse... no place for a baby.

"I need a bigger house," I said again.

"You seem stressed." Azrael's voice behind me almost caused me to pee my pants.

I gasped and spun around to see him leaning against the door-frame of the bedroom. "You scared the crap out of me."

He nodded. "I can tell. What are you doing?"

I scratched my head. "Trying to figure out our living situation. I really don't want the Angel of Death setting up residence in my living room."

"Why don't you ask Detective McNamara to return to his apartment? There is no need for him while I am here," he said.

In the closet, I gathered all my sundresses in my arms. "While I'm sure you see it that way, Nathan won't agree. He won't ever completely trust you. It's not in his nature, so I suggest you start getting used to it." As I walked past him, I motioned to the closet. "Can you grab all the men's clothes hanging up in there and put them on my bed?"

From his annoyed expression I could tell he thought the task was beneath him.

"And then can you grab all the shoes?" I added.

I heard him groan as I walked to my room.

After arranging all of mine and Warren's clothes in my closet, I returned to the guest room. Both of Warren's gun cases were standing open, and Azrael was holding a huge rifle. I froze in the doorway. "How did you get those open? I don't even know the combination."

He grinned over his shoulder at me. "Magic."

I shuddered.

The closet was empty except for the extra sheets for the guest bed. "I think there's room for your stuff in here now," I said.

He nodded. "I'll bring it up in a moment. You should get dressed."

"For what?"

"It's time to go to work," he said.

I looked at the clock on the nightstand. "It's time to go to dinner."

He looked down the barrel of the rifle as it was pointed at the floor. "You have training to do."

"Not today," I whined. "I want dinner and an early bedtime."

He snapped the barrel closed, and put the gun back in the case. "We won't do much today, but I want to get started. You exercising your gift will not only protect you, but it will protect others *from* you. Right now you're a liability."

I frowned. "You don't even know me."

"Maybe not, but I know what you can do. You need to master it." He looked at his watch. "You do this, and I'll treat you to dinner after. Deal?"

I sighed. "Deal. What should I wear?"

"Something warm."

I returned to my room and dressed in jeans and a turtleneck sweater. I pulled on my brown, fuzzy boots and picked up my cell phone off the bed. I tapped out a text message on my phone to Nathan. *Going out to practice my superpowers with Azrael and then to dinner. Be back later.*

As soon I pressed the send button, the phone buzzed in my hand. *Message Undeliverable.*

He obviously hadn't picked up his new phone yet.

When Azrael and I walked outside, he opened up the passenger side door of the truck parked on my curb. I narrowed my eyes and cocked my head to the side.

"What is it?" he asked.

I pointed to the bland black pickup. "I expected something cooler from you, Mr. Archangel. Like a Hummer...or the Batmobile."

He didn't laugh. "I'm sorry to disappoint. Get in."

Once we were inside, he put an address into a GPS device. I couldn't help but snicker. He cut his eyes at me. "Is something funny?"

I folded my hands in my lap. "The Angel of Death needs Garmin?"

"Navigating was much easier and faster when I could cross in and out of this world," he said.

"Like teleporting or apparating?"

He put the truck into gear. "Something like that."

I looked out at the clumps of dirty white snow lining the streets. "That's so cool. Do you miss it?"

"Every single day," he said.

"What's so great about it?" I asked.

He rubbed his hand over his mouth. "Do you remember what it was like the first time you met my son?"

I laughed. "How could I forget? He showed up at my doorstep and scared the hell out of me."

He looked over his shoulder at me. "I'm talking about the first time he ever touched you."

The first time Warren's hand brushed mine, we were sitting on the curb in front of my house. It was like a bolt of electricity pulsing from his body through mine. The memory alone was enough to make me squirm in the passenger's seat of the truck.

The look on my face must have answered Azrael's question. He pointed at me. "That's what my world is like. It is euphoria all the time. You never get used to it. It never gets old. You can never have enough."

"It sounds like you're talking about heroin or something."

"Haven't you ever wondered why the world has so many addicts? So many lost souls seeking after the ultimate high?" he asked.

"Yeah."

He bowed his head slightly. "Now you know."

I laughed, but I didn't exactly think it was funny. "Are you saying drug abuse is linked to God?"

He gave a noncommittal shrug. "I'm saying everyone on this planet is born with the desire for that connection, that feeling. Some try to satisfy it with drugs, and others use sex, money, and even religion. But, ultimately, everyone's after the same thing."

"That's interesting," I said.

Azrael turned onto the interstate. The mountains were speckled with snow against the dreary gray sky. It was getting dark outside. "Where are we going?"

A thin smile spread across his face. "You'll see."

His cool and disconnected tone unnerved me. "Maybe we should try this tomorrow," I said. "It will be dark soon."

"Don't worry. This won't take long," he said.

After ten minutes of driving, he got off the interstate onto a small access road near the Blue Ridge Parkway. My spine tingled as I realized I had been on the road before. Confirming my fear, Azrael turned onto an even more desolate logging road leading up the mountain. My eyes darted around the dim forest. "Why are you bringing me here?"

"You'll see."

I pulled out my phone and tapped a message out to Nathan. *Azrael is taking me to the woods where Billy Stewart tried to kill me. Not sure why.*

I hit send, but the phone buzzed and another *Message Undeliverable* alert popped up on my screen. I gulped, and my heart was racing. "I don't like this. Please turn around."

He kept driving.

My brain was scrambling for a way out, but I was trapped. I knew it, and Azrael knew it. My heart was thumping so hard I could feel it beating against my seat belt. I closed my eyes. "Nathan McNamara," I whispered.

When I looked at Azrael again, his creepy smile turned my stomach.

Finally, he stopped in the middle of the dirt road and slid the transmission into park. "Is this where it happened?" he asked.

"What are we doing here?" I asked, my voice cracking.

"Get out of the truck."

"Azrael, I—"

"Get out of the truck!" he roared.

He wrenched his door open, and I sat frozen in my seat as he got out and slammed his door. I hit the lock button. He looked back at me and grinned, then he held up his hand. The lock clicked and my door flung itself open.

"Damn it," I muttered.

Before I got out, I closed my eyes once more and pictured Nathan's face in my mind. "Nathan, I need you here."

Carefully, I slid out of the cab and tightened the belt of my coat. Snow was sporadically spitting through the high beams from the headlights as I walked in front of the truck. I stood there hugging my arms and shivering, partly from the cold and partly out of sheer terror of what was coming next. Once again, I had walked blindly into the open trap of a demon.

"Are you afraid?" Azrael asked as he took a few slow steps toward me.

There was no point in lying. "Yes."

"Did you summon the detective here?" he asked.

I nodded.

"Good."

He turned away and navigated down the embankment on the side of the road. He motioned his fingers toward me, beckoning me to follow. When I didn't move, a magnetic force pulled my body in his direction, forcing my feet to keep up. I followed Azrael into a small clearing in the woods. Not a hundred feet from where we stood was the spot where serial killer, Billy Stewart, had buried Leslie Bryson and had dug my grave right next to her.

Icy tears slipped down my face.

Azrael turned toward me. "Close your eyes."

I knew if I didn't close them, he would close them for me, so I pressed my eyes shut.

A moment later, I heard twigs cracking under his weight next to me. "Your life is in my hands, Sloan. The life of your child is putty at my fingertips. I can destroy you and your baby, and no one will be able to get to you fast enough." His warm breath singed the exposed skin of my neck. "I want you to burn this feeling into your memory," he hissed.

My shoulders trembled with silent sobs.

"Oh, don't cry," he taunted. "Each tear is your strength dripping off your cheeks. Your tears make you weak."

"Please," I begged.

"Remember this feeling, Sloan. Let it seep into your bones. Let it flow through your veins," he said. "Open your eyes."

When I opened my eyes, Azrael was standing inches in front of me. His hands were outstretched and between them was a razor-sharp, white, pulsing light. It danced violently in the space between his palms. "Hold out your hands," he ordered.

Trembling, I stretched out my freezing hands.

He carefully extended his arms till his hands reached mine. Then, as if passing me a basketball or a loaf of bread, he placed the light in my hands. My eyes widened so far I feared they might freeze that way. The light sizzled like *Pop Rocks* in my hands. It tingled and burned and felt icy hot as it pulsed from one palm to the other. My terror was replaced with fascination as the bolt surged between my fingertips.

Then the light fizzled out.

Azrael's eyes met mine. "You forgot your fear."

My mouth was still hanging open. "What?"

"The fear. That radical feeling of desperation," he said. "That's the key to unlocking your power over death."

I put my hand on my hip. "So you aren't planning to kill me?"

He grinned and shook his head. "Not today." He took a step forward and looked down at me. "I needed to make you fear me and fear for your life and for your daughter. I'm sorry it had to be this way."

I shoved him backward. "That's a jerk move, Azrael!"

He smiled. "It wouldn't work any other way. I could explain it all day long, but you wouldn't understand unless you felt it," he said. "Let's just say this training exercise was done in a secured environment." He gestured toward the truck. "It's freezing. Let's get out of here."

Azrael walked back to the truck, but I stood motionless in the clearing, frozen to the ground, my mind working overtime to process all that had occurred in the five minutes we had been there.

"Are you coming?" Azrael called from the driver side door.

I thrust my hands into my coat pockets and trudged back up

the hill to the road. I got in the passenger's side and slammed the door behind me. "You're such an asshole!"

"Yes," he said as he looked over his shoulder to complete a three-point turn. "Call your detective friend and tell him to meet us for dinner. Does the baby like Mexican food?"

I felt like kicking and screaming. "Azrael! I thought you were going to kill me!"

"I know. That is what I intended you to think. Better me than someone who actually wanted you dead, don't you agree? Now you know how to access your power without me needing to write a textbook about it." He pointed at my phone. "Call your friend."

I sighed. "I can't. His phone isn't working."

Azrael scowled over at me. "You don't need a phone."

Using my gift, I called out to Nathan and after a few moments of silence, my phone rang and his face came up on my screen. "Hello?" I answered.

"Hey. I just got my new phone. Where are you?" he asked.

"Driving. Where are you?"

"Well, I got turned around on the interstate and accidentally wound up in the forest," he said.

I sighed. "It's because I summoned you. I'm fine now, though. Want to meet us for dinner?"

He paused for a moment. "Uh, sure," he said. "Where are you going?"

"Azrael wants Mexican food. How about Papa's and Beer over near your apartment?" I asked.

"I'll see you there in ten minutes," he said and disconnected the call.

Azrael glanced across the cab at me. "Like I said earlier, now that I'm here, there really isn't any need for the detective to stand guard over you all the time."

I smirked. "Try telling him that."

"It really isn't safe for you to be so close to anyone," he said.

"Angels can use other humans to get close to you, even against their will."

I shuddered at his implication and hugged my arms. "Nathan won't leave me, so you're wasting your breath."

"Are you in love with him?" Azrael asked as he drove.

I rolled my eyes. "You dragged me up into the woods like Ted Bundy, and now you want to discuss my love life?"

He reached across the cab and squeezed my shoulder. "I said I was sorry. You learned though, didn't you? Now you will know exactly what I'm talking about when I tell you to focus on your fear."

"Why does it have to be fear?" I asked. "Why can't it be love? Or happiness?"

"Because fear is more powerful than even love," he said. "Fear forces you to reach into places inside yourself to summon courage and power you never thought you had." He cast me a serious look. "Fear is also ultimate respect. And if you are about to end the life of another being—you had better be fearful and certain of that choice."

His words gave me chills. "I really don't want this, Azrael."

He shook his head. "You don't have a choice."

I decided to extend the dinner invitation to Adrianne also, to smooth things over after not calling her about the accident. She said she'd be right behind us.

Nathan was seated at a table when Azrael and I walked into the restaurant. He stood when he saw us. I huffed as I slid into the booth, and he sat next to me. "What have the two of you been up to?" he asked.

I glared across the table at Azrael. "Well, he tried to kill me."

Azrael grinned. "I did not."

I turned toward Nathan. "He took me up to Billy Stewart's

spot in the woods and made me believe he was about to murder me!"

Nathan's eyes darkened, and he looked at Azrael. "You did what?"

"Tell him what else happened," Azrael said to me.

I sighed. "He handed me this lightning ball thing, and I held it till I got distracted and it burned out."

"What?" Nathan asked.

Azrael seemed proud. "I taught her how to harness the power of death on that mountain."

Nathan sighed and looked down at the menu. "Geez, I hope it's happy hour. I have a feeling I'm going to need a drink."

"But the light went out," I said to Azrael. "What good does that do me?"

Azrael looked around the restaurant toward the bar. He held up one finger. "Give me a second."

When he was gone, Nathan tugged on my arm. "You're all right?" he asked.

"I'm fine. I thought I was going to die though."

His eyes followed Azrael. "I'm still not sure about him."

I put my hand on his forearm. "He is unorthodox, but he could've hurt me and he didn't. How was your day? Did you get the stuff with your car straightened out?"

His face fell. "The car was destroyed. Most everything was gone. Almost all my weapons were swept downstream."

I leveled my gaze at him. "Better the weapons than you and me."

"Absolutely."

Azrael walked back to the table. He had a cigarette lighter in each hand. "Are you ready for a cosmic physics lesson?" he asked.

I put my hands in my lap. "Dazzle me."

"OK, this is what happened up on the mountain today." He held up a pink lighter. He pressed the button down. "You can't see it, but you know gas is leaking out of this thing, right?"

Nathan and I both nodded.

Azrael held up the other lighter and struck it with his thumb. A small flame danced at the end. "For lack of a better word, I ignited my power like this little flame. And then"—he held the flame over the other lighter and it ignited also—"I passed off that power to you."

He let his lighter go out and held out the one representing me.

"Your power burned until you forgot how afraid you were," he said. Then he let the flame go out.

"But I can get the flame back?" I asked.

"When the gas is flowing, all you need is a spark." He ignited the lighter again.

"How?" I asked.

He put the lighters on the table and held up his hands in front of him. "You focus the energy to that spot," he said, nodding his head to the space between his hands. "And if you choose to use it on a human, you will separate their spirit from their body."

"And kill them?" Nathan asked.

Azrael glanced at him. "The human spirit is what animates the body, is it not?"

My cheeks puffed out as I blew out a deep sigh. "I'm not mature enough for this kind of responsibility."

Azrael stood back up. "I must return these lighters to their owners."

When Azrael got up, Nathan draped his arm across the back of the seat and leaned into me. "I still think he's nuts."

I agreed. "He is. He's right though. I know exactly what he's talking about."

"You actually held that light?" he asked.

I put my hands up in front of me. "Just like this."

He tugged his ball cap down lower over his eyes. "Remind me not to get on your bad side."

I nudged him in the ribs with my elbow.

After we'd gotten our drinks and ordered our food, I chewed

on the end of my straw, replaying everything he'd taught me. I looked at Azrael. "So does my power only work on humans?"

He shook his head. "No. It would work on me if you chose to use it."

I pointed at him. "I'll remember that."

It was the first time I'd ever heard him laugh.

Nathan tapped my arm. "Your girl's here."

I looked up to see Adrianne walking through the door. Even in yoga pants, she looked classier than me. I waved and called out her name. "Let me out so I can say hello."

"Hey, sorry I'm late," Adrianne said as she approached. "I wouldn't have been if I hadn't been an afterthought." She was glaring at me as Nathan and I slid out of the booth.

I gave her a hug. "You weren't an afterthought. It was a last-minute decision."

Azrael moved over to make room for her on his side of the table.

Adrianne did a double-take when she saw him. "Is this...?"

I pointed at him. "This is Azrael. Warren's dad. Az, this is my best friend, Adrianne Marx."

He slightly bowed his head. "Hello."

She looked him over again, absolutely mesmerized. "Ho...ly... crap. The genes run strong in this family, don't they?"

"They certainly do," I agreed as we all sat down. Nathan took the inside so I could sit across from Adrianne.

She picked up a menu and held it up in front of her face. She mouthed the words 'Oh my god' and dropped her mouth open dramatically.

I rolled my eyes.

"Is he single?" she whispered.

"I don't know, but he has supernatural hearing," I said.

She dropped her menu and looked over at him. He was smiling. Her face turned four different shades of crimson.

Nathan looked at him. "Are you single?"

Azrael's eyes slowly slid toward him. "I hope you're not asking for yourself."

I giggled. "Listen to that. He makes jokes."

Azrael raised an eyebrow. "Who said I was joking?"

Nathan sighed and picked up his drink.

"I am single," he finally said.

Adrianne leaned toward him and stuck her hand out. "It's nice to meet you, Azrael."

"Oh, no! Absolutely none of that," I said.

"None of what?" Adrianne whined, batting her eyelashes at me.

"I know that look," I said. "And I'm putting my foot down now."

She winked at Azrael. "She never lets me have any fun."

He leaned on his elbow a little too close to her. "Somehow I doubt that does much to deter you."

"Mmm, an angel and a mind reader," she said.

I held my hands up. "That's it!" I got up and pulled on her sleeve. "You can sit by Nathan."

She laughed and stood, but she grabbed my hand and cut her eyes at me with a grin. "Can I flirt with him instead?"

"I learned how to kill people today," I warned.

Laughing, she pressed a kiss to my forehead, certainly leaving a bright red lip print behind.

CHAPTER FOURTEEN

That week, refusing to leave my side, Azrael began accompanying me to work every day. While I fielded holiday news requests and worked on my end of the year expense reports, the Angel of Death sat opposite my desk and played Angry Birds on his cell phone.

Each evening we practiced my superpowers. Most of that time was spent teaching me to conjure up my own deadly light ball and project it onto nearby trees and bushes. Note: no natural vegetation was harmed in the practicing of this skill. Despite popular belief in the mountains of North Carolina, trees don't have souls.

I still hadn't heard a word from Warren.

Friday afternoon, I had a scheduled day off for my follow-up doctor's appointment from the accident. Nathan left for work, and I slept in. When I came downstairs around eleven, I found Azrael standing in the middle of my kitchen.

"Let's go out. The baby is craving cheese grits for breakfast," I said as I walked to the refrigerator.

He rolled his eyes. "It's not breakfast anymore, and the baby will have to settle for a sandwich and potato chips. I've got something special planned for today."

He successfully piqued my interest. "What are we doing?"

"Playing with fruit," he answered.

There was a bag of navel oranges on the kitchen counter. My brow scrunched together. "Is this a joke?"

"I never joke," he said as he ripped the bag open.

That was the truth. One thing had become obvious about my mysterious faux-father-in-law: the Almighty didn't instill a sense of humor within His angels. I hopped up on the counter and peeled an orange. Azrael yanked it from my fingers.

"Hey!" I objected.

"This fruit is not for eating," he said.

A thin smile spread across my face. "Is that what God told Adam in the Garden of Eden?"

He pointed a warning finger at me. "You tap dance on blasphemy, you know."

I pretended to zip my lips sealed.

Azrael carried an orange across the kitchen and placed it in the center of the dinette table by the window. He turned to look at me. "I'm going to teach you how to move the orange."

I cocked an eyebrow. "Move it?"

"Without touching it," he added. "Stand up."

Obediently, I jumped down from the counter. With a smile plastered across my face, I walked to the center of the kitchen. I spread my feet apart, bent my knees, and rubbed my palms together furiously. "Let's do this."

Azrael folded his arms across his muscular chest. "I need you to be serious."

I pressed my lips together and straightened my posture. "I'm sorry. I'll be serious."

"Close your eyes," he said. When my eyes were sealed, he continued. "For the next several moments, I want you to forget we are standing in your kitchen. I want you to forget we are even connected to this world you live in."

I wanted to ask if he would be burning incense, but I kept my mouth shut.

"Where you exist, Sloan, is inside this shell called the body." I felt his fingertips tap lightly against my forehead. "The part of you that makes decisions, that loves, that hurts, that fears—that is who you really are. Your body actually limits you. Let's do an exercise," he said. "Where's the most beautiful place on Earth?"

I smiled. "Bora Bora."

"Have you been there?" he asked.

Sadly, I poked out my bottom lip and shook my head.

"That's even better. Can you see it right now?"

I smiled again. "Yeah."

"What's it look like?" he asked.

"I see a turquoise lagoon with thatch-roof bungalows built over the sparkling water. Behind it are green mountains against a bright blue sky," I said.

"Is it warm?"

"Yes, but there's a cool ocean breeze that smells like coconut and limes."

He chuckled. "Now open your eyes."

My eyes popped open, expecting to see that we'd been teleported across the globe to tropical Tahiti. Nope. We were still in the middle of my kitchen. The only thing I could smell was lemon scented bleach from the sink. I shook my head and pointed at him. "That's a dirty trick, Azrael."

He waved his hand down my face. "Close your eyes again."

With a huff, I obeyed.

"Everything in this house, in this city, in this country is standing between you and Bora Bora, correct?" He tapped my forehead again. "You're already back there in your mind, aren't you?"

I was. I was currently peering through the glass bottom floor of my bungalow watching a school of blue and purple fish swim under me.

His large hand gripped my skull. "This is the most powerful

tool you possess, and everything outside of it is simply matter that can be moved and bent to your will."

"Is this like, 'Do not try to bend the spoon, Neo'?," I asked with a grin.

"What?" he asked.

My eyes opened again. "The Matrix? Keanu Reeves?"

Azrael was glaring with disapproval.

"Sorry," I whispered, closing my eyes.

"The art of what you know as telekinesis is really a simple process. Your body is a store of potential energy, and if you consider your potential energy as an accessible entity, you can learn to harness it and project it as kinetic energy onto an external object."

I groaned. "I should have paid more attention in high school physics."

"Please stop talking," he said.

I nodded.

"I want you to try to see that energy inside you, the same way you created your vision of Bora Bora."

My eyes opened again. "Are you serious?"

He was standing only inches in front of me. His expression was a mix of frustration and annoyance. "Yes. Do you want to learn this or not?"

"I'd rather learn how to teleport."

"Someday I'll teach you."

He had my attention. "Really?" I asked.

"Yes, but not today. Focus."

I closed my eyes again and huffed.

Two of his fingers touched my forehead. "You were given creativity for a reason. Use it to create your energy into a viable resource. See it in your mind."

I took a few slow and deep breaths to rid my mind of how ridiculous this all was to me. On the next inhale, I held the breath. It was surprisingly easy to dream up a glowing haze of energy. I imagined it to be like the first orb of light Azrael had passed to me when we were on the mountain road. It sparkled and sizzled and danced around in my mind like static electricity in the clouds on a dry summer night.

He removed his fingers and walked in slow circles around me. "Hold on to that image and then imagine forcing that energy into the space between you and the orange I placed on the table. Use your hands to direct the energy toward the orange, but do not open your eyes."

I raised my hands and imagined sending the ball of sparkling light across the room and into the orange. I slowly exhaled.

A deafening crack exploded behind me and reverberated around the room nearly sending me flying out of my skin. I clapped my hands over my splintered ear drums and opened my eyes in time to see the glass shattering as the orange crashed through the kitchen window. I spun around on Azrael who was holding a small handgun pointed toward the ceiling. He was smiling.

"Jesus, Mary, and Joseph! What did you do?" I screamed.

He tucked the gun into his waistband and grabbed my shoulders. He was laughing with pride. "No! It is what *you* did!" He turned me back toward the window.

"Did you shoot the orange?" I shouted.

"No! I fired a blank!" He pointed toward the window. "You did that! You broke the window!"

My jaw dropped as another piece from the pane of broken glass crashed to the tile floor. I whirled back around and punched him as hard as I could square in the nose. His head snapped back and blood poured down into his mouth, but he was still laughing.

"I absolutely hate you!" I roared. "You are an evil man!"

He pulled his shirt up to catch some of the blood. Even though I really wanted to hit him again, I retrieved a towel from under the sink and handed it to him so he wouldn't track blood all over my house. He pressed it to his nose. With bloody fingers, he pointed to the window again. "You did it, Sloan!"

"Why did you fire a gun in my kitchen?"

He examined the amount of blood on the towel. "Adrenaline makes it easier."

My ears were still ringing, and I pressed my palms against them. "I think you ruptured my eardrums!"

"It's a tiny gun. You'll be fine," he said. "I think you broke my nose."

"I hope I did! You're lucky it wasn't your neck!"

He pulled the bloody towel away and pointed to his crooked nose. "Can you fix this so the bleeding will stop?"

"Fix it yourself," I grumbled.

He shook his head. "I can't. It won't kill me, but I do not heal as you do."

I crossed my arms over my chest. "Well, if it won't kill you, I should let you suffer."

"I'll go sit on your sofa," he warned.

I narrowed my eyes. "You're such a jerk."

"I know."

For the sake of my white upholstery, I placed my hand over Azrael's face. For a moment, I considered cutting off his oxygen supply but healed his nose instead. He winced as the cartilage and bone popped back into place and fused back together. "There," I said when the process was finished. "I hope it hurt like hell."

"It did. I'm going to go wash the blood off upstairs."

I pointed to the window. "I hope God gave you some carpentry skills because I expect you to fix this!"

"Don't worry, I will."

I still hadn't completely regained my hearing by the time we reached my doctor's office downtown. While we waited in the lobby, Azrael thumbed through a pregnancy magazine.

I looked over at him. "Can I ask you a question?"

He put the magazine down. "Of course."

"I'm sorry for the way I brought this up before, but will you tell me more about Warren's mother?" I asked.

His hands and the magazine dropped into his lap. He looked at the floor.

I leaned into him. "I understand if you don't want to talk about it."

He sighed. "I don't like to talk about Nadine."

"That's a pretty name," I said.

"She was a beautiful person." He looked over at me. "What would you like to know?"

"Where did you meet?"

He closed the magazine and put it on the table. "Nadine was a field nurse in Vietnam during the war." Leaning sideways in his chair, he pulled his wallet from the back pocket of his jeans. He opened it, took out a small picture, and handed it to me.

It looked like a copy of a Polaroid yellowed with age. The woman in the photo was standing next to a window in a short white tank top dress with a wide patterned sash around her waist. Her long, straight dark hair fell around her shoulders, the front pulled to the side and fastened with a barrette. She was laughing.

"Warren has her smile," I said.

He tucked the photo back into his wallet. "I stayed close to her for several months, and after the fall of Saigon, I returned with her to Chicago."

"Did she love you?"

He chuckled. "She didn't like me at first. I terrified her."

"Warren terrifies people when I'm not around him," I said.

He shrugged his shoulders. "Humans naturally fear death. But Nadine was different. She could *see* me."

I turned toward him. "What do you mean?"

"There are a few humans born with the ability to see us. They get glimpses of the spirit world. It's called the gift of discernment," he said. "Nadine was one of those few."

I was skeptical. "I can't even see other angels. Kasyade said it was my humanity that prevented me from seeing."

"That's true. Your human spirit doesn't have the gift."

Looking down at the photo, I studied Nadine's exotically beautiful face again. "What was she like?"

Had I blinked, I might have missed the split second Azrael's dark eyes glazed with the unmistakable swell of sweet remembrance. "She was feisty."

Not exactly the answer I expected.

"She knew her own mind, didn't back down to anyone. And she was tough. She never once flinched during that war, and it was brutal." A hint of a smile tugged at the corners of his mouth. "Maybe she flinched once." His expression was fascinating as he traced the line of the scar down his face. "She was with me when I got this."

I'd always been curious about that scar but too afraid to ask. "Oh, I have to hear that story."

"We slipped away from the hospital one night to an abandoned hut in a village the Viet Cong had lost to the army. On our way through the village, I ran up ahead and ripped down the Vietnam flag left behind." He looked away, but I swear I saw a tinge of pink rise in his cheeks.

"And?"

"The flag was rigged with a grenade."

My hands flew to cover my mouth.

He laughed. "Blew half my damn head off."

"Are you serious?"

He nodded, still shaking with chuckles. "Yeah. It took a while to come back from that one." He looked over at me. "Needless to say, my seductive plans for that night were thwarted by my own stupidity."

"Did she freak out?"

"Of course she did, but by then she knew I'd come back." Azrael's laughter subsided. "She never let me forget it though."

I gave the photo back to him. "What happened to her?"

"She died when Warren was born." He shifted uncomfortably in his seat and cast his eyes down at the floor. "There were complications during his delivery that were compounded by Warren and I being what we are. The doctors couldn't stop the bleeding, and her heart gave out."

My heart ached. "I'm sorry."

He forced a smile.

"Warren refuses to go around sick people with me because he says his presence makes them worse," I said.

He nodded. "That's true."

We were both quiet for a while. I touched my stomach. "Azrael, when this baby is born, will I die?"

He gently took my hand. "No. Warren's birth was complicated, and his mother was not an Angel of Life, as you are. I'm sure you'll be fine."

I sighed with relief and relaxed in my chair.

A nurse walked into the waiting room. "Sloan Jordan?"

We both stood.

She looked up at Azrael. "Is this the baby's father?"

"No, this is the baby's..." I caught myself before I said *grandfather*.

Azrael stretched out his hand. "I'm the father's brother."

She smiled, obviously confused. "Oh, OK." She looked at me. "Well, this appointment won't be as invasive as the last. Dr. Watts is going to do a different type of ultrasound if you would like for the baby's uncle to come with you."

I looked at Azrael. "Want to come see your *niece?*"

A genuine smile came over his face. "I would love to."

"Follow me," she said.

We walked back to an exam room. The nurse opened the door,

and we followed her inside. She motioned to the weight scale by the window. "I need to get your weight and your vitals," she said.

I kicked off my tennis shoes and stepped onto the scale. I had gained two pounds since my last appointment. She took my blood pressure and temperature and then pointed to the exam table. "Go ahead and have a seat. Dr. Watts will be in shortly."

When she left the room, I looked over at Azrael who was studying a three-dimensional model of a pregnant woman. It was cut in half to show her insides. He touched it, and the fake baby toppled out of the model's uterus and bounced across the floor.

I laughed.

Dr. Watts came in, hugging her clipboard. "Hello again, Sloan."

I smiled. "Hello."

She stuck out her hand toward Azrael, and he actually shook it. "I hear you're the baby's uncle. Welcome."

"Thank you," he replied.

She put the clipboard down by the sink and sat on a chair with wheels. "How are you feeling these days, Sloan?"

"Tired and I cry *all the time*. Is that normal?" I asked.

She chuckled. "Yes. It's perfectly normal and it may get worse." She patted the pillow behind me. "Sloan, you can go ahead and lie back. No need for a gown this time. Just pull your shirt up," she said.

Obediently, I lay back on the table and tugged my sweatshirt up to my ribs.

She rolled the ultrasound machine over beside the table. "Normally, I don't do ultrasounds this early, but with your accident a few weeks ago, I would rather play it safe."

"I understand," I said.

"I read the report. That must have been quite the ordeal," she said as she turned the machine on.

I nodded. "It was terrifying."

"I'm glad you were able to get out of the car."

"Me too."

"Me three," Azrael added.

Dr. Watts squeezed warm blue jelly out of a bottle onto my stomach. Then she rolled a wand around in the jelly, pressing it into my abdomen. After a moment, we all heard a fast *bump, bump, bump.*

"Is that the baby's heartbeat?" I asked.

She smiled and nodded her head. "Yes, and it's very strong." She put her finger on the screen. "See the little blinking light? That's the heart."

Azrael leaned close to the screen and sucked in a deep breath. "That's the baby?" he asked.

"That's him," she said.

"Or her," he corrected.

She laughed. "Yes. She looks wonderful, Sloan."

I sat up on my elbows for a better view. The little bean actually looked like a baby this time. It had tiny arms and legs and a giant head in comparison to the body. My eyes prickled with tears.

Azrael was completely mesmerized by the screen. "It's really real," he said.

"It's quite a miracle, isn't it?" Dr. Watts asked.

He looked back at me. "You have no idea what a miracle it is."

Dr. Watts printed out a photo for me to take home, and I tucked it into my purse. Before I left, she asked me a ton of questions about my health. Have I had any abnormal bleeding? Have I had problems with my anxiety? Have I had any more migraines? I assured her all was well, and we were free to leave.

On our way back to the car, Azrael looked over at me. "What do you think about the migraines?"

I groaned. "They're terrible. That's actually how I knew I was pregnant. I didn't have a migraine when we dropped Warren off at the military station."

He nodded. "Even though I've never been pregnant, that makes sense. When I left Warren at the church in Chicago, I was sick for a week."

"I believe it," I said. "Warren figured out our migraines usually start around the thirty mile mark of us being separated. Is that how it works?"

He shook his head. "Not exactly. Your power is limited by distance, but it's not an exact science. The closer two angels are in proximity, the worse the separation."

"Is that why Warren never had migraines before me?" I asked. "Because you kept your distance?"

"Correct. His side effects would have been mild."

For a moment, my mind replayed the horrific headaches I'd experience. "I guess that makes sense. My first migraine happened immediately after Warren left, certainly not after thirty miles."

"And Warren's likely happened later," he said. "Warren's body was more adjusted to the physiological response than yours was."

I stopped walking.

He turned toward me. "What is it?"

"When I figured out Kasyade was my mother, I called her, and she was out of town. When I talked to her in Texas, she said she had a headache when she got back. She was with another angel while she was traveling."

He raised an eyebrow. "Did she say where she went?"

I shook my head. "No, but I'll bet we can find out." I tugged on his arm. "Come on. We need to find Nathan."

When we got back to my house, Azrael yanked my keys out of my hand when I tried to use them at the front door. "You don't need them anymore."

"My bladder says otherwise," I answered.

He dangled them in the air, just out of my reach. "I guess you have some good motivation then."

"Some days I think you're a demon."

He winked. "Some days I would agree." He pointed to the lock. "Focus like you did this morning."

For five full minutes, I focused on the damn deadbolt. And for five minutes, nothing happened. "You're not projecting your energy into the lock," he said. "See it in your mind. Slide the bolt open."

My knees were pinched together, and I was bouncing. "I see it in my mind, and I'm sliding the stupid bolt open. It's not working."

Suddenly, the door swung open. But it wasn't my supernatural doing. It was Nathan. "The door's unlocked," he said.

I spun with a glare toward Azrael. "How can I unlock an unlocked door, you stupid angel?"

He laughed, holding his hands up in the surrender position. "Maybe you should've tried the handle first."

With a huff of frustration, I thrust my purse in to Nathan's arms and ran past him into the house. I took the steps two at a time upstairs to the closest bathroom. When I was finished, I trudged back to the living room. Nathan was sitting on the sofa watching the news. He looked up at me. "Still haven't mastered your superpowers, huh?"

"Maybe I have. I guess we'll never know," I said, sitting down next to him on the arm of the couch.

He gestured toward the door. "I can lock you outside if you like."

I rolled my eyes.

He handed me my purse. "How was the doctor's appointment?"

"Oh!" I found the photo Dr. Watts had given me and thrust it in front of his face. "Look!"

He smiled. "That's awesome. She looks just like you." He turned in his seat to look at me. "Did you know the kitchen window is busted?"

I pointed at Azrael as he walked in with water from the

kitchen. "He did it."

He pointed back at me. "You did it."

"Only because you fired a gun next to my head!"

Nathan jerked his head toward Azrael. "You fired a gun in the house?"

Azrael shrugged his shoulders. "They were blanks."

"Still!" Nathan shouted. "What the hell were you doing?"

I crossed my legs and let them dangle off the arm of the sofa. "Azrael was teaching me how to move things with my mind."

Nathan was almost too angry to laugh. Almost. "What?"

Azrael put his hand on my shoulder. "She did it too. That's how the window was broken."

Nathan narrowed his eyes. "Is that why I found an orange on the sidewalk?"

I patted him on the back. "Good work, Detective."

He sighed and shook his head.

I grabbed his shoulder. "Speaking of detective work, guess what I figured out?"

He looked up at me. "What?"

"I'll bet Kasyade visited Ysha or Phenex, or maybe both, right before the second trip we made to Texas. If we can get ahold of her travel records, then we can possibly find them," I said.

"What makes you think that?" he asked.

"Because she had a migraine when she got back which means she was with another angel," I said.

He laughed. "I want to be on the line when you explain this theory to the FBI."

"It's possible to find out though, right?" I asked.

"Yeah, it's possible."

"And if we find the other two sisters, then we find Kasyade and end this thing," I said.

"There is a lot of *ifs* in that assumption," Nathan said. "*If* we find them and *if* she's with them and *if* they don't kill us all before we can do anything about it." He looked back at Azrael. "I'm not even so sure it's such a good idea to go looking for them if we have no way of killing them. What's the point?"

Azrael opened his mouth to answer, but the doorbell rang.

Nathan looked at me. "You expecting company?"

I shook my head and moved to get up.

The doorbell rang again.

Azrael held up a hand and signaled for me to stop.

It rang a third time.

Then a fourth.

And a fifth.

I sent out my evil radar.

Nothing human was pressing the doorbell as it chimed over and over and over again...

CHAPTER FIFTEEN

Nathan stayed in front of me as a shield as we turned and watched Azrael walk to the door. His heavy footfalls on the hardwood creating an eerie sound against the incessant chimes. Without looking through the peephole, he opened the door.

And through it fell the red-haired woman, tattered and bloody.

I gripped Nathan's arm as I peered over his shoulder.

Azrael caught her as she collapsed over the threshold, and I relaxed when I realized she was unconscious.

"Where can I put her?" he asked, lifting her limp body into the air.

"On the couch," I said.

She wore a pair of thin sweatpants and a men's v-neck white t-shirt. That was it. It was freezing outside. Blood was crusted on most of her skin, except for the places it was still sticky on arms and feet. Azrael hesitated before laying her down on my white furniture.

"It's only a couch," I told him. "Put her down."

Her body was emaciated, like something off the cover of a National Geographic story on third world poverty. Her skin was so thin it was translucent, showcasing thin blue veins and tendons everywhere clear enough to be visible. Her sunken eyes were open but fixed on the ceiling, staring into nothingness, or maybe not staring at all.

Nathan felt for a pulse. "She's alive." He stretched out one of her arms along the sofa. My name was still freshly carved into her flesh. I shuddered.

Her pale lips were cracked and raw. She looked like a corpse—and felt like one too.

I looked at Azrael. "This is Ysha's daughter? What happened to her?"

He took a step back. "My guess is she was raised by Ysha."

"I thought that wasn't allowed or something," Nathan said.

"It's not." I looked at Azrael. "This is why, isn't it?"

He nodded. "That is correct. Imagine a lifetime of constant electroshock. It breaks the mind which all of us still have. This, or some version of this, is always the result."

"Can I heal her?" I asked.

He looked at me with sadness in his eyes. "She's like you. She already has your healing power."

My shoulders sagged. Had different choices been made for me, I could have ended up on someone's couch, clinging to life or standing half-naked in the middle of the road in the dead of winter.

Nathan stretched out her other arm. "Azrael, what does this mean? *Kotailis.*"

"The kotailis is the time the earth is most inclined toward the sun. Light is greater than darkness on that day," he explained.

I frowned. "Are you speaking literally or figuratively?"

He pointed out the window. "Right now it is dark. In the morning, it will be light."

I relaxed again.

"In America we call it the first day of summer," Nathan said.

"What does that have to do with anything?" I asked.

Azrael simply turned his palms up in question.

"What do we do with her?" I asked.

Nathan pulled out his cell phone. "I'll have a car come pick her up and take her to the station."

I grabbed the phone out of his hand. "No! You can't do that."

His eyes widened. "Why not?"

Gripping the phone with both hands, I shook my head. "Because if she's like me…Nathan, you can't lock her up in jail. I would rather you shoot me between the eyes. Nobody deserves that."

He put his hands on his hips. "Well, what else can we do?"

I gave him his phone back. "We'll have to keep her here."

Nathan swore. "Are you kidding me?"

Azrael folded his arms over his massive chest. "This woman is completely unpredictable, Sloan. We don't know why she's here or what she wants with you."

"Look at her," I said. "I could kill her with a fly swatter."

Nathan paced the room. "She's been court ordered to be in that facility. They'll keep looking for her."

I pulled the blanket off the back of the couch and gently draped it over her. "I'm not sending her away so she can wind up in jail again. Besides, I want to talk to her and find out why she's here and why the heck my name is engraved on her skin."

"She doesn't speak English, remember?" Nathan asked.

"Yeah." I pointed at Azrael. "But I'll bet he can translate."

From the expression on Nathan's face, it was clear he was surprised he hadn't thought of that. He looked at Azrael. "What language do you speak?"

"*En makkai est molingui ine tempronera.* It is called *Katavukai.*"

Suddenly, the woman on the couch convulsed like she'd been electrocuted. She jumped upright and scrambled into the corner of the couch, facing away from us. I ducked behind Azrael.

Nathan crossed his arms. "Looks like you said the magic words, Az."

The woman's head turned slightly, just enough for one glassy eye to peek back over her shoulder. Then she jumped over the arm of the couch, sending the side table lamp crashing to the floor as she scurried toward the corner. She was terrified, shielding her face with her arms, crouched like a wild animal against the wall.

"Azrael, say something to her," I said, grabbing his sleeve and pushing him forward.

"*Nankal taracebit amaityano.*" He cautiously moved toward her with his hands raised. "*Amaityano. Nakal uteves auxil.*"

She was peeping through the crack made by her arms. I'd never seen anyone look so afraid...except Kayleigh Neeland after she'd been kidnapped, beaten, and left to die in a dark attic. My eyes teared up imagining what this poor creature had endured.

Azrael's voice was barely above a whisper. "*Nakal uteves auxil.*"

She slowly unveiled her face.

"*Quid peyar?*" Azrael asked.

"*Taiya.*" If mice could speak, that's what she'd sound like.

Azrael looked over at us. "Her name is Taiya."

"Ty-ah," Nathan said slowly.

The woman stretched out her arm and burst into tears. She pointed to my name.

Taking that as my cue, I slowly walked over to her and knelt down. She grabbed my hand, still sobbing. Puzzled, I looked at Azrael. "Ask her how I can help her."

"*Taiya, auxi uta Sloan,*" he said.

"*Nadas auxi,*" she replied.

"She cannot help me," he translated.

"*Nadas auxi,*" she said again. "*Praea morteirakka.*"

I gulped. "She just said I'm going to die."

Azrael's face snapped toward me.

Nathan walked over. "How do you know that?"

"Praea is the name Kasyade gave me, and I know enough Latin to know *morte*-anything is probably bad news." I looked at Azrael. "Am I right?"

He nodded.

The woman babbled to Azrael, her words coming out so fast Azrael squinted like it was difficult to keep up. I heard a few words I recognized. *Kasyade* was one of them. *Ysha* was another. My name was said a lot.

"What's she saying?" Nathan asked.

Azrael held up his hand to silence him. He said something to the woman instead that sounded like a question.

Then the woman looked at me. "*Morteira kotailis.*"

By some miracle, I made it out the back door and over the porch railing before dispelling the contents of my stomach onto the frozen ground. It wasn't exactly new information. I'd known for a while I was a target. But now I knew the demons had a timetable; they were planning to kill me on the first day of summer.

A hand rested on my back. "You know I've seen you puke more times than I've seen all my other friends and family puke combined." Nathan's tone was light. I knew it was to calm my nerves. It didn't help. "It was very considerate of them," he continued, "to give you the date of your demise."

I spat on the ground. "Indeed. It was very thoughtful."

He tugged on the hem of my shirt. "Come here."

I turned and stepped into his arms.

"This doesn't change anything," he said quietly. "We still won't let anything happen to you, and actually knowing this will help us do that."

That did help me feel a little better.

He pulled back. "Let's go in before we freeze to death and the demons aren't a problem anymore."

Back inside, Azrael had coaxed Taiya into the kitchen. She was drinking a glass of water, and he appeared to be making her something to eat. As we passed my couch where she'd been lying, I sighed. The white fabric was defiled with blood and grime.

Nathan guided me to the loveseat. "Sit. I'll get you some water."

In the kitchen, I watched Azrael put a plate down in front of Taiya before walking over and sitting on the arm of the couch across from me.

"What else did she tell you?" Nathan asked as he returned with a bottle of water. Without sitting down, he handed it to me.

Azrael hesitated, looking down at me.

"It's OK," I said, unscrewing the cap. "I want to know."

He drew in a deep breath. "As I assumed, she was raised by Ysha, but she was left in the house in Chicago about two months ago. She was taken into custody with the other girls."

In the kitchen, I watched Taiya nibbling on a Pop-Tart. "Why can't I see her soul?"

"Excuse me?" Azrael asked.

I looked at him. "I couldn't see Warren's soul till I was pregnant. I still can't see hers though."

"Taiya's human spirit is very weak," he said. "It's part of the consequence of her upbringing."

A question was bothering me; I was almost afraid to ask it.

Azrael must have noticed. "What's the matter?"

I put my hand on my stomach. "Will I have to give her up?" I asked. "So she doesn't turn out like Taiya?"

He shook his head, offering me a gentle smile. "Your humanity tempers the effect you'll have on her, so you'll be fine to raise her as your own."

"How did she get here?" Nathan asked.

Azrael shrugged. "She escaped the facility where they took all the girls, but she doesn't know how she got here."

I looked again at the woman hunched over the dinette table. I would have been surprised if she could find her way across town, let alone the country.

"She's kinda got a Houdini thing going on. How does she keep escaping these places?" Nathan asked.

Azrael's brow rose. "Don't underestimate her. She's been around angels her whole life. She's more powerful than you think."

Nathan looked over at her. "Is she dangerous?"

Azrael took a deep breath. "I do not yet know."

After I made up a bed for Taiya on the couch, Nathan followed me upstairs. He stopped in the doorway to my bedroom, and I turned back toward him after switching on my bedside lamp. "You never come in here anymore," I observed out loud.

He braced his arms against the doorframe and tapped his fingers against the wood. "It doesn't feel right now," he said.

I smiled. "You're such a good guy."

He laughed. "I promise, I'm really not."

I took a few steps toward him. "Crazy day, huh?"

"I expect no less." He jerked his thumb over his shoulder toward the hall downstairs. "You OK? That was a lot."

I nodded. "I will be. You're right. What she said doesn't change anything. I know I'm safe." *For now*, I added silently.

His face was serious. "You are safe."

I nodded again.

"I'll be in my room if you need me," he said.

"Goodnight," I replied.

When he backed out into the hallway, I gently closed the door. Then I turned the knob lock before shutting off the light.

———

It was still dark in my room when I opened my eyes. The clock on the nightstand said it was just after three. Sleeping through the night was becoming rarer as bathroom trips became more and more frequent. I had assumed bladder control would be one of the final hurrahs of pregnancy. I was wrong.

I also didn't have to pee.

There was a strange noise so soft it was curious rather than terrifying as most noises are in the middle of the night. Maybe a slip of paper had fallen into the air vent. Or maybe a leaf was trapped in the windowsill outside. No. It was more subtle than that, and it was closer than the window. It was a tearing sound.

My heart quickened in my chest, and I sat up in the middle of the bed. Straining my eyes in the dim light of the moon, I searched.

Between my nightstand and the wall, a pair of wild eyes blinked in the corner.

I screamed and scrambled across the bed in the opposite direction, thankfully toward the door. But my legs were tangled in the sheet, and I tumbled off the side of the bed onto the hardwood floor. I half-crawled, half-ran to the door and twisted the handle but it wouldn't budge.

Screaming for help, I yanked as hard as I could, rattling the door against the casing.

There was commotion on the other side. Someone had heard me. Perhaps all of Bradley Avenue.

"Sloan?" It was Nathan's voice.

"Nathan!"

"Sloan, open the door!"

"I can't! It won't open!"

Whatever was in my room, was standing right behind me. I had to get out.

There was a click, and the door swung toward me.

Then I was through it and into Azrael's arms on the other side.

Nathan was cursing behind him. "What the...?"

I didn't want to look, but I did.

Taiya was standing a few feet behind me in the long white night gown I'd given her to wear. Her empty eyes were glassy and slightly crossed. At her sides, her bony hands were covered in tangles of her long orange hair. I buried my face in Azrael's chest again.

He spoke to her in their language.

"Taiya," he said louder. "Taiya! *Auyuketkai!*"

Azrael pushed me behind him.

Nathan grabbed the sides of my face. "Did she hurt you?"

I was still shaking so much I could hardly move my head from side to side.

He pulled me backwards across the hall into his room and closed the door behind us. "What happened?" he asked, looking me over for injuries. "Your knee." He nudged me toward the bed where I sat down and he knelt beside me.

My knee was flushed bright red and split open straight down the middle. Blood was trickling out. "I...I f...fell off the b...bed."

He stood. "I have a first aid kit out in my trunk—"

"No!" I grasped the tail of his white t-shirt.

"Shh." He sat and pulled me into his arms. "It's over."

I sobbed against his shoulder until the door creaked open. It was Azrael.

"Are you OK?" he asked, stepping into the room. He was fully dressed, of course.

I straightened and swiped my fingers under my eyes. "She was in my room! She was ripping her hair out, watching me sleep!"

"What was she doing in there?" Nathan asked, tightening his arm protectively around my shoulders.

Azrael crossed his arms. "Something like sleepwalking. I don't believe she was conscious."

"Where is she now?" Nathan asked.

"Back asleep on the couch," Azrael answered.

I raked both hands back through my hair, still heaving for oxygen. "I can't do this!"

Nathan shook his head. "I'm calling dispatch to have her taken in."

Azrael held up his hand. "Let's wait. I'll sit and watch her till morning and we can—"

"You were supposed to be watching her tonight!" Nathan shouted, cutting him off.

"She went to the bathroom," Azrael said.

"She moved through a locked door!" I cried.

Azrael dropped his gaze to me. "It's not that hard to do."

"Thanks, that makes me feel a lot better!"

The angel wasn't moved by my hysteria. "Let's wait until morning to decide her fate. If she was going to harm you, she would have."

I buried my face in my hands. "Just go watch her and make sure she doesn't budge off that sofa."

Without a word, he walked out of the room.

When he was gone, Nathan turned to me. "Forget about what he said. What do you want me to do? I can get her out of here tonight."

Pressing my eyes closed, I sucked in a deep breath. "Right now, help me clean up my leg."

When I looked at him again, he was nodding. "Can I get a washcloth from the bathroom?"

"I'll come with you."

He helped me to my feet. There was no pain in my leg. I looked down to see the blood had stopped oozing and was starting to crust, and while the wound hadn't closed, it did already look like a fresh scar.

Nathan's eyes widened. "You're getting better at this."

I groaned as we went to the bathroom. "Great. Maybe my head will reattach itself when she severs it in my sleep."

CHAPTER SIXTEEN

The next day, I didn't send Taiya to jail. When I left my bedroom, I stepped on a plate with a peeled brownish banana, a handful of crackers, and a bite-size Milky Way. Beside the plate was a pink sticky note from the pad I kept in the kitchen. I picked it up and read, *I sory. Taiya.* The handwriting reminded me of Kayleigh. I'd have to be a demon for that not to melt the ice around my heart. Pun intended.

Azrael made waffles.

"What will we do with her long term?" Nathan asked, pointing at Taiya. She was next to me, swiping up syrup with her finger. "Is she going to live here too?"

I leaned my elbow on the table and rested my chin in my hand. "I guess she can stay on the couch."

Nathan looked around the room. "This place is getting crowded."

I rolled my eyes. "It's been crowded since Warren moved in."

Behind his hand, Nathan snickered.

"Shut up, Nathan," I said.

"You said it, not me," he defended.

Azrael cleared his throat. "Nathan, you don't have to stay. I'm fully capable of taking care of things here on my own."

Nathan's fork clanged against his plate when he dropped it. "Like you took care of things last night?"

"Boys," I said with a warning tone. "I am in no mood to referee this morning. Last night sucked, but it's over. Let it go." I looked at Nathan. "Do you have to work today?"

He shook his head. "I'm off all weekend."

"Can you take me shopping?" I asked. "I want to get her some clothes that fit. Mine swallow her up."

His entire countenance fell. I might as well have asked him to take me to the third ring of hell. "Why can't Azrael take you?"

I pointed at Taiya. "Would you rather stay here with her?"

He huffed. "No."

"It's settled then," I said.

"What will happen when we both go back to work?" he asked. "Azrael won't stay here with her, and he can't bring her to your office."

"Well, if we can figure out Monday, I'll talk to my boss about working from home this week." I wiped my mouth with a napkin and dropped it on my empty plate. "I'll blame it on pregnancy stuff."

"How are you feeling these days?" Nathan asked.

"I'm finally over the caffeine headaches," I said. "I still feel kind of queasy on and off through the day, but other than that, I'm OK." That wasn't the complete truth, but I didn't feel like talking to Nathan and Warren's dad about my overactive bladder and painful boobs.

"Ding, dong," Taiya said, reminding us all of her presence at the table.

We all looked at her, just as the doorbell rang.

I looked at Nathan as he got up. "That's freaking creepy," I whispered.

He answered the door.

"Morning, Nate!" Adrianne was entirely too chipper for so early in the morning. She rushed in, unwrapping her bright red scarf as she came. "It is freezing out there!" She slid to a stop in the middle of the kitchen and froze at the sight of our new house-guest. "Uhh…"

I looked up at her. "Adrianne, this is—"

She held up her hand. "I know who this is. She tried to kill you. Why is she…" Her head angled sideways. "Why is she drinking maple syrup out of the bottle?"

I turned to look as Azrael snatched the bottle from Taiya's hands. "Nil," he said, wagging his finger in her face.

Taiya dropped her hands in her lap. Pouting was clear in any language.

I jerked my thumb toward her as I turned back to my best friend. "This is Taiya. She's a long story. What are you doing here? Aren't you working today?"

Nathan pulled out his chair for her. "Have a seat, Adrianne. You want some coffee?"

She held up the travel mug she'd carried in. "I'm all set. Thanks." She flashed a flirty smile at Azrael. "Morning, Az."

I groaned.

Laughing, she plopped down into the chair and crossed her long legs. "I took today off because I have done zero Christmas shopping."

"Crap," I said. "Me either."

She slapped my leg. "Good. I came to make you go with me."

"We were literally just talking about shopping when you walked in," I said. "I need to go get our new friend some clothes."

Nathan was at the refrigerator, but he spun around with a bright smile. "Hey! We can give Adrianne some money and we can stay here."

I rolled my eyes. "Nice try. We're going."

His shoulders slumped again.

"Great." She gripped my arm. "We can buy maternity clothes!"

Behind me, Nathan mumbled, "Kill me now."

"I *so* do not need maternity clothes yet," I argued.

"You'll need them soon enough." She pointed back toward the stairs. "Go get dressed. The mall will be nuts today. We'll probably be there all day as it is."

Nathan cursed under his breath.

Nuts didn't begin to describe the state of the Asheville Mall. We parked in the last space of the highest deck of the parking garage and entered into the overwhelming lingerie section of a department store. We were greeted by women dressed as elves handing out coupons as *Hark the Herald Angels Sing* blared over the store's sound system.

Nathan put his hands on his hips and looked at me, shaking his head. "The things I do for you."

I pinched his nose. "Santa's going to bring you an extra big present this year."

"Speaking of Christmas," Adrianne said as we wound our way through the crowded department store. "My boss won a private dinner party at the Deerpark restaurant at Biltmore next weekend. She's out of town and offered me the tickets. You guys want to go?"

"I don't know." I looked back over my shoulder. Nathan's eyes darted in every direction, and his hand was poised to grab the handgun I knew was tucked under his jacket. I giggled. "Nathan, did you hear Adrianne?"

He looked at me. "Huh?"

"Do we have plans next weekend?"

He dodged left out of the way of a woman with two armloads of shopping bags. "I don't think so."

Adrianne looped her arm through mine. "It would be so much

fun. We can get all dressed up and wine and dine like royalty. What do you think?"

The corners of my mouth dipped into a frown. "Can't have wine."

"Well, you can have chocolate cake for two."

My mouth watered at the mention of chocolate.

"Did I hear something about getting dressed up?" Nathan asked, doing a double-step to catch up with Adrianne's long stride. "If so, I'd like to vote no."

She looked at him over her shoulder. "You don't get a vote, McNamara."

He grumbled something too low for me to hear.

"What do you say?" She bumped me with her hip. "I bought a new dress for that hot father-in-law of yours."

"Good luck getting him into it," I said.

She rolled her eyes. "You know what I mean."

I sighed, exasperated. "You have the worst taste in men."

Her bottom lip poked out. "I thought you liked him. How could he be bad for me?"

"For starters, he's not human." I held up two fingers. "Secondly: He's. Not. Human."

"Warren's not human," she said.

I tugged her on toward the junior's department. "Yes, he is."

"I agree with Adrianne," Nathan interjected behind us.

"Your opinion doesn't count," I called over my shoulder.

She leaned against me. "But he's beautiful, smart, and kind... and he can cook."

I stopped walking and looked up at her. "He's the Angel of Death, Adrianne. The Grim Reaper. Death personified!"

Nathan laughed. "You have to admit, he's still a step up from that Mark guy she dated."

I jabbed my finger down my throat and faked a vomiting noise.

"Look! Baby clothes!" Adrianne squealed. She dropped my arm

and quickened her pace toward a rack covered with Christmas dresses for babies…or dolls, I wasn't sure which. She held up a red sequined, velvet Santa dress with cuffed, fuzzy white sleeves and a big white bow around the middle.

I put my hands over my stomach. "I think it's a little big for her."

Nathan snickered beside me.

Adrianne held the dress against her chest. "Little Adrianne can wear it next Christmas."

"Little Adrianne?" Nathan asked.

She nodded. "Of course."

"And if it's a boy, same name spelled with an I-A-N. *Adrian*," she said.

"Azrael says it's a girl," I told her.

She dangled the dress on the tip of her finger. "Then it's perfect! I'm buying it."

Nathan looked at me. "I feel bad for this kid already."

I chuckled.

"Nathan! Sloan!" a familiar female voice called out behind us.

Nathan's head fell back, and he pressed his eyes closed in agony. "Dear God, why?"

We both slowly turned around.

Shannon Green's hips were swinging from side to side so dramatically she cleared a path all the way to us. As usual, she was overdressed in a long wool winter green coat…or maybe it was a dress, with her blond curls dangling beneath a leopard print beret. She wore more makeup than I'd worn all year collectively, and I could smell her pungent perfume from fifteen feet away. "Fancy meeting the two of you here." She tossed her hair back over her shoulder as she stopped in front of Nathan.

He forced a smile. "Hello, Shannon."

She blinked her heavy eyelashes at him. "I'm a little surprised to see you here, Nathan." She glanced at me. "Or, maybe I'm not."

"How have you been, Shannon? I haven't seen you at all since we got back from Texas," I said.

She shrugged. "Why would you?" Her eyes ran the length of my body like she had X-Ray vision and she was giving me a body scan. "I hear you're pregnant."

"That's right," I said.

She looked at Nathan. "Dare I ask?"

Nathan rolled his eyes. "I'm not the father, Shannon."

"Where's Warren?" she asked me.

"He was deployed," I answered.

She waved her finger between me and Nathan. "I'll bet he loves this arrangement. I've heard you're living together. Is it true?"

Nathan crossed his arms. "I'm not sure how that's any of your business."

She jabbed her fingernail into the center of his chest. "Because everyone is talking about it. You and I just broke up!"

Adrianne raised an eyebrow. "It's been like two months."

She cut an evil glare at Adrianne. "Was I talking to you?"

Adrianne took a step toward her. "Oh, you don't *want* to talk to me!"

My eyes widened. "It's like we've time-warped back to 1997." I stepped between Adrianne and Shannon. "It's Christmas. Let's all be nice."

Tears were brimming in the corners of Shannon's eyes. "I really hate you, Sloan."

Ouch.

She spun on her heel and stalked away, the heels of her knee-high boots tapping out a sharp staccato against the tiles. I jogged to catch up with her. "Shannon, wait."

"What?" she snapped, spinning to face me. She tried to catch a rogue tear on her sleeve before I saw it.

"For what it's worth, I'm really sorry about you and Nathan," I said. "And I hope someday you'll be able to forgive me for whatever part I may have played in it. I never meant any harm."

She sniffed.

I smiled and touched her arm. "Have a Merry Christmas, Shannon."

As I turned to leave, she called out after me. "Sloan."

I looked back at her.

She didn't say anything. She just stared at me for a second, then walked away. We might never be actual friends, but I didn't hate Shannon anymore. And as hard is it was for me to admit, in more ways than one, she was a better person than I'd ever be.

It took begging and extortion, but Adrianne finally agreed to hang out with Taiya for the day on Monday while Azrael went with me to work. Mary agreed for me to work from home for the rest of the week, and the following week was Christmas. Hopefully by the New Year, we'd have a permanent solution to our babysitting problem with Taiya.

When we got home that evening, my kitchen looked like a crime scene, the weapon of choice—hairdresser's scissors. Bright orange locks lay all around the dinette table, and Adrianne stood in front of Taiya with her head cocked to the side and her scissors raised at the ready.

It was like a sacrificial offering to the gods of cosmetology.

Taiya looked stoned.

"Did you drug her to get her to sit still?" I asked, walking up next to Adrianne.

Adrianne shook her head. "I gave her wine and melatonin." She snapped her fingers. "Works like a charm."

Taiya's hair was cut in an angled bob just above her shoulders. It had been blown dry with mousse, flat-ironed, teased, and hosed down with enough hairspray to freeze time. I looked up at my friend. "Give her some big earrings and a guitar, and she could be the lost ginger from Jem and the Holograms."

Adrianne's face scrunched up. "I know. I'm not sure it works for her."

"Taiya?" Azrael asked.

She blinked up at him and smiled.

He rolled his eyes.

Behind us, the front door opened and Nathan walked in. His eyes widened as he looked around the kitchen. "What happened in here?"

"Adrianne has been playing a game called *Give the Angel a Makeover*," I answered.

"Cool." He looked over at me. "Are you next?"

I rolled my eyes. "Funny."

He nudged my arm. "I need to talk to you, and you'll want to sit down." His tone was unnerving.

"OK. What's going on?"

Azrael and I followed him to the living room, where we sat on my sofa that was covered with a bed sheet. He opened a file folder he was carrying and handed me a piece of paper. "I got ahold of Kasyade's travel record for around the time right before you went back to Texas."

"Great!" I scanned the paper. "Where was she?"

"Here."

I looked up at Nathan. "What?"

He leaned toward me and pointed to a line item on the page. "Look. She was in Asheville the day she confirmed she was your mother on the phone."

The paper clearly said she flew into Asheville on Wednesday that week and flew back to San Antonio on Friday. "How can that be possible? What was she doing here?"

He shrugged. "The bigger question is—"

"Who was she with, and what was she doing while she was here?" Azrael interrupted.

Nathan tapped his finger on the paper. "I'm sure the FBI is asking the same questions."

I looked at Azrael. "Do you think Ysha or Phenex is here?"

He stared out the window. "The presence of the angelic has been so concentrated since your child's conception that it's hard to say. I believe so, and I know they have both been here before, but as good as I am at tracking, they are equally good at evading."

"Can you dig around some more?" Nathan asked.

Azrael was thoughtful. "I've already got some contacts working on it, but I'll go out tonight and see if I can find anything close by."

I stood. "Well, let's get a move on because I promised Adrianne dinner at Chestnut tonight."

Azrael nodded. "OK. We'll rendezvous here later then. I'm not sure how long I'll be—"

I held up my hand to silence him. "No. You'll have to go after dinner." I rolled my eyes toward Adrianne who was grinning mischievously at me from the kitchen. Then I looked back up at him. "Dinner with you was the deal."

CHAPTER SEVENTEEN

"Adrianne has balls," Nathan said as we sat in the living room eating Chinese takeout in our pajamas.

I popped a forkful of sesame chicken into my mouth. "That she does," I replied around the bite.

Azrael had been grinning—quite a feat for him—when he left the house with Adrianne for dinner. She was a crafty one. Not only did she force me to relinquish my stance on her chastity where he was concerned, she cornered him into the date whether he wanted it or not. They'd been gone for a while and I hadn't heard a word from either of them, except for a photograph Adrianne had taken with her phone at the bar. Both of them were smiling, a feat for Azrael.

Nathan crossed his socked feet at the ankles on top of my coffee table. "Do you think he's interested in her like that?"

"How am I supposed to know?" I asked. "He's about as readable as braille on sandpaper."

"True."

He chewed in silence for a moment. "Do you trust him?" he finally asked.

I looked over at him. "With Adrianne or in general?"

"In general."

"That's an odd question."

He jammed his fork into the container of fried rice and put the container on the floor. "I feel like he's hiding something from us. I mean, we still don't know anything about him. I thought about trying to pull his travel records today and realized we don't even know his last name."

"Does he have a last name?" I asked.

His expression was smug. "Do you see my point?"

"I don't think I *don't* trust him," I said.

He chuckled. "That's a solid position. You either trust him or you don't."

"I trust him," I said, trying to sound more confident. "It's hard when things fell apart so quickly with Abigail."

"I know what you mean."

"What will you do about it?" I asked.

"Dig. I nosed around in his stuff a little when he first showed up, but didn't find anything. I might try to lift some prints or find out who that truck was rented to," he answered.

"It's a rental?"

He nodded.

"Why don't we ask him?"

He picked up the remote control. "Because everyone lies. It's better to find out via other methods."

I smiled. "Do you lie?"

"Never," he said with a wink. "Were you lying to Shannon yesterday when you told her you were sorry?"

It was a valid question, and I thoughtfully considered it for a moment. "Actually, no. That was the truth. I am sorry for whatever role I played in her getting her heart broken. As much as I don't like her, I wouldn't wish that on her."

He raised a skeptical eyebrow.

I laughed. "OK, maybe I would have wished it on her in high school but not now. We're not the same people we used to be."

"Just for the record, you weren't the reason I broke it off with her," he said.

"I know."

He nudged my ribs with his elbow. "I will admit I wanted you to be the reason."

I knew that too.

"Can I tell you something that's been bothering me for a while now?" he asked quietly.

I put the rest of my food on the table. "Of course you can."

He turned slightly toward me. "The night we got into the fight about you saying I was only attracted to you because of your power, I've thought about it every day since. Honestly, I've hoped it was true."

His words stung, but I understood what he meant.

"But it's not true," he said. "It can't be."

His tone wasn't wistful or amorous. Nathan was in detective-mode and stating facts.

"Why?" I asked, genuinely curious.

He draped his arm across the back of the couch. "Remember what Azrael said. Your power is limited. Maybe the thirty-mile theory was off base, but at some physical distance your power loses effect." He lowered his voice. "How many times in the past few months have I been gone to Raleigh or Greensboro or Winston-Salem? For god's sake, when you were in Texas, I dropped fifteen hundred dollars on a plane ticket to come see you."

"But the investigation—"

He cut me off. "Screw the investigation, Sloan. I came because you were there. I came because there is no force in this world—or the next—strong enough to change how I feel about you."

Sometime during his explanation, his tone had changed. So had the distance between his face and mine. I sucked in a deep breath and laughed to cover my nerves or keep from bursting into tears. I scooted back several inches on the sofa.

He obviously realized the conversation took a turn he didn't intend, and he held his hands up. "I'm sorry. I didn't mean to—"

Shaking my head, I stood. "No, don't be sorry." I wiped my sweaty palms on my pants and looked at the clock. "Wow, it's gotten late." It was four minutes after eleven.

"Yeah, we should probably get to bed. I've got work in the morning."

"So do I," I said.

He motioned toward the coffee table. "I'll clean up our mess. You go on up."

I forced a smile. "Thank you."

My tears stayed corralled till I reached my room, but when the door was secured behind me, I fell spectacularly apart. Nathan was right, and I'd known it all along, but that only made everything infinitely harder. I collapsed onto my unmade bed and sobbed into the pillow.

There was a soft knock on my door. As Nathan opened it, I quickly dried my eyes on the sheet. "Can I come in?"

I sniffed and wiped my eyes with the edge of the sheet.

He walked slowly across the room. "I heard you crying." He sank down on the side of the bed. "Are you OK?"

I nodded.

He winked and pointed at me. "See, I told you everyone lies."

Through my tears, I genuinely smiled.

Nathan pulled the comforter up over me. When he started to get up, I grabbed his hand. "Will you stay with me till I fall asleep?" Even to me, I sounded pathetic.

He hesitated for a second. "Sure."

Sliding down in bed beside me, he pulled the covers up over us. Against both our better judgements, he pulled me close and I rested my head on his shoulder. My soft sobs subsided as I paced my breathing against the warmth of his neck. Still, tears slid down onto his t-shirt. "I'm sorry for all this. I'm so sorry I hurt you."

He pulled my hand up and rested it over his heart.

"I love you, Nathan."

His breath caught in his chest.

When he remembered to inhale again, his hand traced the shape of my arm all the way up until his fingers raked through my hair. He paused for a moment while he certainly contemplated the consequences of his next move. My fingers curled into the center of his chest, and that was all the encouragement he needed. He rolled toward me, and in the darkness, his lips found mine.

For so long I had dreamed about feeling the warmth of his body on top of mine, and the reality of it was so much sweeter than the fantasy. My fingers gripped the hem of his t-shirt, and I tugged it up until he grabbed the back of it and pulled it off in one fluid motion. He tossed the shirt on the floor before covering my body again. My fingernails traced the gentle waves of the muscles in his back as his tongue explored my mouth, and his hands explored my body. I pushed with my hips and rolled him onto his back, sitting up in the moonlight and dropping my knees on either side of his hips.

His stomach flexed as he curled up to grasp my tank top and pull it over my head. He smoothed my hair back into place as his mouth covered mine once again. His hand trembled as it touched my breast for the first time. The sensation of his cool fingers against my warm skin triggered a desperate whimper I barely recognized as my own.

Breathless, he pulled away and graced the bottom of my throat with his lips. "If you're going to say no, please say it fast."

In response, I tightened my thighs against his and pulled his head back by his hair to kiss him as I scraped my nails down his spine.

He rolled again, discarding his shorts in the process, until he rested on me so my heart beat against his. He braced my arms against the pillows over my head and breathed into my neck. "Do you really love me?"

"Yes."

"Say it again," he whispered.

"I love you, Nathan."

His hands slid carefully down the length of my arms to my collar bone as he pressed his hips into mine. "Do you love me enough to die for me?"

My eyes fluttered open. "What?"

His fingers closed around my throat. The streaks of light from the window danced across his perfect face, and when his eyes met mine, they were a sea of black.

I grasped at his hands, trying to pry his fingers away, but his grasp was too tight. He pressed in as he constricted my throat against the pillows. I clawed at his chest, drawing blood with my fingernails, but he wouldn't stop. The blood vessels in my face throbbed, some bursting and splintering my skin in agony.

I heard Azrael's voice in the back of my mind. *Hold on to your fear.*

I drew my hands together, and a flash of light appeared between my fingertips. As I drowned in the void of oxygen, I prayed to not have to kill my best friend. Then, as the life drained out of me, I pressed the light into Nathan's chest. Sparks exploded around the room and screams echoed through the night.

"Sloan!"

Taiya was shaking me, and Nathan was shouting. I blinked. Panic was etched on both their faces.

"Sloan, are you awake?" Nathan asked.

My eyes focused on him, and I recoiled from his touch. "What happened?"

"You were screaming," he said. "In your sleep. We both ran in here. Taiya unlocked the door."

I was panting so hard I felt light-headed. I looked down for my shirt; I was still wearing it. Then I dropped my face into my palms and cried.

"Are you OK?" Nathan asked as the bed dipped under his weight.

My eyes pouring tears, I glanced up at the clock. It was 3:04 AM. My hands were still shaking.

"Where's Azrael?" I asked.

Nathan shook his head. "I don't think he's back yet."

"Call him," I cried.

"OK."

When he moved off the bed, Taiya took his spot. She placed her hands against my face, and immediately peace washed over me. My breathing slowed to almost normal.

"They come," she said. "They come in sleep."

"You can speak English?" My voice was quaked.

She smiled gently. "Little."

Nathan returned with his phone in his hand. "He's on his way back now," he said. "What can I do?"

I shook my head. "Nothing. I want to go downstairs. I can't stay in here."

He offered me his hand, but I refused it.

"I'm OK," I insisted, standing up.

"Look at me," he said, putting a hand under my chin. He turned my face toward him. "Your neck."

I touched my fingers to my throat and felt pain.

"It's really red. Looks like bruising," he said, alarm rising in his voice.

Nathan faltered back a step, quickly withdrawing his hands from me. Terror flashed in his eyes.

A chill rippled through me. "What is it?"

He slowly pulled up the front of his shirt. First, I saw his chiseled abs. Then I saw the long, bloody scratches down his chest.

CHAPTER EIGHTEEN

"Tell me *exactly* what happened." Azrael sat on the coffee table to face me without even removing his coat. "Start at the beginning."

Nathan was pacing in front of the fireplace. Taiya had fallen back to sleep with her head in my lap since I was sitting on her bed, the sofa. "I don't know what the beginning was. None of it felt like a dream," I admitted. "I don't even remember going to bed."

"You fell asleep on the couch," Nathan said. "I carried you to your room, then I went to bed."

"We ate Chinese food?" I asked.

He nodded. "We had it delivered."

"Where was Taiya?" Azrael asked.

Nathan pointed to a spot on the floor, but Azrael held up his hand to silence him. "I only want Sloan to answer."

I closed my eyes and tried to remember. "She wasn't there," I said, looking at him.

He touched my knee. "Of course she wasn't because you can only see her physical form."

Holy crap. He's right.

"What else happened?" he asked.

"Nathan and I were talking about a fight we had a few weeks ago. I had told him his feelings for me existed because of my power, and he got upset. Last night he said he'd figured out that wasn't true because of what you'd told us about my power being limited by distance."

Azrael shook his head. "Nathan wasn't there when I told you your power was limited. That happened when we left your doctor's office."

"Oh, that's true," I said. I rubbed my hands over my face. "I can't tell what's real and what's not anymore."

He leaned toward me. "Sloan, it's all real. Do you not realize that?"

My chin quivered.

"What else happened?"

I swallowed hard. "Um...I went to my room and cried. Nathan heard me and came in to comfort me. We started to...um..."

Nathan turned his back to us, his hands folded on top off his head.

"Did you have sex?" he asked.

"No," I answered. "Before that happened, he tried to kill me."

Azrael tilted my chin up. "He choked you?"

I nodded.

"I swear, I was asleep in my room the whole time. I woke up to her screaming and ran across the hall," Nathan said. "The door was even locked. Taiya had to open it."

Azrael silenced him with his hand again. "Sloan, how did you stop it?"

I covered my face as the tears spilled out. "I used my power. There was a huge explosion, and I killed him."

Azrael's mouth fell open a fraction of an inch.

Nathan walked around to face him and pulled up his shirt, displaying the marks on his torso. "Azrael, what does this mean?"

The Angel of Death straightened and looked at him. "It means, Detective McNamara, you are *very* lucky to be alive."

I'm pretty sure Azrael used his magic to put me back to sleep for several hours, and when I woke up again, it was daylight and Nathan was gone. Azrael and Taiya were talking quietly at the table in the kitchen when I came downstairs. "Good morning," I said to both of them.

"Good afternoon," Azrael corrected me. "Do you feel better?"

"No."

"How is your throat?"

"It's better," I said. "Did Nathan go to work?"

"Several hours ago." He pushed the chair out across from him with his foot. "Sit down. We have things to discuss."

"Azrael, I'm too tired for deep conversation this morning."

"I don't care."

After retrieving a water from the refrigerator, I sat in the chair. He reached around to my prenatals on the counter behind him. He slid the bottle toward me. I dropped one in my mouth, washed it down with a gulp of water, and slid the bottle back to him. "All right, what do you want to discuss?"

"You're not safe like this," he said with zero emotion.

I tapped my finger on the table. "I'm fine as long as you're here and you weren't here last night. Where were you, anyway?"

He leaned his elbows on the table. "You know where I was. I was looking for Ysha and Phenex."

"Were you?" I asked. "Or were you fooling around with my best friend?"

His face slipped into a scowl. "I was *exactly* where I said I was. My involvement with Adrianne was *your* doing. Don't forget that."

I rubbed my hands over my face. "I'm sorry. I'm tired and completely freaked out today."

"Which is why we must change our situation here. You're not safe. Humans are too vulnerable," he said. "And that puts you and my granddaughter in danger."

"I'm not leaving Nathan," I said.

He folded his arms over his chest. "How long do you think you can keep this up with him, Sloan? Will you be able to leave Nathan when Warren comes home? How about when your child is born? Where will you draw the line?"

"It's not that easy," I said.

"Let me make it easy." He slammed his index finger onto the table. "This child holds the fate of humanity, and compared to that, your *feelings* are worthless. This is your destiny."

I smirked. "You sound like my demon mother right now."

"Perhaps I do, but that doesn't make me wrong," he said. "And if you're so in love with him, do you not even care you could've taken his life last night?"

"Of course I care!" I screamed. "I've already lost him once. I don't want it to happen again."

Azrael leaned back. "Lost him when?"

"Kasyade killed him in Texas," I said. "I brought him back."

He sat back in his chair, dropping his hands into his lap. "That explains a lot."

I pushed back from the table in frustration. "Well, explain it to me."

"You cannot kill what you've already saved and vice versa," he said. "If you used your power to heal him—"

"I used my power to bring him back from the dead," I said.

"If you used your power *at all,* you can't harm him."

I stood. "Great. It's settled then." I put a hand on the table and leaned over it. "He's staying."

"No, I'm not." Nathan's voice came from behind me, but I hadn't even heard him come in.

I spun around toward him.

He looked around me to Azrael. "Can I talk to Sloan alone?"

Azrael said something to Taiya in Katavukai, then I heard their chairs move. A second later they both walked past me toward the door. "We'll be outside," Azrael said.

When they were gone, Nathan gestured toward the loveseat. "Can we sit?"

I followed him across the room and sat down beside him. "Nathan, I don't know—"

"Let me talk first," he said, interrupting me.

I bit down on the insides of my lips and relaxed back in my seat.

He gathered my hands in his and looked down at them for a long while before he finally spoke. "I need you to allow me to take a step back from this."

"Did Azrael put you up to this?" I asked.

He shook his head. "Azrael has nothing to do with it. This isn't about what physical danger you or I might be in. This is about me not being able to stop my mind from replaying being in your bed last night."

I was surprised. "You remember it?"

"It's jumbled and doesn't make much sense, but yeah." He let out a deep sigh. "It doesn't matter if I was in control of myself or not; what matters is I don't want to be in control anymore. I want all of you, and it's too damn hard being this close and not being able to have you."

He gripped my hands tighter, still not meeting my eyes. "I've been an asshole, and I've passed the responsibility of what happens with us completely to you. I've stayed right here because I told myself I was doing it to protect you and that I was doing it because Warren asked me to. And while those things are true, they're also bullshit. I did it for me because I can't stand being away from you."

We were both quiet as I let his words sink in. He was doing it. He was really saying goodbye.

"I do love you, Nathan." My voice was barely a whisper.

When he finally looked up, his gray eyes were glassy. "I know you do, and somewhere in another lifetime, I'm sure we have an awesome life together." He tucked a loose strand of hair behind my ear. "It's just not in this one."

"Where will you go?" I asked softly.

He shrugged. "I don't know. Maybe back to Raleigh."

I looked down and tears splashed in speckled shapes onto my pants.

Nathan put his hand under my chin and lifted my face to meet my eyes. "I need you to be OK though, and I need you to be happy."

"How can I be happy?"

His smile was gentle. "It'll come. Warren will be home soon, your daughter will be born, and you'll have a good life with them."

"What about you?"

He winked at me. "I've always got bad guys, booze, and college basketball."

I laughed and wiped my eyes.

"Look at me, Sloan," he said.

Nathan studied my face carefully for a moment, like he knew it was the last time he'd see it. Then without hesitation or apology, he slid his hands up my jaw and pulled my lips to meet his.

The kiss was long and slow. Deep and memorable…because that's exactly what we both knew it would become.

A very distant memory.

CHAPTER NINETEEN

Nathan took all his stuff back to his apartment without even a final goodbye before he left. No matter how many times Azrael said the words *'he did the right thing,'* nothing made Nathan's departure any easier. By lunchtime the next day, I still hadn't gotten out of bed.

"Knock, knock," Adrianne said, announcing her presence as she pushed open my door.

I looked around the pillow I was hugging. "Hey."

"Hey," she said.

"What are you doing here?"

"I'm on my lunch break. Your dad called me. He's really worried about you," she said, sitting down next to me.

"I'm fine," I mumbled.

She frowned. "I'm looking at your hair. You are *not* fine."

"You're right," I said, rolling over to look at her. "I'm not. I'm a horrible person, destined for hell or equally bad things."

"I can't argue with you there," she said, grinning at me.

I threw the pillow at her.

"Get in the shower, you nasty skank," she said. "And get your ass out of bed. Geez, this isn't a moody teen melodrama. You need real food and real human interaction...or at least non-human interaction. Just get up."

I snuggled further under my blankets. "I'm so tired."

With an exasperated huff, Adrianne yanked back my comforter. "Get up!" She stood and pointed at me. "Don't make me push a pregnant lady on the floor."

Obediently, I sat up in the bed.

She aimed her finger at the master bath. "Shower. *Now.*"

Twenty minutes later, I came downstairs, showered and dressed for the first time since we'd all gone Christmas shopping. Adrianne was sitting next to Azrael on the couch, a little closer to him than I was comfortable with. Taiya was sitting on the floor with a coloring book. She clapped when she saw me.

Adrianne and Azrael looked up.

"Back from the dead," Adrianne announced.

Azrael looked at her. "You're a miracle worker."

"Stop being dramatic," I said. "It's only been a day."

Adrianne put her hand on Azrael's arm. "You have no idea the miracles I can work."

I wanted to throw up. "Move over," I said, pushing them apart and dropping down in the seat between them.

"Are you hungry?" Azrael motioned to the box of pizza on the coffee table. "It's extra meat and extra cheese."

"Azrael, you eat like you're preparing for a reality show intervention someday, but you never work out. How is it you're built like a tank?" I asked.

Adrianne made a soft purring noise beside me.

I rolled my eyes.

"The cells in this body are programmed to work at maximum efficiency all the time," he said. "Outside factors have no influence on them."

"I hate you," I said, leaning toward the pizza box.

He grabbed my arm and pulled me back. "No. I'm sorry. You have to work for your dinner."

I was confused. "What?"

"If you want pizza, you can't use your hands."

"Are you serious?" I asked.

He let go of my arm. "You can use your hands to eat it, but not to get it."

"Azrael," I whined.

"Close your eyes," he instructed.

With a huff, I pressed my eyes closed.

"Think about what you want to happen. Visualize it. Use the space around you to move the pizza onto the plate and not your lap," he said.

Adrianne burst out in nervous laughter beside me. "What kind of voodoo shit is this?"

I cracked up, and my eyes popped open.

She leaned over, dropped a slice of pizza onto a plate and handed it to me. "Problem solved," she said.

Frustrated, Azrael sighed and shook his head.

"I have to get back to work before you two circus monkeys get any weirder." Adrianne stood, then leaned down to look at me. "Will you be OK?"

"I'm fine. Thanks for dragging me out of bed."

She pointed at me. "No more sulking."

"Yes, ma'am."

"I love you, freak."

"I love you too."

She tousled Taiya's hair. "Goodbye, beautiful."

Taiya waved at her, smiling from ear to ear.

Azrael walked her to the door.

"So...will I see you on Friday?" she asked, running a finger under the collar of the jacket he was wearing.

I groaned.

"I'll let you know," he said, opening the front door.

She held her pinky and her thumb in the shape of a phone up to the side of her face. "Call me."

When she was gone, he brought me a bottle of water from the kitchen before reclaiming his spot on the sofa. "Here," he said.

"Thanks." I pointed the bottle at him. "What's happening on Friday?"

He cleared his throat. "She said we're all going to some fancy dinner thing."

I groaned. "I forgot about that. We're having dinner at the Deerpark restaurant."

"I don't know what that is," he said.

"It's probably the most romantic restaurant in all of North Carolina." I sighed. "Just the perfect place for me to have my debut starring role as a third wheel." I pointed at Taiya. "What about her?"

"She'll have to go with us, I guess," he answered.

"Is that a good idea? Taking her out in public?" I asked.

He shrugged. "Taiya's not exactly a wanted criminal. Besides, I doubt anyone would even recognize her now."

That was the truth. Between her haircut, her new clothes, and the five pounds she'd packed on in the week she'd been at my house, Taiya looked like a completely different person.

"Adrianne really worked some magic on her, didn't she?" he asked.

The melodic notes of his tone caught my attention. I looked over at him. "What's going on with you and my best friend?"

He shook his head. "Nothing."

"Liar."

"She's nice," he said. "And she's tall. I like that."

I took a long drink of water. "She's off limits."

He turned toward me. "How come?"

"Because you're a dead guy!"

His brow crumpled. "I am most certainly *not* a dead guy."

"You're not a human," I said.

"That's correct." He winked at me. "I'm better."

I picked up my slice of pizza again. "You can't give her a future, and she deserves one. I don't want her to wind up with a broken heart."

"I have no intention of breaking anything," he said, putting his feet up on the coffee table.

"You'd better not. I'm just getting used to having you around, so I'd hate to have to use my light ball on you."

He watched me retrieve a second slice of pizza from the box. The thick mozzarella drew out into a long greasy string for as high up as I could reach. I had to use my other fingers to break it.

"Do you ever plan on practicing your skills, Sloan?" he asked with a hint of exasperation.

"Of course," I said.

He crossed his arms. "When?"

I lowered the stringy cheese into my mouth and winked at him. "It's my New Year's resolution. I promise."

On Friday afternoon, Adrianne came to my house to get ready for the party. She claimed it was so we could all ride together, but I really knew it was so she could make sure I looked presentable next to her in public. "You should wear the black Ivis Mishi dress I got you," she said as she pinned a hot roller into my hair.

I made a sour face. "The monstrosity that looks like a jeweled garbage sack?"

She made a sharp screeching sound that echoed around the bathroom. "You take that back!"

"I wish you'd taken that dress back," I teased.

She yanked on my hair.

"Ow!"

"You're such a brat," she said, rolling her eyes at me in the mirror.

I slathered on a layer of sheer lip-gloss. "I know."

"You look so hot in that dress," she whined.

My heart sank. Nathan had said the same thing not too long ago. In the five months we'd known each other, hardly a day had passed that I hadn't heard his voice until that week. He'd been gone four whole days.

"Earth to Sloan," Adrianne said.

My eyes snapped up. "Sorry."

"What's the matter?"

I scrunched up my nose. "Thinking about Nathan."

"Have you talked to him at all?" she asked.

I shook my head. "Not even a text message."

She twisted another long strand of my hair around a hot roller. "Was it really that bad? You never told me exactly what happened."

I sighed. "Yeah, it was *that* bad. The night you were out with Azrael, I had another one of those crazy weird nightmares. Only this time, Nathan was a part of it. It was pretty, um..." My cheeks flushed red.

"Explicit?" she asked.

"Very. But then he tried to kill me in the dream and I almost killed him."

She looked confused. "But it was a dream."

"Well, somehow I woke up with bruises around my throat, and he had bloody scratches down his chest. God only knows what really happened."

"That's terrifying."

"Yeah."

She hosed down the set curlers with hairspray. "So that's why he left?"

"That and he said he's tired of being so close and not being able to have me," I said.

Her bottom lip poked out. "Ohh...that's so sad."

"I know." I slumped in my chair. "And he kissed me."

"Shut up. Really?"

I nodded.

"Like a real kiss?" she asked.

"Closed eyes and everything."

She gasped. "Not closed eyes."

"And face-holding," I added.

She put her hands on my shoulders. "You poor thing."

"And now he's gone," I said. "We weren't even a couple, and it's still the worst breakup I've ever been through."

She grimaced. "Will you tell Warren? He's going to know something major is wrong if he comes home and Nathan is gone."

"I don't want to lie to him," I answered.

Adrianne shook her head. "No. You can't do that. Maybe he won't ask."

I laughed. "Right. Because Warren is about as oblivious as a hawk at dinnertime."

"Sorry."

I waved her off. "Let's talk about something else before I start crying and ruin my makeup."

"Right! There will be absolutely no sad tears tonight. This will be a glorious evening!" She spun around toward my closet. "Now, what are you going to wear?"

"I look like a California Raisin," I grumbled, tugging at the hem of my skirt as I followed Adrianne and Azrael—who were locked at the elbows—up the stone steps to the glass front doors of the Deerpark Restaurant.

Adrianne flashed a painted smile back at me. "You look gorgeous."

"I look *alone*," I corrected her.

Azrael, who was wearing a black suit against his will at Adrianne's insistence, glanced over his shoulder. "Not true. You've got Taiya."

Taiya.

I stopped walking and looked around for her. It was the

second time we'd lost her that evening, and we'd only left the house a half hour before. The first time, she'd disappeared through my neighbor's backyard to the street behind my house. Azrael had brought her back. This time, she was wandering down the cobblestone handicap ramp. I shouted her name, but she was looking everywhere but at me.

"*Eshta!*" Azrael called out.

Taiya spun toward us, causing the short skirt of her dark blue velvet dress to swirl around her thighs. Adrianne had found the frock in the children's department at the mall, and it almost fit perfectly, except for the sleeves which were barely long enough to cover her scars. The square heels of her strap-on dress shoes clopped against the path as she ran over.

I took her hand. "Stay with us." I pulled a pen out of my purse, yanked up Taiya's sleeve and on the outside of her pale forearm I wrote my phone number and *If found, please call Sloan Jordan.*

She ignored me and smacked her lips together like she had been doing ever since Adrianne put pink lipstick on her at the house.

"Azrael, tell her to quit doing that. She looks like a guppy," Adrianne said.

"Oh, leave her alone." Azrael reached for the door handle and held it open for all of us.

I imagine there are few places in the world as grand and spectacular as the Biltmore Estate. The 250 room home, nestled against the backdrop of the Blue Ridge Mountains, was nothing shy of a fairytale castle. Even in my current, irrevocable state of melancholy, it was hard to be blasé about the Biltmore at Christmas.

Inside the spacious restaurant lobby, we were greeted by ten-foot, flawless Frasier firs sparkling with white twinkle lights and silver jingle bells. Fresh pine garland and poinsettias of every size garnished every stationary furnishing in the room. Soft Christmas music drifted from the instruments of a string quartet somewhere nearby.

Dinner at the Deerpark was like dining inside a Hallmark snow globe.

I missed Warren.

And Nathan.

The hostess led us through a maze of banquet tables and buffet stations. Taiya swiped a handful of cheese cubes from an artisan platter as we passed by. Our round table, draped with a pristine white tablecloth and set for a party of six, was tucked into the corner beside the windows that overlooked the center outdoor courtyard hidden at the heart of the restaurant. Adrianne and I had attended our high school prom out in that magical space beneath the stars. I smiled as I pulled out the chair closest to the window.

Adrianne grabbed my hand. "Let me sit there. You know I hate having my back to the action."

Rolling my eyes, I stepped back beside Taiya while Adrianne eased into the seat right next to Azrael.

Deep inside my belly, a distinct flutter tickled my bladder.

My hands covered my stomach. "Whoa."

Azrael looked up with alarm. "What's the matter?"

I giggled. "I think I felt the baby move."

Adrianne clasped her hands together. "Really?"

"I think so." I froze, waiting to feel it again.

Everyone was watching me. Well, everyone except Taiya. She had walked around to the window and was pressing her cheek against the glass.

Azrael snapped his fingers in her direction. "*Eshta. Por dova.*" He pointed to her chair, and obediently she pulled it out and sat down.

Giving up on feeling the flutter a second time, I sank down beside her. "That was weird."

"What did it feel like?" Adrianne asked.

I bit my lower lip. "Kind of like I had to go to the bathroom."

Adrianne's face soured. "That's gross. Isn't it kind of early to be feeling her kick? When my boss was pregnant, she felt her son the first time at the salon and she was further along."

Azrael shook his head. "You can't expect this to be a normal pregnancy. It's not a normal child."

Even if it was true, I didn't like him calling my baby abnormal.

A waitress took our drink orders and invited us all to help ourselves to the buffet tables. Normally, I didn't like buffets. It reminded me of cattle being herded to a trough, but for the Biltmore, I'd make an exception. And since my dad wasn't there to argue, I started at the dessert table.

It was clear from Azrael's scowl that he didn't approve of my chocolate raspberry cheesecake and triple chocolate mousse. "The baby needs calcium," I said, putting my plate down on the table.

Perhaps she heard me using her as my gluttony defense because she moved again.

I smoothed the soft fabric over my midsection. "I feel her again!"

When I glanced toward Adrianne, movement behind her in the courtyard caught my attention. A tall, broad figure was poised in the moonlight, and when he looked up, his black eyes locked on mine.

It was Warren.

CHAPTER TWENTY

Gasping, I covered my mouth. "Oh my god."

Everyone in earshot turned to look outside.

Warren stuffed his hands into his pockets, smiling from ear to ear.

In my haste toward the door, I knocked over two chairs and caused an older gentleman to dump his untouched slice of cheesecake onto the floor. I didn't even stop to apologize. My feet didn't stop till I was through the door, across the courtyard, and on top of him. "Warren!" Under the canopy of stars in the cloudless sky above, every nerve ending in my body came alive when his strong arms closed around me. He lifted my feet from the ground and stumbled backward from the force of my impact.

I buried my face in the bend of his neck and cried. "I can't believe you're here!"

He set me down on my heels and pulled back enough to see my face. "Surprise!" Tears sparkled at the corners of his eyes as he cupped my face in his strong hands and pressed his lips to mine. The baby tumbled in my stomach as his energy surged with mine. When he finally broke the kiss, he rested his forehead against mine, sliding his hands down my bare arms till his fingers tangled with mine.

"Are you real?" I asked quietly.

He chuckled. "Of course I'm real. What kind of question is that?"

"A valid one," I said, rubbing my nose against his. "Weirder things have happened lately." I opened my eyes and looked into his. "What are you doing here?"

"We got back yesterday," he said. "I have until Monday to spend at home before I have to go back and process out."

"How did you know…" I blinked up at him. "Adrianne organized this, didn't she?"

He grinned. "Yeah. I called her last week. I wasn't exactly sure this would work out, so I didn't want to get your hopes up."

His black hair was growing back out, and he was as formal as Warren ever got: nice dark jeans that clung to all the right muscle groups, a fitted, black button-up shirt covered by a steel-gray jacket. The jacket looked amazing, but I knew it hadn't been a fashion choice; Warren likely hid an arsenal beneath it. I slipped my finger between two buttons on his chest. "Is this new?"

"I literally bought it"—he glanced down at the tactical watch tucked under his sleeve—"forty-seven minutes ago. Adrianne told me to dress up."

"You look amazing."

"*You* look amazing," he said. "And you look cold. Let's go inside."

I grabbed his hand to stop him. "Wait. Before we go in, I need to tell you something." Over dinner was not how I wanted to tell him about the baby and waiting till after wouldn't be an option given my new affinity for chocolate as an appetizer.

Concern flashed in his eyes. "What's going on?"

Standing in front of him, I sucked in a deep breath and held it.

"Sloan?"

Say it.

"Warren, I'm pregnant."

His face froze.

"Warren?"

Nothing.

I stepped to the side, but his eyes stayed fixed on the spot I'd vacated. I waved my hand in front of his face. "Warren?"

He blinked twice, his mouth gaping. "You're pregnant?"

I nodded.

"Pregnant?"

I nodded again. "I didn't want to tell you inside with everyone."

His gaze fell to our feet. "Are you sure?"

"She's due in July."

"She?" His voice broke.

I shrugged. "Your father says it's a girl."

His eyes doubled in size and he angled his ear toward me. "My *father?*"

Crap.

I covered my mouth with my hands. "Oh, geez. Warren, we have so much we have to talk about."

He looked around the courtyard. "I think I need to sit down."

Behind us was a waist-high wall built in a semicircle. I tugged him toward it. "Here."

Carefully, he sat down on top of the bricks, and I stood wringing my cold hands in front of him. "I'm sorry this is a lot of overwhelming information to dump on you."

He held up his index finger. "One thing at a time. Are you really pregnant?"

"Yes. I'm sorry I didn't tell you sooner. I didn't figure it out till you were gone." I put my hands over my stomach. "Please don't be mad."

In an instant, he was on his feet in front me. He gripped my hands in his and held them against his chest. "Sloan, I could never be mad about that." He blinked back tears. "I'm going to be a dad."

"Yeah." I laughed and burst out crying at the same time.

Warren pulled me into his arms and kissed me, his tears mixing with mine. He was breathless when he pulled away. "This is the absolute best news I could come home to. I love you so much."

I gathered the fabric of his jacket in my hands. "I love you too."

His large hand rested against my stomach, and the baby fluttered again.

I laughed. "I think she's kicking."

His eyes whipped up to meet mine. "Really? I can't feel anything."

"I think it's too soon. I never felt her before tonight."

"Are you feeling OK? Have you been sick?" he asked.

I sighed. "Honestly, with all the drama, there's not been much time for normal pregnancy stuff. But I'm healthy, and so is she, I think."

"She," he whispered.

Gripping his forearm with one hand, I pointed back to the restaurant with the other. Our party was watching us intently on the other side of the glass. "The guy next to Adrianne is Azrael."

Warren's shoulders dropped and his jaw slowly opened.

"He's your father," I said.

All the blood drained from Warren's handsome face. He ran his fingers over his head, raking his hair back till it stood on end and then fell in different directions.

"He showed up a few weeks ago and has been taking care of me," I said.

"How did he find you?" he asked, still staring at Azrael.

I tightened my grip on his arm. "He says he's been watching you your entire life. He came straight here when he found out about the baby."

Warren looked up at the sky and blew out a long sigh. "This is a lot to take in. A baby and a father in five minutes."

"I'm sorry." I tugged on his sleeve. "Let's go meet him."

His Adam's apple bobbed with a hard swallow. He nodded. "OK."

I'd never thought it was possible for Warren Parish to look nervous. I was wrong. Before we walked through the door, he pulled me to stop. "Do you trust him?" he asked. "We've not had such good luck with biological parents."

"Well, he could have killed me plenty of times since he got here and he didn't." I shrugged. "He's a bit unconventional, but he's not like Kasyade."

Warren relaxed. "Thank God." He gazed through the window again. "Did he tell you anything about *my* mother?"

I laced my fingers between his and hesitated.

He looked down at me. "She's dead, isn't she?"

I nodded and squinted up at him. "How did you know?"

His eyes darted from mine. "Do you remember that I can see the number of people a person has killed?"

My shoulders sagged with the weight of the statement I knew he was about to make next. "Yes."

"Every time I look in the mirror, I see one death I can't account for." He looked at the ground. "I've always wondered if somehow I killed her."

I squeezed his hand. "There were complications when you were born. She loved you too much to be separated from you."

His jaw was set, and he nodded stiffly, still not meeting my eyes.

I stretched up on my tip-toes and kissed his cool cheek. "Come on. Let's go in." I pushed the door open, and he followed me inside.

Azrael stood as we approached the table and when they were face to face, Azrael extended his hand. "Hello, Warren."

When their hands touched, Warren straightened with a jolt.

Azrael's lips spread into a thin smile. "It's nice to finally meet you, son."

Warren cleared his throat. "Uh...it's nice to meet you too."

His tone wasn't convincing. The pleasantry sounded like it needed a question mark at the end. Warren was studying his father's face like he was preparing for a quiz, and Azrael was having one of those rare moments where he genuinely looked happy.

Realizing the two men were both too stunned or awkward to speak, Adrianne broke the silence by getting up and pushing her way in between them. She threw her arms around Warren's neck. "Welcome home, Warren!"

He pulled back and smiled at her. "Thank you, Adrianne." He reached back for my hand. "And thank you for being my co-conspirator in all this."

"I'm just glad it all worked out so you could come. Sorry I couldn't warn you about everything else." She gestured between me and Azrael.

"I'm a little impressed you kept your mouth shut," I said.

She put a hand on her hip. "You didn't make it easy with all your moping around lately."

My eyes flashed at her, and I bit down on the insides of my mouth. The last thing I wanted to discuss right then was my McNamara-induced funk.

Adrianne took the hint. "She's been absolutely miserable without you, Warren."

He pulled me under his arm and kissed the side of my forehead. "I know the feeling."

I noticed the empty chair next to mine. "Where's Taiya?"

"Who?" Warren asked.

My gaze followed the direction of Azrael's finger across the room.

She was making her way across the dining room with a salad plate piled high with deviled eggs. I couldn't help but smile.

Taiya froze when she looked up and saw Warren. Her cheeks flushed red and her hands went limp, spilling the eggs from her plate and sending them bouncing across the tiles. She dropped to her knees, crouching behind the tablecloth of an empty table near us.

"Taiya?" I called out.

She gathered up a few scattered eggs and peeked between the tables at us.

"*Por ata dova, Taiya,*" Azrael called out. "*Misha forste Warren.*"

The surrounding patrons were mortified. Either by Azrael's strange language or probably by the grown woman crawling under the tables of the four-star establishment.

"*Por ata dova,*" Azrael said again.

"What's going on?" Warren whispered in my ear.

I pointed to Taiya. "She's a little skittish."

"Who is she?" Warren asked.

I sighed. "She's a long story. Her name is Taiya. She's Seramorta like us."

His head snapped back. "Really?"

"Yeah. She showed up in town around Thanksgiving," I said, purposefully omitting a lot of details. "She's the daughter of one of Kasyade's cohorts named Ysha. She's with us now. I think."

"Kasyade has cohorts?" The alarm in his voice was obvious.

"Two of them, unfortunately." I looked up at him. "We have a lot to talk about."

"I'll say."

"Be right back." I walked down the aisle, picking up stray eggs as I passed them. When I reached the last table before the salad buffet station, I lifted the skirt of the tablecloth and peeked under it. "Taiya."

She was hiding her red face behind her hands.

"What are you doing under here?" I asked.

She shook her head wildly.

I reached under for her arm. "Come on. Come meet Warren."

"*Keshtaka mi noviombre uta.*"

I had no idea what she was saying. "Come on," I said again. "You'll love him."

"Love him," she softly echoed.

"That's right." My fingers found her wrist. Gently, I pulled her out from under the table.

As she stood upright, she swiped an egg off the floor and stuffed it into her mouth before I could stop her. I almost puked on my shoes. I steered her by the shoulders back to our table, apologizing to each table on the way for the scene we'd created.

Taiya pushed back against me when we got closer to Warren.

I looked over his shoulder. "Taiya, this is Warren."

"Hello," he said, offering her his hand.

She tugged the collar of her shirt up over her face and squealed.

Adrianne giggled. "Look at her. She's totally crushing on him."

"Of course she is," I said. "He's beautiful."

Warren rolled his eyes.

Azrael pointed at Warren. "She's probably been told her whole life that she'll be with him, remember?"

"What?" Warren asked.

My heart sank. "Oh, that's sad." I looked at Warren. "You'll have to let her down easy."

Warren tossed his hands into the air. "What the hell are you guys talking about?"

Adrianne walked around the table and took Taiya's hand. "I'm going to go fix her a plate while you start explaining to your poor boyfriend what all is going on." She looked over at Warren. "I hope you brought something to take notes with."

Azrael and I took turns filling Warren in on the details about Taiya, Ysha, and Phenex. I told him about the FBI investigating me and about Azrael pulling me out of the river. Azrael spoke about the angel world and about teaching me to use my powers. We talked about the baby and the demon's plan to kill me in the summer. By the time I finished my chocolate mousse, Warren's head was resting in his hands with his elbows propped up on the table.

I squeezed his knee under the table. "I'm sure this overload isn't what you had planned for tonight."

He looked up and chuckled. "I really expect no less from you, my dear." He crossed his arms on the tabletop. "I do have another question though."

"What?" I asked.

"Where's Nate?"

My mouth snapped shut. Adrianne stopped chewing. Azrael's face was set like stone. Taiya was swirling ketchup into her mashed potatoes.

Warren glanced around the table. "OK, this can't be good. Where is he?"

There was another beat of awkward silence.

"Ice fishing!" Adrianne blurted out.

We all looked at her.

"He went on an ice fishing trip to..." She looked at Azrael for help.

"Alaska?" Azrael said.

Adrianne nodded. "Yes. Alaska."

Now it was my turn to want to crawl under the table.

Warren raised a skeptical eyebrow. "Alaska?"

"He won a trip on the radio," Adrianne added.

Oh, geez. It wasn't any wonder that we never got away with breaking curfew in high school.

It was obvious that Warren was debating calling us all out at the table or trusting that our lie was with good reason. He pointed across the room. "I'm going to go get some more prime rib. Anybody need anything?"

I slouched in my chair. "No, thank you."

He was still eyeing me curiously as he got up from the table.

When he was out of earshot, I glared at Adrianne. "Ice fishing? Really?"

She held up her hands. "It's the first thing that popped into my head."

Groaning, I buried my face in my hands.

Adrianne smacked me across the top of my head. "Don't you dare spoil his first night back with your guilty conscience."

Knowing the Angel of Death would have a strong opinion, I turned my gaze to him.

Azrael shook his head. "She's right. He's been through enough tonight. Wait till tomorrow, but you'd better tell him soon. This kind of news only festers with time."

When Warren returned with his second plate of beef and mashed potatoes, I was anxious to avoid revisiting the subject of Nathan's phony fishing trip. "Can you tell us now where you've been?"

Warren scanned the room, then lowered his voice. "We were right about them sending me after the terrorist in Lebanon." He looked over at me. "But we were wrong about him being a demon. He was dead."

"Really?" I asked.

Warren nodded. "And he'd been dead for quite a while when I found him. They believe he was killed by a US drone months ago."

Adrianne seemed confused. "Why would they send you across the world for a dead guy?"

Warren sliced into his meat. "They weren't a hundred percent sure they'd killed him since his terrorist organization keeps releasing propaganda with his name and picture on it. Now that the US has his body, the organization loses a lot of their power."

I drummed my nails on the tabletop. "It seems strange they would send you of all people in the military."

Warren shrugged. "I found all those bodies Billy Stewart hid in the mountains. I guess they figured I knew what I was doing."

"Will they discharge you now?" Azrael asked.

Warren nodded. "This week I'll process out. They said we'll be back home by Christmas Eve."

"And be done for good?" I asked, perking up in my seat.

He reached over and squeezed my hand. "And be done for good."

When dinner was finished, the five of us walked out to the parking lot. Warren tried to put his arm around me as we ducked into the cold, but Taiya wedged herself between us and held onto my arm. When he tried to talk to her, she giggled and slipped around my back to my other side. It was adorable, and a little sad.

"Did you drive here?" I asked as we neared Adrianne's car.

He pointed to a gray sedan parked at the end of the row. "I rented a car this morning."

I split a glance between Adrianne and Azrael. "I want to ride with Warren, so we'll see you at the house."

Warren's hand tightened around mine. "No you won't."

I looked up at him. "I won't?"

He laughed. "If you don't mind, I'd like to have you all to myself for tonight. I've made other plans. *Private* plans."

My heart quickened at the thought.

Azrael shook his head. "That's not possible."

Warren's brow lifted, and he was trying and almost succeeding at suppressing the smirk on his face. "No offense, *Dad*, but I didn't ask you."

I bit down on the insides of my lips.

Adrianne's eyes widened.

Azrael took a step toward his son. It was creepy how much they looked alike. "Warren, things are not the same as you left them. Sloan is in danger and she needs—"

Warren held up his hand. "I'll be the judge of what she needs. Tonight, she's spending with me, so you might as well save your breath."

The two stared at each other with so much intensity I worried one or both of their heads might start smoking at any second.

Warren finally pointed at Adrianne. "She knows where to find us if there's an emergency, and we won't be too far from home."

The muscles around Azrael's eyes softened just enough to make it clear he knew he'd lost the argument. He looked at me. "Keep your phone on. If the weather changes or if you dream, call me at once."

Warren pulled me close. "I don't intend on letting her sleep."

There was a small squeak in the back of my throat, and I hid my face behind my hands.

"I mean it," Azrael snapped.

Still cringing with embarrassment, I nodded. "I promise."

Warren wrapped his hand around mine and pulled me in the direction of his car before anyone could say anything else.

"You two have fun!" Adrianne called after us.

I waved back over my shoulder.

When we got to the car, Warren opened my door. "Is he always like that?"

"Hard-headed and argumentative?" I laughed as I got into the car. "You haven't seen anything yet."

Warren had booked a king sized room at the Inn on Biltmore Estate, just up the road from the Deerpark. It had only been open a couple of years, and I'd never been inside it. Like every other property on the lavish estate, the Inn was fit for American royalty with a grand mix of gothic elegance and contemporary comfort. To be honest, I felt a little out of place as we walked up to the registration counter to check in.

"You're fidgeting," Warren said, leaning against the marble counter.

I hadn't realized I was. Perhaps it was the ritzy hotel. Or maybe it was my nerves about the whole thing with Nathan. Hell, maybe it was the ungodly amount of sugar I'd consumed at dinner.

He ran his fingers down my arm. "Would you be more comfortable at home? I should've asked that earlier."

I snuggled under his arm. "No way. This is wonderful. Thank you for planning something so special."

He looked down at me, his face a mix of concern and hesitation. "I feel like we need to talk about stuff."

"I won't lie and say we don't, but I'd rather save it for later. It's nothing that can't wait till tomorrow."

He was obviously skeptical. "Are you sure?"

I smiled. "I promise."

Our room was on the third floor. It had an oversized mahogany bed with a pristine white comforter and fluffy white pillows. There were two leather wingback chairs with footstools facing the private terrace which I was sure had a glorious view of the mountains in the daylight.

Behind me, Warren wrapped his arms around my waist. "I missed you, Sloan."

I covered his arms with my own. "I missed you too, so very much."

He pressed warm kisses to the side of my neck sending tingles rippling down my spine as his fingers worked loose the buttons on the front of my winter coat. Slowly, he peeled it back off my shoulders before draping it over the back of one of the chairs. His hands slid across the smooth fabric covering my stomach.

"I still can't believe you're pregnant," he said quietly in my ear.

I turned around in his arms and locked my fingers behind his neck. "Are you ready to be a dad?"

"Nope." He laughed and pulled me closer. "But I'll figure it out."

"I'm sure you will," I said.

He dipped his head and pressed his lips to mine. The room seemed to spin around us as I melted into his strong arms. I had almost forgotten how it felt to be wrapped up with him—like the earth could implode, and it wouldn't even matter. His hands slid down the curves of my back till they settled behind my thighs. He lifted me up until my legs draped across his hips, and my curls spilled down over his shoulders. I cradled his head in my arms as he kissed me. Carefully, he slid one arm behind my back and used the other to brace himself against the bed as he lowered me down onto it.

As he knelt between my legs, he shrugged out of his jacket and tossed it on the chair with mine. He unclasped his double holster, slipped it off his shoulders, and lowered his two guns carefully to the ground. He unbuttoned his shirt and peeled it back off his shoulders. Then with one hand, he reached back between his shoulder blades, grasped his white t-shirt, and tugged it off over his head. Over his chest was a tribal dragon's talon tattooed across his shoulder and down the center of his torso. On his waist, just above the normal resting place for his sidearm, was the name Azrael. I dragged my nails down his stomach till they found the clasp for his black belt. He slid out of his slacks as he bent down over me.

He undressed me slowly, taking extra care to trace every inch of the new landscape of my figure. "You've never been more beautiful," he whispered as he trailed kisses down the center of my tender, swollen breasts to my stomach and then back up again.

Warren was hesitant, nervous even, to cover my body with the full force of his weight, but I pushed his support arm up toward my head forcing him to settle slowly on top of me. He hooked his hand behind my knee and drew my leg up toward his hip. After that, everything swirled out of focus.

———

True to his word, Warren didn't let me sleep. Not much anyway. We'd dozed on and off between sweaty bouts of lovemaking. It was the best non-sleep I'd ever had, and that was saying some-thing. My lips were raw and my legs felt like Jello by sunrise.

When we pulled up in front of my house, Adrianne's red sports car was still parked at the curb. I frowned. "That's not good."

Warren slid the transmission to park. "She stayed the night?"

"Looks like it," I grumbled.

He looked over at me. "I gather from your tone this isn't exactly great news."

I glared at him.

"You can't protect her from everything," he said.

"I can't protect her from *anything*, Warren. She never listens to me."

He pointed toward the house. "Do you think she needs protecting from him?"

I groaned. "I think best-case scenario is that she'll wind up hurt when he can't give her what she wants."

We walked inside to find Taiya watching cartoons on the couch and no one else around. Upstairs I heard the sound of the shower in the guest bathroom. "Good morning, Taiya," I said as I dropped my purse on the floor with a heavy thud and kicked off my high heels.

Her face broke out in a wide smile when her eyes settled on Warren. He waved, and she ducked her head into her pillow.

"She lives here now too?" he asked, following me to the kitchen to get my prenatal vitamins.

I nodded. "Yeah. It's been a little less crowded since Nathan moved out, but it's still—"

He cut me off. "Nathan was living here?"

My back was to him at the refrigerator so he couldn't see me cringe. I grabbed the orange juice and carried it to the counter. "I was attacked while I was home alone one night. After that, Nathan moved into the guest room."

Warren pulled out the chair at the dinette table and sat down.

"Are you ready to tell me where he really is and not that bullshit story about ice fishing?"

My bottom lip poked out. "No."

He crossed his arms. "Babe, I promise you don't want to leave this one to my imagination."

Sadly, I feared his imagination couldn't be much worse than the truth. But the last thing I wanted was to tell him the truth and then send him away for a few days to stew on it. So, instead, I shook the carton of Tropicana in his direction. "Do you want some orange juice?"

"No, Sloan. I don't want any juice," he said, his voice dark and bordering on anger.

Buying myself a few more seconds of pre-fight peace and happiness, I dropped the vitamin into my mouth and drained the entire glass of juice. When I finished, I washed the glass by hand in the sink, dried it slowly, then tucked it away in the cabinet. When I turned around to look at him, Warren's jaw was twitching. That was never a good sign.

I leaned back against the counter for support. "You asked Nathan to take care of me while you were gone, remember?"

His eyes tightened, and he drew in a deep breath. "Yes."

I looked down at the tiles. "Well, things with us—"

Just then, Adrianne jogged down the stairs wearing a pair of my sweatpants—that only reached half-way down her calves— and one of Azrael's shirts. I was almost too relieved by her interruption to still be mad at her. She froze when she saw us in the kitchen.

I put my hands on my hips. "What are you doing here?"

A sly grin was on her face. "Good morning to you too, sunshine."

I rolled my eyes as she entered the kitchen. "I don't even want to know."

"You probably don't." She winked at me as she grabbed a banana out of the fruit basket. "How was the hotel last night?"

"Really nice," I said. "Have you been there?"

She nodded. "I've done hair for a few bridal parties there."

Warren cleared his throat. "Not to be rude or anything, but Sloan and I are kind of in the middle of something."

Adrianne cringed. "That doesn't sound good."

I jerked my thumb toward the stairs and looked at Warren. "Come on. Let's go talk upstairs in our room."

He got up and walked toward me. Over his shoulder, I saw Adrianne mouth the words *good luck*.

I practiced deep breathing as we crossed the living room.

"Ding dong," Taiya said from the floor.

My eyes widened, and I looked at the door just as the bell rang.

"Did she do that?" Warren asked, confused.

My heart pounded in my chest. I knew somehow I'd slipped up and summoned Nathan McNamara, possibly to his death. Warren must have realized the same thing because we both bolted toward the door at the same time. My hand reached the knob first.

"Sloan, wait!" I heard Azrael shout upstairs.

But it was too late.

I pulled the door open.

It was Agent Silvers...and a team of other officers.

"Sloan Jordan, you're under arrest."

CHAPTER TWENTY-ONE

"Please state your last name."

My wrists ached from where they'd just removed the handcuffs. I rubbed the red marks left behind. "Jordan."

Agent Silvers looked up from the paper. "And your first name?"

I looked at her in disbelief. "You know my name."

"This is procedural, Ms. Jordan. Please answer the question."

"My first name is Sloan."

"Middle name?"

"Bridgett."

"Can you spell that please?"

"B-R-I-D-G-E-T-T."

"Date of birth?"

"January 24th, 1986."

We went through a list of *procedural* information before Agent Silvers let me go to the bathroom and get some water. I'd cried the entire drive in the back of the unmarked car, until I realized they weren't taking me to jail as I'd assumed. I had driven past the stone and glass building on Patton Avenue a thousand times but had never been inside. Little did I know the FBI field office was housed there.

When we came back into the interrogation room, someone else, a man who looked like he might play golf with my dad, stared at me from across the table. Agent Silvers excused herself and left, closing the door behind her.

The man extended his hand to me. "Hi, Ms. Jordan, I'm Special Agent Elijah Voss. It's nice to meet you. I'm sorry it had to be under these circumstances."

My smile was awkward.

"Ms. Jordan, as you know, we've been investigating Abigail Smith for the past several weeks, and in the course of our investigation, we have discovered substantial evidence that brings us back to you. Now, I'm pretty new on this case, so I'm hoping you can explain to me how an upstanding county employee such as yourself has gotten mixed up in a federal investigation." He smiled. "You have certain rights I'm obligated to advise you of before I talk to you. You have the right to remain silent. Anything you say can and will be used against you in a court of law. You have the right to talk to an attorney before answering any questioning or making any statements now or in the future. If you can't afford an attorney, one will be appointed for you before any questioning if you wish. Do you understand?"

I nodded.

"You can decide at any time to exercise these rights and not answer any questions or make any statements." He folded his hands on top of his notepad and file folder. "Now, knowing and understanding your rights as I have explained them to you, are you willing to answer my questions without an attorney present?"

This is the part where you're supposed to say no.

But I didn't. "Yes."

My curiosity about what evidence they'd come up with outweighed my good sense in the matter.

"How do you know Abigail?"

"I really don't know her well. I met her a couple of times in Texas," I said.

"What took you to Texas?" he asked.

This was one of those questions, I knew I shouldn't answer since we'd already lied about it the first time we met with Agent Silvers. "I'd rather speak to my attorney about that."

He made some notes. "Very well. Will you tell me how you came across the information that led to human trafficking charges being brought against Ms. Smith?"

"She invited me to her home, and while I was there, I was snooping in her office. I found bond paperwork on an individual I knew had been arrested for trafficking," I said. All of that was completely true.

Thin lines of confusion rippled his brow. "Why were you snooping in her office?"

I shrugged my shoulders and kept my mouth shut. The truth was a voice in my head told me to go in there, but that wasn't the sort of thing you tell a detective...or anyone.

"What happened after you found the paperwork?" he asked.

"I heard Abigail on the phone in the other room, and then I left her home," I said.

He tapped his pen against the pad. "What was she saying on the phone?"

"It's in the notes from my previous statement," I said.

"I'd rather you tell me."

I stared back at him. "I'd rather you look them up."

"Are you refusing to answer the question?" he asked.

"Yes."

He looked annoyed, but he didn't say anything. "Are you aware surveillance photos and other information spanning most of your life were found at the residence of Abigail Smith?"

I nodded. "Agent Silvers showed me some of the photos."

"Any guess as to why she would have such information on you?"

I shook my head. "I wish I knew."

While that was true, I also had a very good idea why she would have kept close tabs on me over the years. She'd had a plan my entire life that brought me to where I was presently—pregnant with Warren's kid.

"Where were you on the morning of October 31st?" he asked.

"Halloween," I clarified.

"Yes. Halloween."

That was the day I called Abigail and asked if she was my biological mother. That week, Warren had stayed with my dad while I dipped in and out of my office trying to catch up from being gone and trying to prevent falling even further behind.

"I went into work that morning." I thought for a moment. "I remember sending out something to our newsletter subscribers about trick-or-treating safety."

He made some notes. "What else did you do that day?"

"I left work early—"

"At what time?"

I thought back. "It's hard to remember exactly, but it was probably around four or so. I remember skipping lunch so I could leave early."

"And where did you go?" he asked.

"Back to my father's house. My boyfriend and I stayed with him all week because my mother had just died," I said.

"I'm sorry to hear that. Your boyfriend...Detective Nathan McNamara?"

I rolled my eyes. "No. My boyfriend's name is Warren Parish. I have had a close relationship with Detective McNamara, but I was with Warren on Halloween. We had dinner at the Sunny Point Cafe, then went back to my father's house in time for trick-or-treaters to show up. Oh yeah, and we stopped to buy candy for them on the way home."

"Anything else happen that day?" he asked.

I swallowed. "I spoke to Abigail on the phone. She asked me to come back to Texas for a meeting."

"Did she call you or did you call her?"

This was a test to see if I'd tell the truth. I was sure he'd already seen my phone records.

"I called her."

He blinked with fake surprise. "You called her? Why?"

I shook my head. "I'll only answer that question with my attorney."

For a moment, we stared at each other in a battle of wills. I won, and he looked at his pad of paper again. "Did you visit anywhere else on the day of October 31st?"

"No."

He nodded and made some notes.

"Sloan, where do you bank?"

That was an odd question. "Western Carolina Credit Union, why?"

He glanced up at me. "Do you utilize any other financial service institutions?"

I thought for a second. "I have a deferred compensation retirement plan through my work, plus a Roth IRA through Smithson Investors Services."

"No others?"

I smirked. "Are you planning on freezing my assets or something?"

He just stared at me.

I sank in my chair. "No other institutions. I want to contact an attorney. I won't answer any more questions."

"We haven't even discussed the—"

I cut him off. "I don't care. I'm exercising my rights. I want an attorney."

He closed his notebook. "Very well."

Never in my life had I needed an attorney for anything other than closing on my new house. I knew a few from my dealings with work, but those were generally prosecutors or sleaze bags covered in the media. But my dad knew lots of people, so I called him. When he answered the collect call, he sounded panicked. "Are you OK?" he asked before even saying hello.

"I'm OK. I'm in an interrogation room downtown," I said. "I need you to call Nathan, and I need you to find a federal criminal attorney."

"We've already made some calls. I came to your house as soon as Warren called me. Azrael and Nathan are both here with us as well," he said.

Relief washed over me. "Thank you."

There was some commotion on his end of the line. "Nathan says they'll take you to appear before the federal magistrate and they'll set bail. We'll get you out then."

"OK. Please find someone quickly."

"We will, sweetheart. Be brave."

I heard Nathan in the background. "Keep your mouth shut, Sloan."

"Tell him I will," I said. "I love you, Dad."

"I love you, Sloan. We'll figure this out."

"I know." I almost believed it too.

When I hung up the phone, Agent Silvers returned to the room. "Were you able to contact an attorney?" she asked.

"My father's handling it," I answered. "When will I see the magistrate?"

A thin smile spread across her painted lips as she looked down at her watch. "In a few days once you're back in Texas."

My heartbeat quickened. "Texas?"

"Correct. Your transport has already been arranged."

My lower lip quivered. "What will happen to me until then?"

She walked toward the door, then paused and looked back over her shoulder. "I think you're familiar with the Buncombe County Jail."

By the time we reached the Buncombe County Jail well after midnight, I was in the fetal position in the back of the car. Rather than parking in the front lot and going through the main doors, we were admitted through a high gate covered in barbed wire to a back covered entrance I'd never seen before. The car door opened, and one of the male federal officers pulled me out by my handcuffs. My legs faltered and before I could get my feet underneath me, my knees buckled and slammed into the concrete.

"I'll take it from here!" an angry voice shouted.

A man hooked his arms under mine and hoisted me to my feet. I recognized his face but didn't know his name. His eyes were full of confusion and pity. "Are you OK?" he asked quietly in my ear.

All I could do was shake my head.

"I've got you," he said, wrapping an arm around my waist to help me walk. "Baynard, get me a wheelchair!"

They helped me sit down and wheeled me inside.

Movement in the far corner of the room caught my attention. "Sloan!"

My blurry eyes focused on Nathan just as two deputies caught him by the chest to prevent him from reaching me.

"Get him out of here!" a gruff voice I didn't recognize barked from a nearby hallway.

"We're working on getting you out of here!" Nathan shouted before he was forced through a door and out of my view.

The deputy who had brought me in wheeled my chair up to a tall counter and handcuffed my arm to it.

Behind us, there were murmurings from the federal agents warning the deputies about procedures and preferential treatment. The woman behind the counter looked terrified to talk to me. I didn't know her, but it was obvious she knew me. And judging from the whispers and wide eyes around the room, she wasn't the only one.

She slid a sheet of paper and a pen toward me. The top of the page read *Female Inmate Intake Form.* I shuddered. "Please fill this out," she said.

There was an entire section about pregnancy. I snorted at the line, *Is your pregnancy high risk?*

When I was finished, she placed a clear plastic box in front of me. "Ms. Jordan, I need you to place all your personal belongings inside this container for inventory."

They hadn't even allowed me to change out of my dress before taking me into custody, so I took off all my jewelry and put it in the box.

"I'll need your shoes as well," she added.

I slipped off my heels and dropped them into the box. The deputy who had gotten the wheelchair brought a pair of rubber, slide-on flip-flops. He knelt down and slipped them onto my bare feet. He stood and un-cuffed me from the counter, then helped me to my feet.

"We need to get your photos," he explained. "Can you walk?"

I nodded but leaned heavily on his arm for support.

He backed me up against a wall marked with measurements for height and took a step back. Another woman tapped a webcam positioned on top of a computer. "Please look here, Ms. Jordan," she said.

When my mugshots were finished, they took me to a computer that electronically scanned my fingerprints. "Your dad treated my grandmother last year," the deputy at the computer said.

I tried to smile.

After he clicked a few more buttons, he motioned toward a woman standing behind me. "Deputy Knox will take you back to shower and change," he said.

I shook my head. "I don't need a shower."

He grimaced. "It's policy. You don't have a choice."

Deputy Knox took my arm. "This way, Sloan."

Her tone caught my attention, and I looked at her. Her name when I'd known her had been Kellie Bryant. "Kellie?" I asked.

She cast her gaze at the floor.

Ten years before, Kellie had been on the high school cheerleading squad with me and Adrianne. We had shared a lab table in Advanced Placement Chemistry and had ridden the same school bus before her family moved to Arden. Now she was escorting me across the booking room toward a curtained hallway wearing rubber gloves. That could only mean one thing.

"Do you want me to get someone else?" she asked, still refusing to meet my eyes.

My chin was quivering. "No. Thank you, though."

Once we were behind the curtain, she stood behind me and held my arms out to the side. She proceeded to thoroughly canvas my body, from my ears to my ankles. "Turn around, please," she said.

I turned to face her, and she lifted my arms up again. Then she completely patted down my front, swiping under my boobs and between my legs. I refused to cry, but I'd never been so mortified and shamed in all my life. That is, until she instructed me to disrobe, squat...and cough.

"I'm so sorry," she whispered.

I stood back up, covering myself as much as I could with my arms.

She motioned to a concrete shower with no curtain and a chipped floor behind her. "Step into the shower and use the lice shampoo. Everyone has to do it. It will sit on your hair for three minutes, and then you can wash it out. There's regular shampoo in there you can use after."

I nodded my understanding.

"Your dress and undergarments will be inventoried with the rest of your things," she said. "You'll get them back when you leave."

I thought about telling her she could just trash the dress, but in that moment, I wanted nothing more than that expensive ugly garbage bag.

My teeth chattered as I soaked my head under the ice-cold water. Then, naked and shivering, I leaned against the concrete wall while the lice shampoo burned into my scalp. I slid down the concrete blocks and wrapped my arms around my legs, my tears mixing with the suds as I cried into my knees.

When I was finished, Kellie waited for me with a white cotton sports bra and panties, a white thermal undershirt, a pair of drawstring orange pants and matching top, thick white socks, and black slide flip-flops. As I pulled up the orange pants, I noticed the elastic strain as it went up over my belly.

How lovely.

My first memory of my baby bump would be forever tainted with the scent of lice killer and the cold steel of handcuffs.

CHAPTER TWENTY-TWO

When I was a child, maybe four or five, I had a horrific nightmare after attending an Easter egg hunt at my Aunt Joan's church. Twenty years later, graphic details of that dream were crystal clear in my memory.

I was dragged to the basement of the building by a scaly creature with a forked tongue and razor-sharp claws. It had glowing amber eyes and smelled of sulfur, rotten eggs. The thing slithered through a door, slamming me against the doorframe as we moved.

I knew there were hundreds of people on the floor above the basement, but something invisible, with the weight of a thousand bricks, was crushing my windpipe. I couldn't scream.

With a violent fling, I was slammed against the cold, wet tiles of a bathroom. They were tiny tiles, maybe an inch in size, and they were green, a fluorescent lime that gave the room a sinister glow. Something sticky was splattered on the tiles; I assumed it was blood, but it had the consistency of tar and the tackiness of superglue. In my discarded heap, I was paralyzed, unable to move. Or run. Or fight.

The creature opened a long box—a vertical, wide coffin, maybe—that was nailed to the wall in front of me. Inside it, were my parents, seemingly made of stone with their eyes fixed but full of terror. Hot tears stung my cheeks, but I couldn't cry because I couldn't breathe.

Helpless and screaming on the inside, I watched the creature use its claw to dissect the body of my mother first. Her dripping bowels splashed into a puddle of blood on the floor. I could feel her pain. Every bit of it, but there was nothing I could do to save her—or save myself.

That panic. That nightmare. That feeling—magnified tenfold —was what the inside of my cell at the Buncombe County Jail felt like. All night long. It was an all-consuming nightmare from which I could not escape.

Because of the baby and my hysteria, I wasn't put into the general population. I was put in a cell on the medical floor, as far away from the other inmates as possible, but that was little consolation. Under my metal bed, I curled into a ball with the itchy down pillow clamped down tight over my head. My face was slick against the polished concrete floor, resting in a pool of tears, snot, and saliva.

For hours and hours, I couldn't stop the shaking.

At some point, I heard my name. "Sloan? Sloan, can you hear me?"

Prying open one of my eyes, I saw the face of Virginia Clay-brooks peeking under my bed. Her hand closed around my wrist, yanking me along the smooth floor out into the halogen light of my cell. She plopped down on her backside and pulled my head into her lap. Stroking my hair, she quietly sang a song I'd never heard.

"When peace, like a river, attendeth my way, when sorrows like sea billows roll; whatever my lot, Thou hast taught me to say, it is well, it is well with my soul..."

I tried to focus on her words, but the melody was like a baby's mobile lullaby chiming in a horror house.

"The sheriff is coming," someone said.

Virginia flinched.

Heavy footfalls echoed down the hall, then a gruff male voice was in the room. "Virginia, you aren't authorized to be in here."

"I know that, Sheriff, but you can't blame me," Virginia said. "So fire me if you want. I ain't sorry."

He grunted his disapproval. "Go on now," he said. "Get out of here before I have to put you in handcuffs."

Squeezing her shin as much as I could, I moved off her lap back to the cold tiles.

The sheriff dropped to a knee beside me. "Sloan, are you all right?"

I wanted to scream at him, *Do I look all right?* But I couldn't, and I wouldn't.

"Do you have meds you need to be taking?" he asked.

It was a fair question because I was acting like a lunatic. I was sure my doctor would have deemed this a "Xanax-essential" situation, but I shook my head.

"They tell me you're not eating or drinking any fluids. That's not healthy for you or the baby. You know that," he said.

Honestly, I hadn't even noticed.

"McNamara's been here all night, of course, but you know I can't let him back here to see you," he said. "Your lawyer just got here, so you'll see him in a little while."

I pulled my knees up to my chest. "Thank you," I whispered.

He squeezed my hand where it lay on the floor. "I hate this, Sloan. I wish you the best of luck."

Before he left, he took the blanket off my bed and draped it over me.

A little while later, I heard footsteps again. "Jordan," a man said.

I forced myself to look up.

The deputy didn't look old enough to be a deputy. "Ms. Jordan, I need to cuff you to take you down to see your attorney. Can you come put your hands through this slot in the door?"

It took a few tries and several deep breathing exercises to get me off the floor. When I finally made it to the door, I stuck my hands through it and let him put handcuffs back on my bruised wrists.

The kid held onto my arm as we shuffled down the hallway. He smelled of Axe Body Spray and had teenage boy acne and a taser. I felt very safe.

We turned a corner and stopped in front of a bright white room. Inside, a man with strawberry blond hair and pale skin was looking through a file folder on the table in front of him. Alarm bells went off in my head. *Not human. Not human. Not human.*

Then the man looked up and ice ran through my veins when I locked on his eyes. They were striking blue, the same color as Taiya's.

Ysha.

The boy-deputy urged me forward, but I dug the heels of my flip-flops against the concrete floor. "Ms. Jordan, I need you to move your feet," he said, looking at me like I was crazy. Maybe I was.

The angel stood when we entered. He was dressed in a tailored, navy suit and tie. A briefcase was laying on the table with pens and a legal pad. He certainly looked the part of a lawyer.

"Let me get those," the deputy said, snapping me out of a fearful daze. He turned me toward him and removed the handcuffs.

"Are you leaving me in here?" I whispered.

He nodded. "Attorney-client privilege. Your meeting will be videotaped, but there will be no audio recording."

I rubbed my aching wrists as he backed out the room, closing the door behind him. A clock on the wall said it was almost four. I'd already spent all night and all day in jail.

"Good evening, Sloan." The angel's voice was deep and melodic, and even though I was terrified of him, his simple presence calmed my nerves.

Slowly, I turned to face him, and he extended his hand. I didn't accept it; I took a step back.

He squeezed a fist and dropped it to his side. "My name is Abner Tuinstra. Azrael sent me today when you were arrested."

"You're lying," I said, stepping back into the corner.

He studied me for a moment, then his face split into a creepy smile. "What makes you say that?"

"I know who you are," I said.

He unbuttoned his jacket and sat down. "And who is it that you think I am?"

"You're Ysha, aren't you?" I asked.

He smiled again. "How did you know?"

Azrael could have mentioned Ysha was a man, not a woman as I'd assumed. Maybe gender was an extraneous detail in the supernatural world.

"I know your daughter, Taiya."

His head bowed slightly. "Ahh, yes. My little half-wit puppet. How is she?"

I could have clawed his perfect eyeballs out. "You destroyed her."

"Oh, nonsense," he said. "I made her better."

"Better?"

He sighed and folded his hands together on the tabletop. "Humans are so much more efficient after they've been broken down and rebuilt. Empires have been conquered on the backs of broken humans. Ask that military boyfriend of yours."

"But there's no sense in what you did to her."

"I don't do anything without reason, Sloan. You have no idea what I have planned for my daughter."

"You're sick," I said.

"I've been called worse." He motioned to the chair across from him. "Please have a seat, Sloan." His eyes snapped up. "Or should I call you Praea?"

My jaw clenched. "My name is Sloan."

"Your mother would argue," he replied. "But it doesn't matter. Please sit."

I shook my head. "No."

He glared at me. "You're of no use to me dead, my dear. I won't hurt you." He pulled a file folder from his briefcase. "I do, however, have a copy of your arrest paperwork. I'm sure you're curious to see it."

He was right.

"How do you have it?" I asked.

The angel turned his palms up. "I'm an attorney."

"A real attorney?"

"Of course." He touched the ID wallet hanging around his neck. "Would you like to see my Bar Association credentials?"

I sucked in a deep breath.

He offered me the folder. "Take this then."

Ysha must have realized that, even for the paperwork, I wouldn't budge from my spot in the corner. He opened the folder and took out the papers. "Shall I read it?" When I didn't respond, he nodded. "It's quite a list: conspiracy to commit sex trafficking, conspiracy to harbor aliens, money laundering, forgery, obstruction, perjury..."

My mouth fell open. "But that's not true! How can they arrest me for something there's no proof of? You and I both know I had nothing to do with that."

"Do we?" The pleasure on his face was grotesque.

"What?" I asked.

He flipped to another sheet of paper. "According to this affidavit, there is video surveillance footage of you entering the Asheville Savings and Trust on Merrimon Avenue at 10:19 AM on Thursday, October 31st in the company of Abigail Smith."

"What the hell?" I shouted.

"Apparently, you opened a safe deposit box." Abner rifled through some paperwork, then slid a sheet of paper toward me. "Is this your signature?"

It was.

"I never visited any bank or opened any safe deposit box!"

He read over another sheet of paper. "Inside the box, they found a forged passport with your photograph, a new Texas driver's license, a new social security card"—he looked up at me —"and a hundred thousand dollars in cash."

I gripped the side of my face. "What is happening?"

And then it hit me.

I heard Abigail's voice in my head when she was talking to me about how she raped my biological father. "*When I summon someone for a purpose, they often don't remember it.*"

I slid down the wall till my knees touched my chin.

Abner stood and walked around the table, sitting on the corner of it. "This is quite the predicament you're in, isn't it?"

Refusing to cry, I glared up at him. "So this is your master plan? Plant evidence to have me locked up while I'm pregnant?"

He shook his head. "No. It had been our hope you would come willingly, but I must say, this is one hell of a backup plan." He chuckled as he swung his leg back and forth. "With this evidence, you'll certainly be denied bail once you get to Texas, and when the case goes to trial, it will be a slam-dunk for the prosecution. Then we wait till that precious little asset growing in your womb doesn't need you anymore, and you'll officially be"—he held up his hands—"case closed."

I wanted to throw up. "Did you just come here to torture me?"

He glanced up at the halogen lights, then back down at me on the floor. "Yes."

Slowly, I rose to my feet. "I don't have to listen to this." I banged my fist against the door. The deputy opened it. "Please take me back to my cell," I said holding my wrists toward him.

He looked surprised.

I glanced over my shoulder at the demon. "And please tell Sheriff Davis not to allow Mr. Tuinstra in here again to see me."

The lawyer stood, shaking his head as he closed his briefcase.

He walked past us as the deputy put me in handcuffs. He winked at my jailer. "Some prisoners don't know when they've been beaten, do they, son?"

The kid seemed too confused to answer.

Abner walked down the hall. "I'll see you soon, Sloan."

"Go to hell, Ysha."

He cackled till he was out of sight.

I spent the next twenty minutes vomiting bile into my metal commode.

My assumption about Abigail being with another angel during her travels had been correct, except instead of Ysha or Phenex...it was me. And with no way to argue otherwise, I would spend the rest of my life in prison. Not the county jail. Federal prison.

That is if I survived giving birth which was more doubtful than ever.

For hours, I prayed for sleep to come. It never did. Each time I closed my eyes, the room would spin and the nausea would return. Somewhere a woman was screaming, and I couldn't tell if it was inside the jail or only inside my head. Sweat soaked through my clothes and bed sheets.

Sometime, when all was quiet, I heard the bolt of the cell door slide open. I prayed whoever it was would kill me and end my misery.

Instead, I felt a hand on my back. Tingling warmth spread through me and immediately my nerves began to settle. I inhaled the deepest breath I'd taken in hours and blew it out slowly.

When I looked up, a pair of sapphire eyes sparkled down at me in the faint glow of the security lights.

It was Taiya.

I pushed myself up to face her. She was wearing the same jail issued uniform that I was. "What are you doing here?"

She smiled and pushed my matted hair out of my face. "Help."

I grabbed the crazy waif and hugged her. "Thank you."

When I pulled back, she stood and pointed to the open cell door. "Go."

Shaking my head, I gulped. "Taiya, we can't go!"

Her eyes widened, and she raised her hands in question. "Stay?" she asked, genuinely puzzled.

Wait. Who am I talking to? "Let's get out of here, Houdini."

Taiya was truly a master at getting out of places. She knew when to hide, when to duck security cameras, and most importantly...how to open locked doors without a key. She took me down a couple of hallways I'd never visited and out a side emergency door. She was even able to silence the alarm.

We were in the yard but still behind a locked security fence when I felt the presence of two humans coming toward us. Back inside was the only way to go, and that wasn't an option. She looked at me with wide eyes. "Run."

Grabbing my hand, she bolted in the direction I'd felt the people coming. I had no choice but to follow. We turned a corner and passed two unsuspecting guards who were sharing a cigarette as they patrolled the grounds. Immediately, they were shouting and running after us, but Taiya didn't slow or stop. She ran directly toward the huge gate meant for vehicles.

She threw her hands toward it and slowly it slid open. She jerked my arm forward, pulling me in front of her. "Run!" she screamed again.

I raced through the gate but looked back in time to see Taiya tackle the two guards, clotheslining them with her outstretched arms.

I'd been in the parking lot of the jail a million times but never at night and never running like a madwoman on foot. As fast as my feet would carry me, I ran toward the street. Suddenly, headlights flickered on behind me accompanied by the loud roar of a souped-up engine.

My jail-issued flip-flops pounded the asphalt as the car raced up next to me. It was Warren's black Dodge Challenger.

The driver's side window slid down. "Good evening, ma'am, would you like a ride?"

It was Nathan.

CHAPTER TWENTY-THREE

Never in my life was I a rule breaker. I'd never so much as gotten a detention in school or even let a library book go overdue. But getting in the passenger side of that getaway car was the easiest choice I ever made. Once my seatbelt was fastened, Nathan stepped on the gas, slamming my head back against the leather headrest. "Hang on!"

The car's tires screamed around the right turn onto College Street, then laid rubber tracks down as we cut a left onto Charlotte. A half a second later, we were barreling down Interstate 240, and I turned to look behind us. No one was following. The city planners certainly hadn't put a lot of forethought into the road system when they built the jail.

Nathan was furiously shifting gears and checking the rearview mirror. He relaxed a tad when he merged onto Interstate 40 East, and still no one was behind us. He grasped my hand. "Are you OK?"

"Oh my god! You broke me out of jail!" I leaned over the middle console and wrapped my arms around his neck. "Oh my god! Thank you, thank you, thank you!"

"Technically, Taiya broke you out," he said.

I covered my mouth with my hands. "Oh no. They got her."

He glanced over at me. "Something tells me, she won't be there for long."

I planted a loud, wet kiss on his cheek. "You're my hero."

He shook his head and checked the rearview mirror again. "Don't call me that till we get out of this mess," he said.

I gasped. "They're gonna know it was you. Nathan, you're going to lose your job."

He laughed. "Sloan, if they catch us, I won't have to worry about a job because I'll be in jail."

"Where's Warren?" I asked.

Nathan checked the rearview. "We'll see him shortly." He jerked his thumb back over his shoulder. "In the back is a bag with some clothes in it and your purse."

I found the backpack in the back floorboard, and I pulled out my purse that was laying on top in the main compartment. I dug around inside it for my phone.

"Where's my cell?" I asked.

"At home. Those things can be tracked." He looked over at me. "My sweatshirt is in that bag. You're going to need it."

I pulled out the black S.W.A.T. team hoodie that was inside. In any other situation, I would've at least laughed, but about that time, blue lights flashed inside our car. I squealed with panic as I yanked the sweatshirt over my head.

Nathan pressed the gas again. "You buckled?"

I clicked the belt back into place. "Yes."

"Good."

The engine roared as we sped down the interstate, weaving around the few cars we passed. There were more flashing lights behind us, but they were pretty far off in the distance, and they kept disappearing around the hills and curves through the mountains. Nathan took the exit to Black Mountain. It was a death trap of dangerous roads, but I kept my mouth shut till he dipped off the shoulder of the road and began driving through a field.

"Have you lost your mind?" I shouted, gripping the handle above my door.

"Obviously so," he answered.

Just then, up ahead of us, lights descended from above. I bent and looked up to see a helicopter lowering toward the tall grass. "Where the hell did you get a helicopter?"

"Long story. When we stop, get ready to run," he said. "And bring the bag because that may be the only change of clothes you get for a while."

He slammed down hard on the brakes when we were closer, throwing me toward the dashboard. I cursed and caught myself with my arms.

"Go! Go! Go!" he was screaming.

Hugging the backpack to my chest, I pushed my door open and was knocked backward by the force of the wind from the propellers. Nathan grabbed my hand as we ran toward the chopper. The machine was as black as the night around us, except for the lights and the shiny gold letters down the tail: *Claymore.*

Claymore Worldwide Security had employed Warren as a mercenary till he quit and moved in with me.

A man dressed all in black tactical clothes with an assault rifle slung across his chest, jumped down to the ground. Before I even saw his painted black face, I knew it was Warren. He grabbed my face and studied me for a second, relief evident in his eyes. Then he thrust me up into the open door on the side of the helicopter.

Nathan, who had already gotten in, pulled me up beside him. Warren climbed in behind me as Nathan pushed me into the very back seat. Warren closed the door, just as headlights and flashing blue lights lit up the field.

"Put these on!" Nathan shouted over the noise, handing me a headset.

Obediently, I slipped it over my head as he dropped into the seat next to me. Just then, the helicopter rocked slightly, then lifted into the air.

In the seats in front of us, Warren buckled himself in then watched carefully out the window as we rose into the air. In the cockpit, the pilot and co-pilot were dressed in full tactical gear. When the pilot turned toward the side window, I was surprised to see she was a woman.

When we were well into the air, Warren turned in his seat to look at me. He pulled the microphone on his headset up to his mouth. "Are you all right?"

I nodded. "I am now. You called Claymore?"

Warren exchanged a curious glance with Nathan, then he looked back at me and shook his head. "Azrael did."

My head tilted to the side. "Azrael has connections at Claymore?"

"Sloan, Azrael *is* Claymore," Warren said.

My mouth fell open. "What?"

Nathan leaned his shoulder against mine. "I was right about him hiding something from us. The name on his driver's license is Damon Claymore."

My brain was suffering from information whiplash. I gripped the sides of my skull. "You're joking."

Nathan shook his head. "Nope."

I pointed at my boyfriend. "You didn't know?"

He shook his head. "I've heard the name for years, but never met the man."

I looked around the helicopter. "Well, where is he now?"

Warren shrugged. "We have no idea."

Nathan looked at me. "He took off last night when I got the call from Sheriff Davis saying you'd been visited by a lawyer named Tuinstra," he said. "What the heck was that about? Your dad said he sent a lawyer, a woman—"

I held up a hand to save his breath. "Tuinstra was Ysha," I said. "Taiya's father."

Nathan's head snapped back. "No shit? I assumed Ysha was a chick like Abigail."

"Nope," I told them. "He's a lawyer, and he showed up to see me at the jail tonight."

Nathan sat back in his seat, bewildered. "Az must've known, but he didn't tell us."

"He just left and told us to carry out the plan without him," Warren said. "What did the lawyer want?"

"To gloat, I think," I answered. "The only good thing about his visit is I now know why I was arrested."

Warren nodded. "We found out too."

"About the video?"

"Yeah," Nathan said. "Care to explain?"

I shrugged my shoulders. "I wish I could. All I know is Abigail once told me she has the ability to make people do things without them remembering it. That was her argument for not telling me who my father was."

Warren let out a deep sigh. "If I didn't know you so well, I'd never believe a word of this."

"I fear a jury will feel the same way," Nathan said.

Refusing to break down in tears yet again that day, I looked out the side of the helicopter and watched the red and blue flashing lights getting smaller and smaller in the distance. The pilot said something to Warren about positioning and rally points and he leaned toward the cockpit to talk to them.

Nathan nudged me with his arm. "I told you I wouldn't let them have you. Sorry it took me so damn long to keep my word."

"I still can't believe you did it," I said. "I was honestly beginning to wonder if I would ever see you again."

He rolled his eyes. "Well, next time just summon me. Or hell, call me on the phone. Don't go and get yourself arrested by the FBI in hopes that I'll stage a rescue. Geez."

I laughed for the first time in days. "I missed you. I've been a wreck since you left."

He patted his flat stomach. "I was so upset I couldn't even eat Skittles."

The tension eased in my neck and shoulders. I looked out over the dark mountains, barely lit by moonlight. "Where are we going?"

Nathan shook his head. "I actually have no idea."

Sometime during the flight, I'd fallen asleep with my head against the vibrating wall of the helicopter. I woke up to Warren squeezing my shoulder. He turned the knob on my headphones as my eyes fluttered open. "We're landing," he said.

It was still dark out. I looked at his watch. I'd been asleep for over an hour which was pretty impressive considering helicopters are probably ranked among the worst places to take a nap.

The pilot looked back over her shoulder. "A car is waiting on the ground to take you to your next destination."

"You're not coming with us?" I asked.

The co-pilot shook his head. "No, ma'am. We have orders to return to headquarters."

"We appreciate the safe ride," Warren said to them.

They both nodded. "Our pleasure," the man replied.

When the chopper was safely on the ground, Warren, Nathan, and I unbuckled our harnesses and thanked the pilots one more time. Another soldier in full uniform with green night vision glasses on, approached the side to help us out.

Warren grabbed him by the arm. "Enzo?"

The man smiled and nodded his head. He motioned back toward the black SUV that was waiting across the field. We all slowly jogged across the grass and out of the screaming wind from the propeller blades.

"Good to see you again, Parish," the soldier said to Warren.

The two shook hands. Warren pointed to me and Nathan. "This is Detective McNamara and my girlfriend, Sloan." Warren looked at us. "Enzo and I did field training together when I first went to work at Claymore."

Enzo's face was curious. "So I guess the secret is out now?"

Warren crossed his arms. "About our boss being my dad? Yeah, you can say that. You knew?"

Enzo nodded. "I've worked for Azrael almost since the beginning."

"Of time?" Nathan asked.

I snickered.

Enzo apparently didn't get the joke. "For a little over ten years, ma'am."

Nathan was still chuckling.

"What's the plan, Enzo?" Warren asked.

"I'll be taking you to the compound," he said.

"Is it close?" I asked.

He nodded, opening up the back door of a black SUV. "Thirty miles or so."

I grimaced. "Can we stop and use the bathroom?"

"I'm sorry, ma'am. My orders are to not stop till we reach the compound," he said.

We were in the middle of nowhere. Nathan jerked his thumb toward the tree line. "You can go squat in the woods."

"Ew. No," I answered.

"Thirty miles," Warren said. "Could be an hour before we get there."

My mouth dropped open. "I *cannot* pee outside."

Nathan smirked. "Of course you can. It's not that hard."

"Maybe not for you," I said.

"Come on. You're a mountain girl. It's in your blood," he said.

"That's"—I wanted to say 'sexist', but that wasn't the right term —"*regionalistic*! Stop assuming things about me because I live in Asheville. I don't know how to shoot and I can't pee in the woods!"

Nathan doubled over laughing. Warren and Enzo laughed too.

"Besides, I'm from Florida, remember?" I asked with my hands on my hips.

"So you're gonna hold it?" Warren asked.

"Yes." I turned toward the SUV. "No. Damn it!"

"Would you like a flashlight?" Enzo asked.

My bottom lip poked out. "Please."

Enzo reached into the front of the SUV and came out with a flashlight as long as my arm. "Here you are, ma'am."

"Come on," Warren said, offering me his hand.

"Dude, be sure to check for bears," Nathan said.

I glared back at him. "I hate you."

He just grinned.

"Don't worry ma'am," Enzo called after us. "We haven't seen any bears around here in almost two years!"

Warren and I walked through the tall, dead grass. "If that kid calls me 'ma'am' one more time, I'll beat him with his giant flashlight."

Warren grinned down at me. "Aw, did prison make you tough?"

I stuck my tongue out at him.

When we reached the tree line, he scoured the area with the flashlight. "The area is clear, just don't fall down the hill," he said.

"Did you check for snakes?" I asked as he handed me the flashlight and walked past me toward the car.

"It's December, babe," he said.

"That doesn't answer my question, Warren!"

"Yes, it does. Hurry up. It's cold!"

I shined the flashlight over the area and decided to go far enough downhill so my butt would be hidden if anyone tried to peek. I laid the flashlight in the grass and pushed down my prison pants. Squatting with my backside against the hill, so I wouldn't roll backward, I waited. And waited. And waited.

"Sloan!" Nathan yelled. "You're gonna get frostbite on your ass if you don't hurry!"

I ignored him, but my butt *was* numb, hanging out in the cold. Finally relief came, soaking my white socks as it ran down the hill. I screamed.

I heard feet pounding in my direction. "No! No! Stop! I'm fine!" I yelled before they reached me.

"What's going on?" Warren asked.

"Are you all right, ma'am?" Enzo called.

"Ugh." I yanked up my pants. "I'm fine."

"What happened?" I could almost hear Nathan trying not to smile.

I pulled off my wet socks, exposing my toes to the icy air. "I hate my life."

Thankfully, by some miracle, my pants were completely dry. I prayed for forgiveness for littering and left my socks in the grass before trudging back to my waiting companions. "We can go now," I said, walking past them.

"You OK?" Warren's tone was more curious than concerned.

"Yes. Let's just go." I opened the back door and climbed inside.

Warren followed me. Enzo got behind the wheel and Nathan got in the passenger's seat in front of me.

Before he closed the door, Warren dropped my backpack on the floorboard and his eyes fell on my bare feet. "Sloan, where are your socks?"

I balanced my elbow on the armrest and rested my chin into my hand. "I don't want to talk about it."

Chuckling, he closed his door and the interior light flickered out.

We drove for a while on small, narrow roads that aggravated a case of car sickness I didn't know I had. Maybe it was yet another pregnancy side-effect. We passed a feed store and The Honey Pot Cafe, and then there was nothing but trees for miles and miles. At some point, I began whistling the theme song to *Deliverance*, and Nathan told me to knock it off.

A road sign caught my attention. "Did that sign say 'Calfkiller Highway'?"

"It's named after Calfkiller River," Enzo answered.

I sucked in a deep breath and blew it out slowly. "Oh, boy."

"Where are we?" Nathan asked.

"Halifax County, sir. Between Raleigh and the coast, about ninety miles away from headquarters."

Warren stretched his arm across the back of my seat. "Claymore uses this place for escape and evasion training."

"You've been here before?" I asked.

He nodded.

"And sometimes we get to deer hunt," Enzo added.

After what felt like an eternity, he turned left onto a dirt road that was blocked by a metal chain strung between two wooden posts. "Sit tight," Enzo told us as he got out of the car. In front of the headlights, he used a key to open a single padlock.

"Very secure. That will keep demons and the FBI out for sure," I said, looking at Warren with wide eyes.

He grinned.

The truck bounced over a washed out dirt road for another mile before lights speckled the darkness. He rolled to a stop in front of a handful of pull-behind campers that looked like set props from a National Lampoon movie. They were arranged in a semicircle with a fire pit in the middle.

I looked around. "This is it?"

"Yes, ma'am," Enzo answered. "You'll want to watch your step getting out."

When my feet hit the ground, they sank down into a deep hole filled with squishy, cold mud. I groaned and pulled my feet up. The mud sucked off one of my flip flops. "Nathan, help," I whined.

He shook his head. "I'm not touching those shoes."

I whimpered.

Enzo grabbed my arm and helped me onto solid ground. "Thank you, Enzo."

He tipped the bill of his camouflage hat. "My pleasure, ma'am."

"Sloan," I corrected him as Warren walked up beside me. "Just call me Sloan."

"Yes, ma'am."

I rolled my eyes.

"Detective McNamara," Enzo said. He held up a set of keys then tossed them to Nathan. "You and I can bunk together in the gold Jayco."

Nathan nodded and started off across the yard.

"Come on," Enzo said to us. "I'll show you two to your home away from home."

Three wobbly and rusted steps led the three of us inside the largest soup can I had ever seen. The carpet had been stripped out, leaving only the sub flooring. There was half of a kitchen, a coffee pot, no television, two twin bunk beds in the corner, and lawn chairs instead of furniture. I put my hands on my hips. "I feel like Mother Mary in the stable in Bethlehem."

Warren laughed.

Enzo knelt down and turned on an electric heater that was on the floor. "I don't recommend running this all night for safety reasons, but you shouldn't need it once you go to bed. There are sub-zero sleeping bags in the closet with hand warmers you can toss in the bottom."

"Is there food?" I asked, moving closer to the heater.

He stood and pointed to the cabinets. "MREs and bottled waters. There's also a small amount of hot water if you want to take a shower, but I suggest you make it fast."

"Do you know when we might see Azrael?" Warren asked.

Enzo shook his head. "No, sir. He didn't give us an ETA." He held up a finger. "But he did have me pack a rifle case for you. It's in the back of the car."

Warren nodded. "I'll come grab it." He kissed my forehead. "I'll be right back."

As the two of them left the camper, they passed Nathan at the bottom of the steps. He held up the backpack he'd brought for me. "I forgot to give Sloan her bag."

Warren tipped his head up in approval, then followed Enzo into the darkness.

Nathan came inside and looked around. He pointed to the lawn chairs. "At least you have furniture. We've got hard-side coolers to sit on in our camper."

"It's better than a jail cell," I said. "I wouldn't have made it through another night in there. Thank you."

His eyes fell to my feet. "I tried so hard to get you out of there, Sloan."

I bent to look him in the eye. "You did get me out."

He shook his head. "Not fast enough. I know firsthand what that place does to you."

"It's over now."

Nathan opened his mouth to speak, but he didn't. Instead, he handed me the backpack. "There's a toothbrush in there. I know you can't stand not being able to brush your teeth."

He remembered my freaking toothbrush.

The simple thoughtfulness was enough to bring me to tears again.

I wanted to hug him, but I couldn't. Swallowing back every emotion inside me, I pulled the backpack into my arms instead of the man holding it. "Thank you, Nathan," I whispered.

Neither of us spoke for several moments, then finally, he put his hand under my chin and tugged at my lower lip with this thumb. His eyes were fixed on my mouth. "I need you to do something for me," he said quietly.

I blinked up at him.

His lips spread into a thin smile as he met my eyes and lowered his voice to a whisper. "Please go wash your feet."

I laughed and wiped my eyes on the back of my sleeve...his

sleeve. "Shut up, Nathan."

He smiled. "I've actually missed hearing you say that." He stared at me for a second, then he turned toward the door. "Good-night, Sloan."

He opened the door, just as Warren stepped up on the first step outside.

Nathan stood back out of his way to let him in. Warren came inside and put the big, black rifle case down on the counter.

Nathan nodded toward the door. "I'll see you guys in the morning if none of us freeze to death."

"Hey," Warren called out as Nathan stepped toward the door. He reached out his hand to him. "Thank you, Nate. I couldn't have done this without you."

Nathan nodded and gripped Warren's hand. He smiled over at me. "Of course."

When he was gone, Warren came to face me. His eyes were bloodshot with heavy, dark bags under them. "Come here," he said, pulling me into his arms.

All at once, I fell apart. My knees went weak as I cried, but Warren held me tight against him. He stroked my hair as he eased me over to the bed.

I was a mess for a lot of reasons. Adrenaline was leaving my bloodstream, and a slight case of shock was settling in. I hadn't really slept in...I literally couldn't remember when. On top of it all, I was pregnant—enough said.

But I was mostly a mess because I was tired of being dishonest. Dishonest with Nathan, dishonest with Warren, and dishonest with myself.

Tears streamed down my cheeks as I looked at my baby's father. "I need to talk to you."

He brushed my tears away with his thumbs and studied my face carefully. "Not tonight." There was a perceptive resolve in the way he studied my face. "It's nothing that can't wait till tomorrow."

CHAPTER TWENTY-FOUR

The sound of a car's engine woke me from a deep sleep the next morning. I sat up and looked around the dingy camper. Warren was gone, and I was alone. I shimmied out of the cozy sleeping bag and into the brisk mountain air. Male voices were outside. One of them was Azrael. I hurried to the bathroom to brush my teeth, then slipped on the sneakers Nathan had packed for me. My flip-flops were in the trashcan.

A fist pounded against the front door. "Anybody hungry in there?" Azrael called out.

I ran across the camper and threw the door open, only touching the top step before jumping into his unsuspecting arms. He laughed as he set me on the ground. He pulled back and tucked my tangled hair behind my ears. "You gave us quite a scare, young lady."

I hugged him around the neck again. "You saved me."

He shook his head. "My son and McNamara saved you. And Taiya. I only provided the ride." He squeezed my shoulders. "And the FBI won't find you till we're ready for them to."

"How can you be sure?" I asked.

He winked a black eye at me. "You don't walk the Earth for thousands of years without picking up a few tricks along the way."

I laughed and looked around for Warren. I spotted Nathan instead sitting at a picnic table with a plate of eggs and bacon and a large blue thermos. "Where's Warren?" I asked.

Azrael pointed to the trees in the distance. "He's out with some of my guys securing the perimeter. Did you sleep well?"

I smiled. "Your son is home. Of course I did."

Several men in multi-cam were carrying boxes, bags, and military-grade weapons from two more SUVs, one of which was pulling a large white trailer.

I put my hands on my hips. "I still can't believe you own Claymore."

Azrael shrugged. "We all have our secrets." He gestured toward the table. "Let's get you some breakfast, and then I'll answer all the questions you want. I'm sure you have lots of them."

"You bet I do," I said with a warning tone.

"Good morning," Nathan said as we approached.

I smiled and sat beside him. "Morning."

"Morning," he said, handing me a plate from a box on the ground near his feet.

Azrael sat across the table from us.

"Who made breakfast?" I asked, lifting the lid off of a cast-iron skillet.

Nathan glanced toward one of the other campers. "Enzo."

"God bless him," I said as I piled eggs onto my plate.

"I trust you were in good hands last night," Azrael said.

I nodded. "Your team was great."

"They really were," Nathan agreed.

Behind us, the loud rumble of a motor fired up. I turned in time to see one of the soldiers driving one of the biggest, camouflaged ATV's I'd ever seen. I counted four, maybe six, seats. Another ATV followed behind that one. I chuckled. "I didn't know they made ATV buses."

"We call them HOKs," Azrael said. "High-occupancy karts."

I used a piece of bacon as a pointing device, motioning all around the camp. "I don't understand though. How is it you came to own one of the biggest private military companies in the world?"

He sprinkled a ton of salt onto his food, far more than any human heart should have to suffer. "I started it when Warren joined the Marine Corps. I had to find some way to keep up with him. Turned out to be a profitable idea."

"But how did he not know his own boss?" I asked.

"Claymore has thirty thousand employees and contractors spread over four continents. I'm everyone's boss and no one's." He pointed to the guys who were still carrying stuff in and out of the campers. "These guys are part of a core group I work with directly, but they're an exclusive bunch. Most people who work for my company never see my face."

I thought back over everything Warren had told me about the company he had worked for in various capacities since his release from active duty with the Marines. I found it hard to believe that after three years there would be so much disconnect between him and the company's owner. Then it occurred to me the disconnect was certainly intentional. Azrael would have made sure to stay off Warren's radar, all while calling the shots like an intergalactic puppeteer.

My mouth dropped open. "Just after we met, Claymore offered him a lucrative transfer to the West Coast." My fork clanged against the plate when I dropped it. "That was you!"

Nathan scooted closer to me on the bench.

Azrael stared at me without speaking.

Bits of information were snapping together in my mind like loose pieces of a jigsaw puzzle. "*You* offered him the job in Oregon, didn't you?"

He nodded slowly.

I gasped and covered my mouth. "You tried to split us up!"

Nathan scooted even closer to me. "He did split you up," he mumbled.

"Wait." I looked at Nathan. "What do you mean?"

Nathan pressed his lips together, refusing to answer.

I shot my gaze back at Azrael, who was holding up his hands in defense. "Sloan, you must understand how detrimental this child has the potential to be for all of us."

"What did you do?" I demanded.

He hesitated.

I threw a slice of bacon at him. "Azrael!"

"The US government has contracted my company for years to handle situations all around the globe, so I have plenty of friends at the Pentagon—"

I jumped up from the table. Nathan's hands grabbed me to hold me back.

"You had him recalled to the Marines!" I yelled.

Azrael stood and stepped away from the table—away from me. "I may have suggested he would be able to deal with their terrorist problem in Palestine. I knew Warren would be able to find the body of Shallah."

I lunged at him over the table, but Nathan stood and held me tight. "I'm going to kill you!" I screamed.

"I told you she'd take this news well," Nathan said sarcastically over my shoulder.

A couple of Azrael's soldiers had cautiously started in our direction. Azrael held up a hand to stop them.

"Nathan, let me go," I ordered.

He didn't. "Sloan, you're going to hurt yourself. Consider the possible outcomes of this. He's the Angel of Death."

"Yeah? Well, so am I!"

"Dude, she has a point," Nathan told him.

Azrael still kept his distance. "Hate me if you will, but I would do it again if it might save us from this fate. Surely, you must be feeling the same way."

I pointed an angry finger at him. "I would never wish Warren away from me."

"Perhaps not, but your world and mine are now at stake," he said.

Taking a deep breath, I tried to relax but it was hard. I wanted to claw his angel eyeballs out.

Nathan shook my shoulders. "Come on," he said. "Let's sit back down like civilized people and talk this out."

I huffed, but I sat down.

Cautiously, Azrael returned to his seat as well. "I'm sorry I deceived you, Sloan."

Refusing to look at him or accept his apology, I stabbed at my eggs with the fork.

Nathan squeezed my shoulder. "It's water under the bridge now. We've got bigger things to worry about."

Azrael wiped his mouth on a napkin and leaned his elbows on the table. "Sloan, are you aware of who you met during your time in jail?"

"Ysha. How did you know who the lawyer was?" I asked.

He smiled. "The name, Abner. It literally means *the father of life and light*."

"Seriously?" I asked.

"Seriously."

"Was it Abner you went after?" Nathan asked.

Azrael drummed his fingers on the tabletop. "Not exactly."

"Then what were you doing while I was rotting in prison?" I asked.

Azrael frowned. "You're so dramatic."

Nathan's eyebrow peaked. "Still a valid question."

"I was preparing," Azrael said, "to lead Ysha here."

My head snapped back with shock. "You were doing what?"

His smile was wild and mildly frightening. "It's the perfect plan, really. Here we have the upper hand. There are no witnesses, no risk for human casualties, and we'll be ready."

I laughed toward the sky. "You're insane! What if Ysha shows up with all his friends?" I asked.

He rubbed his palms together. "I'm counting on it."

"Even if those friends include Phenex and Kasyade?" I pointed between me and Nathan. "We took on just one of that trio by ourselves not too long ago. It didn't go well."

He jabbed his thumb into the center of his chest. "You underestimate me, my dear. And you certainly underestimate yourself."

I cackled in mockery. "I think I've done an excellent job at proving exactly what my estimation is lately. I've spent the past twenty-four hours barely containing my bladder because I was locked inside a building with petty thieves and wife beaters!"

He stood and leaned on his arms toward me. "You chose those bars, Sloan Jordan. You weren't locked inside anywhere." His words stung almost as much as the look in his eyes.

Nathan held his hand up. "Whoa, whoa, whoa. That's over the line, Az."

Azrael smacked Nathan's hand away. "I wasn't talking to you, McNamara."

What the...

I jumped out of my seat and walked around the table till I was in the angel's face. "I don't know where you get off, but while you were out playing *Marco Polo* with the *father of life and light"*—I used air quotes for dramatic effect—"*McNamara* was busy protecting the life of your precious granddaughter!"

"She's not his responsibility!" he roared, taking a step toward me. "You failed her, and you failed yourself!"

My hands were shaking I was so angry. I turned to stalk back to the camper.

"That's right. Run away, Sloan," he taunted after me. "You were right when you said you weren't capable of saving anyone. You aren't capable of—"

I whirled around to lunge in his direction, but he was knocked sideways and backward off his feet by an invisible force radiating from my fingertips. The Archangel of Death crash-landed into the center of the picnic table sending the skillet, eggs, and bacon flying in every direction.

I froze, my hands in mid-air.

Nathan's mouth was gaping.

Azrael started laughing and clapping his hands wildly in the air.

"Holy shit," Nathan muttered.

The angel sat up. He was still clapping. "Congratulations."

I dropped my hands. "What is wrong with you?" I shrieked.

He pushed himself up, walked over, and put his hands on my shoulders. "You must stop doubting yourself, Sloan. You are more powerful than you know."

"You are a madman!" My fists were balled at my sides.

He leaned toward me, smiling. "You will be ready," he said. "I promise."

I shook my head. "You have egg in your hair. I can't even take you seriously right now."

Nathan was still mesmerized at the table. His eyes fixed on me, he pointed at Azrael. "I can't believe you did that."

"I can't either," I said, reclaiming my seat beside him.

Azrael shook the scrambled eggs out of his black hair. "It really isn't complicated." He looked at me and pointed to his head. "Did I get all of it?"

I nodded. "Egg free."

"Not complicated?" Nathan asked. "How do you figure?"

He sat across from us and motioned between himself and Nathan. "What's between us right now?" he asked.

"Uh, the table," Nathan answered.

Azrael put his hands on the table. "Correct. What else?"

Nathan looked curiously around. "I dunno. About three feet of space."

Azrael didn't laugh. "Yes, and that space is made of millions of particles." He counted on his fingers. "Oxygen, nitrogen—"

I raised my hand. "Carbon dioxide."

Azrael nodded. "Yeah. Methane and argon. What else?"

Nathan and I looked at each other, confused.

"What about dust?" Azrael asked.

"Pollen?" Nathan asked.

I looked at him. "Not at this time of year."

He chuckled.

"Close your eyes," Azrael said. "Breathe in."

We obeyed.

"What do you smell?"

"Pine," I answered.

At the same time Nathan said, "Smoke."

"All those things are particles that make up what you perceive as the empty three feet of space between us," Azrael said.

Nathan raised an eyebrow. "OK."

"If I were to stand and push this table, you'd feel it, right?" Azrael asked him.

Nathan cringed. "Probably more than I'd want to. Please don't throw the table at me."

Azrael smiled. "What if I push the air? Would you feel that?"

Nathan smirked. "Sure. If *you* did it."

Azrael looked surprised. "Really? Then what's the purpose of fanning your face when it's hot outside? Your hand creates force against the air, causing those particles to move."

I held my hands up. "Hey, that's true."

Nathan looked impressed.

"What Sloan did to me is no different, except she—instead of the hand—is the force against the air."

A wide grin spread across my face. "That's badass."

Nathan laughed, but he nodded in agreement. "That's definitely badass."

I leaned my elbow on the table. "So why did you say all those mean things?"

"A few reasons," he said. "Adrenaline makes it easier, as I told you the day I shot the gun in your kitchen."

I scowled at him.

"And you were visualizing exactly what you wanted to do to me if you could get your hands on me fast enough, correct?"

"I wanted to backhand you across the face," I admitted.

He pointed at me. "And by taunting you, I made you specifically think about accessing your power the way I showed you."

I nodded, impressed with his teaching skills. "That's all correct."

Nathan winked at me. "I feel safer already."

"Ha." I smirked and rolled my eyes. "It's all well and good that I can throw one angel across a table, sure. But we'll need a lot stronger supernatural power than just me."

Azrael got up from the table. "Speaking of strong supernatural powers, I need to find my son. I suggest the two of you get some rest."

When he was gone, Nathan looked over at me. "What do you think he meant by leading the demons here? How will he do that?"

I thought about it. "Well, Samael said the whole spirit world can see me now. He made it sound like this baby is some kind of supernatural homing beacon."

He picked up his coffee cup. "I don't think so. If it were that easy, Azrael wouldn't have had people out looking."

I shrugged. "I don't know."

Nathan pointed toward the woods in the distance. "You haven't told Warren yet, have you?"

"No."

"Are you going to?" he asked, not meeting my eyes.

I shoved my hands into the front pocket of Nathan's sweatshirt I was still wearing. "Of course. I don't want to lie to him."

He shook his head. "I don't either, but who's going to do it?"

"Want to flip for it?" I asked, smiling as I nudged him with my elbow.

He laughed out loud. "Hell no. I already died once because of you. It's your turn."

While Nathan took a nap, I sat at the table and practiced picking up and putting down the iron skillet without touching it. After an hour, I was able to lift it into the air, move it all the way to the steps of the camper, and bring it back to the table without so much as a wobble.

"Very good, my little protégé," Azrael said from behind me.

Startled, I dropped the pan, and it crashed onto the metal camper steps.

"Geez, you scared me!" I spun around to see him clapping.

"My apologies," he said.

The camper door flew open, and a red-eyed, squinting Nathan stumbled outside. "What's going on?"

"Sloan's throwing pots and pans," Azrael said.

"Nathan, look!" I held my hand up, and the pan flew into it with so much force it stung my palm.

He nodded. "Nice. I'm going back to bed."

"Hold up," Azrael called out. "We have a camp-wide meeting in five."

Nathan groaned and disappeared back into the camper.

"Mortals need their sleep," I said, cutting my eyes up at Azrael.

Azrael's finger pointed up at the sky. "No time for sleep. Do you hear that?"

The sky was gray with clouds, and there was a low rumble in the distance. "A storm's coming?"

He walked past the table toward the campfire. "You could say that."

I got up and followed him. "What's going on?"

"That isn't thunder." He put more logs into the fire pit. "That's the sound of company arriving early."

I listened again. "Are you sure?"

"One of these days you're going to trust me." He clenched a fist, and when he opened it, a crackling flame danced in his hand. He knelt down and lit a small pile of kindling on fire.

"Whoa," I whispered.

He dusted his hands off as he stood.

"Where's Warren?" I asked.

His head tilted toward the field beyond the campers. I looked out to see three of Azrael's soldiers and Warren carrying shovels and duffel bags toward us. Nathan appeared at my side, yawning and rubbing his eyes. "What's going on?" he asked.

I turned my palms up. "I don't know. Azrael says the thunder isn't really thunder."

Nathan sighed and rolled his eyes. "Of course it's not." He looked at Azrael. "What now?"

"Nate, I need you to grab chairs out of the blue camper, and Sloan, bring the picnic table over here by the fire so no one freezes to death," Azrael said.

"Are you joking?" I asked.

He shook his head. "It's twenty-four degrees out here."

I put my hands on my hips "Not what I meant."

"I know what you meant. Bring it over here."

"Az, that thing's made out of concrete," I said.

He shrugged. "And?"

Nathan looked at me and laughed as he folded his arms over his chest. "I want to see this."

Blowing out a sigh that puffed out my cheeks, I turned toward the table and raised my hands. My fingers strained and trembled as I tried to move the table. It wouldn't budge.

"Close your eyes," Azrael said behind me.

My index finger whirled in his direction. "I swear to God I'll kill you if you fire a gun near my head."

The Angel of Death chuckled. "Close your eyes."

I closed my eyes and relaxed my shoulders.

"Now lift it," he said.

I could feel the weight of the table as it lifted off the ground.

"Good," Azrael said. "Now open your eyes so you don't clunk anyone over the head with that thing."

When I looked again, the table was floating inches off the ground. I pulled it toward me...and it came. Nathan was slowly clapping beside me as I turned, moving the table around us toward the fire. Gently, I set it down on the grass.

"When the hell did you learn how to do that?" Warren asked, walking up on the other side of the fire pit with his mouth gaping in awe.

I smiled as I sat down at the newly positioned table. "Lots has changed since you've been gone, Mr. Parish."

He straddled the bench next to me and leaned in for a kiss. "I like it."

Azrael gripped Enzo's shoulder when he approached. "Get the map for me."

Enzo nodded and carried his load toward his camper.

Nathan unfolded a few metal chairs around the table, then sat on the other side of Warren. The other soldiers unloaded their equipment before joining us.

I leaned toward Warren and lowered my voice. "I feel like there were more army dudes this morning."

"There are more of them," Azrael answered. "And they're not *army dudes.*"

I forgot he could hear everything.

"Some of his guys are already in position around the perimeter," Warren said, swinging his leg over the bench and leaning his elbows on the table.

Enzo walked over and spread a large topographical map on the table, then went and stood beside his boss.

Azrael used his finger to draw an imaginary circle around the map. "This is where we are. Approximately four hundred untouched acres with one road in and one road out. I've got five armed guys watching the perimeter, and we've got cameras posted here, here, here, and here." His finger moved to four different spots around the circle, then he looked out over the mountains on the horizon. "They're coming in from the east."

"How do you know that?" Nathan asked.

"The thunder," Enzo answered. "It's in the east."

Nathan's brow crumpled in confusion. "What?"

"When spirits cross into this world, it creates an effect similar to the sonic boom of an object breaking the sound barrier." Enzo's answer was so nonchalant he might as well have been explaining the process of making our morning scrambled eggs. "To us, it sounds like thunder."

Warren's head fell to the side, baffled. "How the hell do you know that?"

Enzo seemed equally puzzled. "You don't?"

Azrael held up a hand to silence them. "I'm sorry. I believe proper introductions are in order." He pointed around our group. "This is Enzo, Special Operations Director of SF-12."

I turned my ear toward him and raised an eyebrow. "SF-12?"

Enzo turned toward me. "SF-12 is a covert division of Claymore, kept completely off the corporate books and out of the main organizational structure."

"Like *Ocean's Eleven*?" I asked with a grin.

"Twelve, Sloan," Nathan corrected me.

I giggled but forced a straight face. "It has a nice ring to it, *Azrael's Twelve*."

Azrael wasn't amused, as usual. "SF-12 works directly with me. Most of them, like Enzo, have been with me almost since the company's inception."

"They know what you are?" Nathan asked.

"Yes," Azrael said.

Enzo looked at me. "And we know what you are."

My heart stopped when I met his gaze. Enzo knew what I was because he could see me. He could *really* see me. And he had one blue eye...and one green.

CHAPTER TWENTY-FIVE

Had I not been sitting, I would've fallen down. I gripped the side of the table and stared at the concrete while my mind raced in a thousand different directions. Only one other person I'd ever met had eyes like Enzo's, and she'd been the first person ever to call me an angel.

Kayleigh.

"What is it?" Warren asked, concerned.

I looked at Azrael. "Enzo is like Warren's mother."

Azrael nodded.

"It's the eyes?" I asked him.

"It's the eyes," he said.

Warren rubbed his forehead, squinting in confusion. "My mother?"

I gripped Warren's arm. "Enzo can see angels. So could your mother. It's called a discerning power."

Nathan glanced around. "Will someone please explain what they're talking about?"

I beckoned Enzo to come closer, then I pointed to Nathan. "Nathan, look at him."

Nathan and Enzo stared at each other. "His eyes are blue and green," Nathan said. "That means he can see angels?"

"Yes. And who else has eyes like that?" I asked.

His mouth fell open a bit. "Kayleigh Neeland."

"Who?" Azrael asked.

I raked my fingernails back through my hair. "When Nathan and I first met, I helped him rescue a little girl named Kayleigh. She's five. She told me I was an angel." I chuckled in awe. "I thought she was being metaphorical."

Azrael smiled. Even he looked impressed.

"So all of *Azrael's Twelve* can see angels?" Nathan asked.

Azrael rolled his eyes. "SF-12," he corrected. "And no. Several of them can." He pointed around the circle. "Enzo and Kane can."

Kane pulled off his hat and glasses. His eyes were blue and green as well.

"Cooper and Lex cannot, but they've seen enough to know what we're up against," Azrael said, gesturing toward the two men. "A couple of the guys in the field can see as well."

"And NAG, sir," Enzo said.

Azrael nodded. "Oh yes. NAG, your pilot last night. She can see you as well."

I blinked. "Her name is NAG?"

Enzo chuckled. "I believe her real name is Mandi. NAG is her call sign. It means *Not A Guy*."

The rest of us laughed.

Warren rubbed his palms together. "I'm feeling much better about our odds now." He looked up at Azrael. "Finish explaining the plan."

Azrael smiled and leaned back over the map. "By my estimation, Ysha and his crew will arrive on foot maybe this time tomorrow."

I raised my hand. "His crew?"

"I hope Phenex and Kasyade will be with him, but I'm sure he'll bring others as well."

"Other demons or humans?" Nathan asked.

"Both," Azrael answered.

Enzo crossed his arms. "We've had no sign of Phenex, sir."

"We might still get lucky," Azrael said.

"And by our last count, Ysha travels with two humans, one with sight, and two AOPs, Mihan and The Destroyer," Enzo said.

Warren looked up. "AOPs?"

"Protection, warrior angels," Azrael said.

I looked at Azrael with alarm. "You've mentioned The Destroyer before. You said Samael decides who can cross the spirit line, who must suffer the second death, and who must be turned over to The Destroyer. Are we talking about the same person?"

"The Destroyer is not a person," Enzo said.

I rolled my eyes. "Is it the same *Destroyer*?"

Azrael nodded. "That is correct."

My stomach churned. I held up five fingers. "That's five potential angels, one of which is like the worst tormentor on the planet, and they're all showing up here tomorrow. And we've only got you on our side?"

"And you and Warren."

I groaned. "Oh my god, whatever."

"And Reuel," Enzo added.

Azrael pointed toward the woods. "Reuel, our own AOP, is on the perimeter. Abaddon, The Destroyer, will be his responsibility. Ysha will flank us. He won't come by the road, and we've got every measure possible to slow him down out there," Azrael said.

"Like what?" I asked.

"Snipers, for starters," Azrael answered, looking at Warren.

Nathan turned his palms up in question. "What good will guns do us? When we were in Texas, I emptied a clip into Sloan's demon mom, and I might as well have been pelting her with Cheerios. The bullet holes closed right up."

Enzo spoke first. "The whole group isn't immortal. We can

certainly pick off the humans and have less bullets flying through the air."

I nodded. "And Kasyade was different. Not all of them will heal the way she does." I pointed at Az. "I broke his nose in my kitchen, and then I had to fix it."

"Correct," Azrael said. "Ysha is the only one with the power to heal as Kasyade does. Mihan and Abaddon can be injured."

Kane and Enzo exchanged a glance. "If you can hit them," Kane said.

Warren looked at the two men. "Where's the list of stuff we still need?"

Enzo pulled a small pad from the chest pocket on his camouflage jacket. "Got it."

"Pick up as many packs of tent stakes you can buy. The sharpened metal kind." Warren held his hands about a foot apart. "Maybe twelve to eighteen inches or so."

I looked up at him. "Stakes? They're demons, not vampires."

Warren smiled. "I'm aware. We'll dig a trench, and when the demons step into it, their legs will be impaled on the stakes. It might buy us some time."

"You scare me sometimes," I said.

He nodded. "Good."

"So how do we kill them?" Nathan asked.

There was silence all around the group. Finally, Azrael shook his head. "We don't." Then he turned toward me. "Sloan does."

My head snapped toward him. "Excuse me?"

He leaned against the table. "I told you. The Vitamorte has the power to control life and death." He lowered his voice. "That power is not limited to human life."

My mouth was gaping. "Are you saying I have the power to destroy angels?"

He just stared at me.

I balanced my elbows on the table and dropped my face into my hands.

His hand rested on my shoulder. "You're the only one, Sloan."

Azrael had once told me that my fizzling light ball would work on him if I chose to use it, but I didn't realize it would do more than just separate him from his human form. If he'd kept that information from me to prevent more tears and vomiting, he'd been smart. My stomach felt queasy and my hands trembled.

His hand tightened around the back of my neck. "Look at me."

I looked up into his stern face.

"Remember, you were created for this. Even your enemies know how strong you are. They wouldn't try so hard to break you if they weren't afraid of what you can do." He bent so we were eye to eye. "You're even more powerful than me. Don't you forget it."

I sincerely wished that made me feel better. It didn't.

He lifted my chin. "Faith without doubt isn't faith at all. Just because you don't believe it right now doesn't make it any less true."

And as if adding a cosmic exclamation point at the end of his sentence, another loud boom of thunder shook the mountains in the east.

Before Enzo and Kane left to make a run to the store back near the exit we'd taken off the interstate, I added a few more things to their list including clothes, socks, underwear, and a hair dryer. While they were gone, I retreated to the camper to take a nap, but sleep was elusive. Every time I closed my eyes, all I saw was Ysha's hateful, jeering eyes.

The door creaked open. "You awake?" Warren asked softly.

"Yeah," I replied.

He walked inside, ducking through the doorway. "Did you sleep at all?"

I laughed sarcastically in response.

The dusty old mattress dipped under his weight as he sat down beside me.

"Where have you been?" I asked, rolling onto my back to look at him.

"Digging trenches." He slid his hand over my stomach. "Are you feeling OK?"

I smiled. "I'm good, just tired."

"Can we have that talk now?"

Reluctantly, I held up my hand. "Yeah. Help me up."

Warren pulled me up, and I slid out of the warm sleeping bag. I groaned, slumping forward and balancing my elbows on my knees. "You know how much I love you, right?" I asked.

There was a deep rumble in his throat. "I don't like how this is starting out."

I turned toward him, studied his worried face for a moment, then drew in a deep, brave breath. "Back around Thanksgiving, you know I went to Raleigh for Nathan's sister's burial service, right?"

He nodded.

"Things were really emotional, as you can imagine." My hands started to sweat. "I hadn't told Nathan about the baby—or anyone besides my dad and my doctor, for that matter. Well, after the funeral, he was really upset, and he kissed me, but I stopped it before things went too far and told him I was pregnant."

Warren's Adam's apple bobbed with a strained swallow. He was clenching his jaw. "He kissed you?"

"Yes, but then he told me the whole 'Nathan and Sloan drama' had to end and he needed to put some distance between us," I said.

He relaxed a little. "OK."

I scrunched up my nose. "Well, that didn't exactly happen."

His eyes darkened.

"I started having all these crazy nightmares, like demons trying to choke me in my sleep and stuff."

"You told me about that."

"He kind of moved into the guest bedroom after that." I quickly held up my hands. "But absolutely nothing happened."

The muscle in his jaw was working again. "OK."

"Like a week later was the car wreck and from that night on, Azrael lived with us. Then Taiya moved in."

"Did Nathan leave when Azrael showed up?" he asked.

My head fell to the side. "You know Nathan better than that. He doesn't completely trust Az."

Warren crossed his arms. "That's not why he stayed, and you know it."

My shoulders dropped. "I know, but that's beside the point."

"What is the point?"

"As long as Azrael was with us, I didn't have any of the crazy dreams, but one night he went out looking for Ysha and Phenex, and I had another nightmare." I hesitated, then cut my eyes up at him. "I won't lie to you, all right?"

He held his breath. "All right."

"I dreamed I was crying and Nathan came into my room to console me." I took a deep breath. "Things got really physical, but then he started choking me to death, and I started clawing at him to get him to stop. When he wouldn't, I used my power to kill him."

He cocked an eyebrow. "So, you dream cheated on me?"

I rubbed my palms on my jeans. "Well, I woke up screaming with Nathan and Taiya both shaking me. He had been asleep in the guest room the whole time." I touched my neck. "But I had bruises on my throat, and he had really bad claw marks down his chest." For the safety of everyone, I left out the part about my lips being bruised from Nathan's kisses.

He was staring at me, his expression caught somewhere between hostile and confused.

I held my hands out. "I really don't know what happened that night, Warren. But the next day, Nathan moved out because he didn't want to take any more chances."

He frowned. "He moved out because he's in love with you and couldn't take it anymore."

"Well…"

He rubbed his palm down his face. "That's it?"

I bit down on the insides of my lips till I tasted blood.

He groaned and cursed under his breath. "What else?"

"When he told me he was leaving…" I sucked in a deep breath and closed my eyes. "We kissed. I was fully awake and knew exactly what I was doing, and I kissed him."

Warren's head dropped. He didn't look up at me. "You kissed him?"

"Yes."

He was silent for a long time, staring at his boots. Finally, he cut his eyes up at me. "I want the truth, Sloan. No lies to protect me. No lies to protect him."

Hesitantly, I nodded.

He stared at me. "Are you in love with him?"

My heart was pounding so hard I felt dizzy. "Yes."

He cringed and pinched the bridge of his nose. "Are you still in love with me?"

I gripped his arm. "Yes."

He pushed himself up and walked over to the counter where his guns were spread out and ready to be used. He gripped the tabletop and hung his head. His knuckles went white, and the sound of splintering wood crackled around the camper.

I struggled to my feet and cautiously walked over to him. Tears were building in my eyes as I reached to touch his arm. He flinched away from me. "Please talk to me," I begged.

He released the counter and folded his hands over the top of his head.

I placed my hands on his sides. "I *choose* you. I *choose* us."

He blew out a deep breath slowly and turned around. He stared down at me, his black eyes smoldering like hot coals. I had never felt so small standing in front of him.

Just then, a fist pounded against the door. "Hey, guys! Enzo and Kane are back from the store and they brought food!" Nathan shouted.

Warren's eyes widened and shot toward the door. He turned, and before I could grab him, he was across the room and exploding through the door. All I could do was scream.

"Nathan, run!"

Sheer panic flashed across Nathan's face before Warren rained down on top of him, tackling him onto the ground. I ran to the door in time to see Warren's fist come up and slam onto Nathan's face. My feet couldn't get down the steps fast enough, and before I jumped onto Warren's back, he got at least three solid punches into Nathan's skull.

"Warren, stop!" I shrieked as I pulled on his shoulders with all the strength I had.

My hands slipped, and I stumbled backward till I landed on my butt in the grass behind them. I pushed myself up on my elbows to see Warren's fist drop to his side. He rolled off Nathan onto the ground and sat there, fuming. Nathan was too stunned to move, or maybe he was unconscious, I wasn't sure.

Laughter was coming from the campfire. I looked over to see it was Azrael, standing and holding Enzo back to prevent him from intervening.

Covered in dirt and grass stains, I pushed myself up and crawled over to Nathan. He was panting with wide eyes and sweat rolling off his forehead. The side of his jaw was bent at an awkward angle and starting to swell. His cheek bone was bright red, and blood poured from his nose.

Warren sat motionless except for massaging his knuckles.

"I think your jaw is broken," I said. "Maybe your cheek bone too."

"He's lucky it wasn't his neck," Warren grumbled.

I leaned over top of Nathan and pressed my hands to both sides of his lower jaw till I felt the bones grind and snap back into place. He winced with pain and swore as tears leaked from the corners of his eyes. When it was over, he opened his mouth and moved his jaw around but didn't dare speak. I gave him a hand and helped him up till he was sitting.

Warren pulled his knees up and draped his arms over them, staring out into the field beyond the campers.

Nathan rubbed his swollen jaw. "I guess you told him what happened."

I bit my lower lip.

"Warren, I'm really sorry—" he began.

Warren snapped. "Shut the hell up, Nathan." He pushed himself off the ground and walked back inside the camper, slamming the door behind him with so much force a side window fell open.

Nathan sighed. "Well, at least he didn't kill me."

I shook my head. "I wouldn't be too relieved just yet. He's got a lot of guns and ammo in there."

A shadow fell over us. It was Az, offering a hand to pull Nathan up. "Can't say you didn't deserve that one." He pulled Nathan to his feet.

"I know," Nathan said.

I stood and slapped Azrael's chest. "You could have stopped that."

He rested his arm across my shoulders, turning me back toward the fire. "My dear, had I stopped it, Warren would have come up with nineteen ways to kill Nathan before sundown. And we don't have time for that."

"I should go talk to him," I said.

Azrael held me still. "No. You need to let him cool down. Then you can talk." He pointed toward a chair. "Sit."

Rather than taking the empty seat beside me, Nathan sat on

the opposite side of the fire. Enzo handed him an ice pack from the cooler, and he pressed it against the side of his face.

"Here," Azrael said, handing me a plate of gas station fried chicken.

"Thank you, but I'm really not hungry."

He sat down next to me. "Your daughter is hungry."

"Do you have a course on guilt trips in the spirit world?" I asked, accepting the paper plate.

He just smiled. "I need to talk to you about something, and I want it to stay between us."

That didn't sound good. I frowned. "Why do I have a feeling this is very bad news?"

"It isn't news at all." He rested his arm along the back of my chair and leaned into me. "What was the FBI agent's name who arrested you?"

I pulled the skin off the chicken leg on my plate. "Sharvell Silvers."

"I want you to summon her here," he said.

"You want me to do what?" The question definitely went well beyond the volume of 'just us' dialogue. Everyone looked our way.

He rolled his eyes. "Keep your voice down."

When the rest of the group returned to their own conversations, he continued. "Sloan, the government will never believe you're completely ignorant to everything Kasyade's been up to. Every shred of evidence they find against her will always point back to you because you're central to her plot. Don't you realize that by now?"

I stared into the fire, knowing he was right. I'd known it since the first night Nathan and I sat across from Agent Silvers in Texas.

"If you bring her here, she'll see for herself what you could never explain." He pressed his finger into my shoulder. "She'll see what no jury will ever believe."

I dropped my chicken leg. "And what will stop her from hauling me back to jail when she gets here?"

He motioned around the campfire. "No one here will allow her to haul you anywhere. Besides, she'll be completely unprepared to encounter you. She won't know where she's going, remember?"

"This is a bad idea."

He bent forward to look me in the eye. "Sloan, trust me."

Across the campfire, Nathan was watching me, obviously curious as to what we were so deep in discussion about.

"Why don't you want anyone to know?" I asked.

Azrael's gaze shifted to Nathan, but he kept his voice low. "You know as well as I do that my son and Nathan will do everything they can to keep you from going back to jail." His eyes snapped to mine. "But nothing they can do will actually work aside from keeping you hidden for as long as possible. Is that what you want? To sleep in that camper or something similar for the rest of your life, always on the run and always looking over your shoulder? To ruin Nathan's career and make them both accomplices to crimes you can't prove you're innocent of?"

Looking down at my chicken, I felt sick. A bloody vein ran through the dark hunk of meat bared by the missing skin. I added it to my newly written mental list of food aversions in my first trimester, right behind deviled eggs—thank you, Taiya.

"You need to decide this for you, Sloan." He stood, but he paused before walking away and looked down at me. "Let me know what choice you make."

Unable to eat, I put my plate on the ground and tugged my sleeves over my cold, bare hands. I stared at my feet as my mind played out all the possible scenarios that could unfold if I did as Azrael suggested. Maybe it would clear my name if Silvers were allowed to peek behind the curtain to the supernatural world. Or maybe instead of prison, she'd have me committed. Given my recent string of luck, Silvers would probably wind up dead and I'd be able to add homicide to my long list of federal charges.

But I had more than just me to consider. Rusty and dilapidated campers I could live with; ruining Nathan's life and Warren's, I could not.

I closed my eyes and reached into the universe with my gift. In the darkness, I found Agent Silvers' spirit and before I could convince myself otherwise, I pulled her to me.

"What are you so lost in thought about?"

Nathan's voice snapped my attention back to reality. He sat down in the seat Az had vacated. His face was still swollen, and the redness was deepening to purple.

I looked away. "So much has happened in the past few days, I might never find my mental way back here again."

"I can sympathize with that." He nodded toward Azrael. "What did he say to you?"

I shook my head. "Nothing important."

"Liar."

I didn't even bother to argue.

Dark blue blood had begun to pool under his left eye, and the skin was split just above his cheekbone. "How's your face?" I asked.

He pulled back the slide on one of the Glocks. "It's throbbing, but it isn't broken anymore. Thank you."

"Do you want me to fix that gash under your eye?" I asked.

He shook his head and laughed. "Nah, it's all right. It will probably make Warren feel better to look at it."

I nudged him with my shoulder. "I guess I have to forgive you for leaving me, huh?"

He pointed to his face. "Yes. You have to give me a pass for all transgressions past, present, and future because I haven't taken a beating like that in my life."

I poked out my bottom lip. "I'm sorry."

He shook his head. "Don't be. It's my fault. I would have kicked my ass too."

Behind us, the door to my camper flew open and Warren

stomped down the metal stairs. Nathan was out of his seat and five feet away before Warren looked in our direction. He stopped near the pile of shopping bags Enzo and Kane had brought back. After rummaging through them and repacking some of the contents, he slung a bag over one shoulder, his rifle over the other, and picked up two cans of gasoline. He walked by me without so much as a glance in my direction.

"Where are you going?" Nathan called out.

"To the woods to think about killing you," Warren replied, storming off toward the field.

Nathan put his hands on his hips, hung his head, and groaned. "Well, that's great."

I pointed at Warren. "Seriously, where's he going with the gas?"

He nodded toward the trees. "Probably to mix napalm and fantasize about burning me up with it."

"Warren's making napalm? That's frightening."

He nodded. "You've got a Recon Marine for a boyfriend, Sloan. Napalm is pretty low on the frightening scale of what he's capable of."

"How long do you think he'll be pissed off?" I asked, leaning on my elbow.

Nathan looked up as Warren cut through a pile of brush. "If I were him, forever."

The sun was low in the sky by the time Warren returned from the woods. He glanced at me by the fire as he walked wordlessly to our camper. I took that as my invitation to follow him.

Inside, I sat down on the bed as he silently unloaded his gear by the sinister red-orange glow of the space heater. "Are you going to talk to me?" I asked.

There was no answer.

Instead of joining me on the bed, he sat in one of the rickety lawn chairs. Its hinges creaked under his weight. He didn't even look at me.

After what felt like eternity, his deep voice echoed off the metal walls. "Is it over now with you and him?"

I got up and crept over beside him. "It will never happen again. I promise."

His eyes reflected the burning coils of the heater when he turned his head to look at me. "You didn't answer my question. Is it over?"

"I think so." It was the most truthful answer I could give. "I want it to be."

He looked out the window.

Dropping my head, I took a step backward. But he grabbed my hand, pulling me down till I straddled his lap. Studying my face, his hands gripped my hips, then he stood and carried me to the counter. With his arms braced beside my thighs, he dropped his face and cut his black eyes up at me. "It's him or me. I love you and I will always take care of our daughter, but I will not share you. Ever. Do you understand?"

I nodded. "I swear, I'm yours. Please forgive me."

"Not today."

I gulped. At least I couldn't fault his honesty.

Warren straightened, his eyes still smoldering as they searched me. His fingers found the hem of Nathan's sweatshirt I was still wearing, and silently, he yanked it up and over my head. "I never want to see you in this again." He threw the shirt toward the door.

I nodded, hugging myself to shield my bare skin from the chill of the room.

He peeled my arms from around my body, and his warm hands slid up my sides, slipping underneath the white cotton of my prison-issued sports bra. Sexy.

As he dropped it on the floor with one hand, the other raked through my hair till he could pull my mouth down onto his. The kiss was fierce, hot, and angry. His teeth scraped across my lower lip as he worked the button on my jeans. When he got them down to my ankles, he freed one leg from the denim and didn't bother with the other before he buried himself inside me.

And in that moment, we both knew it.

I'd made my choice.

I was irrevocably his.

CHAPTER TWENTY-SIX

My stomach rumbled so loud Warren raised up on his elbow and looked down at me. I laughed and covered my face with my hands. "I haven't consumed enough calories today to do what we just did."

Smiling for the first time since that morning, he settled back down on the pillow beside me, resting his hand on my stomach where we lay, our naked and sweaty limbs tangled under the mound of thick sleeping bags. "We should fight more often," he growled in my ear. "That was amazing."

I snuggled against him. "I think I blacked out a couple of times."

He laughed and tightened his arm around me. "Is that a good thing or a bad thing?"

"Definitely a good thing." My stomach growled again. "I smell burgers."

He pushed himself up. "Let's go grab something to eat before it's all gone."

As he stood, he pulled his cargos up over his bare, perfect butt. I smiled, enjoying the view. I reached for his hand and tugged him back toward the bed. He sat down beside me and pushed my hair out of my face. "Are we OK?" I asked.

"We will be," he said. "But I meant what I said. My patience has run out and I'm not doing this wishy-washy bullshit anymore." He tugged the blanket up around my shoulders. "Do you swear you told me everything? No more secrets."

"I swear," I said.

He was quiet for a moment, and then he leaned down pressed a kiss to my forehead. "I forgive you. Let's try to forget about it."

As if on cue, we heard Azrael's voice outside. "Nate, are those burgers about ready?"

I grimaced and traced my finger along the thick black line of the tattoo down the center of Warren's chest. "Will you forgive Nathan?"

He shook his head. "Probably not, but we do need him to help fight a war."

I caught his eye. "And it sounds like he has dinner."

Warren smiled again. "I am pretty hungry." He grabbed my hand and pulled me up. "Get dressed. Enzo bought you some clothes earlier."

He crossed the dark room and flipped on the light switch. By the door were a few shopping bags. He tossed me one that was tied shut. Inside was a black thermal shirt, some black jogging pants, a fleece pullover, and three plastic packages of women's underwear. I looked up at him. "Eighteen pairs of underwear? How long will we be here?"

He shrugged. "I have no idea."

There was a pack of granny panties, a pack of bikini briefs, and a pack of animal print thongs. I held up the last one over my head. "Seriously?"

He stopped tying his boots and pointed at me. "Speaking for all men everywhere, cut them some slack. We don't have any business shopping for women's underwear if it's not split crotch and covered in lace." He stood and zipped up his coat. "I'll see you out there."

The campfire cast an ominous glow over our group as we ate charred burgers and canned baked beans. No one said it out loud, but despite Azrael's confidence, we all knew it could be the last peaceful dinner we ever ate. And 'peaceful' was a generous description of the meal. The tension between Warren and Nathan was almost palpable across the campfire.

Breaking the silence, Azrael cleared his throat and poked the embers with a long stick. "Tomorrow, we're moving away from the campsite," he announced. "This area is too wide open with too little cover."

"Where will we go?" I asked between bites of my hamburger.

"There's a mountain spring that serves as the headwaters of Calfkiller Creek about a half a mile, directly north of here. It will give us a high vantage point because everything below and around the spring is an open meadow."

"Plenty of spots to pick people off from above," Kane added.

Warren looked at me. "And there's a cave back in the rocks where the spring is."

My eyes widened. "I hope you're not insinuating the cave is for me."

He shrugged. "Just in case."

I shook my head. "I'd rather be out fighting demons than be stuffed into a dirty cave with spiders and snakes and god-only-knows-what-else."

Nathan sighed. "You're so weird. Do you even hear yourself?"

I nodded. "Ysha, I can see coming. A brown recluse can slip into my shoe and inject me with skin-rotting poison while I shop for shoes on my cell phone. Those things are no joke."

The guys around the fire were softly chuckling.

Azrael held up his hand to silence us all. "Quiet."

I didn't hear anything.

Azrael tossed his paper plate into the fire and slowly rose from his seat, his ear angled up toward the sky.

"What is it?" I asked.

"Silence!" Azrael demanded, walking closer to me.

I bit down on the inside of my lips.

"Surround positions!" Azrael called out.

What the hell...

The unmistakable sound of gravel grinding under tires came from the road. I watched the soldiers scatter from the campfire and put on gear waiting at the ready nearby. They moved like pieces of a well-oiled machine. I, on the other hand, ran in circles like a squirrel stuck in rush hour traffic.

I grabbed Azrael's arm. "I forgot to tell you!"

"You summoned her?" he asked.

I nodded.

He patted my back. "Good girl. You stay behind Warren, no matter what." Before I could say anything, he turned away, slipping an earpiece into his ear. He pulled on a pair of black gloves that had been tucked into his pocket and handed Warren the assault rifle that had been sitting next to his camping chair.

Warren slipped the gun's strap over his head. "Sloan, what's going on?"

"I need to tell you something."

He looked down at me. "What now?"

I covered my mouth with my hands. "I summoned the FBI here."

His head snapped back. "You did *what?*"

I ducked behind his back as headlights flashed through the sky. "It was Azrael's idea. He told me to summon Silvers here to let her see what's going on. He said it's the only way to prove my innocence."

He raised the rifle to his shoulder. "Why the hell didn't you tell me?"

"Azrael told me not to." I gripped his sides. "And, honestly, I kind of forgot about it with…you know, everything else."

The black sedan rolled to a stop behind one of Azrael's SUVs.

Nathan appeared at Warren's side. "Human or supe?" he asked, looking at Warren.

"Human," Warren answered. "Sloan summoned the feds here."

Nathan's angry gaze shot to me. "Excuse me?"

Before I could explain, we heard more than one car door open.

"I guess she brought friends," Warren said.

I balled my fists at my sides in frustration. "I don't know why I listen to that guy!"

Suddenly, the faces of Agent Silvers and Agent Voss were lit up by the flashlights mounted on the assault rifles pointed at them by Azrael's men.

"Who's the guy?" Warren asked me over his shoulder.

"He's the agent who questioned me at the federal building," I answered.

Sharvell Silvers looked surprised but not the least bit intimidated. "My name is Agent Silvers, and I work for the Federal Bureau of Investigation. I must advise you of—"

Azrael took a few steps forward and held up a hand to silence her. "Lady, I don't care who you are or who you work for. You're in my world now." He pointed to her chest. There were two bright red dots from laser sights gleaming in the center of her breast bone.

Even from our distance, I could see her gulp.

"I don't want to kill you." Azrael spread out his hands as he walked to face her. "But I will."

His malevolent threat was enough to make me shudder.

Sharvell shifted on her feet.

Azrael crossed his arms and cocked his head to the side. "Stand down, Agent. You and I both know the government doesn't pay you enough to put your family through a funeral at Christmas." He put his hand over the top of her pistol.

She hesitated for a second, then released it into his grasp.

Agent Voss lowered his gun as well, and Cooper came out of the darkness and immediately disarmed him.

Satisfied, Azrael took a step back. He raised a finger in the air and swirled it around. "Check that car, boys," he said into his microphone.

Enzo and Lex walked to the sedan, keeping their aim on the driver who was still seated behind the wheel with his hands raised in the air.

Azrael reached into the pocket on the front of his vest and tossed a handful of zip-ties to Warren. "Staff Sergeant, you and Nate make our guests comfortable."

That's when Sharvell saw Nathan and her expression morphed from anger to confusion. "Detective McNamara?"

He groaned as he walked up and grabbed her hands. "Yeah."

"Is Sloan here as well?" she asked as he tied her wrists together with the plastic strip.

I walked straight up to her, much braver with her in restraints. "Nice to see you again, Sharvell."

Her mouth was hanging open.

I shook my head. "Don't try to make sense of what's happening to you right now. I do promise I won't let them hurt you."

Nathan and Warren walked the two agents over to the campfire and pushed them down carefully onto the ground. Enzo brought over the driver, Agent Clark if I remembered correctly, and put him down beside them as well.

Nathan dusted his hands off and looked at the agents. "It's nothing personal guys."

"Your career is finished, Detective," Sharvell spat at him.

"Yeah, I figured. But I have a feeling you'll see why."

Her brow rose, and she glared at me before mumbling something to her partner.

Azrael walked up beside me. "You made the right choice, Sloan."

Warren spun around toward him. "What were you thinking, Azrael?"

Azrael held his hands up in defense. "This is the only way the three of you get to go home again."

"Home again?" Sharvell asked from the ground. "You're harboring a fugitive from federal custody. No one here is going home."

Azrael smiled. "Those are mighty words from where you sit in the dirt." He looked around at us and his men. "Nothing changes tomorrow." He gestured toward the agents. "They'll be coming with us."

There was a collective gasp around the circle, along with lots of wide eyes and dropped jaws.

Warren crossed his arms over his chest. "You can't be serious. You're going to let them see everything?"

Azrael put his hand on Warren's shoulder. "Son, sometimes it's in everyone's best interest to not keep things hidden. This will certainly be what's best for you."

"Will you leave them tied up?" Nathan asked. "They'll get killed out there!"

Azrael nodded. "It's possible."

The agents squirmed uncomfortably, but none of them spoke.

Nathan scowled. "They may be sorely misguided in their attempts to uphold justice, but they're still the good guys."

Azrael grinned at me. "Maybe I'll stick them in Sloan's hideout cave."

I held up my hands. "As long as you don't expect me to go in there too."

"I demand to know what's going on here!" Sharvell shouted.

Azrael walked over and knelt down in front of her, leaning forward on his knee for support and intimidation. It worked because Sharvell shrank back. "Tomorrow will be a war unlike anything you've ever seen. You can decide which side of that war you want to be on. I trust you'll recognize where you went wrong in this whole mix up."

"There is no mix up," she argued. "We have Sloan on videotape working with Abigail Smith."

"Perhaps," he said. "But tomorrow you'll see that not everything you believe to be true actually is."

"Who are you?" she barked viciously at him.

Slowly, he rose till he towered over them again. "My name is Azrael. And I'm the Angel of Death."

The next morning, I was awake before the sun which by itself was a miracle. Warren was still sleeping, also a miracle. Maybe it would be a good day for miraculous things to happen. God knows, we needed all the help we could get.

It was so cold I could see my breath, but I was snug under the weight of several sleeping bags and the heavy arm of the man of my dreams and beyond. His breath was warm against the back of my neck where he was curled protectively around me from behind. Our legs were tangled under the blanket.

Outside, hushed voices carried over the sound of something sizzling in a pan over the open fire. It smelled like sausage.

Warren stirred slightly, then I felt his lips grace the back of my shoulder. "Good morning," he whispered in the early morning light.

I snuggled closer into him. "Good morning."

His arm tightened around me. "I need about four more hours of shut-eye."

"I didn't sleep well either," I said, lacing my fingers between his under the blanket. He slid our locked hands down to my stomach, and the baby's tiny body fluttered. I glanced back at him over my shoulder. "I think she can sense you. She's moving again."

He flattened his palm against my stomach. "I still can't believe you're pregnant."

"Some days, neither can I." I rolled over till we were almost nose-to-nose and I curled my arms up under the pillow. I studied his handsome face to burn all his features into my memory.

"What are you thinking about?" he whispered.

"If something happens today—"

He shook his head to cut me off. "Don't talk like that. We're going to win, you'll see."

"You don't know that, Warren." I hugged the pillow a little tighter. "If something happens to me, I want you to know how much I love you."

The corner of his mouth tipped up into a smile. "You showed me pretty well last night, a few times."

I didn't laugh. "I'm serious."

He pushed my hair behind my ear. "I love you too, Sloan. This will all be behind us soon. We'll go home and have a beautiful little girl, and we are going to be happy. You'll see."

I smiled and wanted to believe him, but it was hard considering that the hounds of hell were coming with the day.

"I hope she has your eyes," he said.

I grinned. "I hope she has your hair."

He laughed and rolled over on top of me.

When Warren and I walked out of the camper later that morning, Nathan was sitting at the table alone, buttering a piece of toast. He was wearing multi-cam like the rest of Azrael's soldiers, and his face was flushed with bright shades of blue and purple. His eyes widened with worry as we approached and sat down. Cautiously, and silently, he slid a couple of empty plates toward us.

Warren poured two cups of coffee from the aluminum pot on the table and handed one to me.

"She can't have that—" Nathan began, then quickly snapped his mouth closed.

Warren glowered across the table.

Not another word was spoken as we ate, and Nathan chewed his food slowly as though it may be the last meal he would ever taste. Warren punished his eggs with his fork, clanging the tines so hard against the plate that the birds in the nearby tree line scattered each time he went for a bite. I nibbled a piece of sausage, praying for something to break the awkward tension.

That something turned out to be one of the HOKs appearing in the field from the tree line. Driving it was Azrael, and in the passenger seat was another man—no, *angel*—that I didn't know. They rolled to a stop about twenty feet away. "Good morning, all," Azrael said when he was close enough.

I smiled up at him. "Good morning."

Azrael leaned against the table. "Have we all kissed and made up?" His smile was taunting.

Warren nor Nathan even looked up.

Azrael laughed. "Well, if you'd all take a break from your brooding this morning, I'd like you to meet a friend of mine." He turned toward the man with him. "This is Reuel. We spoke of him yesterday."

Reuel was twice Azrael's size, a remarkable achievement by anyone's standard. He reminded me of a life-size action figure— or a professional wrestling entertainer, like John Cena without a soul. Reuel was terrifying.

Azrael spoke to him in Katavukai and told him all our names.

Unsure of angelic introduction protocol, given Azrael's aversion to hand-shaking, I waved awkwardly from my seat. "Nice to meet you, Reuel."

Azrael shook his head. "Reuel, doesn't speak English. He understands it perfectly well, but he never speaks it."

Weird.

I motioned toward the food. "Are you hungry?"

"We already ate," he answered. "I came to make sure everyone is up and moving. It will be a busy day."

"Where did you stash the FBI?" Warren asked.

Azrael pointed to his camper behind us. "I hope they enjoyed their accommodations." He turned in the direction he had pointed and began to walk. "Let's go find out."

A few minutes later, Azrael, Reuel, Kane, and Enzo escorted the FBI team out to the campfire. They looked awful, sleepless and afraid, and they were all still bound at the wrists. I knew what that felt like. "Are the wrist ties really necessary?" I asked.

"Yes," everyone else answered at the same time.

"They don't have weapons and they can't go anywhere," I reasoned.

"Not happening, Sloan," Azrael said. "Let it go."

I got up from the table. "Have you at least given them water or food?"

"No," Agent Clark answered.

I put my hands on my hips and looked at Az in disbelief. "Seriously? They're not our prisoners. Bring me some bottles of water."

Azrael looked annoyed, but then he smiled. "OK, but you have to get it yourself."

With a huff, I turned toward the cooler and took a step.

"No!" he shouted.

I looked back at him.

"You can't use your hands."

"Fine," I said, pushing up my sleeves.

Everyone was watching me. I took a deep breath and focused on the blue and white cooler sitting outside of Azrael's camper.

This will be tricky. I need to open the cooler, then somehow count out three bottles of water. Hmm. A smile spread across my face. *Or...*

Much easier than I expected, I lifted the entire cooler off the ground. Just like an invisible person was carrying it, it traveled across the lot, past me, and directly at Azrael's face. I dropped it with a thud right at his toes, making him jump out of the way.

The entire campsite exploded into cheers.

Warren's mouth was gaping at the table, and he was clapping his hands.

Nathan cupped his hands around his mouth and yelled, "Woohoo!"

Laughing, Azrael bent, pulled out three waters and carried them over to me. "Nicely done, Ms. Jordan. Nicely done."

"Thank you," I said, bowing before my teacher.

We unscrewed the caps and passed the waters out to the dumbfounded FBI agents. I saved Sharvell for last. "Here," I said, handing it to her.

"Thank you."

When she reached up and grabbed it, I held on. "I'm not who you think I am."

She stared at me, indignant but maybe mildly impressed.

Warren was still grinning from ear to ear when I walked back around to my place at the table and sat down. "When in the hell did you learn how to do that?"

"Baby, lots has changed since you've been gone," I said, smiling.

He leaned over and gave me a quick peck on the lips. "That's clear." He pushed his plate away and looked up at his father. "I'm assuming you've got an armory around here somewhere. I'm a little low on ammo."

Kane chuckled. "Yeah, we have an armory."

Nathan turned toward Azrael. "Speaking of weapons, I can't tell demons apart. I won't know who I can kill and who I can't."

Enzo looked at him. "Shoot all of them in the head, and if they get back up, blow out their kneecaps."

Nathan nodded. "I can do that."

I glanced sideways at our FBI friends. A couple of them were whispering with each other, but Sharvell's hateful gaze was fixed on me. I smiled and gave her a tiny wave with my finger.

Warren pointed at me. "What about Sloan? What's her role in all this?"

Azrael looked at me. "Sloan will be on the ground with me tonight."

Warren's eyes widened. "In the middle of everything?"

"Correct."

"Absolutely not," Warren said.

Azrael turned his palms up. "Warren, you don't have a choice. We're the offensive team here. I brought them out here so Sloan can kill them."

"So *Sloan* can kill them?" Warren asked, pointing at me in case anyone was confused by who Sloan was, apparently.

"She's the only one who can," Azrael said.

Warren's tone was laden with sarcasm. "Her little mind movement trick is really *neat* and all, but do you really think I'm going to allow the mother of my child to be—"

As if of their own accord, my hands began flailing wildly in the air. "*Allow* me?"

Out of the corner of my eye, I saw Nathan's hand clamp over his mouth. Muffled chuckles were coming from Azrael and his crew.

Warren shifted in my direction, glaring as he waited for my outburst.

I lifted my eyebrows and blinked. "Allow me?" I asked again.

Nathan's head was hung, and his shoulders were shaking with silent giggles.

Warren crossed his thick arms. "You can't expect me to be all right with the thought of my pregnant girlfriend battling a bunch of demons out in the middle the woods."

I scowled. "I don't expect you to be *happy* about it, but just because I'm pregnant doesn't mean you get to make decisions for me."

Azrael walked around the table and leaned between us. "OK, kids. Calm down." He draped his arm around Warren's shoulders. "I understand your hesitation about this. I really do. But she's more capable of ending this, once and for all, than any of us. I'll keep her safe, but I need her with me."

Warren looked at him. "Then you'll have me with you too."

Azrael tapped his finger on the table. "You're the best long-range shooter we've got. You can protect her better from somewhere else."

"He's right, Warren," Nathan said. "You're far better than anyone I've ever seen with a rifle."

It was obvious Warren didn't completely trust his father, which was understandable given how much of a whack-job my demon mother turned out to be and given Azrael's track record for keeping his own counsel. After a long moment of obvious internal debate, he looked at Nathan with a pained expression.

Nathan must have understood because he nodded. "I won't leave her."

Azrael glanced around our group. "It's settled then?"

Warren gave a thumbs-up, but he didn't look happy about it.

"She'll be safe in my charge," Azrael said.

I raised my hands again. "I don't take orders from you either, Oh-Archangel-of-Death."

Warren looked at Azrael. "She's always this difficult, so get used to it."

Azrael slapped him on the back. "Tell me something I don't know."

"I'll tell you something you don't know." Enzo's voice caught us all by surprise as he pushed his way into the center of our group with his finger pushed against the speaker in his ear. "We've got heavy movement coming in the back east quadrant."

Azrael shoved his earpiece into his ear, and after a second looked around at all of us. "Our guests are early."

CHAPTER TWENTY-SEVEN

"All right, boys. Let's go to work!" Azrael announced. "Enzo and Kane, you've got the HOKs. I want you to take Sloan, Warren, Nate, and our FBI friends to the clearing. Haul as much shit as you can. Reuel and I will take care of the rest."

"Roger that," Enzo said.

Azrael looked at Lex. "Lex, hook Warren up with the ghillie suit you found last night."

"Sweet," Warren said, getting up and then following Lex across the camp.

Azrael pointed at Nathan. "You've got my M-4, right?"

Nathan nodded. "Do you need it back?"

Azrael shook his head. "Nope. Keep it. You got mags?"

"Yes, sir."

I held up both my hands. "What do you want me to do?"

Azrael smiled. "Don't get killed."

"Not encouraging," I said, shaking my head furiously.

"Just kidding." He held up his hand. "Enzo! You've got two minutes to fit Sloan with some body armor!"

"Roger that, sir!"

Azrael pointed at me, then pointed at Enzo, whose head was

sticking out of Azrael's camper. I jumped up from the table and scurried across the grounds. Enzo offered me a hand and pulled me up into the RV so sharply that I missed the top step.

The inside of Azrael's camper was worse than ours. His bunks didn't even have a mattress. It smelled like mold and there were rat droppings on the floor. "Ew," I said, looking around.

With a loaded smile, Enzo reached into the closet. I heard a switch followed by the unmistakable sound of hydraulics. The bottom bunk slowly lifted a few inches into the air, and Enzo swung it sideways on a hinge back against the wall. My bottom jaw dropped. "What the hell?"

There was a staircase underneath and halogen lights flickered on.

Enzo started down the stairs. "We're down to seventy-eight seconds, ma'am. Please hurry."

I followed him down into the underground bunker. "Shut up!" My voice echoed off the walls.

There were rows of barracks-style bunk beds, lockers along the walls, a large lunchroom table with bench seats, and even a door marked as a bathroom. At the far end, Enzo unlocked a large steel cage. "We're down to a minute, Ms. Jordan."

I shook my head to clear it. "Sorry." I scurried into the cage where he helped me put on the smallest vest they had. The bulky, camouflage Kevlar hung off my chest, even after he'd tightened it to the end of the Velcro strap. "I feel like a turtle," I told him, unable to lay my arms down flat against my sides.

"I'm sorry we don't have anything that fits better. I don't think we've ever even had a woman here before besides NAG and she took all her gear with her," he said.

I shook my head. "It's OK. I'm more pissed off I've been sleeping in that tin stable out there while you guys have been living it up down here in the Taj Mahal of hidey-holes ."

"The boss doesn't let us open it if he's not here. And last night, you and Staff Sergeant Parish crashed out early before we had a chance to move your stuff."

"I think Az just wanted me to suffer," I said.

"I doubt that, ma'am," he replied. "I'll see you on the HOK."

Just then, Cooper and Warren jogged down the stairs. Warren's reaction had to have been similar to my own, but he got over it a lot quicker than I did. "Don't you look hot?" he asked, grabbing me by the collar of my vest and kissing me before brushing past me into the cage.

"Have you ever seen anything like this place?" I asked.

He nodded as Cooper handed him a box full of ammunition. "Yes."

I rolled my eyes. "Of course you have. I need to grab a few things from the camper. I'll see you up top."

Warren didn't reply. He was distracted by all the big guns.

Less than ten minutes later, I was in the back seat of Enzo's HOK with Warren. Agent Silvers was stuffed into the passenger's seat up front, and Nathan was riding with Agent Voss in the very back. All our laps were loaded down with everything from grenades to gauze. My vest rode up over my chin the second I sat down, making it hard for me to talk as the group discussed the danger zone we were entering.

I had nothing helpful to add, anyway. Regardless of what everyone thought they knew, no one really had any idea what was coming our way. And we had no idea if we would win—or even survive. The battle in Texas with Kasyade hadn't gone well, and this one promised to make that look like a cat fight. I pressed my eyes closed and talked to the only person who could hear me behind my oversized armor.

Dear God, we need help.

It was a quick ride to the mountain spring in the middle of the plot of land. Enzo parked the HOK in the middle of the worn grassy path. "We'll unload here, then I'm stashing this thing in the woods."

We all got out, and I took in our surroundings. Up ahead was a rocky and shallow creek. The path opened up to an unleveled clearing with tall grass and thick leaves left to decay during the winter. Beyond the grass, a large rock jutted out from the earth forming a long crack in the mountainside, and toward the top, a small stream of water trickled out onto the rocks below. Near the bottom, a larger swell of the waterfall splashed into a rocky pool. And between the two spouts was an open, jagged space in the rock formation.

I pointed to it. "If that's the cave, which I'm sure it is, I'm putting everyone on notice, there's no way in hell I'm going in there."

"What are you mortals waiting for?" Azrael shouted down from the top of the rock.

I looked at Warren. "I thought he was behind us?"

"So did I," he said.

Warren draped the M-4's strap around his neck and reached for my hand. "Let's go."

It was at least thirty yards straight up the side of that *hill.* Warren looked back over his shoulder. "Hey, Nate. What does this remind you of?"

Behind us, Nathan began mimicking my voice. "I'm tired. My legs hurt. This is too steep. I want to go to the car."

If I had something I could throw at him, I would have.

Warren was chuckling. A good sign, considering he'd almost killed Nathan hours before.

Azrael was waving us forward when we reached the top of the falls. "Bring it in," he said. "We've got lots to cover in a short timeframe."

We all gathered around him, including the FBI.

"We already have eyes on at least six targets, three humans and three angels, including Abaddon. Reuel is en route to the border, to Abaddon's last known position. Do *not* engage with him. He's known as The Destroyer for a reason."

I shuddered. That didn't sound good.

"Any questions?" he asked.

"What about us?" Agent Voss asked, holding up his hands that were still bound at the wrists.

"Kane and Enzo will escort you to the cave." He lowered his glasses and glared at him. "I suggest you stay in it." Azrael looked around our group and used both hands to motion all the way around us. "These woods are rigged to kill people. If you don't want to die a painful and fiery death, don't cross the tree line."

As soon as the words left his mouth, a deafening blast shattered the silence of the woods. A black billow of smoke rose above the trees against the gray winter sky. A blood-curdling scream echoed through the forest, accompanied by the sound of startled woodland creatures scuttling through the fallen leaves. The screams sickened me as much as they brought me hope. Then, as if silenced by a cosmic mute button, the shrieks abruptly ceased, and the land was silent again. A chill ran down my spine, and I shuddered under Warren's arm.

"One down." Azrael's voice was even and sinister. "Get to your positions."

Warren grasped my arm and turned me around to face him. "Are you armed?"

I shook my head. "I should keep my hands free. Besides, there's no point. You know I can't shoot."

He pulled me close and pressed his lips to mine. "I love you, Sloan."

"I love you too."

He tucked my hair behind my ear. "Stay with Nate and don't do anything stupid."

I kissed him again.

"Ready?" Nathan asked, stepping to my side.

Warren grabbed him by the front of his vest. "Don't you leave her."

"You know I won't." Nathan stepped back and offered Warren his hand.

Warren looked at it before accepting. "Thank you," he said.

Nathan nodded. "Stay safe."

They stared at each other a moment, some sort of unsaid sentiment passing between them.

"Warren, get in position," Azrael ordered.

Warren turned to look at him. He pointed his finger at his father's face. "You'd better not let anything happen to her."

"You have my word, son," Azrael replied.

After a bit of heated staring, Warren nodded. He looked at me one last time before turning and jogging toward the trees.

"We've got to go," Azrael said, taking me by the arm.

Going down the mountain wasn't much easier than going up. Azrael had to hold me vertical to keep me from sliding down on my backside. I watched the three agents duck into the cave, then Enzo and Kane scaled off the falls to meet us at the bottom.

Back to back, Azrael, Nathan, and I formed a triangle, looking out toward the trees. Enzo and Kane were in opposite corners of the clearing.

For what felt like hours, but could have only been minutes, my eyes scanned the layers of the knotty pine trunks in front of me. I could only see about fifty feet beyond the tree line before the brush became too dense and the shade of the trees became too dark. There was no movement except for the pine needles that were rustled by the breeze.

The loud crack of a rifle rang out over our heads, followed by angry men shouting in a language I was becoming more and more familiar with—Katavukai. I shifted my weight from foot to foot and ground the toes of my boots into the earth. There was a second blast from a rifle, and after a moment, another one. More shots crackled through the woods, overlapping each other as the assailants in the woods returned fire. Then, *pop pop pop...pop pop pop...pop pop pop...pop pop pop!*

"They already switched from long range to assault rifles," Nathan said. "That's not a good sign."

There was commotion behind me, and Nathan opened fire. I spun around in time to see a man—a wicked human—dressed in all black, go down sideways in a trench. His light eyes bulged as he cried out in pain. The life extinguished in his expression as he fell backward into the leaves.

There was another explosion from a mine closest to Enzo's post, followed by more shots from the assault rifle and gunfire on the ground. My heart was pounding so loud it seemed to harmonize with the sound of the gunshots. Azrael sent a fireball into the woods, sending everything in its path up in flames.

Another demon—a woman with short brown hair—came through the trees where the first man had fallen. She extended her arms and two trees uprooted themselves. She flung them in our direction. Azrael caught them in midair, but gunfire on my other side caught my attention.

I turned in time to see Enzo fly backward off his feet amid a shower of bullets.

Before Azrael or Nathan could stop me, I sprinted toward him, my helmet clanging against my skull as I ran.

When I dropped onto the ground at his side, blood was gurgling out of his mouth as he struggled to breathe. A crimson stain spread from under his left arm where a bullet had caught him between the plates of his body armor.

"Stay with me, Enzo," I shouted, shoving my hand into the bloody cavern on his side.

As my healing power swelled at my fingertips, two more men, one human with a huge gun and one demon with empty hands, ran through the tree line toward me. I collapsed over Enzo's chest, and a sharp crack sailed through the air. A bullet caught the human directly in his right eye socket, exploding his skull in a shower of blood and bone as it knocked his body sideways onto the ground.

The demon kept charging like an angry bull until another bullet caught him in the knee. He faltered but kept coming.

Just before he collided with me on the ground, a brilliant white light exploded in every direction. The demon flew backward, feet over his head, taking out two small pines as he skidded into the woods.

When the light dissolved around us, a figure cloaked in what appeared to be fabric made of the night sky turned to face me. "You called for help?" Samael asked, his golden eyes dancing like flames.

"Sloan!" Azrael shouted.

I looked to see him pinning the brunette demon against the ground. Enzo gasped for air underneath me. "Can you breathe?" I asked.

He nodded. "Yes. Go."

I leapt from the grass, and Samael followed me to Azrael. Nathan was firing into his side of the woods. "Is that Phenex?" I asked as we ran up on them.

Azrael shook his. "No, but kill her anyway. She tried to club me over the head with an oak tree."

The woman's throat was caught under Azrael's hand, but she was cackling anyway. "This bitch can't kill me," she croaked out.

I opened my fingers and a bright light burst to life in my palm. "Wanna bet?" I slammed the light down right into the dead center of her chest.

The light splintered through her body quickly before it detonated with the force of a nuclear warhead. Azrael, Samael, and myself were all blown back by the explosion. The ground shook like an earthquake and shattered the rocks around the waterfall. Dazed and deaf, I sat up and looked around. The blast had leveled everyone on the field. And the spot where the brunette had been was black and covered in something that looked like shiny salt.

Azrael and Samael looked as shocked as I felt as they struggled to their feet.

An arm scooped me up around the waist and hauled me up. I turned to see Nathan, blinking like he was dizzy.

"Are you OK?" his lips asked. My hearing was slowly returning, but he sounded hollow and muffled.

I nodded. "Are you?"

He gripped the side of his head. "I think so."

An electric charge surged through me as a hand closed around my arm. It was Azrael, and he spun me around toward the woods. "He is here," he said, his voice so calm it made me shiver.

In front of us, there was an explosion of a different kind. Shards of broken earth shot up and speckled the sky as the sound of splintering wood and crashing trees reverberated through the forest. I needed no explanation. Like Azrael said, they called him The Destroyer for a reason. And he was coming.

I inhaled and stretched my fingers as trees toppled like bowling pins in front of us. A land mine detonated under the force of a fallen tree, erupting the timber into a blaze. Fiery napalm showered down onto Abaddon, clinging to his clothes and skin as it burned. Still, in the firelight, I saw him walking toward us with so much power the woodland floor vibrated with each step. The flames cast wicked shadows of his figure dancing among the trees.

Abaddon's hands shot forward, sending me sailing backward into Nathan. I toppled him over, landing hard on the solid earth. Pain radiated through my bones. I rolled onto my side in time to see Abaddon cross over the dismembered tree line into the clearing. All I could think of was The Incredible Hulk, except Abaddon wasn't green…he was black, charred by the napalm which still burned in some places on his massive frame.

A gun shot cracked through the sky and knocked him sideways, but he regained his footing quickly and charged me. I threw my hands toward him, sending up an invisible wall that knocked him completely off his feet.

I seized the moment and leapt to my feet as Azrael lifted Abaddon's stunned body into the air. He slammed him into a nearby tree, causing the demon to bounce like a giant pinball back to the ground. Without pausing to recover, Abaddon waved his arm toward the blaze behind him, sending a wave of fire over his head and through the clearing straight at us.

I shielded my face in time, but my hands were burned and the smell of burning hair turned my stomach. Samael's arms reached toward the stars, and a shower from a cloudless sky rained down and extinguished the flames.

Abaddon was on his feet and barreling toward us. More bullets sailed through the air in bursts from Nathan's assault rifle, but the demon wasn't deterred. Azrael sprinted toward him, then dove at his legs. The two collided and tumbled together into the woods, sending dirt, leaves, and brush flying like shrapnel.

Out of the corner of my eye, Kane was tackled to the ground by the demon Samael had knocked into the woods moments earlier. He outweighed Kane by at least a hundred pounds. With fists flying faster than I could see, the demon pounded Kane's face. My hands rose in their direction, the sizzling charge of light dancing at my fingertips, and I hurled the death blow into the demon's torso when he rose up to slam Kane again.

Another blast like before knocked everyone back again, and Kane's broken body was showered with electrified, glowing ash.

I scrambled toward him as Nathan and a bloody Enzo aimed and fired their weapons into the woods. Kane was wiping blood from his eyes with the back of his sleeve. "I'm OK," he said. "Thank you."

He may not have been dying, but he was far from OK. Had I not known who he was, I wouldn't have recognized him. I gently touched the sides of his face.

"The rocks," he choked out.

My head whipped toward the waterfall. Another demon was standing on the rocks, dangling Cooper over the side by his vest. When the inhuman man caught my eye, he laughed.

Then he dropped the soldier.

I screamed, throwing my hands in her direction. Cooper froze in the air, inches above the jagged rocks in the bottom pool. I exhaled so heavily, I almost collapsed. On the far side of the field, Samael seemed to vaporize into a cloud, then the cloud sailed through the air and collided with the demon on the rocks. The two of them disappeared into thin air with a crack.

"Sloan, look out!" Nathan shrieked.

Before I could react, my body sailed into the air, the force of gravity against the power holding me, nearly ripped my body in two. I cried out in pain as I hung suspended fifteen feet off the ground, my arms plastered against my sides, immovable. All I could think of was my baby.

There was a loud explosion from one of the mines in the distance followed by a fireball that rose through the trees. Azrael was nowhere to be seen.

Beneath me was Ysha.

"You don't want me to drop her," he said, daring Nathan and Enzo with his wild eyes. His hand that was stretched toward me, bent my body to an excruciating degree.

My piercing scream echoed around the woods.

They cautiously lowered their weapons.

"Come out! Come out!" Ysha called. "Warren, I know you're up there! Drag your friends out here too!"

A moment later, at the top of the waterfall, Warren in a ghillie suit walked out to the edge with his rifle raised over his head. Lex walked up beside him.

"Drop your guns!" Ysha told them.

Warren and Lex slowly slid their rifles off the edge of the rock they were standing on and they clattered down the side of the mountain.

There was another loud crash of trees somewhere in the distance.

With a satisfied nod, Ysha lowered me a few feet, then he let me fall. I crashed to the ground, my leg crumpling at an awkward angle underneath me. I screamed again. The blistering pain rendering me helpless. I looked down to see bloody bone poking through my pants.

Nathan lunged toward me, but Ysha flung his hand towards him, knocking him off his feet.

Ysha grasped hold of my hair, tearing strands from my scalp as he ripped me off the ground. Somehow, through my hysterics, I managed to conjure up a flicker of my killing power, but before I could touch him with it, Ysha slammed me into the ground again.

He jerked my head up to look at him. "Did Azrael tell you what happens if you kill me?"

I could hardly see him through my blinding tears, but I could feel his hot and sticky breath on my face.

"If you kill me, Taiya dies instantly," he hissed. "I suggest you come quietly."

Without another word, I was dragged by my hair across the terrain. Jagged rocks from the creek bed ripped through my clothes and into my flesh. The lower half of my leg slapped against every surface it hit like dead fish. The icy water burned instead of numbed my skin as Ysha jerked my body through the stream. With one hand I fought against him while the other covered my belly. His merciless stride didn't slow as he ascended the mossy rocks. Where he was taking me, I wasn't sure, but my skull clanged against every rock he climbed.

Halfway up a huge boulder, the blast from a gun sounded over our heads. Ysha's grip went slack as he fell backward, taking me with him. Over his shoulder in the middle of our free fall, I caught a glimpse of smoke rising from the barrel of Warren's discarded rifle and, through the haze, I saw Sharvell Silvers holding it.

CHAPTER TWENTY-EIGHT

We crashed into the shallow pool, Ysha's full weight on top of me. My tailbone snapped and the back of my skull smacked against the rocks. Somehow I didn't die.

Ysha thrashed until he got his hands on me. My face broke the surface at the same instant his hands closed around my throat. Before he submerged my head again, I saw that half his skull had been blown away by the gun shot.

It didn't stop him from drowning me.

I had no other choice.

My baby and I would die if I didn't act.

This was my only chance.

My power surged into him and detonated.

The blast knocked me unconscious.

Nathan's face was the first thing I saw when I opened my eyes and inhaled for the first time since I'd gone under the water. He was hauling me out of the icy pool by the front of my body armor. We fell in a heap with my broken body landing across his lap. Inside my chest, bones were broken. I coughed and a shower of blood splattered back down onto my face.

"Can you breathe?" he asked.

Sort of. I nodded.

"The baby...are you cramping at all?"

I shook my head, gingerly touching my fingers to my stomach. "I think she's fine."

Sharvell sloshed her way through the water toward us. "What can I do?" she asked, dropping to her knees beside me.

"Someone has to put my leg back together and hold it," I said through my sobs.

She looked at me like I was crazy.

"Please," I begged.

Warren jumped down from one of the rocks. "Move," he said to her.

Sharvell crawled back out of his way as Warren pulled a knife from his vest. He knelt down next to my leg and cut my pant leg off.

"Don't look," he said.

I was struggling to breathe. "Warren, you have to put the bone back in. It can't heal like that."

"We need to get you to the hospital and let them—"

"Do it!" I shouted.

Warren unvelcroed his vest and dropped it on the ground. He peeled off his camouflage shirt and tossed it to Sharvell. "Here. Cut this up. I need something to bind her leg." Warren looked at Nathan. "You'll have to hold her still."

Nathan pulled me back against his chest, wrapping his arms around me as tight as he could.

My blood-curdling scream pierced my own eardrums as Warren grabbed the dangling piece of my lower limb. When he shoved it back in place, the world went black again.

"What happened?" I asked when I woke up. My leg still hurt like hell, but the worst of it was over. The bone under the bandages felt wrong, but solid. My chin was quivering from shock and the freezing air against my wet clothes.

Warren was holding me on the ground. "You're like the bionic woman. I don't know how the hell you survived that."

"I told you. Things have changed." I looked around. Nathan, Cooper, and Lex were gathering up the weapons. Enzo and Kane were carrying another soldier out of the woods. And the FBI agents were sitting on the ground a few feet away from us. "Where's Azrael?"

He shook his head. "I'm not sure. Shit got crazy between him and the big guy. The woods went silent not long after you killed the ginger."

The ginger.

"Taiya," I said, slumping in his arms.

"What?"

I looked up at him with tears in my eyes. "Ysha said if I killed him, Taiya would die."

He didn't say anything. He just kissed the top of my head.

Something heavy was coming through the woods to our right. When we looked, Reuel stumbled into the clearing. The trunk of a tree, at least four feet long and six inches in diameter was running through his chest between his right shoulder and his breast bone.

When he saw us, his shoulders wilted with relief.

Warren gently slid me off his lap and got up. He jogged over and caught Reuel under his left arm before the big guy stumbled. I gasped and struggled to my feet.

My left leg was significantly shorter than it had been before the break. The bone had healed at a horrible angle, but it was a small issue compared to the man standing before me who was impaled by a poplar.

"I guess this explains where you were when shit got ugly," Warren said as helped Reuel kneel down.

Reuel grunted.

He looked up at me, his eyes pleading.

I grimaced. "I'll heal you, but we've got to get that thing out first."

He nodded.

"Dude," Nathan said as he and Enzo walked over.

"I'll hold his chest, if you want to push," Enzo offered, looking at Warren.

"You sound experienced in this," I said.

Enzo smiled. "It's happened to Azrael more than once."

Warren blew out a heavy sigh, shaking his head. "Let's get this over with."

Enzo braced Reuel from the front while Warren pushed the log forward. Nathan ended up having to help him. It was the nastiest thing I'd ever seen which was saying quite a lot. It took forever to heal. Everyone else began packing up the HOKs while I closed the gaping hole in Reuel's chest.

"You owe me big time for this," I said.

He chuckled, though it was obviously painful.

"I wonder what would happen if I didn't heal it."

Reuel's head jerked up and he looked around.

"What is it?"

"Shh."

The look on his face was worrisome.

He grabbed my arm, his eyes wide with alarm.

The second I looked up, the sound of rapid-fire gunshots ricocheted off the falls again. Most everyone dove to the ground, except Enzo, who face-planted in the grass. Reuel pulled me behind him and Warren and Nathan ducked behind one of the HOKs. Agent Silvers showered the area in bullets with an M-4, shooting Agent Voss in the head and blowing out the kneecap of one of Azrael's soldiers I didn't know.

Then she stopped, but she didn't lower the weapon.

"Silvers, what are you doing?" Agent Clark shouted.

She didn't respond. Her eyes were glazed over and not really staring anywhere in particular. I'd seen the same look on Warren's face when Kasyade was controlling him in San Antonio.

Suddenly, the HOK flipped forward, landing upside down a few feet from me and Reuel, leaving Nathan and Warren exposed and vulnerable. Silvers turned the gun toward them.

Lex raised his sidearm in her direction, but before he could fire, he was knocked sideways off his feet by an invisible blow. My eyes frantically scanned the area, looking for the demon responsible. Then I saw her. A young Hispanic girl, maybe thirteen, standing at the edge of the woods.

Reuel saw her too. "Phenex."

I expected someone older.

"Kill them," she said, her calm voice eerily amplified for all of us to hear.

She aimed the rifle at Nathan.

I screamed.

Silvers fired.

And Warren jumped in front of the bullets.

———

Azrael had once told me that adrenalin makes everything easier, which explained why I broke from Reuel's powerful grasp like his fingers were coated with butter. Power exploded from my fingertips like a nuclear explosion blasting the Hispanic girl off her feet. Before she hit the ground, Samael appeared out of nowhere, grabbing her and vanishing into the air.

Another agent fired a round from a handgun into Silvers from behind. She toppled forward, losing her grip on the rifle. Lex jumped on her, and someone else grabbed the gun.

Warren landed on top of Nathan.

Blood was everywhere.

I ran across the field, falling twice before I reached Warren.

The front of his shirt was riddled with bullet holes and soaked with blood. His dark eyes were vacant and staring into the sky.

Nathan was checking for a pulse.

A pulse I knew he wouldn't find.

"Get out of my way!" I yelled at him, fanning out my fingers, igniting my fingers with every ounce of power I had. As I reached toward his lifeless body, Samael descended on top of me, yanking me away and holding me back.

"Sloan, you must not!" Samael's lips pressed against my ear.

With all my strength, I kicked, elbowed, and punched him. "Let me go!"

He held me firm, covering my arms with his own to keep me from using my power on him. "Listen to me!" His voice was unyielding. "If you succeed in summoning him back to this body, his being will be splintered between this world and the next." He shook me. "He will likely die a painful death, regardless. And if he lives…it's not a fate that should be sentenced on anyone."

I crumpled in his arms, but continued to writhe against him. "I have to bring him back!" I screamed through my tears.

Samael tightened his grasp. "You must not. You must love him enough to let him go."

His words jarred me. My father had said those words before.

CHAPTER TWENTY-NINE

Samael held me as I cried. When he finally released his grasp, I sank to my knees next to Warren and touched his blood-speckled face. Tears streamed from my eyes and mixed with the blood on his cheeks. I cradled his head in my arms, and our daughter kicked in my womb as I bent and kissed his frozen mouth.

Someone else was sobbing behind me. I glanced back to see Nathan seated in the grass, his eyes buried in his palm as tears dripped off his chin. Samael put a hand on his shoulder, but Nathan flinched away from his touch. He pushed himself off the ground and walked away from us all.

A few feet away, Warren's armored vest lay draped over the rucksack he'd carried in.

As I withered into hysterics again, the air came alive, buzzing with energy all around me. I looked at Samael, just as his face snapped up. Across the clearing, Reuel stood to his feet, angling his ear toward the sky.

Impulsively, Samael grabbed me again, hooking his arms under mine and pulling me swiftly backward. Warren's upper body slumped onto the grass as I was dragged from under him.

A gentle vibration grew beneath us, spreading and building

until all the terrain rumbled violently. The rocks along the waterfall split open and tumbled into the waters below. Nathan and the few soldiers who had been standing fell to the their knees.

"What's happening?" I shouted over the thunderous quake.

A violent wind rushed over us, and the air around Warren's body visibly fractured in a thousand different directions. The space suddenly erupted into the most brilliant light I had ever witnessed. It was both blinding and inviting—the whitest white, icy and warm at the same time.

Samael's arm shielded our eyes against it as splintered through the sky.

There was another flash and as the light dissolved around us, the storm faded. Then standing before us was Azrael...and Warren.

His strong chest heaved with heavy breaths.

My heart stopped.

I'd slammed my skull pretty hard during my fall with Ysha, certainly bruising my brain. Maybe this was a hallucination. Maybe I was dreaming again. Maybe I had actually died and this was some vision of the afterlife. But the pressure from Samael's grip on my arm when we stood, convinced me it was reality.

"What. The. Hell?" Nathan's words were slow and over-enunciated as he walked up beside us.

Warren took a step forward. "Sloan." It was his voice, strong and even.

My feet were rooted to the forest floor.

He closed the space between us, and then his arms were around me. I couldn't move, and I stood there like a mannequin, petrified in place as he lifted me from the ground. His body was no longer rigid with death, his warmth seeped into my skin, and his energy surged through my nerve endings, stronger than it ever had before. I remembered to breathe as he settled me on my feet again. Our daughter fluttered in my belly.

Everyone else withdrew a few steps in horror.

"Sloan," Warren said again.

I pressed my eyes closed, and then reopened them. "You're alive?" I stammered.

He nodded. "I'm alive."

I shook my head. "No. This isn't possible. You were dead."

"I'm not dead anymore."

Carefully, I searched his face. There was no trace of blood on his skin or on his clothes. His eyes were sparkling in the mid-day sun that was peeking through the dissipating gray clouds, but something about him was alarmingly different.

I couldn't see his soul.

Recoiling from his touch, I grasped the sides of my head, fearing my skull might explode. "No, this isn't you. You're different."

Azrael appeared at his side. He was smiling. "You're right. He is better. Much better. He no longer has the weaknesses of humanity."

My head snapped back. "No longer human?" I started laughing. Hysterical, maniacal laughter. I spun on my heel and walked away from them, still shaking my head and holding my head together with my hands. Nathan, with his mouth hanging open, grabbed me by the arm to stop me. I looked into his eyes and pointed back over my shoulder. "You're seeing this shit too, right?"

He nodded but didn't, or couldn't, speak.

Warren spoke behind me. "Sloan, look at me."

I turned back around.

Slowly, he approached with his hands up in surrender. "Everything we've been told is true. Our little girl is very special. Now I have the power to protect her, and you." He took my hands and pulled them against his chest. I could feel his heart beating. "Please trust me."

For a long time, I stared at him. I touched his cheek, and his eyes closed as my fingertips graced his warm skin. When he reopened his eyes, peace washed over me. Tears slipped down my face. "You were dead."

He swiped his thumbs under my eyes. "And now you'll never worry about that again." He leaned in and kissed me, his power making me dizzy.

When he released me, Nathan was waiting with his hand outstretched. Again, Warren looked at it for a moment. Then, instead of shaking it, he stepped forward and embraced him. Neither of them spoke, but neither of them had to.

Azrael's hand came to rest on my shoulder. He looked down at me. "I assumed you would have known I'd have the power to bring him back."

"Seriously?" I asked, crossing my arms.

"You have the ability to control the human spirit; I command the Angels of Death. I thought this would be a natural conclusion given our circumstances."

I shook my head. "Not really. An explanation would be helpful."

"I'll explain everything soon," he said.

My eyes narrowed at him. "Where were you?"

"Trying unsuccessfully to subdue The Destroyer," he said.

"Where is he now?"

Azrael shrugged. "I couldn't stay with him and go after my son."

A thought occurred to me. "Can I recall Warren's human side now, so he'd be the same as he was before?"

Azrael sighed and shook his head. "Warren's human spirit is gone forever."

"But Samael said he can't survive if—"

Azrael cut me off. "As a human, he could not easily survive without the power his body has become dependent on over the years." He touched my forehead. "Remember those migraines?"

"It would kill him," I said quietly.

"Most likely."

"What about Taiya?" I asked. "Could she still be alive?"

He hung his head. "It's doubtful."

Tears pooled in my eyes. "I killed her."

He gripped my shoulders. "You can't think that way. It was not your choice." He pulled me against his chest as I began to cry. Of all the things Azrael was capable of, I was surprised tenderness was one of them. He dipped his head and spoke quietly just to me. "And you know it is not an empty platitude when I tell you if she is gone, she's in a better place."

His words made me feel better, but only slightly.

Just then, sirens howled in the distance.

"Someone must have heard all the explosions," Nathan said. "We're about to have some confused and angry deputies on our hands."

My eyes widened at the mention of law enforcement. The rest of our group was still scattered around the field. I took a step in their direction, but Azrael put a hand on my chest to stop me. "Agent Voss is dead."

I looked at him.

He pointed to the field where Agent Clark was performing triage on Agent Silvers. "This is your opportunity to do more than just bring someone back."

I rubbed my palms together. "It's time to clear my name."

The Halifax County Sheriff's Department was thoroughly perplexed when they descended on Calfkiller Creek and found the FBI and Claymore Worldwide cleaning up from a "training exercise." I don't know what the agents told them, and I didn't care. All that mattered was I wasn't going back to jail...not yet, anyway.

Just as I had no memory of being with Kasyade at the bank in Asheville, Sharvell Silvers had no memory of trying to kill us all with the M-4. Before she'd fallen under Phenex's control, she and the other agents had been able to sever their restraints on the jagged rocks inside the cave. They had freed themselves at just about the time that Ysha was dragging me up the rocks. Silvers had found Warren's rifle and shot Ysha in the face blowing us both off the rocks into the stream below.

Before the cops showed up, I healed her shoulder and, in front of all of them, brought Agent Voss back to life. He was in severe pain and completely freaked out, but he was alive.

Warren slipped an arm around my shoulders. "Are you all right?"

I leaned my head against his chest. "This was a terrifying day."

"I agree."

I looked up at him. "Kasyade wasn't here, Warren. That means this still isn't over."

"I know," he said. "But we'll be ready for her next time."

"Sloan?" Agent Silver asked behind us.

We turned to see her walking over from where the agents were loading up the helicopter. She had a thick file folder in her hand. She offered it to me when she was close enough.

"What is this?" I asked.

She crossed her arms. "It's a copy of all the information I have on Abigail Smith."

I raised it in my hand. "You realize it's kind of worthless, right?"

"You might be surprised," she said. "I'm fairly certain the young girl who..."

Warren's head tilted. "Who took control of your mind and forced you to go full-blown Scarface on all of us?"

Her gaze fell to the ground. "Yes. I'm sure she's in this information."

"Interesting," I said. "Thank you."

After a moment, she glanced back up at me. "You were right."

"About what?" I asked.

"You're not who I thought you were," she said.

I rocked back and forth on my heels. "I hope that means you won't send me to prison."

She shook her head. "No, I won't. I'll make sure the charges are dropped and the evidence against you is destroyed."

I pointed across the camp to where Nathan was eating Skittles by the fire. "And what about Detective McNamara?"

She shrugged. "Maybe he was with his family for the holiday."

I smiled. "Thank you."

"No. Thank you." She tapped the top of the file folder. "Let me know if you need any help. Just please find Abigail and the others." She cut her eyes up at me. "And when you do, make sure you kill them."

"I will."

CHAPTER THIRTY

All I wanted to do was go home and crawl into my bed, but a lot of business still had to be handled. A larger Claymore helicopter picked us up and flew us to Azrael's headquarters in New Hope. Over dinner in his conference room, Azrael explained how he'd been fighting Abaddon when he felt Warren die. For the first time in three decades, the Archangel of Death was released from his confinement to this world, and he crossed the spirit line to find his son. He said in order to bring Warren back, Warren had to choose for his human spirit to be completely destroyed.

"You *chose* to come back?" I asked, putting my fork down.

He nodded. "Of course I did. I couldn't leave you here alone."

"I don't understand." I looked at Azrael. "How does that work?"

Azrael pushed his plate back and crossed his arms on the tabletop. "Human spirits are not able to come back into this world once they cross the spirit line."

"Then how did Sloan bring me back?" Nathan asked before Azrael could continue.

"She brought you back before you crossed over," he explained. "Because Warren is my son, he basically went straight to the front of the line and passed through before anything could stop him.

Even if Warren hadn't crossed the spirit line, Sloan would only have been able to recall his human spirit to his body, splintering him between both worlds. It would likely kill him, and if it didn't we'd all be sorry he lived."

That was what Samael had tried to explain to me on the battlefield.

"So what did you do to bring him back like this?" Nathan asked.

"As the archangel, I have the power to inflict the second death. I cannot destroy another angel, but I can completely obliterate a human soul." Azrael seemed sickeningly pleased. "Without the hindrance of his humanity, Warren stepped fully into his power and is now able to pass freely between this world and my own."

"Even with the baby? Isn't he *bound* here, or whatever?" I asked, pointing to my own stomach.

Azrael shook his head. "I told you, your child is different."

Nathan seemed confused. "But he was dead for maybe five minutes. How did you pull all that off?"

Warren looked at him. "Time does absolutely not work the same way on the other side. I felt like I was gone for hours."

"Correct," Azrael agreed.

"What was it like?" I asked Warren.

He leaned back in his chair and thought for a moment. "It really wasn't that different than here. More peaceful maybe and definitely more beautiful. There was so much sunlight." His voice had a note of wonder to it. "A lot happened that I can't explain. Something really weird happened with my body."

"Yeah," Nathan said with a chuckle. "It was blown full of bullet holes."

Warren shook his head. "No, after." He looked to Azrael for an explanation.

"Your physical body evolved," Azrael said. "Bullets will no longer be a problem."

I raised my hand into the air. "But at what price?"

Azrael was obviously surprised by my question. "At the price of weakness," he answered.

I was skeptical. "You keep saying that, but there must be something that makes us favored above the angels, right?" No one said anything. "Warren lost whatever that is. It's got to be a pretty big deal."

A muscle was working in Azrael's jaw. "This was the only way."

"And I appreciate that," I said. "I'm just not naive enough anymore to believe that such a miracle won't come with some consequences."

Nathan knocked his knuckles against the table, then lifted his beer into the air. "Well, let's not worry about it tonight. This day has sucked enough." He looked at Warren. "For whatever reason, I'm glad you're still here."

All our eyes widened with surprise.

Grinning, Warren raised his glass. "Thanks, Nate. Even though we all know it's a load of bullshit."

Everyone burst out laughing.

Some things with Warren were definitely improved. I found that out the nice way when we went to bed in a private housing unit after dinner. Like Azrael, he didn't really need to rest anymore. That had all kinds of benefits for both of us.

The next morning was Christmas, but it certainly didn't feel like it. Azrael gave us an SUV to drive to Camp Lejeune so Warren could collect his things from the barracks and deal with his command. Azrael stayed behind to take care of some business, but he promised to see us before the new year.

Nathan and I spent an hour at a sports bar on base while we waited for Warren to return.

"Did you call your dad?" Nathan asked, pointing to an old pay phone.

I nodded. "I called him from Claymore when we got there, and I called him this morning to wish him a Merry Christmas. Did you call your family?"

He nodded. "Mom said to give you a hug and she invited you to come celebrate the new year with us."

I smiled. "I love your family."

"They love you too," he replied.

"Have you checked in at work yet?" I asked.

Nathan sipped his beer. "Yeah, I called the sheriff last night. He asked if I was having a good vacation."

"That was it?"

"That was it. He played completely ignorant of everything else."

"Thank God. Did he say anything about Taiya?" I asked.

His face fell as he shook his head. "She escaped from the jail shortly after you did, but they haven't seen her since. I will find her, I promise." He tapped his fingers on the outside of his glass. "What did Azrael say about her?"

I sighed. "He said it's true. She probably would have died when I killed Ysha."

He frowned. "That sucks. I was starting to like her."

I slouched in my seat. "I know."

"Things will be very different when we get home," he said.

I stared at the table. "About that…"

Nathan took a deep breath. "You're going to marry him, aren't you?"

"Yes."

He forced a smile. "Congratulations."

"Will you forgive me?" I asked.

He reached over and squeezed my forearm. "There's nothing to forgive. It's how it should be."

"Will you come to the wedding?"

"I wouldn't miss it for anything."

Just then, the front door chimed when Warren walked inside.

He was smiling, but it quickly faded as he approached the table. "It looks like someone died. Everything OK?"

I nodded. "Yeah. How'd it go?"

He handed me a white envelope and put a plastic bag down on the table as he slid into the booth beside me.

"What's this?" I asked, sliding the papers out.

"My discharge paperwork."

I looked briefly at the papers and then back at him. "Does this mean you're completely done?"

He nodded. "Completely finished."

I sighed with relief.

"You're officially out of the Marines?" Nathan asked.

"I'm out of the Marines," Warren said.

Nathan cracked a smile over the rim of his glass. "That's convenient now that you're in the Lord's Army."

Warren narrowed his eyes and Nathan's beer sloshed out across the front of his shirt.

"Damn it, Warren!" Nathan cursed, slamming the beer down on the table and grabbing a fistful of napkins.

I laughed and Warren winked at me.

Leaning back in my seat, I folded my hands over my stomach. "I see you're not having any issues using your powers. It took me forever to learn how to do that."

He grinned and stretched out his fingers. "I've gotten a bit better."

Warren's veiled modesty wasn't fooling anyone. While we waited for him to return, Nathan and I had discussed at length what had happened in the woods. Without a mortal soul, there would be nothing to dilute Warren's power. The thought was creepy but comforting when I considered Kasyade and Phenex were still out there somewhere.

I nodded toward the bag. "Did you buy me a present?"

His head snapped up. "Oh, I almost forgot." He handed the bag to Nathan. "It's actually for you. I found it at the MPX on base. Merry Christmas."

Nathan's eyes widened with curiosity as he accepted it. He reached into the bag and pulled out a small rectangle. His brow crumpled, and he scowled at Warren. "Really?"

Warren dropped his forehead onto the table and laughed harder than I had ever seen him laugh before. I held out my hand. "What is it?"

Nathan huffed and handed it to me. "It's a patch for my hat."

I turned the brown patch over in my hand. The front of it read, *REGULAR GUY.*

I covered my mouth with my hand and tried to suppress my chuckles. I wasn't sure what was funnier: the patch or Warren so tickled over it.

Nathan smacked Warren across the back of his head. "Asshole."

When Warren sat up, there were tears in his eyes from laughing. He held up his hands in defense. "Man, I'm only trying to help. Sloan told me you lost all your patches in the accident."

Nathan held up his middle finger and drained the last of his beer.

Warren regained his composure and pulled the car keys from his pocket. "I don't know about you guys, but I'm beyond ready to go home."

Home. From his lips, the word had a nice new ring to it.

We said goodbye to Nathan in our driveway when we got home. He promised to work on getting Warren's car out of impound and then bid us farewell with a cheesy, "I'll see you next year."

Even though we knew we'd see him again in the next couple of days, there was an odd finality to our waving goodbye from the front porch. Judging from Warren's heavy sigh, he felt it too.

A glint in the sky caught my attention. I looked up to see the angels standing guard. I pointed. "Can you see them now?"

Warren followed the direction of my finger. Then he looked at me. "There are more than just those, babe. Angels are everywhere."

I looped my arms around his neck. "I only need one."

He smiled. "Speaking of that." He reached into his jacket and pulled out a ring box. "Are you ready to wear this thing now?"

"You still want me to?" I asked, heat rising in my cheeks.

He flipped the box open. "Sloan, I never stopped."

My hand trembled as he slid the diamond on my finger. "Will you marry me?" he asked.

Happy tears almost froze to my face. "Absolutely." I stretched up on my tip-toes and kissed him. "I love you, Warren."

He cradled my face in his strong hands. "I love you too."

I squealed with glee as I held my hand up to watch the ring twinkle in the last rays from the pink sunset. "I want to go call Adrianne."

He laughed and picked up our bags off the porch. "I expect no less, but you'd better hurry. We need to get to your dad's."

Without touching the front door, I unlocked it and we walked inside. Someone had left my phone plugged in and laying on the coffee table. I skipped across the room and picked it up.

On the screen I had eleven missed calls and more text messages than I could scroll through. But one of them caught my attention; it was a picture message time-stamped that morning.

I clicked it open.

The picture showed Taiya tied to a chair. Her blue eyes were open, but they were dangerously weak. Someone held out her arm toward the camera.

If found, please call Sloan Jordan.

THANK YOU FOR READING!
Please consider leaving a review! Reviews help indie authors like me find new readers and get advertising. If you enjoyed this book, please tell your friends!
REVIEW

Book 4 - The Taken

Order It Now

Want more of your favorite detective?
THE DETECTIVE
A Nathan McNamara Story

Here's a FREE GIFT for you!
Download The Detective at
www.thesoulsummoner.com

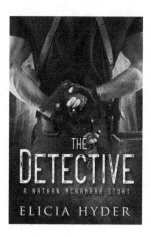

ALSO BY ELICIA HYDER

Be brave. Be strong. Be badass.

Roll into the exciting world of women's flat track roller derby, where the women are the heroes, and the men will make you weak in the kneepads.

A brand new romantic comedy series from Author Elicia Hyder.

ALSO BY ELICIA HYDER

Lights Out Lucy: Roller Derby 101

Welcome to the exciting world of women's roller derby, where the women are the heroes and the men will make you weak in the knee pads.

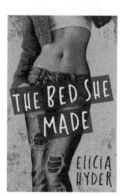

The Bed She Made

2015 Watty Award Winner for Best New Adult Romance

During her wild and crazy teenage years, Journey Durant's father warned her that someday she'd have to lie in the bed she made. But she didn't believe him until her ex-boyfriend is released from prison and he threatens to bring her troubled past home with him.

To Be Her First

The Young Adult Prequel to The Bed She Made

At sixteen, Journey Durant hasn't yet experienced her first anything. No first boyfriend. No first date. No first kiss. But that's all about to change. Two boys at West Emerson High are vying for her attention: the MVP quarterback and the school's reigning bad boy.

ABOUT THE AUTHOR

In the dawning age of scrunchies and 'Hammer Pants', a small-town musician with big-city talent found out she was expecting her third child a staggering eleven years after her last one. From that moment on, Susie Waldrop referred to her daughter Elicia as a 'blessing' which is loosely translated as an accident, albeit a pleasant one.

In true youngest-sibling fashion, Elicia lived up to the birth order standard by being fun-loving, outgoing, self-centered, and rebellious throughout her formative years. She excelled academically—a feat her sister attributes to her being the only child who was breastfed—but abandoned her studies to live in a tent in the national forest with her dogs: a Rottweiler named Bodhisattva and a Pit Bull named Sativa. The ensuing months were very hazy.

In the late 90's, during a stint in rehab, Elicia was approached by a prophet who said, "Someday you will write a book."

She was right.

Now a firm believer in the prophetic word, Elicia Hyder is a full-time writer and freelance editor living in central Florida with her husband and five children. Eventually she did make it to college, and she studied literature and creative writing at the American Military University.

Her debut novel, **The Bed She Made**, is very loosely based on the stranger-than-fiction events of her life.

www.eliciahyder.com
elicia@eliciahyder.com